Raves for the novels

"Superb characters living with a detective story that just sucks you right into the storyline. Marshall Ryan Maresca impressed me with *The Thorn of Dentonhill*, but *A Murder of Mages* has secured me as a fan." —*Fresh Fiction*

"*A Murder of Mages* was another hit for me, a fantastic read from a new talent whose star continues to be on the rise." —Bibliosanctum

"Books like this are just fun to read." —The Tenacious Reader

"*[A Murder of Mages]* is the perfect combination of urban fantasy, magic, and mystery." —Kings River Life Magazine

"Marshall Ryan Maresca has done it again. After introducing readers to Maradaine through the eyes of criminals in *The Thorn of Dentonhill*, he focuses now on the constabulary, the ones catching the criminals, in *A Murder of Mages*....Another rollicking adventure of magic and mayhem." —The Qwillery

"Maresca's debut is smart, fast, and engaging fantasy crime in the mold of Brent Weeks and Harry Harrison. Just perfect." —Kat Richardson, national bestselling author of *Revenant*

"Fantasy adventure readers, especially fans of spell-wielding students, will enjoy these lively characters and their high-energy story." —*Publishers Weekly*

DAW Books presents the
novels of Marshall Ryan Maresca:

THE THORN OF DENTONHILL
THE ALCHEMY OF CHAOS
THE IMPOSTERS OF AVENTIL*

*

A MURDER OF MAGES
AN IMPORT OF INTRIGUE

*

THE HOLVER ALLEY CREW

*Coming soon from DAW

Maresca, Marshall Ryan,
The Holver Alley crew /
2017.
33305239707643
ca   10/17/17

RESCA

THE HOLVER ALLEY CREW

A novel of the
Streets of Maradaine

DAW BOOKS, INC.

DONALD A. WOLLHEIM, FOUNDER
375 Hudson Street, New York, NY 10014

ELIZABETH R. WOLLHEIM
SHEILA E. GILBERT
PUBLISHERS
www.dawbooks.com

Copyright © 2017 by Marshall Ryan Maresca.

All Rights Reserved.

Cover art by Paul Young.

Cover design by G-Force Design.

DAW Book Collectors No. 1753.

Published by DAW Books, Inc.
375 Hudson Street, New York, NY 10014.

All characters and events in this book are fictitious.
Any resemblance to persons living or dead is strictly coincidental.

If you purchased this book without a cover you should be aware that this book
may have been stolen property and reported as "unsold and destroyed" to the
publisher. In such case neither the author nor the publisher has received any
payment for this "stripped book."

The scanning, uploading, and distribution of this book via the Internet or via any
other means without the permission of the publisher is illegal, and punishable by
law. Please purchase only authorized electronic editions, and do not participate
in or encourage the electronic piracy of copyrighted materials. Your support of
the author's rights is appreciated.

First Printing, March 2017
1 2 3 4 5 6 7 8 9

DAW TRADEMARK REGISTERED
U.S. PAT. AND TM. OFF. AND FOREIGN COUNTRIES
—MARCA REGISTRADA
HECHO EN U.S.A.
PRINTED IN THE U.S.A.

Acknowledgments

A few acknowledgments of the people who helped make this book possible:

This time I'm going to begin with Daniel J. Fawcett, who has been a sounding board for my crazy creative ideas for as long as I've known him, which is a rather long time. The city of Maradaine, and the world that surrounds it, has been enriched by his influence. But specifically in the case of *The Holver Alley Crew*, the characters of Asti and Verci Rynax were very much midwifed by him. I very much doubt I would have created them, as they are here, without his help.

Early drafts of the manuscript were read and torn apart by Kevin Jewell (always a rock), Abby Goldsmith, Ellen van Hensbergen, Kelli Meyer, Katy Stauber, and Miriam Robinson Gould. They all did their part in making it stronger.

Stina Leicht and Melissa Tyler were running the Armadilloic Con Writers Workshop back when I wrote the earliest draft of this novel, and it was this rough draft of the first chapter of this book that first got their attention. Melissa, in particular, has been a fan of this story, so she'll be especially happy to see it in print. And in every previous acknowledgments, I've gushed about Stina Leicht, and I could continue to do so here. I'm very lucky to have her as a friend.

My agent, Mike Kabongo, has been an advocate of my work as well as a fan. I love that he doesn't like to read my outlines of future novels because *he doesn't want spoilers*.

The entire team at DAW and Penguin has been a godsend, and I am immensely grateful to be working with them: Katie Hoffman, Sarah Guan, Joshua Starr, Briar Herrera-Ludwig, Alexis Nixon, Nita Basu, Betsy Wollheim, and, of course, my editor Sheila Gilbert.

Finally, there's my family. This is a wide circle that includes my son Nicholas, my parents Louis and Nancy, and my mother-in-law Kateri. The most important is my wife, Deidre Kateri Aragon. Deidre has been a beacon of strength and support who has always believed that I could be successful as a writer. That, given my early work, was quite an act of faith.

THE HOLVER ALLEY CREW

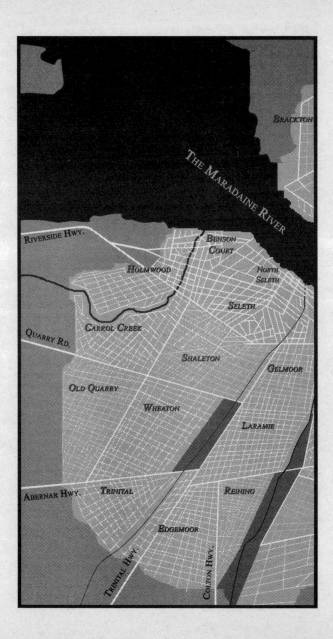

THE MARADAINE RIVER

BRACKTON

RIVERSIDE HWY.

BENSON COURT

HOLMWOOD

NORTH SELETH

SELETH

CARROL CREEK

QUARRY RD.

SHALETON

GELMOOR

OLD QUARRY

WHEATON

LARAMIE

ABERNAR HWY.

TRINITAL

REINING

EDGEMOOR

TRINITAL HWY.

COLTON HWY.

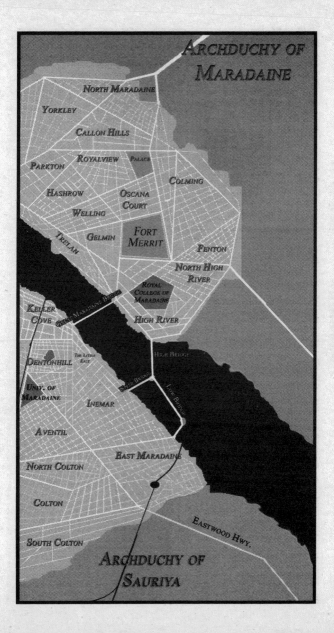

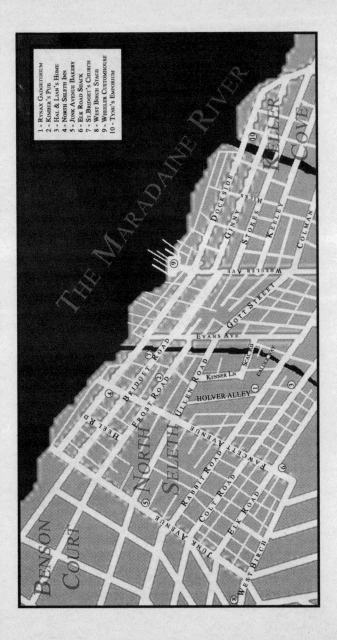

THE MARADAINE RIVER

KELLER COVE

1 - RYNAX GADGETERIUM
2 - KIMBER's PUB
3 - HAL & IAN's HOME
4 - NORTH SELETH INN
5 - JUNK AVENUE BAKERY
6 - ELK ROAD SHACK
7 - ST. BRIDGET's CHURCH
8 - WEST BIRCH STAGE
9 - WHEELER CUSTOMHOUSE
10 - TYNE's EMPORIUM

BENSON COURT

NORTH SELETH

HEEL RD

BRIDGET ROAD

FROST ROAD

ULLEN ROAD

KENNER LN

HOLVER ALLEY

EVANS AVE

GOTT STREET

SCARO

CALBERT WY

JUNK AVENUE

FAWCETT AVENUE

RABBIT ROAD

COLT ROAD

ELK ROAD

WEST BIRCH

WHEELER AVE

DOCKSIDE

GINNY

HICKS

STOKES

KEELEY

COLMAN

Chapter 1

ASTI RYNAX COULDN'T SLEEP. The bedroll wasn't the problem. He'd slept plenty of nights in jail cells, road ditches, even trapped inside a wooden crate. The problem was sleeping on a hot wooden floor in the single-room flop, his younger brother, brother's wife, and crying baby just ten feet away behind a thin cloth. He craved his own flop, his own space, without families, babies, or smoke.

Smoke.

Asti sat up, smelling the air.

Definitely smoke. And not from the oil lamps.

Asti sprang to his feet. "Verci. Wake up."

"What, what is it?"

"Smoke."

Verci was out of the bed, crossing over to Asti in a flash, despite being naked. Asti's eyes went to the slight paunch his brother was getting. Married life was taking its toll on his normally lean body. "You're right."

"It's just the Greenfields' kitchen," Raych mumbled from the bed.

"No, it's too strong," Asti said. He glanced back at Verci. "Put something on."

Verci waved him off, taking another smell. "Much too strong."

Asti touched the door. It was warm. Cautiously he cracked it open. The hallway glowed with crackling flames. He dashed back over to the kitchen and grabbed the bed-roll and blanket.

"Blasted saints," Verci muttered. "Raych, wake up."

"Wha—"

"Get up. Get the baby." Each word was like an arrow. Verci grabbed his pants off the back of a chair and pulled them on.

Asti held the blanket over his face. In the hallway the flames were licking up the walls and ceiling, wooden support beams already cracking. Asti swung the bedroll at the fire, beating it down. Useless. The smoke was getting thicker, the fire hotter, despite his efforts.

"Can you get to the stairs?" Verci called.

Asti pushed forward. The stairs leading outside were only eight steps away. Eight impossible steps. He could race past the fire to reach them, if he went right this moment. The stairway was engulfed, but he could leap down the flight. He would reach the bottom with a few singes and roll on the ground when he landed, snuffing out his clothes if they caught flame on the way down. He could do it, and be outside and safe in seven seconds. He imagined the whole plan in an instant, his body tensing in anticipation.

Verci could do it too, if he called out, told him to run, to go now.

Raych and the baby could never make it.

He beat down the instinct to run.

"No chance," Asti replied. The fire filled the hallway, rac-ing along to block him from the apartment door. Lungs and eyes burning, he beat a clear path back and slammed the door shut.

"How bad is it?" Raych asked. She was out of bed, wrapped in a loose dressing gown, caramel hair framing her pretty face, with the baby clutched to her.

Asti could barely speak through hacking coughs. "Very," was all he managed. He shoved the bedroll under the crack in the door, blocking the smoke that was starting to pour in.

"How are we going to get out, then?" she asked. Her voice cracked with fear.

Asti didn't answer, but he heard a slight snort from his brother. Verci covered it with a cough, but Asti knew exactly why he laughed: Verci never walked into a room without immediately finding every way to get out.

Verci went over to the trunk by the bed and opened it up. While he rummaged through it, Asti pulled on a shirt and boots and grabbed his pack. Everything in the apartment that he owned was in the pack.

"Plan?" he asked Verci.

"That window," Verci said, pointing to the one by the stove. "But not yet." He pulled out an empty pack from the trunk.

"Verci, what are we—" Raych started.

Verci tossed the empty pack to Asti as he went over to Raych.

"Give me Corsi and get dressed," he said. "We have to move quickly."

"Quickly?" She looked stunned, but relinquished the baby to Verci.

"Put that on, Asti," Verci said, crossing over to the kitchen with the baby. "Wear it across your chest." Asti did it, and Verci put his son into the pack. He tightened the straps on the side so the baby was snug, close against Asti's body.

"Verci Rynax, what the blazes are you doing?" Raych asked, pulling on a cotton dress.

"Keeping our son safe," Verci said. He turned to Asti, "Get the window open and get out there."

"If you think I'm going to let my baby . . ."

Verci went back to the trunk. "We need to climb down from the window, Raych. You can't do that while carrying him." He pulled on a shirt and grabbed another pack.

"Then you carry him!"

"I'll be helping you, love," Verci said. He threw a few more things into the pack. Smoke was filling the room. "No time to argue."

Asti went out the window. There was a slight ledge, only a few inches, just enough for him to stand on. Above him there was only smoke and darkness; he knew both moons were roughly half full, but he couldn't see them. The street below was chaotic, people shouting and pointing, running around in their nightclothes while the fire crackled all around. Directly below him was the canvas awning of Greenfield's locksmith shop, stretched wide and tight.

"Awning, slide, street?" Asti called to Verci.

"Right," Verci said. "Move."

"Hold on, little man," Asti said, rubbing the head of the baby. For his part, he was quiet, his big blue eyes staring up at Asti.

Asti sat down on the ledge, his feet a short drop from the top of the awning. Keeping one hand on the ledge, he dropped off, using his arm to keep his full weight from hitting the awning. Once his body was on the canvas, he let go, sliding down over the lip of it. A second later his boots hit the dirt. He stumbled forward, almost needing to fall into a roll, but he clutched at the baby and lurched backward, keeping his balance. Several people on the street cried and cheered.

Up on the ledge Raych cried, "I'm going to break my neck if I do that."

"No, you won't," Verci said.

Asti looked back at the building. The whole place was on fire, smoke pouring out the windows. Verci lowered his wife onto the awning. Her eyes were locked on Asti, focused on the bundle strapped to his chest. Asti looked at the baby again, who was gurgling and smiling.

"He's fine, Raych. Come on." Asti held out a hand, though he knew it was a meaningless gesture. Verci stretched out, easing Raych down the awning until she was as far as he could get her without stepping on the awning himself.

"Ready?" Verci called.

"Do it!" she said. He let go of her hand, and she slid off to the ground. Her landing was sloppy, almost falling on her face before Asti caught her. Raych gasped and clutched at Asti. A moment later she was fumbling at the straps, desperate to get the baby out of his pack. Verci slid down, landing on the ground with practiced grace.

"That's the whole place," Asti said. The locksmith shop and the apartments above it were all burning.

The shop next door was burning as well. And the one next to it. The fire spread down Holver Alley as far as Asti could see. Every building was wood and plaster, pressed next to each other, nothing to stop it all from catching.

An old man grabbed Asti's shoulder. "Look at that, Rynax! That's magic fire, isn't it? Has to be!"

"No, no," he said, coming up with an answer that was somewhere between fabrication and gut instinct. "Magical fire always burns hotter, with blue and white flames." Asti knew hardly anything about magic, but that was more than anyone else in Holver Alley. His word might be enough to quell wild rumors about mages starting this.

"Where's Win?" Verci asked, looking around the crowd. "And the girls?" Asti glanced about. Winthym Greenfield wasn't anywhere, nor were his wife and daughters.

"Did they get out on the other side?" Raych asked, holding her baby close to her chest.

"No chance," Verci said. Asti knew the question was ridiculous, but bit his tongue. Greenfield's shop was built right up against a solid brick wall, the back of the row houses on Kenner Street.

"They must be trapped," Asti said. The shop windows were dark, covered in iron bars. No way to see in or break through. Asti touched the door of the shop. It was still cool.

"Asti, what are you doing?" Raych cried.

Asti tried the door, but it was locked. Of course it would be. "Verci, can you . . ." he called out, but his brother was already at his side.

Verci looked at the lock carefully. "Win's very good," he muttered. "It would take me at least five minutes."

"No time for that," Asti said. He scanned the crowd. Raych was in the center of his vision, screaming at them. Far behind her, towering over the crowd, was just the person he was hoping to find. Julien Kesser, the biggest bruiser on Holver Alley.

"Julien!" he called. The big man pushed his way through the crowd, Asti meeting him partway. "You all right, Jules? Your house all right?"

"No," Julien said, his wide, sad face covered in ash and soot.

"I'm sorry, Julien," Asti said. "Win Greenfield and his family are still trapped."

Julien nodded, and charged without further prodding. Verci scrambled out of the way as Julien smashed his shoulder into the door. It splintered and cracked.

"Asti Rynax, what in the name of the blasted saints do you think you're doing?" Helene Kesser, Julien's cousin, had come up right behind him, grabbing his wrist tightly. Her face and nightclothes were covered in ashes, black hair a tangled mess, and bare arms scraped and bleeding. "I barely got Jules out of our house. Don't you dare have him—"

"I just need the door open," Asti said. He glanced over at Raych, still crying at Verci to come away from the burning building. "Keep everyone else out, Hel. Especially Verci."

"How the blazes—"

"Just do it," Asti said. He took off his pack and handed it to Helene. Without another word, he pulled a cloak out and took it to the well spigot nearest Greenfield's shop. He pumped it hard, but only a trickle of water came out. While he was doing that, Julien broke the door off its hinges with a loud crunch. Smoke poured out through the open frame.

Asti took a deep breath, put on the damp cloak, and ran into the shop. He could hear Helene yelling from outside, telling Julien not to go in after him.

Asti couldn't see anything; thick smoke filled the shop. Eyes shut, cloak over his face, he went by memory to the back counter. He didn't need to see to find his way; it was five steps straight, and then three to the right to the door leading to Win's workshop.

"Win!" he called out. He could barely hear his own voice over the roar of fire. Blindly he found the door to the back room, and gave a silent prayer that it would be unlocked. He pushed his way in and tripped over something on the ground.

The fire blazed throughout the workshop, but on the floor the smoke was thinner. He had tripped over Greenfield's body. Winthym lay flat on his face, breathing shallowly.

Asti shook him. "Win, come on." Asti shook him again, but he didn't wake.

Through the smoke, a hand touched Asti on the shoulder. Verci came crawling in, stopping right in front of Win's body.

"What are you doing?" Asti shouted at his brother.

"Same as you," Verci said. The ceiling crackled and creaked above them.

"Fine. You get him out, I'll—"

"You'll nothing." Verci pointed to the stairway to the Greenfields' rooms, blocked by the fire. "You can't get up there."

"Get him out! Maybe I can—" He got to his feet.

"There's no chance, Asti!" Verci yanked him back down. A moment later the ceiling came crashing down in the middle of the workroom, bringing fresh flames from above. One timber knocked Asti on the arm. Verci grabbed the damp cloak and beat out the fire on Asti's sleeve.

"We can't leave them!" Asti shouted over the screaming blaze.

"No one is alive up there! We need to get out now!"

"But—"

"Help me!" Verci draped Win over his shoulder, and Asti did the same on the other side. They traced the steps through the black smoke, back out to the street. Julien came over and took Greenfield from them. They all hurried away from the blaze, dropping to their knees once they were clear. Asti took several deep breaths of sweet, cool air, while Verci hacked and wheezed next to him.

"Verci Rynax, how *dare* you . . ." Raych started.

"I'm fine, Raych," Verci said, even if his cough belied that. He reached up and cupped her face tenderly. Her eyes welled up with tears.

"You are not fine, that was a stupid, reckless—"

"I'm fine as well, you know," Asti said. He left his brother and went to where Julien had laid Greenfield on the ground. Asti knelt down and touched Win's head and chest.

"What you think, Rynax?" Helene said, hovering over him.

"He'll probably have a blazes of a cough, but I think he'll

live," Asti said. He looked back up. Every shop and house on the east side of Holver Alley was on fire now.

Their shop was on the east side.

"Where is the blasted Fire Brigade?" Asti muttered.

"Don't know," Helene said. "Don't think we can count on them now, can we?"

"Right," Asti said. The crowd stood staring at the fire, people screaming or crying, but no one doing a blasted thing. "Julien, take Win to Kimber's Pub over on Frost. Doc Gelson is usually deep in the cider over there all night. Hel—"

"Don't think you can order me and my cousin around, Rynax," Helene said, emphasizing her point by shoving his pack back in his hands.

"I'm not ordering, Helene!" Asti snapped at her. "I'm asking for help."

"Asking sounds a lot different."

"Blasted damn saints, Hel, the whole alley is burning down!" Asti's guts were churning; he fought down the bile forcing its way up his throat.

Helene grit her teeth. "What you want, Rynax?"

"Get people away from the fire," he said. "Make sure Raych goes."

"I'm not gonna be your blasted runnin' girl, Asti," Helene said. "You know I'm worth more than that."

"I know," Asti said. "But I don't need you putting an arrow in anyone tonight. Not yet, anyhow."

"Right," Helene said. Julien had Win picked up in his massive arms, looking to his cousin for her cue. "If you do, though . . ." She let it hang there.

"Wouldn't call on anyone else."

Helene nodded and went into the crowd, telling people to head over to Frost. People started shuffling away. Asti went back to Verci and Raych.

"Raych, get out of here, go over to your sister's," Asti said. "Come on, brother."

"Where are you going?" she asked him, grabbing her husband by the arm.

"We've got a shop down on the other end, case you forgot," Asti said.

Verci nodded, touching Raych's hand. "Every crown we have is put in there."

"Right," she said, resigned. She glanced back over to the locksmith shop, now completely ablaze. "Don't do anything else so stupid as that, though."

"I'll do all the stupid things," Asti said. "Come on." He raced down the alley. His brother was right at his heels. He didn't need to look behind to know, he could feel it.

Holver Alley was a quarter mile long. If Asti ran full tilt, he could cross it in a minute. With the panicked crowd, the flames, the choking smoke, Asti had to fight for every step.

Every shop, every home, every building on the east side of the alley was on fire. Asti almost tripped over Missus Hoskins, who sat on the dirt with her grandchildren, all wailing and screaming while their house burned. Jared Scall, the butcher, was held back by three others while he desperately clawed toward his shop and house. His children were nowhere to be seen. A dark-haired street girl stood in the middle of the road, staring blankly up at the conflagration.

"Asti!" Verci shouted. He pointed to a wrought-iron balcony three flights up. Hexie Matlin, the crazy fortune-teller, trembled with her little dog clutched to her chest. The fire raged inside her flop, trapping her. She cried out for help, panic cracking her voice.

"We have to go—" Asti started.

"Asti!" Verci didn't need to say anything else, it was all in his face. Hexie had been a good friend to their mother; they had known her all their lives.

"Fine," Asti said. "But I promised your wife I'd do the stupid things."

"I'm the better climber," Verci said.

"Then figure out how I'm getting her down." Asti gave a quick point up to Hexie's balcony and then to the barbershop on the other side of the alley. With two quick bounds, he was up on the doorframe of the barbershop, and then scrambling up the windows, finding whatever handholds he could.

He reached the roof, forty feet above the alley. From up here he would normally be able to see most of the city of

Maradaine, or at least the west side. But now smoke filled his vision, obscuring even the view of the North Seleth neighborhood. He could still see the alley below, the balcony across, and Hexie's panicked face.

Verci came up over the edge of the roof, quickly getting his pack off.

"I told you to stay down there."

"You told me to not do anything stupid." He pulled out a rope and a gear-and-pulley device from the pack. "Trust me, I'm leaving that to you." He tossed one end of the rope to Asti.

"What's the plan?" Asti asked.

"You know damn well what the plan is," Verci said. "Like the gig for Tolman five years ago."

"Right." Asti hated that gig.

He tied the rope around his waist and dropped his pack. He darted over to the far end of the roof. "This is the dumbest thing I've done in a long time."

"At least a month," Verci said. He held on to his end of the rope. "Go!"

Asti dashed across the roof and leaped off, sailing across the alley. A second later he crashed onto the balcony next to Hexie's.

"You missed!" Verci shouted from the rooftop.

"Shut it!"

Asti climbed up on the rail of his balcony, the metal creaking under him. He jumped the few feet over to Hexie, who screamed when he landed. The balcony shuddered with his weight.

"Get me out of here!" she cried.

"That's the plan," he said, untying the rope from his waist. The balcony buckled again.

"Hurry!" She clutched her dog tighter.

"I really am going as fast as I can," he said. He stood behind her, wrapping the rope around the both of them as he held her tight.

"Now, Asti!"

"Yes, ma'am," he said. A loud crack came from behind them, and the balcony came loose on one side. The two of them lurched, and Hexie screamed again. Asti saw Verci working frantically with his device. He threaded the rope through it, and then coiled it around his waist.

"Blessed saints, forgive me my sins," Hexie cried.

"You'd think you'd have seen this coming, Hexie," Asti said. He wrapped his arms around her. The rope pulled taut from Verci cranking the gears on his device.

"I didn't—I couldn't—I . . ." Hexie stammered out. The balcony was about to give way. No more time.

"Verci, now!" Asti shouted, and he jumped. The balcony collapsed, crashing down to the alley below, onlookers scattering to avoid being crushed. Verci jumped over the ledge at the same time. He drifted down, while Asti and Hexie shot up, flying across the alley. Asti braced himself, both feet hitting the brick wall of the building with a hard sting. Hexie and her dog both cried out, but they seemed unhurt.

"Oh, blessed saints, blessed saints," Hexie whispered.

Asti looked down to the ground. Verci started uncoiling the rope, controlling Asti and Hexie's descent. His hands worked quickly, his arms straining, until they reached the ground safely. As soon as their feet made contact, Asti let her go, untying the rope around them. She collapsed to the ground, still giving prayers, her little dog running in crazy circles around her.

"Gadget worked this time," Asti said as he freed himself from the rope.

"Of course it did," Verci swiped back. He bent over Hexie. "Safe and sound, Missus Matlin?"

"Thank you, blessed saints," she said. "Oh, thank you, boys. Your mother would be so proud of you."

"It was nothing," Verci said with a smile.

"It was nothing for you," Asti said, elbowing his brother in the ribs.

"You promised to do the stupid things," Verci said.

"Stupid promise," Asti muttered. "You all right now, Hexie? We have to check our shop."

"I'm fine, boys," she said unconvincingly. She looked around at the fire and madness surrounding them.

"Our packs are still on the roof," Verci said.

"Later," Asti muttered. He grabbed Verci's arm and pulled him down the alley.

The Rynax Gadgeterium hadn't even opened yet. Not one customer, not one sale. They had bought the shop less than a month ago and had been working on getting it fixed up enough to open. They had put down most every crown they had to buy the place from Old Spence, and they still owed him quite a bit of silver. It wasn't a great bargain, but it was better than owing money to one of the ankle-breakers in Keller Cove.

Old Spence had let the place become a wreck, and it had taken a lot of work on their part to make it presentable. Asti had figured it would only be a couple more days before they could open. The flops above the store were still unlivable, but when the shop was open, they planned to clean and fix them so they could move in.

The Rynax Gadgeterium was nothing but a burning husk now, a handful of beams and stones in the rough skeleton of a building, the sad corpse of their plans.

Verci stood agape in front of what had been their shop, not moving an inch as he stared at the smoldering remnants.

Asti's blood boiled, a rush of mixed emotions, rage winning.

It took a moment for Asti to realize there was a cry from inside Almer Cort's chemist shop across the street from the Gadgeterium. Cort's shop wasn't burning, but the door was broken open. Asti ran inside.

Five young toughs were in the shop. Two of them held Cort up against the wall, working him over. The other three were rifling through the shop, knocking over shelves and glass bottles. "Where's your lockbox?" one of them shouted.

Asti charged right in at the two boys holding on to Cort. His building rage finally had a target, five stupid faces for him to hit. He launched at the one he figured to be the leader of this gang, grabbing the hooligan about the waist and ripping him away from Cort. That one dealt with for the moment, he kicked the other one in the knee.

"Run!" Asti shouted to Cort, who was still up against the wall, gasping for breath. Cort managed to stumble to the door of his back room. Asti turned to the hooligans.

Just a glance was all he needed to figure this bunch out. Street scrappers, every one, no real training. The closest two had knives. The other three, back by the shelves, didn't have any obvious weapons. Asti knew he didn't look too intimidating, given his short stature and wiry frame. If it wasn't for the layer of unshaven scruff on his face, they might think he was just a kid. Still, they hung back, each one waiting for someone else to pounce.

Asti didn't give them a chance. Since he was unarmed, he went for the closest one, the one with two knives. Asti needed those knives. The kid held his guard up, tried to slash at Asti. Wasn't fast enough, and Asti dove in, taking the cuts on his arms. He gave two sharp punches at the kid's shoulders. Before the others could react, Asti grabbed him by the wrists and spun him around. The knives clattered to the ground.

Asti was about to push the kid at the other armed one. Before he could, the hooligan swung back his head, cracking Asti's nose.

Everything went red.

Chapter 2

VERCI DIDN'T KNOW HOW long he stood staring at the smoldering remains of his shop. He couldn't even wrap his head around what was lost. Tools. Inventions. Every crown they owned, every ounce of work they had put into it. All gone.

Screams from Cort's shop snapped Verci out of his reverie. Three boys ran out of the shop, screaming. They ran like they were on fire. They ran like death was after them.

Asti wasn't next to him anymore. Verci hadn't noticed him leave.

"Asti," Verci whispered, racing into the shop.

Shelves were knocked over, bottles broken. The place was a wreck. A street boy was dead on the floor, two knives buried in his chest.

Asti was on top of another one, pinning him to the ground with his knees while pummeling his face. There was no struggle, no resistance. Just his brother pounding his fists into a senseless mass of blood and meat.

Verci grabbed Asti's shoulder. Asti reacted instantly, spinning around and grabbing Verci by the throat. His face was twisted, covered in blood and ash, his eyes burning with empty rage. Verci clawed at his brother's hand, trying to get it free of his neck. Asti lifted him up off the ground.

"As—" was all Verci could gasp out. He batted at Asti's head, a futile effort. Asti wasn't letting go. Verci was about to black out.

A hand appeared from nowhere and smeared a paste under Asti's nose. A moment later Asti went limp and crumpled to the ground. Verci managed to land on his feet, woozy but stable. Almer Cort was standing there, a small man with a thick graying beard and wide spectacles. He wiped off his finger on the front of his leather apron.

"You all right?" Cort asked. Schooling had blunted his West Maradaine accent, but not eliminated it.

"Think so," Verci said. "How long will he be out?"

"A few minutes." Cort pulled out a handkerchief and wiped the gunk from Asti's face. "Shouldn't leave it there very long, though."

"What happened?"

"Some rats cracked into my shop," Cort said. "They were roughing me up when he came in and . . ." Cort looked at the two dead bodies on the floor of the shop. "He . . . he just went crazy on them."

"Yeah." Verci shook his head. Blazes. Not again. Asti had been getting better. "Night like this, could make anyone snap." Cort ought to buy that.

"What's happening out there?" Cort asked.

"Fire," Verci said. "The whole east side of the alley."

"Fire Brigade?"

"Haven't seen them yet," Verci said. "It's insane out there."

"It's insane in here," Cort said, looking down at Asti. "He going to go berserk when he comes to?"

"No." Said it too quick. Too suspicious. "I don't think so, at any rate."

Cort picked up another bottle. "He gets this in his face if he does."

"He'll be fine!" Verci snapped. "Think you can do something about the fire?"

Cort looked around at the broken shelves. "Nothing on a large scale. This building should be safe if the fire jumps across. Solid brick."

"Small comfort," Verci said. Asti groaned and stirred. "Hey, brother. You all right?"

Asti woke with a startled jerk. Eyes bulging, he clutched out and grabbed Verci's shirt.

"Verci," he said, looking around. "Where are we?"

"Cort's shop," Verci said.

"When did we—" Asti looked at his hands, covered with blood. "Did I . . ." He faltered, looking back at Verci.

"You did," Verci said. "Some street rats were hurting Almer, and you . . . you got rid of them."

"Not all of them," Asti said. The mutilated bodies were still lying on the ground near them. He sat up, burying his face in his hands. "Blazes, brother, I don't know if I can go through this again."

"It's all right, Asti," Verci said, crouching down. "It's been a crazy night. Anyone could lose it. Right? Anyone." He signaled in Cort's direction with his eyes.

Asti didn't care. "There's two dead bodies here, Verci! What are we going to do about that when Constabulary comes?"

"I can take care of that," Cort offered. He opened up one bottle and poured a light powder on top of the two bodies. They both started sizzling, the flesh burning away. "We've got half the alley burning down, I can slip them into one of the burned buildings. Constabs won't be looking too hard at two more corpses in this mess."

"This 'mess' is our homes, our businesses, Almer," Asti snapped. "Friends. Lives!"

"I know that!" Cort stalked over to the door, looking out at the wreckage across the street. "And snots like these boys tried to take advantage. You took care of it, Asti. I'm not gonna let you take a hit, get sent over to Quarrygate or something, for helping me. Least I can do."

"We appreciate it, Almer," Verci said.

Cort pulled on some heavy gloves and dragged the first body out of the shop.

Asti paced about, hands clenched in tight fists. "Not again, Verci. I can't—"

"Don't say that." He took Asti by the shoulders. "Don't you dare tell me you can't."

Asti shook his head, looking at the ground. "I'm not any better. Head's still cracking."

"Look at me!" Verci grabbed his brother's head, forcing him to meet his eyes. He'd be damned if he let Asti slip off on him now. Not in the middle of this. "Job ain't over, and we're skunked. You hear me?"

"Job ain't skunked until you're pinched or dead," Asti whispered. One of Dad's rules.

"Are we pinched?" Verci asked.

"No."

"Dead?"

"Not yet." A hint of a smile crossed Asti's lips.

"Then we drive forward, hmm?"

"Forward." Asti nodded and stepped away. Now his chin was high, eyes full of thought. He stripped out of his bloody clothes, throwing them on the remaining body. "Where's my pack?"

"Still up on that roof."

"Go get them," Asti said. "I need fresh clothes."

"Good," Verci said. He went to the door. "Tell me you have a plan."

"I always have a plan, brother."

"And what's that?"

"We're going to go see the Old Lady."

※

There were no lamps burning in the windows of the Junk Avenue Bakery. Several blocks away from Holver Alley, it was a quiet night. No panic in the street, hardly any stirring at all. The only sound was Asti pounding on the bakery door.

"She's probably asleep," Verci said. He didn't want to do this. Not in the middle of the night. Not without checking on Raych first. Asti insisted, though, his mind whirring like a clockwork box again. Verci would go all night if it kept Asti on this side of sanity.

Asti shook his head. "The question is if she's here at all tonight."

"She's here," Verci said. He didn't have his ear to the ground like he used to, but if she had gone somewhere else, he probably would have heard about it. "Question is if she'll see us."

"She will."

"She never liked that you left," Verci said.

Asti shrugged. "She'll still see us. She likes you." He pounded the door again. After a moment it creaked open a crack. A small man looked out through the crack.

"What do you want? It's the middle of the night."

"We need the Old Lady," Asti said. "Is she here?"

"I don't know what you mean."

"Oh, come off it, Mersh," Verci said. "Look at us. It's Asti and Verci Rynax." The man peered closer.

"Sorry, couldn't see you." He added pointedly, "It's dark. It being the middle of the night when you came banging." He opened the door and let them in. "Been a while since you've been here."

Verci looked around the bakery as Mersh went about lighting lamps. He hadn't been in the place for over a year. The place still smelled the same as it had a year ago, when he did that last job for her. A lifetime ago.

"You two look awful," Mersh said once he had a light on. "What happened?"

"The whole alley burned down tonight."

"What?" said Mersh. "What do you mean? Which alley?"

"Holver Alley. Every single shop and house on the east side," said Asti, "From Ullen Street to Rabbit."

"Great blessed saints," said Mersh. "How? Is anyone hurt, or ..." He let it hang.

"A lot of people dead, Mersh," Asti snarled.

"We don't know all what happened yet," Verci said. "Stay awake and start baking, though. There's a few more hungry people with no homes out there today."

Mersh kissed his knuckle and pressed it to his forehead, whispering a quick prayer. Three knocks pounded from below the shop. Mersh went over by the oven and twisted a few hidden levers. A small trapdoor opened in the wall by the counter.

"Sounds like she'll see you. Go on down."

Asti crouched to enter the hatch.

"Boys, leave the packs. And any weapons."

"Right," Asti said, sliding the pack off his shoulders and handing it over to Mersh. He crawled down the hatch. Verci slid his own pack off, grabbed a lamp, and followed him.

The passage was a narrow staircase, the ceiling not more than five feet high. The two of them needed to crouch low to work their way down, one step at a time. As soon as they were both going down, the hatch door shut behind them.

"How the blazes does she get down this way?" Asti asked.

"I don't think this is the way she takes," Verci said. "I've never gone down this way." A sudden sense of dread filled him. "Asti, stop!"

"What is it?" Asti asked. He put his foot down on the next step, and as he did it Verci heard a gentle click. Asti looked up at Verci. "Oh, sweet blasted saints, is this what I think it is?"

"Stay perfectly still, Asti."

"She blasted well had us sent down a blazing trapped staircase?" Asti shouted. "Played us for rabbits?"

"Shush!" Verci hissed. Slowly he moved down to the step above Asti's and handed him the lamp. "I think it's an arm-and-release. We'll be all right as long as you don't move."

"And what will happen if I do?"

Verci gently touched the step. There was just a hint of quiver to it, barely noticeable. He reached down to the next step and touched it. No quiver, no give. It was stable. Stretching around Asti, he moved down to it.

"Blazes you doing?"

"Getting a better view," Verci said. "Don't move."

"Don't knock me over."

Verci got on the lower step and crouched down to Asti's feet. The steps were wooden, and Asti's had two small grooves in the back that allowed it to slide down the quarter inch it needed to arm the trap.

"What will it do when it goes off, Verci?"

"Working on that," Verci said. He could feel a slight vibration somewhere near him. He touched the wall. That was the source. He ran his fingers down to the base, where the wall met the steps. Sure enough, there was just a slight gap, a hint of a draft coming from the crack.

"This wall will close in on us."

"We're going to be crushed?" Asti started swearing profusely. Verci looked along the wood grain of the step. There were slight scrapes, ending two-thirds of the way across.

"No, it doesn't close completely. We'll just be pinned. A few broken bones."

"Slow or fast?"

Verci placed his hand back on the wall. "I'm thinking this is being held back by tension. Its natural position is to be closed in. I think it'll slam on us."

"I'm going to kill that blasted doxy," Asti said.

"Just stay still," Verci said. He tapped along the back of the steps. Hollow. He took off his shirt and wrapped it around one hand.

"What are you doing?"

"Don't have many tools," Verci said. "Have to get into the guts of this trap somehow."

He punched into the back wall of the step.

"Saint Keller!" Asti shouted. "Won't that set it off?"

"Hope not."

"Hope not?"

Verci punched again. The wood cracked. The panel on the back step wasn't very thick. Verci punched again. The panel gave way enough to get a few fingers inside it. He unwrapped his hand and pried the panel off.

"Hand me the lamp."

"Do you know what you're doing?"

"Now you're just insulting me."

The device was not very complicated. It armed when Asti's weight snapped a small pin holding the release trigger in place. Once he moved off the stair, there would be nothing to prevent the trigger from closing, and that would slam the wall on them both. "There must be a lot of counterweights in here somewhere to balance this out."

"That's really fascinating, brother. What can you do?"

"Take off your belt."

"Why my belt?"

"Because I'm not wearing one."

Asti started removing his belt. "Verci, I really feel I have to tell you something."

"Please don't get sentimental on me, brother," Verci said.

"I'm not," Asti said. He handed Verci the belt. "I want to tell you that far too many of your plans involve removing clothing."

"You love it."

"Yes, very much."

Verci pulled off the belt buckle. It was a crude tool, but it would do the job. "Get ready."

"To do what?"

"Very slowly, you're going to remove your weight from the step, and I'm going to wedge the belt buckle into the trigger."

"This is your plan?"

"This is the plan."

"I hate your plan."

"Good," Verci said. He got the buckle in position. "Count of five."

"Do I remove on five, or is a five-count the pace of taking my weight off?"

"Surprise me," Verci said. "One." Asti lifted himself up, the step moving just a hair. "Two. Three. Four." The step moved up a bit more, and Verci pushed the buckle into the trigger. "Five."

Asti was off the step.

The trigger held.

"All right, let's go," Asti said.

"Up or down?"

"Down," Asti said. "We go through that, we're going to see the Old Lady."

They went down the last few steps carefully, making sure that nothing else was rigged. The door at the bottom of the steps had no handle.

"Fake door? A staircase to nowhere?" Asti asked. Verci knocked on it. Hollow.

"There's empty space back there. Just don't know what."

"What do you think?"

"I think that belt buckle isn't going to hold forever, and we want to get out of this stairwell."

"Good thought. Stand back," Asti said. He braced his hands on the sides of the wall, and hit the door with a sharp kick. It came right off the frame. "Easy enough."

"A little crude, though," the Old Lady's voice came from the next room. "Come in, boys."

The room was a small study, warmly lit with several

lamps and candles. Verci hated this room. There were no obvious exits, save the broken door they just came through. He couldn't even spot the entrance he had always used in the past. The Old Lady made every way in and out a hidden passage. Verci darted his eyes about, trying to determine what in the room could be a secret lever, a hidden catch, anything that would open the way out. Knowing her, there was a good chance any door he found would lead to a trapped dead end.

There were several soft chairs at a round table. The table was covered in loose papers. The Old Lady, Missus Josefine Holt, was sitting at the table. Slowly she gathered up some of the papers and put them in a neat pile.

"Sit down," she said. She stood up from her chair, picking up a cane and using it to support herself as she crossed over to a metal pipe. She banged it twice with the cane, and pulled a lever next to it.

She looked much older than she had a year ago. Her curly bush of hair had gone from dark brown with a few single grays to having large streaks of white. Her clothes were simple: modest cotton blouse, practical wool skirt. No jewelry or other adornments. No one glancing at her would suspect she was one of the richest people in the North Seleth neighborhood. She was stooped slightly, as if she was carrying a heavy weight. Verci knew she had been reliant on the cane for years, but now it seemed far more necessary than ever before. It almost broke his heart to see her like this. Almost.

"Why did you try and kill us?" he asked. Asti, he could tell, was steaming, too angry to speak yet.

"Please, Verci," she said as she returned to the table. "If that little thing had killed you, then you wouldn't be worth talking to anyway. And put your shirt on."

"So that's why you sent us down that way?" Verci asked as he dressed. "See if I still had the goods to get through a trap like that?"

"I'm disappointed that you triggered it at all, frankly."

"So am I," Verci said. "Careless and amateur."

"You do that on a real job, you'd get pegged for sure."

"Real job I'd be long gone by now," Verci said. "And I wouldn't have left my gear with a front man."

"Fair enough," she said. "So you passed well enough to get to see me."

"A test?" Asti shouted.

"Don't you scream at me, Asti Rynax," she snapped. "You come to me after years, years since you decided to cut out on me and go straight. Your brother had the decency to go straight honestly, telling me to my face that he was out of the business. But you—"

"What about me, Josie?"

"There's going straight and going square."

"I ain't square," Asti said.

"That's the word out there," she said. "Could be a nice cover. Asti Rynax gets kicked out of Druth Intelligence and worms his way back into the old business. Gets in good and deep."

"That's not it," Verci said. "That's not it at all."

"So you say." She pointed to a cupboard. "Get a bottle of wine from there and pour us some glasses."

Verci went over to get the wine. Asti sat down at the table, leaning in to Josie. "You don't trust me, fine. Trust him."

"When it comes to you?" She shook her head. "Not hardly. He'd walk through fire for you."

"Already did tonight," Verci said. He brought the wine over and poured out three glasses.

"You said some noise about a fire up there. What happened?"

"Holver Alley. The whole thing burned down on the east side. Our shop, Greenfield's shop, everything in between."

Josie whistled low and sipped at her wine. Asti picked up his glass and sniffed at it.

"Problem, Asti?" she asked. "Something wrong with the wine?"

"Not sure," he said. "I'm trying to decide if you are paranoid enough to keep a cabinet full of poisoned wine, dosing yourself with the antidote every day so you can casually offer the wine to someone who comes down here."

"I am," she said, sipping her wine again. "I got pinched and thrown in Quarrygate once. That was plenty. But if I wanted you dead you wouldn't have even made it in here."

"When's the last time you saw sunlight, Josie?"

"I've got safehouses with windows," she said. "I've even got a nice little garden in one."

"Charming," Asti said.

"Quite," she said. "All right, Asti, drink it."

"Pardon?"

"Drink the wine, Asti. Or get out."

Verci had enough of this game. He picked up his glass and drank down the wine in one gulp. Asti shrugged and did the same.

"Can we do some business now?" Verci asked.

"Well, boys, that depends on what your business is. Who do I have here: a disgraced ex-spy and a married shopkeeper? Or do I have the Rynax boys?"

"Josie, we've lost just about everything," Verci said.

"And I need to know why you're here. Are you two locals, standing with hat in hand for a loan? Or are you the sons of Kelsi Rynax, coming to me to get a gig?"

Verci looked over to Asti. He would rather just go for the loan. He'd hoped Asti would feel the same way.

He saw the look in Asti's eye. Asti was here for the gig.

"You want to get back into the business?"

"No," Asti said. "But what the blazes else can we do? We've tried other things, brother, but this is what we've been bred for. This is our blood."

"Touching, Asti," Josie said. "But smart. If I'm right, you boys already have a debt to Old Spence for the shop. Adding a loan at my rates would break your backs."

Verci stared at the empty glass. He didn't like this. He didn't want to go back to it. Raych didn't want him to, either. Raych and Corsi needed a home and money, too. Food on the table.

Josie was right, no matter how much he didn't want her to be.

A few good gigs, they could rebuild the shop, get back on course.

"Only slip-and-grab jobs, though," Verci said. "From cats who can take the hit. No blood runs, no *hassper* or drug deals of any kind."

"I don't do those kinds of deals," Josie said. "Those have moved to the big dogs."

"We won't do them," Verci said.

"Fair enough," she said. "I may have something for you."

"All right," Asti said.

She got up from her chair and hobbled over to a desk in the corner. She took out a small pouch and tossed it over to Asti. "Twenty crowns. As an advance."

"What's the gig?"

"I'll send word with details. I'll be hooking you up with a carriage-man to work it."

"This a three-man job?"

"Don't know for sure," she said. "That's what you do, Asti. You size up the job and figure out what you need. But I've got a carriage-man I want to check out. He's swaddling, but he's eager."

"You want us to train new blood?" Verci asked.

"You're the boys who need the work," she said. "You take what I got, or find someone else who'll even talk to you. I'm only doing it because I feel a little nostalgic about your father."

"We appreciate it," Asti said.

"I'll send him to you at Kimber's, around six bells tomorrow evening."

"How'll we know him?"

"He'll say I sent him," she said flatly. "And he's Ch'omik, so you can't miss him."

Verci was surprised to hear that. Josie Holt usually didn't use talent that stood out in a crowd.

"We'll see him tomorrow, then," Verci said. "How do we get out of here?"

Holt lifted her cane and hooked a wall-mounted lamp near her desk. A hidden door swung open next to her.

"No traps in this one?" Asti asked.

"You tell me," she said with a smile. The two of them went to the door. She stopped them just before they went in. "Boys, I am sorry about the alley, and your shop. We'll get you on your feet quick, all right?" She smiled warmly for the first time.

"Thanks," Verci said.

"We at least could come to you," Asti said. "There's a lot of folks who don't have that option."

"All right, get," she said. "I've had enough of the both of you." They went into the passage and the door closed behind them. A moment later another door opened in front of them, a powerful stench coming in with it.

"Sewer exit," Asti said. "Lovely."

"That way, about a half a mile," Verci said, pointing down the passage. "We come out at the creek."

✦

Asti held his breath for five disgusting minutes until they were back in the open air, wading in Shale Creek, which marked the line between the neighborhoods of Seleth and Keller Cove. Asti breathed deep and looked around. Their packs were hanging on a hook above the sewer entrance.

"Isn't that thoughtful?" Asti said.

"She thinks of everything," Verci said. He climbed up and took their packs while Asti got out of the creek. He threw Asti's pack to him and stripped out of his sewer-stained clothes.

"I'm running out of clothing," Asti said as he took his own off. "Give those to me. I'll bring them to the laundry girl on Kenner in the morning."

"Where are you going now?" Verci asked.

"I'm going to Kimber's," Asti said. He took a few coins out of the purse and tossed it over to Verci. "You're going to Raych's sister's place."

"You could come, too," Verci said.

"I barely get along with Raych, let alone her sister," Asti said. "That flop is going to be crowded enough."

"You sure?"

"Get to your wife, brother." He pulled on his last clean pair of trousers.

Verci started up the embankment. "I'm not happy with this, you know."

Asti didn't know what to make of that. "What the blazes is there to be happy about?"

"Nothing," Verci snapped. "I mean . . . I understand, all right? We're in a bind, we go to Josie, we get a gig, we get on our feet. But that's it, right?"

"Are you asking me if we're going back for good?" Asti

did his best to smile, put on a good face for Verci. "Not on your life."

"Not on Corsi's life, you get it?" Verci said.

Asti got it plenty. Dad had never given either of them much choice, putting them to work almost as soon as they could walk. Verci was adamant about never doing that to his son.

"You'll raise him clean," Asti said. "I'd die before I let otherwise happen."

"Don't talk like that."

Asti waved him off. "I'll see you at six bells tomorrow, all right?"

"All right," Verci said. "You're going to be well, yes?"

"I'm fine, brother," Asti said. It came out shorter than he meant. He knew what Verci was hinting at, but didn't want to talk about when he'd lost control.

"Fine," Verci said. "Tomorrow, then." He went off down the dark street. Asti went the other way, up Frost, until he reached Kimber's Pub. Despite the late hour, the lamps were still lit out front.

Asti found the taproom filled with people. Most of them were from the alley, smeared with ash. Eyes red from smoke or tears. The worst off were laid out on the tables, and Doc Gelson, looking weary and broken, was going around checking the injured. Others were curled up on the floor, wherever there was space.

Helene and Julien were up against one wall, near a table with Winthym Greenfield sleeping on it. Asti started his way over to them.

"Asti." A soft hand touched him on the arm. Kimber, her warm, round face filled with big, sad eyes. "You're hurt." His arms were covered in scrapes and cuts, red welts from the burns.

"It's not much." He pulled his arm away.

"Let's get Gelson to look at it," she said. "I heard you . . . you and your brother . . . you went in there for Win."

"Went in there for all of them. Only got Win."

"But you went in," she said. "Where's Verci? And his wife?"

"Raych has a sister, lives a few blocks from here. They went over there."

"And you came here?"

Asti held up a coin. "I can pay for a room."

She put her hands over his. "No rooms left. Just floor if you can find space, and I'm not charging anyone for that." She beckoned Doc Gelson. "You just take care of yourself right now, all right?"

"Yes, ma'am." She went off as Gelson approached, stinking of cider. Despite that, his hands looked steady and his eyes were focused.

"Rynax," he said. "You really were in the thick of it, eh? Took you a while to get over here."

"Had to take care of things."

"Things." Gelson scowled and took Asti's arm. "Burns aren't too bad. These are knife wounds."

"Taking care of things," Asti said.

"There something we need to tell to Constabulary?"

"Are there any around to tell?"

Gelson shook his head and clucked his tongue. "These aren't so bad as to need stitching. I'll dress the whole arm, burns and cuts."

"A bunch of punks thought they could take advantage. Had to educate them otherwise."

"Wasn't that long ago Rynax boys would have been the ones taking advantage."

Asti resisted the urge to yank his arm away. If Gelson wanted to run his drunk mouth off while patching him, let the man.

"Good," Gelson said once he finished wrapping the arm. "Keep it dry, change the dressing tomorrow night, keep out of trouble. The whole drill."

"Whole drill," Asti whispered.

"You're welcome." Gelson stumbled off.

Asti crossed to the far corner and slumped down by Helene and Julien. In the light, the two of them looked even worse for wear. Helene had taken the pins out of her hair, letting it fall to her shoulders, but it was still a mess of tangles and ash. Julien's short hair was even worse, as a huge chunk on his left side had been burned off.

"What's the word?" Asti asked, nodding at Win's sleeping body.

"He woke up for a bit," Helene said distantly, her green eyes glazed over. "Doc says he took a lot of smoke, but he'll be all right."

"Did . . . did you tell him about his family?"

"Yeah," Helene said. Her voice cracked. Asti had never seen anything choke Helene up before. She was the toughest bird he'd ever known. "It was the first thing he asked."

"I'm sorry about that, Hel," he said.

"Yeah, well," she said. "I was here when he asked. What else could I do?"

"Jules?" Asti asked. "How are you doing?"

"Got no home, Asti," Julien croaked out. "Where is Helene gonna live? Where am I?"

"Don't know yet, Julien," Asti said. "We're all trying to figure that out." He glanced back at Helene, lowering his voice. "You have anything set aside?"

"Nah," Helene said. "And where would we have set it? Wasn't for having that house from our gram, we'd have been flat out a long time ago."

"You're not working?" he whispered to her.

"Not the jobs I want," she said. She locked eyes with Asti. "Nobody wants to give us a gig, not since Holtman's."

"That wasn't your fault," Asti said.

"It was Julien's," she said. "We both know it." She looked over at Julien, who was sitting with his massive legs curled up close to his body. For a moment Asti thought he looked like a giant child.

"What about bare-knuckle bouts?" Asti asked. "Jules could do well enough."

"No chance," she said. Her eyes flamed up. She turned away, looking off in the distance again. "Last thing his head needs is taking a few more shots."

Asti didn't reply. Julien was far from the brightest guy on the block. After he had taken a beating from a gang from Benson Court, he had never recovered. Julien's memory wasn't the same after that. His cousin did her best to take care of him. It was a shame no one would hire her, either. Asti didn't know anyone better with a crossbow.

"I guess you didn't manage a room upstairs," he said.

"Full up already," Helene said. "Kimber told everyone they were welcome to stay the night in the taproom."

Asti looked around the room. Nearly every spare spot to lie or sit was filled with someone. Plenty of people hurt or broken. Plenty more curled up and sleeping wherever they found space. There were faces Asti knew, like Olman and Ellie Hansper, dozing against the wall with their four children asleep in their laps. There were other faces he didn't, like the dark-haired waif girl, barely sixteen, looking like she hadn't had a proper meal in weeks.

He turned back to Helene. "Has anyone official come through here?"

"Official how?"

"Constabulary, Fire Brigade, Yellowshields? Or the Neighborhood Council, if not the Aldermen? Someone from the Duke of Maradaine? Anyone?" He was agitated, and his question was louder than he had meant for it to be.

The dark-haired girl, sitting in the shadow of the bar, answered. "Brigade showed up to tamp it out, eventually. Just one water wagon, after most the alley had burned out. Couple constabs were around the alley, telling folks to get out of there. But they didn't say more than that. Certainly didn't do more."

"Ain't nobody official going to help us," Helene said.

"We look out for each other, then," Julien said, half asleep.

Asti nodded. He wanted to go around, find out more about what happened, what people were doing, but exhaustion had set in. Sitting down on the wooden floor, he could barely keep his eyes open. Closing them, he surrendered to sleep.

Chapter 3

VERCI HAD BEEN ASLEEP for several hours when the prod of someone's foot woke him up. He opened his eyes just enough to determine the identity of the prodder. It was Hal, Raych's sister's prat of a husband. Hal was a lumbering, puffy man, with what little hair he had pulled back by running his greasy, sweaty fingers through it.

"Why're you sleeping on the floor?" Hal asked.

"Once I got in here, couldn't take another step," Verci said. He really hadn't planned to fall asleep on the floor of the cloakroom of Raych's sister's house. He just dropped down as soon as he got in. "Didn't want to wake anyone. Raych upstairs?"

"How did you get in?" Hal waddled over to the front door. "I thought I had locked it."

"Not much of a lock," Verci mumbled.

Hal glanced back at Verci, his face confused. He shook it away after a moment. "Well, Raych was a wreck when she got here, I'll tell you that." He breathed heavy, rubbing his sweaty head. "It sounds like you all had quite the night."

"We lost our home, Hal," Verci said.

"Yeah," Hal said, nodding. "Real . . . real terrible. But you were just renting that, Verci. What about the shop?"

"Shop was lost as well," Verci said. "We lost everything."

"That's just terrible," Hal said, shaking his head some more. Verci had had enough conversations with the man to know this was the limit of Hal's sympathy. "Well, you know, you . . . you, and Raych of course, take a day or two, figure out what you're going to do."

"That's very kind of you, Hal," Verci said flatly.

"You'll work it out," Hal said, looking more at the floor and walls than Verci. "You were, I always said, you were so clever with your bits and gears and twisty things. Clever one, yeah."

"Where is Raych, Hal?"

"Oh, she and Lian are in the kitchen, of course," Hal said. "You better go let her know you're here, because she's still a frightful wreck. I need to go to work, of course."

"Of course," Verci said. Hal was a clerk for one of the exchange and import houses near the river docks of Keller Cove. This was what Raych's sister would often call a "proper, respectable job."

"Yeah, it's just . . . well . . ." Hal hesitated. "You're on my cloak."

"Oh," Verci said, getting up. He had no memory of taking the cloak off its hook and lying down on it. He had been dead exhausted when he came in. He picked up the cloak, lamely dusting it off and handing it to Hal. "Sorry about that."

"No problem," Hal said. "You've, you know, been through a lot." He sniffed at the cloak and then sniffed at Verci. "Did you fall in the sewers or something?"

"Something," Verci said.

"Well, you know, there's the bathhouse down at the corner of the street. I mean, I don't judge a man by how he smells, but you might want to get down there anyway."

"Right," Verci said. "Thanks for the tip. I'm . . . I'm going to go find Raych now."

"Good, good," Hal said, grinning emptily. "I'll be off. Perhaps I'll see you this evening, you can tell me all about your night."

"Sure," Verci said. He waved dismissively at Hal and went to the kitchen.

Raych was pacing back and forth, absently rocking the

baby as she did so. She did look a wreck, her hair pulled up in a disheveled bun, her face still streaked with ash. She was wearing one of Lian's dresses, too loose on her. Lian was by the stove, her hands deep into a bowl, kneading.

Raych and Lian were unmistakably sisters, with the same dark, piercing eyes and beautiful face, though Lian's had far more creases and lines. The differences between the two stood out the most to Verci. Lian was pale and fair-haired, where Raych was dusky, taking after their Acserian mother. Lian was doughy; Raych was lean. They both had the same arms, though: hard, powerful arms with strong hands.

"He'll turn up," Lian said. "He always does."

"I don't suppose there's any tea," Verci said.

Raych gasped and raced over to him, grabbing him in a fervent embrace, awkwardly holding the baby to the side as she did so. She babbled out at him, "I was so worried. I didn't know what happened to you or what fool thing your brother would have you do. I just kept imagining the worst and what happened to the shop and why do you smell so awful?"

Verci stopped her words with a kiss. She responded warmly, then pulled away.

"Seriously, Verci Rynax, where have you been all night?"

"Most of it, sleeping in the cloakroom." He jabbed a thumb in the direction of the front door. "I didn't last a step longer than getting in the house."

"I didn't hear you come in," Lian said coldly.

"No one hears me come in," Verci said.

Raych scowled at him. "No jokes," she said. "Is the shop all right?"

Verci shook his head. "Gone. Everything."

"What are we going to do?"

"First, have some tea," Verci said.

"Lian, could you?" Raych asked her sister. Lian rolled her eyes and went to the stove.

"You know, Verci," Lian said as she poured the tea. "Hal tells me that they always need people at the docks, working the cargo and such. I'm sure he can talk to someone. Or, if your reading is all right ... you can read, yes?" She stood several paces away, keeping his tea close to her chest.

"Yes," Verci said. He reached out and pulled the cup away from her. "I can read just fine." He sipped at the tea, which was terrible, but hot. He sat down at the table, Raych sitting next to him, her free hand caressing his arm.

"Well, that's good," Lian said. "You could become a clerk's apprentice. You know, a path to a proper job. Hal could help you."

Verci was about to snap at Lian when Raych squeezed his arm. He glanced at her, nodding. He had to be polite to her sister.

"That's an idea," he said neutrally. "Asti and I need to talk and figure out our next step."

"Oh, yes, your brother." Lian's voice dropped an octave. "Of course."

Asti woke suddenly, fully alert the moment he opened his eyes. He was still sitting on the dirty wooden floor of Kimber's Pub, slumped to the side and leaning on Julien. Julien was fast asleep, snoring with his mouth open. Helene was curled up in a ball on the floor, her long dark hair covering her face. Sunlight streamed in from the far window.

Asti pulled himself to his feet, his whole body stiff. He stretched his arms out, and then his neck. All his joints cracked loud enough to make Helene stir for a moment. He grabbed his pack and slipped out from behind the tables they had slept under.

The taproom wasn't as crowded as the night before, but plenty of people still slept on the tables and dusty wooden floor, making it challenging to navigate his way out without stepping on anyone. He worked his way across, slow, graceful moves, silent as a mouse. No one disturbed. He chuckled to himself, reminded of a time years before, when he snuck through the sleeping barracks of the City Constabulary in Abernar. The consequences of waking someone up now would be far less dire, but the same instincts drove him until he reached the door.

He glanced back at the room, seeing who was still there. Winthym Greenfield wasn't. Asti wondered where he had gone.

Frost Road was abuzz with morning activity. Mulecarts and wagons lumbered along in both directions. A few boys were unloading sacks of flour at the grocer across the street. A pair of constabs ambled genially, their hands resting on their handsticks, as if expecting to have to club someone down at any moment. A newsboy stood on a crate at the corner of Junk and Frost, holding his newssheets high as he called out the stories of the day. Asti went over to the corner.

"Parliament vote postponed!" the boy shouted. "Members complain about procedural trickery!"

"Oy, newsboy," Asti said. "There a story on the fire?"

"What fire is that?" the kid asked.

"Over on Holver Alley last night." Asti pointed back in the direction of the alley. "A whole mess of houses and shops burned down."

"I ain't heard," the boy said. He looked at his newssheet. "Nothing about a fire."

"What?" Asti said. He grabbed a newssheet away. The big stories were about Parliament parties arguing with each other, a mistress scandal involving City Council Aldermen, and some mages murdered on the east side. Asti flipped through the sheet. Stories about a dockworkers brawl, a tetchball game, and a ceremony for an old admiral. Nothing about the fire.

"Hey!" the kid shouted. "You owe me two ticks!"

"Why isn't there a story about the fire?"

"I don't print it, chief," the kid said. "Newsboys just call it and sell it. Two ticks!"

Asti dug into his coat pocket, taking a couple of copper coins out. "Who prints this one?"

"That's the *West Maradaine Daily*," the boy said. "They do the printing the night before the newsboys get them, you know. If the fire was in the night, they wouldn't have gotten word in time to make today's print."

"So it'll be in tomorrow's print?"

"I just call it and sell it, chief," the kid said. He turned back out to the street at large. "Alderman Strephen ousted! Mistress shatters the City Council! Big tetchball game tonight! Silversmith Guild against the Brewers League! Read it all for only two ticks!"

Asti walked away from the newsboy and almost collided with a pedalcart trundling around the corner.

"Sorry, mate," Asti said. Mersh was the one pedaling the cart. "What are you up to?"

"Spice cakes," Mersh said, noting his cargo. "The Old Lady said most people who got hurt in the fire are in Kimber's."

"You giving or selling?" Asti asked.

"Giving," Mersh said. "Least I can do, you know?" He took a cake out of the cart and handed it to Asti.

"Good man, Mersh," Asti said. He hadn't realized how hungry he was, greedily taking a bite. "These are excellent. I think it'll help a lot in there."

Mersh nodded. "The secret is a spice called *jhektak*."

"That's Poasian, isn't it?" Asti asked. Poasia was far to the west, across the ocean, and Poasians were a horrible, brutal people. Druthal had spent half a century at war with them, with an uneasy peace for the past fifteen years. Asti's time in Druth Intelligence made him very aware how fragile that peace really was. Despite that, the demand for Poasian spices made the spice trade a profitable enterprise.

"It is," Mersh said. "I get mine from a shop over on Heel Street. You know the shop? You might find something you're looking for over there."

Asti did know the shop, all too well.

"I don't do much baking, Mersh."

"Poasian spices have many uses, as I'm sure you know," Mersh said. He gave a nervous glance down the road. Asti didn't notice anyone watching them, but working for the Old Lady would make anyone jumpy. Mersh cleared his throat and gave Asti a sheepish look. "I'm going to bring these over while they're still warm."

"Of course," Asti said. Mersh started pedaling his cart along toward Kimber's. Asti went down Junk, heading back toward the alley.

He wasn't sure why he wanted to go back over there. Something gnawed at him, and he needed to see it in daylight. The whole travesty of it didn't seem real yet. Last night still felt like a horrible nightmare.

It was no nightmare when he reached Ullen Street and the mouth of Holver Alley. The reek of smoke filled the place. The east side was nothing but ashen husks, skeletons of the buildings that had once been there. Ash covered everything: the cobblestones, pushcarts, every window and sign on the east side.

A few people wandered around, their eyes glazed over. A small cadre of the Fire Brigade and Yellowshields were here, clearing the walkway of debris, collecting the dead. Some street kids ran about, even playing in the burned-out buildings. Asti marveled at children's resistance to tragedy, their ability to enjoy themselves amid the destruction.

"Get down from there! Are you crazy? Get down!" Someone was shouting at a boy up on the second floor of a half-collapsed shell of a house. The boy just laughed, ignoring the man shouting at him.

The man was Winthym Greenfield.

"Win?" Asti called, running over to him.

"Get down!" Win shouted again. "Great saints, he's going to get killed!" Win turned to Asti, grabbing him roughly by the shoulders. His face still smeared black with soot, his gray eyes wild. "Doesn't he understand? Doesn't he care?"

"He's just a boy, Win," Asti said. He wasn't sure what else to say.

"Rynax." Win actually looked at Asti, recognizing him. "You pulled me out."

"Yeah, Win," Asti said.

"My girls? My wife?" Win's voice cracked. "Why didn't you get them?"

"I tried, Win," Asti said. Despite himself, he felt his eyes well up. "I really tried, but I couldn't get to them. We were lucky to get you out."

"Lucky." Win snorted. "That's it. Lucky Win." Win walked away in an aimless wander, as if his feet were moving of their own accord. In the distance Asti noticed the dark-haired waif girl watching Win. She stayed out of the way, her head down, long hair obscuring half her face. She did a good job of looking like she was just milling about; most people wouldn't look twice at her—blazes, she was such a tiny, skinny thing, hardly anyone would see her once.

Asti knew how to focus on someone and trail them from

a ways back, without looking like that was what he was doing. He also knew how to spot when someone was doing that. The girl was focused on Win. She started to move when Win did. As she walked, she pushed through a small crowd of people going the other way. Keeping a close eye on her, Asti spotted her hand slip into one man's pocket and back out in that second of pushing through. None of the crowd noticed, as they kept walking while she followed Win.

Asti strolled in the same direction as her. With her attention on Win, she didn't notice Asti until he was right up behind her. He grabbed her by the elbow and matched pace with her.

"Win Greenfield doesn't have any money for you to filch, girl," he whispered.

"I—I don't know what you . . ." she stammered out. She tried to stop walking, but he kept moving, forcing her along.

"I don't care whose pocket you pick. But Win doesn't need any more grief."

"I know that," she said. She yanked her arm out of Asti's grasp. "I know how much he's lost."

"So why are you following him?"

"I saw when he left the pub this morning. I saw the look on his face. I know that look."

"What look is that?" Asti asked.

"A man ready to die," she said. "He'll be lost soon." She kept walking after Win, and Asti kept with her.

"What's your name, girl?"

"Mila." She paused for a moment. "Mila Kendish."

"Kendish?" Asti couldn't place the name at first, though it was familiar.

"Jono Kendish was my father," she said. Asti remembered, though it was from several years ago. He had heard Jono's wife had gotten sick, and he spent all his money on doctors. It hadn't done any good, and after she died he hung himself. He had left behind two daughters.

"Blessed saints," he muttered. "Didn't you and your sister end up with an uncle?"

"Ancient history, Mister Rynax," she said. She clearly knew who he was. "We ran out of there after a month."

"Where's your sister?" he asked.

She pointed to a burned-out building on the alley. "She was sleeping in there." Her voice was dead, empty of any emotion. "I wasn't with her." She looked down the road, her eyes back on Greenfield. "He's still moving."

Asti didn't know this girl, but he had a feeling in his gut that she was the right sort. Plus she had good eyes, quick hands, and decent instincts. She'd need to be taught, but she could be pretty good in the trade.

She reminded him of himself at sixteen.

He also knew she was right, that Win looked like a man who might hurt himself. Someone needed to keep an eye on him, and the girl wanted to do it. She was hungry for a purpose, hungry for approval.

"Keep on him," Asti said. "Steer him back to Kimber's if you can."

She nodded, walking backward so she could face Asti while still going after Greenfield. She looked eager, excited. "Is that where you'll be?"

"For the time being," Asti said. "Go."

She gave another nod, turned, and dashed off.

"Picking them young, aren't ya, pirie?"

The nasally voice over Asti's shoulder sounded irritatingly familiar, and there were only a handful of people who would call him or Verci a "pirie." Most people didn't even take notice of their Kieran heritage. He barely thought of it himself. He let it wash over; he didn't have time to think about it right now.

Asti turned around. "What do you want, Nange?"

Enanger Lesk, face pockmarked and scarred, thin hair sliding from blond to gray, gave Asti the ugly sneer he considered a smile. Nange had two friends at his elbow. Ren Poller was a weasel, sallow face and wispy scruff on his chin. The other one, the thick-necked bull with the baby face, Asti didn't know.

"Just seeing the what-for, pirie, seeing the what-for. Blazes of a thing, ain't it?" Nange's West Maradaine accent was so thick it was almost comical.

"Putting it lightly, Nange."

"Maybe so." Nange picked at his teeth. "Your brother do all right? Him and his bird?"

"We're all breathing." Asti turned away.

"Heard you saw the Old Lady last night."

Asti turned back. "Where'd you hear that?"

Nange shrugged. "I got ears."

"Apparently so. What of it?"

"Sounds like you and Verci are coming back to work."

The bull chuckled, giving a knowing nod. Asti still had no clue who this guy was.

"Something you find funny?"

"You came crawling back," the bull said.

"Who the blazes are you, meat? You think you know me? Or my brother?"

"He's heard enough," Poller wheezed.

Asti's head was pounding. "He ain't heard enough if he thinks it's smart to laugh at me." He didn't have a knife at the ready; both of his blades were in his pack. The bruiser didn't have a weapon either, but he had over a foot in height and almost double the weight. Nange and Poller were likely armed. Blazes, Nange probably had four or five on his person. Including the sheath knife Asti spotted at his hip, covered with the coat.

Nange laughed this time. "We could just make bets on how you two softies fall apart on your next job."

Asti couldn't stand another second of this. He closed the distance between him and Nange before any of them could react, drawing out the knife on Nange's hip and pressing the tip under Nange's armpit. "You want to make that bet?"

Poller and the bull moved in, but Asti hissed at them. "Wouldn't recommend that, boys. Right, Nange?"

"Step off, gents," Nange said quietly. "That's how you play it, pirie?"

Sharp whistle came from a distance away. One of the Brigade officers came up, with two Yellowshields pushing a handcart behind him. "There a problem here?"

"None at all, Officer." Asti stepped away, palming the knife and sliding it up his sleeve. "These boys were ready to head elsewhere." Not that a Brigade officer could arrest anyone.

"Elsewhere is a good place to be," the spark said. "You all move along."

Nange tipped his hat to Asti and the spark, and walked off, his entourage in tow.

"Obliged, Officer," Asti said. "You here to investigate?"

"I said move along, son," the spark said. "Ain't nothing here for you."

"Plenty here for me," Asti said. "I owned a shop at the end of the alley, and I lived right over there."

"Sorry for that, son," the spark said. "But nothing to be done. We're . . ." He paused, looking down at the street. "We're mostly just collecting the dead."

"There's something you should see, Officer Serrick." Almer Cort came over from one of the burned-out buildings—definitely not his shop. He was covered in soot and grime. He might have been the one Asti spotted in there earlier. He squinted over his spectacles. "That you, Asti?"

"Just having a word with Officer Serrick," Asti said. Tal Serrick, on his scorched, tarnished badge.

"I told you to stay out of there, mister," Serrick said to Cort. "That isn't safe."

"I'm confirming a theory," Almer said. He beckoned them to the building, going on ahead. Serrick chased after him, and cautiously Asti followed along. The place was just the bones of a structure, the beams as much ash as wood.

"Let's come on out of there," Serrick said. "I don't want to have to issue a writ to you."

"Come see this, Serrick, and then decide." Cort went into the back room.

The back room was even more burned out, making Asti nervous. The only thing giving him any comfort was bare dirt directly beneath the exposed floor. There was no cellar to fall into if the floor gave way.

"Cort, this isn't safe."

"No, it isn't," Cort said. "But it's very interesting." He pointed at the ash and burn marks along the floor and walls. "See that? The way the color of the ash changes?"

There were differences in the ash, ranging from a dull gray on the outer edges to a bone white in the center of the room. "I see it."

Serrick, for his part, gave it due attention. "What does it mean?"

"You don't know, Officer?"

"I put out the fires, mister."

"Blazes of a job last night," Asti muttered.

"Don't you—" Serrick started, sputtering. "We were . . . I got here as fast as I could."

"From where, Inemar?" Asti's voice was louder than he expected.

"Shaleton," Serrick said quietly. "Readiness drill."

Asti didn't even know how to respond to that. Fortunately Cort spoke up before Asti bit Serrick's head off.

"It means two things. First, it shows that the fire started in the center of this room, at least in part."

"In part?" Serrick asked.

"Yes. It also shows the fire was deliberately set."

A sharp buzz of anger hit Asti in the back of the head. "You're certain?"

"Quite," Cort said. "I found burn markings like this in three other places. Someone wanted to make sure the whole alley burned." He picked up a charred piece of wood and held it out under Asti's nose, then Serrick's.

"Smells strange," Asti said. Smoky, but not a natural smoke. Like the scent from the shipyards.

"Yeah," Almer said, sniffing it himself. "Pitch, I'm pretty sure. Or something like it."

Serrick waved it away. "That could be a coincidence. What was this building? Did they keep dangerous chemicals here?"

Cort shook his head. "It's the same in the other three places."

"So someone burned out the whole alley on purpose," Asti said. "Killed who knows how many, ruined the lives of even more." He almost couldn't see, he was so angry. He stormed out of the back room. He needed fresh air.

"That's what I'm saying." Almer followed him out, Serrick right behind him.

"Who do you think did this?" Asti asked.

Almer shrugged. "I don't know about things like that, Rynax. I'm just telling you what the evidence tells me."

"What about you, spark? You going to go to the constabs with this?"

Serrick looked troubled. "I don't know what to make of this, gents. I should talk to my supervisors."

"That's a plan," Almer said. "For what it's worth."

"Of course it's worth it," Asti said. "Tell me there's a chance for some justice here."

Serrick shrugged. "I'll look into it." He walked back over to the rest of the sparks and shields.

"Don't know," Almer said, watching Serrick go. "You show a stick a dead body, tell them it's murder, they'll do something about it. This here, he tells his bosses what I showed him? Maybe they'll see it. Maybe not."

"I got it," Asti said.

"You've got a good head, Rynax. You see what's going on and put the pieces together."

Asti nodded. He'd already had a feeling that something wrong must have happened for the whole alley to catch fire the way it did. Someone would have to know something. Someone with his ear to the ground.

Someone like the spice merchant Mersh had mentioned.

"Keep talking to them anyway," Asti said. "You never know."

"What are you gonna do?"

"I'm going to go see a man about some spices."

Lian and Hal's house was small, with an even smaller garden in the back, but it was a pleasant and cozy enough place to stay, at least until Verci found something new for himself and his family. He convinced Raych to let her sister watch Corsi while he talked to her out back.

"So how bad is it?" she asked him.

"The shop is gone. So is most of our inventory. We've got nothing but the clothes on our backs and the tools in my pack."

"Not much," she said with a small smile. "But we also have each other."

"True." Verci couldn't help but smile back.

"So what can we do?" She pulled her dress close around her legs as she sat down on the clover patch. "I think I can wheedle as much as a month out of Lian before she and Hal kick us out. But only if they think we have a plan."

"There's always a plan, love," Verci said.

"Is there a plan we can tell them?" she asked. "Something tells me that you aren't going to go for a dockworker job or a clerk's apprenticeship."

"Neither of those pay very well, you know," he said. "Three or four crowns a week to start at best."

Raych touched him on the leg. He had been pacing nervously; he hadn't even realized it until then. "We could get by on that. It wouldn't be easy, but . . ."

Verci interrupted her. "We've got a huge debt to pay to Old Spence."

"The shop is gone, though."

"That won't matter, the debt'll stand," Verci said. "It might help me to coax him a little about payments. That's presuming he doesn't sell the debt to someone else."

"Like who?" she asked.

"Like someone who doesn't know us and doesn't care about our burned-down shop."

Raych's face sank. "You do have a plan, though?"

"We do."

Her eyebrow raised. "Is it your plan or Asti's?"

"It started as Asti's, but I think it's good enough."

"That doesn't convince me, Verci."

"We went to see Missus Holt." He let that hang there, let Raych drink it in.

"You sure?" she said after a bit. "I mean, I know you wanted to get away from that. I want you away from all that."

"I know," Verci said. "Believe me, I know."

"You know you can't trust her," she said.

"I know that all too well," Verci said. "But she respects business, and she's got a gig she wants us to do."

"What's it going to be?" she asked.

"Don't know yet," he said. "We're supposed to find out more at six bells tonight."

Raych reached out her hand, and when he took it she pulled him down to the ground with her. She wrapped her arms around him. "I trust your instincts, Verci. You think this is what you have to do, I'm behind you."

"That means a lot to me, Raych."

"But stay safe, you hear? You do it smart. I know you can. Even with your crazy brother."

Verci flinched when she said that. He tried to turn away, cover it, but Raych followed him, her eyes hard on his face. He never could hide things from Raych.

"What is it?" she asked.

"It happened again to Asti last night," he said.

"What did he do?" Her face was stone.

"Some street kids were roughing up Almer Cort. He went after them and . . . lost it on them. He killed two of them in a blind rage."

"Verci—"

"I don't think it's a problem, Raych."

"Verci." She was sterner.

"Last night . . . last night could make anyone snap, Raych."

"Did you snap, Verci?"

"Well, no, of course I—"

"It's not safe to work with him, Verci."

"He's my brother, Raych," Verci said.

"He's dangerous!"

"He's got a handle on it."

"Until he snaps again. If we share a home with him and that happens? What am I supposed to do?"

Verci turned away from Raych, not wanting her to see the horror on his face. He couldn't let her even guess at the image that crossed his mind: the same gruesome, bloody mess he found Asti in last night, except Raych and baby Corsi in the place of the two street rats.

He knew she had a point, but he had to draw this line. "I'll handle it. I won't abandon him. No matter what."

Raych touched the side of his face tenderly. "I know you wouldn't." She sighed and looked at the ground. "But I don't want to be alone with him. And I never want Corsi alone with him."

Verci nodded. That was fair, he couldn't deny it.

She got to her feet. "You have any money?"

"A bit," he said, pulling the purse from his pocket.

"All right." She took it from him. "When are you meeting Asti to find out about this job?"

"Six bells."

"Then Lian and I will be back by three bells. And you will stay here with Corsi."

Verci scowled at her. He wasn't very pleased at her idea. "Where are you going?"

"To the market." She patted his face. "I suspect that there will be blackberries today."

That changed his mood considerably. Raych's blackberry pie was one of his favorite things in the world. He smiled broadly. "I think that's brilliant."

"Your brother isn't the only one who can make a good plan."

Five crowns wasn't a lot of money, but Asti was able to stretch it out to get bathed, shaved, and his clothes laundered. It took a few favors and promises, and a bit of flirting with the laundress girl, but he got it done. He looked and smelled presentable again, which was very necessary when he went into the spice shop.

Poasians were a meticulous people, easily offended. Coming into the shop poorly dressed and unwashed would be seen as a sign of disrespect, an insult. Khejhaz Nafath was not a typical Poasian, but he still carried a lot of his culture with him.

The shop smelled strongly sweet, assaulting Asti's nostrils as soon as he walked in the door. A bell tied to the inside handle rang as he came in. Nafath came out from the back room. Like all Poasians, his skin was a sickly milk white, his black hair greasy and cut short. Nafath was thin, with a drawn face and spindly fingers. His suit was black, richly embroidered with interwoven symbols.

"Can I help . . . oh, I see." He gave a disturbing smile, as if the act was a practiced show, impossible for him to do naturally. "Asti Rynax. What a pleasure to have you here. You have finally decided you need the finest spices the world has to offer."

"No spices, Nafath," Asti said.

Nafath opened a small jar and held it up to Asti. "*Ujete*? Excellent in stews, especially ones with root vegetables. Beets, you think?"

"No," Asti said.

"Of course, you are a meat eater, I can tell by your complexion."

"Nafath, I said—"

The Poasian ignored him, pulling out another jar. "*Rijetzh*. Deep richness, even you can appreciate."

Asti slapped Nafath's hand, knocking the jar away. Nafath scrambled after it, catching the jar before it shattered on the floor. "Do you have any idea what this is worth, Rynax?"

"I'm looking for information. I think you might have some."

"For you, Asti Rynax?" He chuckled hollowly as he put the jar back on the shelf. "No, my old friend. For you, I don't think I have any information."

"No?" Asti stepped closer, staring hard at Nafath. Poasians didn't scare easy, but it could be done.

"If I were speaking to Asti Rynax, agent of Druth Intelligence, then I might have information. That was a man worth telling things to. But that is not who has come into my shop, is it? No, I have Asti Rynax, keeper of a tinker's shop."

"You think that's all I am?" Asti snapped.

"Sadly, yes," Nafath said. Asti shot his hand out, finding Nafath's bony neck. With practiced ease he lifted the Poasian man off his feet and slammed him against the wall.

"I'm still a dangerous man, Nafath."

"That was never in doubt," Nafath wheezed out. Nafath was sweating now. That was the man's giveaway. He was a Poasian spy, posing as a spice merchant to establish himself in Druthal. For three years he had been a double agent, feeding information to Druth Intelligence, ever since Asti figured out how to flip him over. "But you are a common man as well. You kill me, I'd imagine Druth Intelligence would be even more upset with you. They wouldn't be content to let you live a civilian's life. They'd lock you away."

Asti tightened his grip.

"You are going to tell me what I want to know."

Nafath choked. "What do you want to know?"

Asti relaxed, letting Nafath fall to the ground. "Last night there was a fire. Deliberately set. You know something about it."

"Is that all?" Nafath laughed, a dry rasp of a laugh. "You're worked up over some petty arson?"

"Petty?" Asti snarled. "That was my home, my shop."

Nafath raised an eyebrow. "This is personal, then. Interesting."

"What do you know about who set it?"

"Nothing. Frankly, Rynax, I do not pay attention to the petty squabbles of the Maradaine streets. Neither of my masters care very much about that."

"People live on those streets."

"I am very aware, Rynax." He stood up, straightening out his suit. "That fire was only a few blocks from here. My shop and home, even in this stinking pit of an uncivilized city, is dear to me. I would not want it to be collateral damage in someone else's fight."

"Whose fight?" Asti asked.

"I don't know." Nafath shrugged. Asti ground his teeth. Nafath held up a finger. "I have heard one interesting point, however. The Fire Brigade came far too late, is that right?"

"That's right," Asti said. "Running a drill in another part of town, apparently."

"A drill? That is very interesting. Because not very long ago Holm Yenner—you know who he is?"

"The chief of the Fire Brigade for these neighborhoods."

"Yes. The very man who would set schedules, and decide to run a late-night drill far away. He recently bought himself a new house and a new carriage. They were, I think, somewhat ostentatious for a man of his salary and position."

"That is interesting." Asti nodded his head. "Thank you, Nafath." He turned to the door.

"Druth Intelligence expelled you for your violent temper, did they not, Rynax?" Nafath called after him. "That is what they called it."

"You've heard right," Asti said, his hand on the handle of the door.

"I have not said anything about that to my new handlers, my friend. You and I both know that description is not entirely accurate. Yes?"

"It's their perception of things," Asti said. He did not turn around to look at Nafath.

"I can see why they think that. How long were you imprisoned in Levtha?"

The question hung like a fog in the room. "Seventeen days," Asti whispered.

"Seventeen days," Nafath said. "In that place, that's a lifetime."

Quietly Asti opened the door. He almost looked back at Nafath but couldn't get himself to do it. He walked out of the shop, leaving the stink of Poasian spice behind, just a memory.

Chapter 4

IT WAS THE SEASON for the Maradaine River to be teeming with freshwater mussels; anyone who crawled under the docks could come out with a sack of them. As a child, Asti had run more than one mussel racket to make money. Those were good times.

The more Asti thought about it, the stranger it seemed to think of those times fondly. He and Verci were usually hungry and scraping by, Dad was in and out of Quarrygate, and Druthal was at war. But the war was across the ocean, and the Poasians were a vague fear rather than a real threat. At the time, all it meant to Asti was that there were very few Constabulary on the street, especially on the west side of Maradaine. Nobody bothered him and his crew of kids. Now, most were dead or in Quarrygate.

Kimber had sent some boys down to the river out to collect a few sacks of mussels and she'd made a huge cauldron of mussel stew. She still had a fair-size crowd of refugees from the fire, though most of the displaced had left to stay with family elsewhere in the city. For the refugees, she sold bowls of stew for only two ticks. For anyone else it was six.

Asti was on his second bowl and third beer when Verci came in.

"You're late," he said.

"It's not six bells yet," Verci returned.

"Almost. Our guy will be here any moment."

"And I'm here." Verci sat down at the table with Asti. "Mussel stew?"

"Kimber outdid herself," Asti said. "You have any money left?"

"A bit," Verci said. "Why?"

"I think I'll have to pay for a room tonight. And dinner."

"Right," Verci said. He dug a handful of silver and copper coins out of his pocket.

"You want some stew?"

"I ate already." Verci's face broke out in a huge grin. "Blackberry pie."

"You bastard," Asti said.

"That's you, brother. Dad finally married Mom when I showed up."

"Shut it. More stew for me. Beer?"

"Yes," Verci said. He waved to Kimber and signaled her for a beer.

"So how was your day?" Asti asked.

"My day was far too involved in baby care." Verci shrugged. "It's very exhausting. You?"

"Information-gathering." Asti gave Verci a quick rundown of the things he had learned. Verci listened quietly, sipping his beer once Kimber brought it over. When Asti finished, Verci scowled.

"Something doesn't track," he said.

"What are you thinking?" Asti asked.

"Value," Verci said. "Let's suppose someone spent a fair bit of coin for a big burn job, and bribing Brigade Chief Yenner. What do they get for it?"

"That's what we have to find out."

"We?" Verci's eyebrows went up.

"You know anyone else who will?" Asti felt the fire in his stomach spark again. He took another swig from his beer to quell it.

"Sounds like Cort showed the Brigade. Let them bring it to inspectors to handle it."

Asti nodded, but he wasn't comforted. "If Yenner was

bought, an inspector could be. If we could trust that to get very far."

"Never know. We may get an honest stick."

"That would be just our luck." Asti chuckled and finished his beer. "The spark we talked to, he struck me as a decent sort. But I doubt he's in a position to do much."

A tall, dark-skinned man walked into the pub, his black hair in thick braids. Ch'omik, in heritage if not in dress. He was dressed in a Druth suit, with a leather hunter's coat. He carried a large satchel over his shoulder. Asti noticed the man; he'd stand out in any crowd. The man was searching around the room. Asti realized that there was no point even bothering being secretive.

"Oy," he called out. "Here, mate."

The man approached. "You two the Rynaxes, then?" His accent was eastern Druthal, either Marikar or Vargox. Asti was never good at distinguishing the accents of those cities.

"Sit down, friend," Asti said. "Asti and Verci."

The man joined them at the table. "Kennith Rill."

"That's not a very Ch'omik-sounding name," Verci said.

"How do you think Ch'omik names sound?"

"All sort of guttural and throaty," Verci said. "What was that one chap called on Ben Choney's ship?"

"Ka'jach-ta," Asti supplied.

"That's the one."

"Well, you know all about it then," Kennith said. He scowled at the two of them. "You knew a guy on a ship once."

"I'm just saying it sounds odd, mate," Verci said. He looked over at Asti. "Is Rill even a Druth name?"

"I am Druth," Kennith said. "I was born in Vargox. Moved downriver a few years ago."

"East country," Asti said. All this confirmed what he suspected once Kennith walked in. "Near the border with Kellirac. I'm guessing your parents came to Vargox from Kellirac, probably a little town called Rill, am I right?"

"That's right," Kennith said. His eyes were suspicious on Asti. "I don't consider myself Ch'omik, really."

"And why should you? Your grandparents or great-grandparents fled Ch'omikTaa and emigrated across the desert to Kellirac."

"You seem to know a lot about it," Kennith said.

"Knowing things is my business," Asti said. "It's no matter to worry us. Blazes, it's not like we aren't the same." That's what a lot of North Seleth was: folk who were too Druth for the Little East, but not Druth enough for the rest of Maradaine. He signaled over to Kimber to bring three more beers.

"How are you the same?"

"Rynax isn't a Druth name," Verci said. "Neither are our given names."

"I thought they were a bit odd," Kennith said. "Are they Racquin?"

Verci shook his head. "Kieran. From what our father told us, he escaped from a Kieran prison camp, fled to Maradaine."

"Nobody sees you as Kieran, though," Kennith said.

"You'd be surprised," Verci said. "We get it from time to time."

"Speaking of," Asti said, looking to the door. Nange Lesk and his two friends came in. A third friend was behind them—Kel Essin, decent window-man when he was sober.

Verci turned. "Lesk?"

"He's nosing around."

"Wonderful."

"This going to be a problem?" Kennith asked.

"Hard to say," Asti said. Lesk and his cronies approached the table.

"Two piries and a chomie," Lesk hissed. "What sort of trouble could be brewing here?"

Kennith's jaw set.

"Just having a few beers, Nange," Verci said. "Same as you all, I presume."

Nange nodded. "Something like that. You've got a small table here."

"Plenty of others over there," Asti said. "Sure you can find one for you and yours."

"So what's the news over here?" Nange asked.

"Just having a drink with a friend, Nange. Find your own chair."

"Fair enough," he said, spreading his arms wide. He put

on a big grin and pointed one finger at Asti. "You owe me a knife, pirie."

"I'll give it to you when you need it," Asti said.

Nange laughed and went to an empty table. The others went with him, Essin giving a small salute to Verci as they left.

"What was that?" Kennith asked.

"Small problem, nothing more," Asti said.

Kennith stewed. "Most guys who call me that eat their teeth."

"Keep it in your chair right now."

"Essin think he's as good as me?" Verci asked.

"I think they think we're rusty," Asti said. "Doesn't matter."

"So what do we do? They know we're up to something here."

"Right." Asti turned to Kennith. "Here's the thing. You walked in here, every eye in the bar turned on you and stayed on you. Every person in here is going to remember you, and they'll remember you came and sat with us. Now, Verci and I, we're unremarkable-looking. People look right past us all the time. You . . . I bet that doesn't happen much."

"No, it doesn't." Kennith almost growled when he said it.

"I can imagine," Verci said.

"I can go," Kennith said. "Maybe someone else will want this job."

"No, no," Asti said. He waved his hands to keep Kennith from getting up. "That won't do. Especially with Lesk and his boys in here. They know us, other people know us. That'll just put more eyes on you, eyes on us, burn everything into people's memories. Forty people in here who just saw something interesting, something worth mentioning to someone else. Secrecy goes to the water closet at that point."

Kennith relaxed in his chair, but he still looked put out. "All right. So what do we do?"

"We have a few beers, and we catch up with our old friend we haven't seen in years."

"Who is that?"

"That would be you. We talk about the Parliament and tetchball and a dozen other mundane things." Asti leaned in close and whispered. "We're going to have a good couple hours of absolutely dull, boring, ordinary conversation so people will lose interest in us. After that we'll take our leave of the taproom in the most ordinary and unremarkable way and reassemble in my room upstairs to talk business." He leaned back just as Kimber came over with three beers.

"Who's your friend?" Kimber asked as she put the bottles on the table.

"This is Kennith," Asti said congenially. "He's an old friend from when I was in the service."

"Pleasure," Kimber said with a nod. "Asti, I can count, and I know that's your fourth. Don't make me regret serving it to you."

"Kimber, I would never do that to you." He took one of the silver coins Verci had left on the table and gave it to her.

"Better not," she said, taking the coin.

"Do me a favor," Asti said. "Make sure Lesk and his boys get slow service."

Kimber made a face. "That won't be a problem."

"All right," Asti said as she walked away. "So, old friend, did you see the tetchball game today?"

Over the next hour they made small talk, and once Verci and Kennith got on the subjects of gadgets, tools, and gears, there was no stopping them. They both lit up like schoolboys, giddy with their shared passion for all things mechanical. Asti sat through it, smile on his face, calculating the exact degree of attention the rest of the room was giving them. He scanned the room, noting every time eyes flashed over at them, or when a newcomer would ask, "Who's that with the Rynax boys?"

Time didn't pass fast enough, and Asti felt the itch in his fingers to move on. It was past eight bells, long after Kimber had refused to sell Asti anything but soft cider, when Lesk and his friends slipped out. Attention on them wasn't going to go any lower.

"The problem with that," Kennith said as he made invisible designs on the table with his finger, "is that you can't take horses out of the equation. Additional horses can help ease the weight, but your top carriage speed will always be limited by how fast they run."

"True, true," Verci said. "Unless there was a way to take horses out of the equation."

"But you can't do that. I tried building something like a pedalcart, but I couldn't get something carriage size moving."

"Not surprised. I can't think of a way to remove horses for a long haul. Short term, though, I have an idea. Spring tension."

"Spring tension?"

"Tension can hold enormous power, and if you can ratchet it up and somehow channel it into the wheels of your carriage, then you can get a huge burst of speed."

"Like a catapult?"

"Exactly!"

"That's the craziest idea I've ever heard." Kennith laughed.

"I'm not saying it will work," Verci said. "It's an idea."

"You know," Asti said, "I think we did save one of those spring cranks from the fire. Our packs are up in my room."

"Really?" Verci asked. His expression of surprise flickered slightly. Asti was afraid for a moment that Verci thought he was actually talking about spring cranks. "Well, let's go up and see."

Kennith stood up, taking his satchel with him. "I'd love to see it." He almost made it sound natural.

"Let's go," Asti said. The three of them left the taproom. Asti gave the room one more glance, noting their exit was given nothing but a token regard by anyone there.

The room Asti had rented from Kimber was small, barely any room for anything other than the bed. The three of them managed to squeeze in and shut the door, with Asti and Verci sitting on the bed. One lamp hung from the ceiling, burning with a low, warm glow.

"So what is the job?" Asti asked as soon as they shut the door.

"There's a jade statue arriving in three days on an Acserian ship."

"First of Joram," Verci said absently.

Kennith nodded. "It was bought by a rich merchant who lives in East Maradaine. Someone else has offered a fairly substantial commission to the Old Lady if she gets it for him."

"Sounds pretty straightforward," Verci said. "Define 'substantial.'"

"Our cut is nine hundred crowns. That straightforward?"

"Straight enough," Asti agreed. "What's the catch?"

"I don't know about catch," Kennith said. "The ship will unload at the Wheeler Docks, and the statue will spend one night in the customhouse at Wheeler. Officially."

"And unofficially?"

"It'll leave in the middle of the night, loaded into an armored carriage for the ride to the estate in East Maradaine."

"And you're that carriage driver," Asti said. "You need someone to rob the carriage you're driving."

Verci whistled low. "So you're selling out to the higher price."

"No, that's not it—"

"Hey, I understand, Rill," Verci said. "Most bosses forget to pay the carriage-man well."

"That's true, but not how you're saying," Kennith said.

"So how is it, then?" Asti asked. He could see something fierce in Kennith's eyes. Integrity. This wasn't a man who was just selling out a boss for a few extra crowns.

"I'm not driving!"

Confirmed. Asti asked, "So how are you involved?"

"I built the armored carriage on commission," he said. "They only paid me a third of what was promised."

"Revenge, then," Verci said.

"Justice," Kennith said.

Asti clasped Kennith on the shoulder. "Justice it is, then."

Kennith nodded, his face grim. "That's why I'm in."

Asti shut his eyes, visualizing the docks at Wheeler Street to the best of his memory. "So it's ship to customhouse, then customhouse to carriage, and carriage to estate."

He could see it clearly—the statue being loaded off the ship, put in the customhouse. He could see men putting it in the carriage. The carriage driving down Wheeler then turning east toward the estate.

"How big is the statue?" Asti asked.

"Not sure exactly," Kennith said. "I got the impression it was pretty big. Maybe as tall as a man."

"That big, made of jade?" Verci asked. "We're talking priceless, then."

"Four points," Asti said quietly. "Ship, customhouse, carriage, estate."

"Estate's a hard point," Verci said.

"Hard point?" Kennith asked.

"It's the final resting spot for the merchandise," Verci said. "Since it doesn't need to travel farther, extra measures can be taken to keep it from going anywhere. The other three points are soft points."

"Since the statue needs to move," Kennith said. "Got it. But the carriage isn't a soft point, I can tell you."

Verci shook his head. "I'd much rather not do a carriage job, either. Give me a nice quiet sneak-in any day."

Asti kept his eyes closed. He tried imagining different plans for getting a large jade statue out of the customhouse. Without a sense of the interior of the place, or the security measures, he couldn't see any plan that didn't involve the men at the customhouse being lazy and slipshod.

He needed to know the customhouse.

"So are we settled, then?" Kennith asked. "What do we do next?"

"Well, we need a safehouse, which the Old Lady usually provides," Verci said. "And we meet there next time."

"North Seleth Inn," Kennith said. "I was supposed to tell you that part. I work out of the stable there."

"Well, good," Verci said. "Is there anything else we're supposed to know? Is the statue cursed, perhaps?"

"No, it's not cursed," Kennith said derisively. Then he stopped for a moment. "At least, I don't think it's cursed."

"If it is, we ask for more money," Asti said.

"I am supposed to give you two this," Kennith said, holding up the satchel. "The Old Lady said it belonged to your father."

"What?" Asti yanked the satchel out of Kennith's hand and opened it up. "She's had this all this time?"

"It would be like her," Verci said. "What's there?"

Asti pulled a belt and a bandolier from the satchel. It had been years since he had seen them. The belt had several knives hidden on it, the bandolier a series of darts along it.

"Dad's weapons," Verci said, his throat catching slightly.

"I thought these were lost," Asti said. He handed the bandolier to Verci. "This one suits you better."

"I do have better aim," Verci said numbly. He took the bandolier and held it tightly. Almost reverently.

Asti inspected the belt. Each knife was still razor sharp, not a speck of rust. The Old Lady had kept them well. Asti closed the satchel. "Tomorrow morning at nine bells at the North Seleth Inn?"

"I'll see you both there," Kennith said. "In the stable, of course."

"Of course," Verci said. Kennith nodded to both of them and squeezed himself out the door.

Verci turned back to Asti. "What do you think? Trustworthy?"

"As much as he needs to be. I think he's being up front about the job and why he wants it."

"Good enough," Verci said.

"Nine hundred, three ways . . . that's a good start for getting us out of our debt."

"Which is why I'm on board, brother."

"Glad to hear it," Asti said.

"What do you think Nange is up to?"

"Haven't a clue. He's a nuisance."

Verci's brow furrowed. "Nuisance on the move. He didn't move with Essin before, either."

"Essin is nothing, and you know it."

"He's not bad."

"He's not you, though." Asti reached under the bed and pulled out a crate of things he had purchased earlier that day: dark slacks, coats, gloves, and boots. "What say we suit up, go take a look at the customhouse?"

As much as Verci hated to admit, it felt good to be up on a rooftop, Dad's bandolier slung over his shoulder, and Asti crouching next to him. From their vantage point, even in the weak moonslight, they could see the whole customhouse facility beyond the high wall. There were three brick warehouses on the grounds, with wide walkways between each one—wide enough to bring mulecarts through. Beyond that there were the river docks, with a handful of moored ships. Past the ships, across the wide stretch of the Maradaine River, Verci could just make out the lights of the northern bank.

"What do you think? Can you get in there?" Asti asked.

Verci took his lensescope out of his satchel. "Don't insult me. In is easy." There were light patrols walking through the grounds—men with dogs.

"In is always easy," Asti said. He pointed along the brick wall, where several men with crossbows walked along the top. "Not over the wall, though."

"Course not," Verci said. "The place is a funnel—enter from the river, leave through the gate." He took a closer look at the gate—gates, more correctly. There were two sets, and a space in between. Looked real easy to get trapped in there.

"Or continue up the river, once the ship is cleared."

"You think that's better?"

"I'm thinking it exists as an option," Asti said. "Go out through the gate, you got to have the gate open. Upstream is unprotected."

"River patrol."

Asti shrugged. "A problem, but they mostly stay downstream of the customhouses, making sure smugglers don't unload before they're checked out. The real problem would be getting the goods onto a cleared ship."

"Bribe." Verci knew as soon as he said it how Asti would react.

"Never works. You're just setting yourself up to get caught. You give some stranger money and hope it buys you some trust which—"

Asti had strong opinions about the value of bribes.

"I was joking," Verci said.

"Though you are right about one thing," Asti said. "Best way out with the goods is to slip through with something legit."

"Depends on the goods." Verci had a romantic notion in his head of quietly swimming upstream, skulking into a warehouse, crack a lock or two, grab the target, head back down to the river, and swim out. In and out with no one seeing.

Asti must have been reading his mind. "Those are wide walkways, plenty of lamps. You have to cross thirty feet, minimum, in the wide open. You'd be crossbow-bait."

"Dog-bait, more likely," Verci said. The hounds the guards were leading were more than just sniffers.

"So no chance of a quiet in-out, hmm?"

"I don't see it," Verci said. "Maybe with a distraction of some sort by the gate."

"Distraction games for burgles are always dicey. Might as well take out the guards."

"You're talking about at least twenty. Not to mention dogs."

"I'm not serious," Asti said. "Private guards, even city constabs, that's fair enough. Customhouse is national. King's Marshals, I think."

"Better trained?"

"Blazes to training. I mean you leave a few of them dead, they'll turn the city over to find you." Asti turned around and sat down. He had seen all he needed to see, at least for now.

"I hate leaving bodies for any gig," Verci said. Sometimes it was inevitable, but Verci preferred to be home and in bed before anyone even knew they had been robbed.

"Do we scout closer?" Asti asked. "Or do we go home, sleep on it, and come up with a different plan?"

"I'm tempted to try the upstream swim, just to see if that can work," Verci said. That would help him work out the kinks. Far too out of practice in this sort of thing. The problem with that was, any mistake would get the guards riled up. Verci wasn't too worried about getting caught, but an incident might put the whole place on alert for a few days.

Asti got back onto his knees, and put one hand out. "Scope."

Verci handed the scope over. "What is it?"

"Would you look at that?" Asti said idly. He passed the scope back.

"What am I looking for?" Verci asked, putting the scope to his eye.

"Structure between the warehouse on the right and the kennels. Almost backed to the warehouse."

Verci spotted it. "Too small for a storage shed. Or an armory."

"I've a hunch that's a backhouse."

"Backhouse?" Verci found that hard to believe. Even in North Seleth plenty of places had water closets. A big facility like this, in Keller Cove, had to have gotten rid of their backhouses.

"Right on the bank, everything is going to flow out to the river anyway, why waste the money to install water closets? No one lives there."

Verci looked again. Asti could be right. "Which would mean no piping. Just a disgusting hole to crawl through."

"A disgusting hole that pops you up ten feet from the warehouse. Could work." Asti grinned.

"Frankly, I'd want a daylight scout."

"What for?"

"For one, just to see if that's a backhouse. But more just to feel out our options."

"Con it instead of burgle?"

Verci thought about it. "We don't have time for the kind of long con needed to get the goods. Plus we were never good at the long con."

"Short con to scout, set up the burgle?"

"That's about the size of it. You have an idea?"

"The seeds of one," Asti said. "Let me sleep on it."

"All right," Verci said as he got to his feet and walked over to the edge of the building. "I'll see you in the morning."

"Give Raych my best," Asti said. "Oh, and Verci?"

"What?"

"Bring some pie tomorrow."

Verci grinned. "Get your own pie-baking wife."

"Seems a waste, when you already have one."

"Shut it, brother," Verci said with a smirk. "Good night." He spotted a stable gutter and slid down to the street level.

❖

Asti took his time walking back to Kimber's. The night was cool, but there were still plenty of people walking about, their ways lit by oil-burning street lamps. A block away he spotted the girl he had put on trailing Greenfield. She sat on the stoop of the brick tenement on the other side of the street, her wool hat held out as her eyes met every person who passed her. Asti couldn't help but grin. She was good at this—she locked her gaze on every well-dressed person, gave them a look that filled them with sympathy, demanded they do something to help her. Asti watched several people throw copper and silver into her hat before he crossed over to her.

"Mila, right?" he asked as he sat down on the stoop next to her.

Mila scowled at him. "You're going to skunk me," she whispered.

"Nothing could skunk you here, girl," he said.

"Creepy man who looks like a doxy boss would," she said.

"How do I look like a doxy boss?"

"Because you're sitting on a stoop with a poor, hungry-looking girl who looks just the right innocent age to be taken in and used by a doxy boss."

"You are a dark, twisted girl," Asti said. "That's good. That's honest."

"What do you want, Mister Rynax?"

"How's Greenfield?"

"He made it through today," she said. "Spent a few hours standing on the edge of one of the river docks, looking like he might jump to the bottom."

"He didn't jump, though."

"Good thing, too," she said. "I can't swim." She picked up a rope that was sitting coiled next to her. "Stole this to pull him out if he went."

"You good with a rope?" Asti asked.

"I do all right," she said. "Was that all?" Mila was clearly annoyed at him spoiling her hatshake.

"Yeah," he said. "I want to ask you to do something. Hire you."

She gave him a hard, cold look. "I'm no doxy, Mister Rynax."

"No, no," he said. "Nothing like that at all."

"Good. What, then? It's not like you paid me to watch Greenfield."

"Well, this will make it up, then."

"How much are we talking about?"

"Ten crowns."

Her eyes widened. "Is it illegal?"

"Legally murky."

"But no whoring?"

"No!" Why was her mind on doxies and whores tonight? Then he realized, for her, that was a last resort she could take to survive, and given the situation she was in, the stark reality loomed over her.

"Then I'm in."

"Good," he said. "Tomorrow, nine bells, North Seleth Inn. Stable."

"What about Greenfield?" she asked.

"He made it through today. I'll get Kimber to keep an eye on him."

"No, you owe me for Greenfield today," she said.

"Running out of coins," Asti muttered. He dug into his pocket and threw a few ticks in her hat. "Find a decent flop to sleep in tonight, eh?"

"All right," she said. "Get out of here. Now."

He nodded and jogged across the street. He went back into Kimber's, skipping the taproom and going back up to his room.

Asti pulled off his boots and slid them under the bed, then stripped off the rest of his clothes. He stood up on the bed and turned down the lamp. Lying back down, he realized that while the bed was small and smelled musty, it was the most comfortable place he had slept in weeks.

Chapter 5

MORNING IN HAL AND LIAN'S house was more social than Verci wanted to deal with. All he wanted was to go down to the kitchen, have some tea and biscuits, and get out the door. Raych was even on board with this plan. Hal and Lian did not cooperate.

"Verci, I'm telling you, there are some good opportunities if you just keep your eyes open," Hal said. He was sitting a bit too close to Verci for Verci's own personal comfort.

"I know, Hal," Verci said. "I know plenty about opportunity."

"Good, good," Hal said. "Because you've got one staring you right in the face here and now. I know someone who knows someone who is looking for a man to supervise on the docks."

"Really?" Verci said as flatly as possible.

"I know!" Hal looked triumphant. "A job like that is going to get snatched up but quick, unless you happen to know someone who knows someone, which I do. And thus you do. Good coin for this job, Verci Rynax."

"You didn't have to do that, Hal." Verci tried to stand up from the table and grab a biscuit from Lian's tray, but Hal clapped him on the shoulder and pulled him down again.

"Nonsense. You're family. And, let's face it, we can't have you staying here indefinitely. Am I right?"

"Too right, Hal."

"This is what I'm saying. So get a good, clean outfit on. One with a smart vest and coat. You have one?"

"Not just now he doesn't," Raych said. "He should get one, though. Maybe head off right now and get one."

"Good idea, Raych." Verci stood up from the table.

"Nonsense, it would take too long. I have just the thing."

"Hal, no offense," Verci said, "but you've got three inches over me. In most directions."

Hal laughed, patting his stomach. "Can't help that. But Lian is terrific at fixing clothes. Right, dear?"

"Absolutely," Lian said.

"That's very kind of you," Raych said. "But . . ."

"But Asti and I have a different meeting this morning," Verci said. "Different job."

Someone knocked on the front door. Lian went out to the parlor. Verci tried to leave the kitchen as well, but Hal got up, grasping Verci by both shoulders in an aggressively congenial manner.

"A different job?" he asked. "That's excellent. Where will that be?"

"At, um . . ." Verci hesitated for a moment. Hal always threw him off his game, and Verci never could understand why. "At the customhouse. Over on Wheeler."

"Really?" Hal's eyebrows went up. "That's impressive, Verci. I have an old school friend who works over there. Yen Tolso?"

"Tolso," Verci said, nodding his head in an act of serious thought. "Don't think that's a name I know, but I can ask someone."

"Well," Hal said, clapping Verci on the shoulder. "It's a name you can drop if you need to."

"Thanks, Hal." Verci edged toward the front door. "I really do need to get going."

"Verci, Raych?" Lian called as she came from the front door. "There's someone here to see you."

Verci turned around and stopped short to avoid crashing

into the man who walked into the parlor. He was an older man in a heavy suit, wearing spectacles.

"Mister Rynax?" he asked. "Mister Verci Rynax?"

"That's right," Verci said.

"You are not an easy man to find, Mister Rynax. I took a chance that you might be at the home of your wife's family."

"That was a successful chance, Mister . . ."

"Of course," the man continued, ignoring Verci, "it's perfectly understandable, since your stated residence over the Greenfield locksmith shop no longer exists. Nonetheless, you have not been as easy to find as I would have liked."

"Sir," Verci said forcefully, "who the blazes are you?"

"Verci!" Lian squeaked.

"Of course," the man said. He bowed slightly, removing his hat. "Heston Chell, of Colevar and Associates. I have you at a disadvantage, of course."

"Quite," Verci said. "I don't have time for games, Mister Chell. Even from Colesky and whatever." He pushed past the man and went to the front door.

"Colevar and Associates. We represent the parties who have purchased your debt to Mister Spence."

Verci stopped cold in front of the door.

"I wasn't aware that Old . . . Mister Spence had sold the debt. When did that happen? And who did he sell it to?"

"I'm afraid I'm not at liberty to discuss these matters, Mister Rynax. The debt is, of course, quite sizable. Given the rate of loan which Mister Spence made the deal at, the amount you owe is on the order of two thousand crowns."

"We made an arrangement to pay that at fifty crowns a month," Raych said. "I know well enough to know that your client, whoever he is, cannot change that arrangement at his whim."

"Very true, Missus Rynax," Chell said. "If you wish, you may continue to pay the debt at the agreed upon rate, for six years."

"Excuse me, Mister Chell," Hal said, raising a finger up as he came into the room. "I couldn't help but overhear. That would make thirty-six hundred crowns."

"Yes, if paid over six years," Chell said. "If paid in full today, it would take two thousand. However, given the state of affairs, given the fact that your intended shop is now nearly an ashen pile of nothing . . ."

"Watch it," Verci snapped.

"My apologies," Chell said, holding up a hand as a peace offering. "Since your shop was so tragically lost, paying the debt in either a lump sum or monthly payments seems . . . unlikely at this point."

"Our payment isn't due for fifteen days, Mister Chell," Verci said. "You've got no claim to haul me to court yet."

Chell smiled, a chilling smile that gave Verci a shiver down his back. "Mister Rynax, you misunderstand. Neither I nor my client has any great urge to haul you to court, nor see you jailed for debt. You have been the unfortunate victim of cruel circumstance."

"That's the truth," Verci muttered.

"We'll make our payments, Mister Chell," Raych said, her chin held up defiantly.

"If you wish," Chell said. "However, I'm authorized to remove your debt completely, in exchange for signing over the parcel of land that the shop once resided over."

Raych's eyes went wide, a smile tugged at her lips.

"I have the papers already drawn up, awaiting your signature, Mister Rynax." He pulled a few pages from out of his coat pocket.

"Verci!" Raych exclaimed. "This is perfect."

Too perfect. Too easy.

Verci had spent a good portion of his life with his senses attuned to that little click, those almost imperceptible signs that a trap was about to be sprung. The hairs on the back of his neck would go up whenever his instincts were telling him that danger was right in front of him.

Every hair on the back of his neck was up right now.

"Well," Verci said. "It does sound like you're giving us a good offer, Mister Chell. I need to discuss it with my brother first."

Chell's cold smile wavered, just for an instant, just the slightest twitch of the muscles on his face. "Yes, of course. He is your business partner, I understand, and he has every right to want some say in such a decision. This offer will stand until the fourteenth of Joram, when the first payment of fifty will be due."

Verci nodded. "Understandable."

"I'll leave these papers with you." Chell held out the pages, which Raych snatched away. Chell walked to the door, tipping his hat to the room again. "And I'll be in touch." As he was about to exit the house, he turned back. "Bear in mind, Mister Rynax, should one of those monthly payments be missed, my clients will press their claim and likely receive ownership of the landplot, and you and your brother would be jailed for debt. That would be a terrible shame, when it's so easily avoidable." He left the house.

"Verci," Raych hissed. "What's the matter with you? That's exactly what we need."

"I know it is." Verci gently put his arm around his wife, leading her with him to the door, away from Hal and Lian. "Which sets my head buzzing. It's too easy, too big for someone to just give away."

"What are you saying?"

"I'm saying it doesn't match, Raych," Verci said. He lowered his voice as he pretended to kiss her on the cheek. "Nobody does something for nothing. That plot of land, with nothing on it but an ashen heap, is worth maybe six hundred crowns. Someone bought the debt for a fair chunk more than that, and is then willing to give up years' worth of interest to get that land."

Raych pulled back, looking at him hard in the eyes. "What does that mean?"

"I'm not sure, but it doesn't sit right."

"Does it matter? What do you want to give Corsi? An indebted father, or a clean life?"

"Clean life, no question there." He still didn't like how this felt. He tapped the pages in her hands. "Give me a few days to think on it, all right?"

She nodded, giving a weak smile. "A few days, no more."

He kissed her for real. "I've got to go," he said. "Time to go to work."

Verci walked out to Colt Road, heading toward Fawcett. Walking west through the neighborhood was always a depressing venture. Each block was more impoverished than the last. Each block, the street had more cracks and missing stones. Each block, the clothes were more patched and threadbare. More boys stared with lean and angry faces. More old men sat on the stoops of crowded tenements.

"Verci, old hat!" Kel Essin was approaching, arms and smile both too wide for Verci's sense of comfort. Verci didn't see a blade, but he wasn't going to let Essin embrace him.

"Morning, Essin."

"We didn't talk much last night." Essin wrapped one arm around Verci, and brought his face in far too close for Verci's comfort. Breath stank of cheap beer. "I guess the night got away from us."

"Must have." Verci shrugged the man's arm off. "Surprised to see you up and about this early."

"Dawn took me a bit by surprise," Essin said. He lowered his voice, as if he were speaking in confidence. "Frankly, I was hopeful to find some company for my cot tonight. Figured there'd be easy pickings, you know, given how many slept in the street last night."

Verci did not want to hear more. He started down the street again. "I'm late."

"What for?"

Verci cursed under his breath. He walked into that, no doubt. "I've heard there's a clerk position available in one of the dockhouses. Off to make a good impression."

"A clerk job?" Essin burst with laughter. "Oh, blazes, Verci, I didn't think you'd . . ." He trailed off, his eyes going wide. With an impish giggle, he slipped over to Verci. Verci had to admit, even leftover-drunk from a sleepless night, the man moved like a cat. "I get it, I do." Essin tapped a finger on his nose.

"You got me," Verci said. Let Essin believe whatever he wanted. Two more steps away from the man, into the street.

"Sure it's a good scheme, old hat," Essin said. "Keep your ears up, all right?"

"Always do," Verci said. He took a few more steps away, letting a mulecart trundle between them. As soon as he was out of sight, he darted back and slipped into a side alley. He dashed to a low fence at the back of the alley, bounded over it, and cut through the adjoining back garden to reach the next street. He glanced around. Essin wasn't in sight. Sighing with some relief, he made his way toward the river again.

The North Seleth Inn was up on Fawcett, just a block away from the river docks. The smell from the river—tar, fish, and refuse—was strong without overpowering. The inn was fairly large, taking up half the block with a ceremonial stone wall surrounding the grounds. Verci didn't know its history, but the building looked like something from the last century, during the Poasian Wars. Solid, heavy construction. A small fortification, ready to withstand attack. That was also when Seleth was a more prosperous neighborhood. Now it was struggling to hold its place on a greased slope: not as bad off as the slums of Benson Court to the west but losing more and more jobs and commerce to Keller Cove and eastern neighborhoods.

Seleth didn't even have organized street bosses or crime lords. Verci sometimes wondered how the Old Lady kept her place.

Walking through the gateway of the North Seleth Inn, Verci saw more of how time had ravaged it. Cracks in the plaster that had decayed into chunks and holes. Shingles missing from the roof. An orange cat dozed on the walkway, ignoring the rats that scurried shamelessly past it.

The stable was around the back of the inn. Verci was surprised that there was no one on the grounds to challenge or question him.

The only person he saw at all was a thin, dark-haired girl who slouched by the door of the stable, her hair falling over her face.

"I know you," she said as he walked up.

"You win, then," Verci said. "I've no clue who you are."

"Mila," she said. "You're the other Mister Rynax."

"Meaning my brother is the first?" he asked.

"I guess so," she said. "Where is he?"

"You're expecting him here?"

"Nine bells, stable of the North Seleth Inn." She cocked her head in the direction of a high church tower, visible from two blocks away. "I'm a bit early."

"Early is always good." Verci didn't want to say too much. "Asti forgets that sometimes."

The girl shrugged. "I was awake already. Been up since dawn. Sticks woke me up from my crash."

"Where did you sleep?"

"Under the creek bridge, over on Frost," she said. "It's usually a good enough crash, least it used to be. About ten folks there last night, and the sticks routed us all at sunup."

Verci didn't know what to make of this girl. "Asti told you to be here for this?"

"Didn't I say that?"

"Did he say why? What you would be doing?"

"Said I wouldn't be anyone's whore, that's what." She spat this at him, like an accusation.

"Well, that's . . ." Verci stumbled. "I didn't think that would be what you would be brought on for."

"You can forget all about it if you were thinking that, mate," she said.

"Not thinking it!" Verci almost shouted. "I'm a married man."

"Married man," she scoffed. "They're usually the worst."

"Forget it," he said. "I'm sure Asti knows exactly what he's doing."

"Of course I do." Asti's voice came from behind them. He came up to the both of them, large pack slung over his shoulder. He shook his head and frowned as he held up a newsprint. "Look at this!"

"What about it?" Verci didn't want to ask about the girl in front of her, so it was best to trust Asti and wait for a private moment. He glanced at the print. None of the stories jumped out at him as being significant. "I don't see anything of note. Unless you are interested in what dresses Lady Henterman and Lady Hanson were wearing last night."

"No, that's my point!" Asti snapped. "Two days, and nearly nothing about the fire! A paragraph in the corner."

"Really?" Verci grabbed the sheet from Asti and looked over it again. "That's odd."

"Newsies don't care what happens out here in west-town," Mila said.

The Holver Alley Crew 73

"When did we become westtown?" Verci asked. "I thought you had to go west of Junk for that."

"Westtown has started at the creek as long as I've known," Mila said. "But you two are old men."

"When did I become an old man?" Verci asked. "I'm twenty-four!"

"I guess that's old now," Asti said.

Mila gave a light slap to Asti's shoulder. "So what do you want from me, old man?"

"I want you to do some hatshaking today," Asti said.

"You're paying me to shake my hat?"

"You're paying her to shake her hat?" Verci echoed.

"Yeah," Asti said. "Specifically, I want you to go into Keller Cove, to the end of Wheeler, and shake in the square outside the customhouse gate."

"The customhouse gate?" Mila asked. "Ain't exactly prime territory for shaking, you know?"

"So no one will try and muscle you out," Asti said. "The point isn't what you make."

"Since you're paying me," Mila said.

"How much?" Verci asked.

"Ten crowns," Asti growled. "You watch that gate. You watch the men on the wall. You learn how long they stay on watch. What time they switch. What they eat for lunch. You get it?"

"I think so," Mila said. "Eyes and ears open, learn everything."

"Everything and anything."

The girl shrugged. "That's a good ten crowns," she said. "Now?"

"Now. Go."

She winked at Asti and walked back off down the lane.

Verci took advantage of the moment. "You're bringing in a strange girl to scout for us?"

"An aspect of it," Asti said. He shrugged and lowered his voice. "That's Jono Kendish's kid. You remember him?"

"Vaguely," Verci said. He did recall two little Kendish girls, long time ago.

"Yeah, well, fire hit her as bad as us, you know?"

"So spread some help around," Verci said, nodding. "Works for me, if you're sure about her."

"Sure as anyone," Asti said. He pounded on the door of the stable. After a moment Kennith opened the door.

"Who's the girl?"

"Girl?" Asti asked innocently.

"I heard you two talking with some bird, who is she?"

"Her name's Mila. We're having her scout out the customhouse for us. Let's get inside."

Kennith scowled, but stepped back so they could enter.

The inside of the stable was larger and cleaner than Verci had expected. A small carriage—a two-wheel gig propped up on blocks—dominated the center of the room. There were only two stable stalls, all the way in the back, where two chestnut horses were quietly eating. The wooden floor had been impeccably swept, and the two workbenches on the side wall had all their tools neatly arranged.

"Nice," Asti said, glancing around. "And this is all yours?"

"I'm the only one who comes in here," Kennith said. "I take care of the horses, and drive the carriage if anyone staying at the inn hires it out."

"No one stays at this trap more than a night or two," Verci said. "It's a whore hole, nothing more."

"Used to be a nice place, I'm told," Kennith said. "The old couple who run it are very nice."

"And they won't ask any questions?" Asti asked. He was looking around the back of the stable, where the large carriage doors were.

Kennith coughed and looked to the floor. "They have been told not to. By Missus Holt. I think they have certain debts to her."

"A lot of people do," Verci said. He checked out the workbenches. Kennith was clearly a meticulous worker. He had several bins of nails and gears and other bits and bobs, each one neatly organized.

Asti closed the lock on the back door. "Secure location. Good sightlines to the road. We could set up some alarm wires on the path, yes?"

"I think so," Verci said. He looked back out the door down the drive to the street.

"Alarm wires?" Kenneth asked.

"This is our base right now," Asti said. "We're planning the whole gig in here, and we need to know if anyone is approaching. Precaution is our best friend in this business."

Kenneth looked skeptical. "If you say so."

Verci knew Kenneth was new at this, but his attitude was especially naive. And the twitch in Asti's eye meant he was about to snap at the man. "It's for the best. Essin was on me a bit this morning."

"How?" Asti asked.

"Might have been nothing. Seemed a little odd."

"Just Essin? Alone?"

"As far as I saw. He was on a bit of a next-morning stumble."

"Drunk?"

"What does this have to do with anything?" Kenneth snapped.

Asti raised his eyebrow. "You want Lesk and his boys to poach this gig from us?"

Kenneth scoffed. "They can't poach this from me. It's my gig. I brought it!"

"Doesn't matter if they learn what we're up to and do it first," Asti said.

"Or skunk us out of spite."

"Really? People do that?" Kenneth sat down at one of the workbenches. "You people are crazy."

"Damn right," Asti said. "So moving on?"

"So what's our next step?" Verci asked. "I'm guessing you want me to set up those defenses here while you do the day scouting."

"I'd like you on the scout, though," Asti said. He took the pack off his shoulder and dropped it on the worktable. "I've got a plan."

"I know you have a plan," Verci said. "What's the plan?"

Asti opened the pack, pulling out clothes. "I was thinking of one of Mister Gin's plays. *The Greasy Merchant*?"

"*Greasy Merchant*?" Kenneth asked, his face showing how much the man was in over his head.

"I never remember the names to those games," Verci said.

"Here's the thing," Asti said. "We need to get into the customhouse today, while they're working, to see how it operates on the inside."

"Sounds risky," Kennith said.

"Course it is," Asti said. "See, there's a trick to any one of these plays."

"It's more or less the same trick every time," Verci added. "You make them think they're pulling one over on you."

"So how are you doing that?"

Asti unfolded the clothes. It was a smartly embroidered tunic, Kieran style, with matching hose and cap. Wearing that, Asti would look like a total fop. "Here's how. I'm going to walk right in there, demand to talk to the foreman, and slide a few coins into his hands."

"How does that help?" Kennith asked.

Verci chuckled. "The idea is that the foreman is going to be suspicious of Asti anyway, so Asti will play into that."

"Confirm his suspicions by trying to bribe him, act like I want something he can deliver."

Kennith nodded. "So he'll be so focused on that, he won't notice that you're really scouting the place to rob it."

"Precisely," Asti said. "Greasy Merchant and its ilk work best when the target never even suspects what you're really after. When they don't actually give you anything."

Verci added, "That foreman will walk away with a few extra crowns in his pocket. He'll figure he had a good day for doing nothing."

"So what do I do?" Kennith asked.

"You and Verci have the other side of our scout."

"Other side?"

Verci didn't like the sound of this. "Sewer trawl?"

Asti shrugged. "Has to be done."

"I have to go in the sewer?" Kennith asked.

"Nah." Asti stripped off his clothes. "You are going to take the inn's carriage out near the customhouse. Cut a hole in the bottom of it."

"Owners may not like that."

"Blazes to them. They can complain to the Old Lady.

Verci'll ride in the carriage, which you'll park over a sewer hole. Verci will go out the hole and into the sewer."

"That seems a bit complicated," Verci said. "He'll just sit there?"

"Someone asks, he's been sent by the inn to wait for someone coming out of the customhouse. If someone asks, you hear?"

"Sit and wait quiet?" Kennith confirmed.

Asti put on the tunic. "Worst thing happens, and we've got to bolt fast, you'll be set to get us out of there."

"And I go in the sewers." Verci really didn't care for that part of the plan.

"Things go well," Asti said, struggling with the hose, "I'll send you a mark drop in the backhouse."

"Presuming that is a backhouse."

Asti put on the cap. "How do I look?"

"Like a jerk," Kennith said. "A greasy, Kieran jerk."

"Perfect."

Chapter 6

THE HARDEST PART about faking a Kieran accent was subduing the urge to exaggerate it. There was something about the big, round vowels and soft palate consonants that made Asti want to push it further. Plus the audience almost expected it, as the big, overblown Kieran was a traditional trope of local theater. If he underplayed it, most people wouldn't believe it.

"Most people," though, wouldn't include people who worked the customhouse, who would encounter actual Kierans, and would see through his ruse if he wasn't on point. It didn't help that his costume wasn't perfect. He would have liked some jewelry. A few gaudy rings would make a huge difference. He had to settle for some heavy rouge on his cheeks and lining his eyes. Hopefully the garishness of his face would be enough to keep everyone's attention off his fingers.

"So who do you need to talk to?" the man at the gate asked. Asti had been let inside the first set of gates, leaving him stuck in the box between the two gates. Verci had a theory about the gates, and from what Asti could see, he was right: they were designed so only one gate could open at a time. The customhouse people could trap someone between the gates and wait for the sticks to come.

Not a position Asti enjoyed. Just standing in the box was making his heart race, and every hair on his neck stood on end. He needed to get through quick.

"Your foreman," he said, keeping his Kieran accent in check. "I don't know the man's name."

"But why?"

"Does it really matter?" Asti asked. He took a single crown out of his pocket and flipped it over his fingers. Might as well start a reputation for bribes right away.

"Eh," the man said, snatching the coin away. "I suppose it doesn't." He pulled a lever and opened up the gate.

Asti walked into the grounds. "So who am I looking for here?"

"You want Mister Tolso, right over there." He pointed to a man in a dark gray vest and matching cap.

"You've been of esteemed service, good man," Asti said. He crossed the lot, noting the locations of each of the warehouse doors, marking the distance to the dog kennels. Tolso was near the suspected backhouse, so that made things all the more easy.

Asti approached boldly, hand outstretched. "Tolso, is it? You're the man to talk to I understand."

Tolso didn't accept Asti's hand. The mealy-faced man looked at it as if it were holding a dead fish. "Talk to about what?"

"Forgive me," Asti said, glancing about. He hoped Tolso read him as checking if they had a bit of privacy, though he actually was counting the men on the wall. King's Marshals uniforms. Three on each side, armed with crossbows and swords. Proper longswords at that, not gentlemen's rapiers. "I should introduce myself."

"Please," Tolso said.

"Gestorus is the name," Asti said. "Andio Gestorus. You may recognize the name." The Gestorus family was huge, and did a fair amount of shipping all over Druthal, and had any number of representatives in Maradaine at any given time. A name that provided just the right balance of notoriety and anonymity.

"It's familiar," Tolso said. "There a problem with a shipment?"

"Not yet there isn't," Asti said. "And I'm doing a bit of . . . preventative action to make sure it stays that way."

"Something incoming?"

"Something and someone," Asti leaned in close to whisper, keeping an eye over to the kennels. Close enough to the wall to throw a few morsels of meat? Asti dismissed the idea. Far too amateur.

"We strictly deal in cargo here, Mister Gestorus. You'd have to go to the north bank to discuss passenger clearance."

Asti pulled a coin out of his pocket and slid it into Tolso's hand. "See, that's just it. I'd prefer not to have to deal with the north bank, if you get me."

"Hmm," Tolso said. He did hold on to the coin, though. "When is your cargo arriving? I take it you need it . . . processed quickly? Perishable goods that can't waste time getting to market."

"Quite right, Mister Tolso," Asti said. "I'd hate to lose their market value." He looked back over to the warehouses. The doors were marked with codes of colors and shapes. No written signs. Blasted saints. That wouldn't make finding anything too easy.

"I'm certain arrangements can be made," Tolso said.

"Good, good," Asti said. "I hate to trouble you further, Mister Tolso, but if I might have occasion to use your water closet?"

"No closet," Tolso said, his teeth gritting. "Just the backhouse over there."

Perfect.

"That will have to do," Asti said. "If you'll excuse me?"

Asti went in. The recent run in the sewer had reminded him of how bad these things smelled. He didn't want to have to stay in any longer than necessary. He gave three quick knocks on the seat.

Three knocks returned.

"How easy?" Asti whispered.

"Ridiculous," Verci called back from the darkness. "Which is good, because it's particularly awful down here. How's it on your end?"

"Good as it can be," Asti whispered. "You were right

about the gate being a double-lock. No chance of sneaking through it."

"Figured," Verci said. "I've got an idea of floating downstream with the goods."

"Problem is still getting it," Asti said.

Someone knocked on the door. Asti composed himself and opened up. Tolso stood outside, looking smug.

"Everything well?" Tolso asked.

"As expected," Asti said, bringing back the Kieran accent.

"Well," Tolso said, holding out an arm for Asti to exit. "I think we're done for now. Yes?"

"I think so," Asti said. "You've been very helpful."

"Of course," Tolso said.

Hairs on the back of Asti's neck went up again. He walked out and went to the gate. Tolso walked right with him.

"Our guest is ready to go," Tolso told the man at the gate. The inner gate opened up.

Asti stepped inside. It slammed closed behind him with a solid clang.

"I'll be in touch soon, Mister Tolso," he said.

"I'm sure," Tolso said.

The outer gate was still shut.

Asti's heart started hammering.

He took a hold of the bars and shook it. His hand was trembling.

Tolso's face was unreadable. "It just takes a moment to switch the gears. Sorry for the trouble."

"Not a problem," Asti said. The beast in the back of his head was screaming. He wasn't going to stay in here. Not going to be trapped, not again. He'd tear through the bars and carve up Tolso and the guard and anyone else—

The outer gate opened.

"Then good day, Mister Gestorus." Tolso nodded and walked off. Asti stumbled out into the street. For a moment he couldn't breathe. He almost couldn't see. He leaned against the customhouse wall and willed his heart to slow down, demanded the beast stay on its leash. He wasn't going to let it loose, not again, not over this.

The world around him slowly came back into focus.

Mila was in her place, shaking her hat with an eye on the gates. Asti walked past her, throwing a coin in her hat. "Two bells, Kimber's."

She nodded but said nothing.

He kept walking, back toward the inn and the stable. Time to get out of this Kieran frippery.

Asti couldn't eat. Partly due to his unsettled nerves, but mostly due to Verci's wretched scent. Granted, Verci didn't smell much worse than most of the other patrons at Kimber's, but it was still pretty blazing bad.

"There are bathhouses, you know," Asti said.

"I didn't know what the afternoon would hold," Verci said. "I would hate to have to bathe twice."

"Fair enough," Asti said. "Where's Kennith?"

"Back at the inn. He's fixing the hole in the carriage."

"Good. Here's Mila."

Mila threw herself in the empty chair. She pointed at Asti's untouched stew. "You gonna eat that?"

Asti pushed it over. "What do you have?"

"Where's my ten crowns?"

Asti pulled a few coins out of his pocket and put them on the table. Mila reached out. "Leave it for now," Asti said. "What do you have?"

"Three men on each side of the wall, one at the gate in the morning. They change about every bell and a half. I counted fourteen different men working the wall and gate, and through the gate saw four more walking the dogs."

Verci gave a low whistle.

"Now, after you gave them your shake-up, things changed about . . ."

"My what?" Asti asked.

"I don't know what game you're playing on them," Mila said. "But you went in there looking like a swell, talk and talk, blah blah, you come out. Then your fat friend talked to the boss, and we've got ten on the wall and three on the gate. And they're all grumbling when they lunched at the pub across the street about working double at night."

"Back up," Asti said. "My fat friend?"

"Who's your fat friend?" Verci asked.

"I don't know," Asti said. "Who is this? What happened?"

Mila shrugged. "I thought he was your guy, because he went up as you walked away, talked to the boss at the gate, pointed at you, nodding and stuff."

Verci groaned. "Ruddy man, thinning hair, pudgy baby face?"

"That's him."

"Hal?" Asti asked.

"Hal," Verci said. "Who was the boss you smoked?"

"Guy named Tolso."

"Yen Tolso," Verci said. "He's an old school chum of Hal's."

"Do you think you might have mentioned that earlier?" Asti said.

"So he's your guy or not?" Mila asked.

Asti growled. "He's—he's my idiot brother's stupid wife's poxy sister's dolt of a husband."

"We don't like the man," Verci said.

"Thank you, Mila," Asti said, sliding the coins over. "You can go."

"Can I—"

"Go!"

Mila took the coins and the bowl of stew and scurried over to another table.

"Why was he at the customhouse, Verci?" Asti asked.

"I may have screwed up this morning."

"Really? How?"

"He was, you know, being Hal, bugging me about getting some stupid clerk job, and I should go with him today, and I said, you know, I can't because . . ."

"Because Asti and I are going to case the customhouse? And he said, oh, I have a friend who works there!"

"No," Verci said lamely. "Well, sort of. I said we had a job possibility, and we were going to look into that. Just to get him off my back."

"Well, now you have me on your back," Asti said. "Come on, let's go back to Ken."

☼

"No chance getting it out of the customhouse," Asti said as they came back into the stable.

"Why?" Kennith asked. "What happened?"

"Short of it, we were pretty much made, and they cranked up their guards."

"It's my fault," Verci said.

"I didn't like our chances doing it that way, anyhow," Asti said. "So we have to have a whole new plan. The target is the statue, after all. We have to get it where we can get it, and that's not the customhouse."

"Not anymore," Verci grumbled. "And I can't imagine getting it off the estate."

"You know what that means."

"Hit and grab," Verci said. "I hate hit and grab."

"What's that mean?" Kennith asked.

Verci explained. "It means instead of sneaking in somewhere, nice and quiet, and slipping away with the goods and being home and dry before anyone notices a blasted thing, we've got to pick a point where it's vulnerable, and hit hard, grab the goods, and run like blazes."

Asti nodded. "Which means the carriage transfer."

"It's not vulnerable," Kennith said. "Not this carriage."

"Tell us about it." Asti knew Kennith was proud of his work, eager to tell them.

Kennith's eyes lit up. "It's gorgeous. The body is made with steel, the doors and panels are all lined with it. It locks from the inside, so you can't even get in it from the outside."

"There's always a way," Verci said. "No such thing as the unpickable lock."

"There is if there's nothing to pick," Kennith said. "There's no latch or keyhole on the outside."

"So the man on the inside can just clamp down and wait for the constabs," Asti said.

"An arrow or an axe couldn't get through there," Kennith said.

"A mage could," Verci said.

"We won't have a mage," Asti said.

"Ain't a mage, like, cheating?" Kennith asked.

"If I could get a mage, I'd use one," Asti said. "Use every blasted advantage you can in this business."

"What about—"

"No, we can't get one," Asti said firmly. There were damned few mages who did gigs like these in town, and any that Asti had known had long since moved on or up. Mages could demand top crown for their work, and none were going to take an equal share in a nine-hundred gig.

Asti closed his eyes again, trying to visualize this carriage. In his mind, he saw it, all metal. "Does it have doors, though? Some kind of hatch, even if there's no obvious way to open it from the outside?"

"Right," Verci said. "There's still got to be a crack or a seam where the door opens. You could get a prybar in there."

"You could," Kennith said. "But I'm sorry, none of us are strong enough to wrench it open with a prybar."

"None of us are, true," Asti said. He still saw the carriage in his head, and he tried to place the driver and horses on it. "What about the driver? He'd still be vulnerable."

"That's part of the genius," Kennith said. "The driver is inside the carriage, protected in the armor. The reins are controlled through a system of pulleys."

"He's got to be able to see," Verci said.

"On all sides there are slots to see through." Kennith held up his hands about a foot apart. "No bigger than this. And those can be shut from the inside."

"So an arrow could get in there, as long as the driver doesn't see it coming." Asti looked over at Verci.

"Tough shot while it's moving," Verci said. "And if you take out the horses first, the driver will clamp down."

"There's one thing," Kennith said. "The carriage isn't very fast. It's too heavy. Even with eight draft horses, it's still moving at a crawl."

"That's something," Asti said. "How many men can fit inside, including the driver and the statue?"

"Maybe one more, but it would be a tight fit," Kennith said. "Really, if you want more guards, they'd have to walk on the outside."

"Maybe yes, maybe no," Asti said. "They probably don't

want to make it an obvious target." He closed his eyes again. He played a few plans in his head.

"You have a carriage that can carry the thing and get away fast?" Verci asked.

"I've got something, yeah," Kennith said. "And I've got two good horses that can sprint almost a mile with it loaded."

"So if we can stop their carriage, take out the guards and driver and get it open, and load it in your gig, you can get it to a safehouse quick?"

"If you can do all that, yeah," Kennith said.

One plan solidified in Asti's head, but it would take six people to pull it off. He opened his eyes and looked at his brother.

"What have you got?" Verci asked.

"I've got a way to stop the carriage, take out the driver, and a maybe on opening it."

"I've got a maybe also," Verci said.

"Two maybes make a yes," Asti said.

"What, really?" Kennith asked.

"Tends to be," Verci said. "If neither way works, the job is skunked and we run."

"Then we don't get paid."

Verci shrugged. "Dad always used to say, you've got to drive forward, even if the job turns left. You can't worry too much about what happens if it fails."

"Plan for it not to fail," Asti said.

"And know how to run like blazes if it does."

"Well, I can run. Or drive my girls like blazes, at least." He gave a nod back to the horses. "But if we don't skunk it, then we come back here?"

"Lay low until we do our pay drop," Asti said. "Do we deliver to the Old Lady, or straight to the buyer?"

"Buyer," Kennith said. "They apparently want to do it that night, around three bells."

"Lovely," Verci said. There was no single act as shady as delivering stolen merchandise in the middle of the night. "Not much room for error there."

Asti shrugged. "Beats sitting on the fire for a few days. Get it, drop it, get paid."

"And split it three ways," Kennith said sternly.

"It'll be six ways," Asti said. "We'll need three more bodies to pull it off."

"Blazes, what?" Kennith's voice dropped to a husky growl.

Asti held up his hands, clearly ready to defend himself if it came to that. "Easy, Kennith. You want to get this statue, get paid, we're going to need six in the crew."

"What kind of bodies do we need?" Verci asked.

"A sure-shot and a set of arms. And a kitten."

"What?" Kennith asked. He looked very confused.

"He means we need a crack archer and someone else to be muscle. And someone who looks innocent to be a distraction." Verci rolled his eyes and shook his head. "You'll have to forgive my brother, sometimes he likes to talk in his little codes."

Kennith frowned. "You sure we need six?"

"We do," Asti said. "And six shares of something is a lot better than three shares of nothing."

Kennith shrugged with grudging assent. "Fair enough. But who will you get?"

"You want that girl for the kitten?" Verci asked.

"Mila's already got one toe in, might as well make it both feet."

"And it's obvious who you want for the other two," Verci said. "Helene and Julien?"

"They need it as bad as we do," Asti said. "They've got the skills, and we know them."

Kennith spoke up. "Seems you're padding this with people you know."

Asti grit his teeth. "You know a good crossbow shot or strongman, let me know. Just Helene and Julien are a package, so might as well use them."

"Fine," Kennith said, though he seemed far from pleased. "Six shares, your friends, sure."

"Just get that getaway carriage ready," Asti said. "I'll take care of the rest."

Kennith grumbled and went into the back of the stable.

Verci lowered his voice. "This is still a good gig, right?"

"Of course it is." Asti shrugged. "I'm not crazy about

precisely timed intercept jobs that leave bodies in the street. But I can't see a cleaner way to do it."

"If you think so, we'll keep driving on. Go find those three. I'll stay here and work with Ken. Hopefully turn his mood."

"You want to turn his mood, you might think about hitting the bathhouse."

"The man sleeps with horses."

"Then do it for me."

Chapter 7

THE COUSINS WERE EASY to find. The two of them were sitting down in Kimber's taproom, nursing beers over mussel stew and dark bread. Both of them looked miserable. Julien sat slumped, leaning on his elbow. The whole table leaned to one side from his weight. Helene hadn't yet cleaned up from the fire, ash and dirt still on her face, her long black hair in wild, tangled clumps.

"You two look terrible," Asti said as he sat down with them.

"Any reason why we shouldn't?" Helene asked numbly. "No more house, no more money. No chances."

"No work?" Asti asked.

"We haven't had gigs in over a year, Rynax," Helene said. "All we had was that house and the nest egg our grandma had."

Any fleeting reservations Asti had about bringing the cousins in on the gig left him in that instant.

"You've got one now."

"Job?" Julien asked, his huge face lighting up.

"Don't toy with me, Rynax," Helene said.

"No toying," he said. He put one finger to his lips. "Verci and I have a lead on something."

"You—" Helene started loudly, then hushed as she glanced around. "You two are back in the game?"

"Not much choice," Asti said.

"True that," Helene said.

"That's good, Asti," Julien said sadly. "But no one wants us."

"Hey, I do, Jules," Asti said. "Some people may only think about the last skunked job, but I know better."

"What do you know?" Helene asked.

"I know you need it."

"Don't bring us in for charity, Rynax," she said.

"I'm not, not one drop. I've always said, there's no one better with a crossbow than you, Hel. And that's what I need for this gig."

"And me?" Julien asked.

"Merch will be heavy, and we'll need to move it quick."

"I can do heavy," Julien said. "Have to fight?"

"Not if I can help it. All goes to plan, guards will be dead before you get close."

"Hel?" Julien asked. "What do you think?"

"I think I don't have a crossbow anymore," she said.

"I think we can get you a new one," Asti said. "In or out?"

Helene scowled, conflict played over her face. She glanced back at Julien. "Blazes, Rynax. It worth it?"

"Nine, split six ways. That'll get you secure, yeah?"

"Yeah." She leaned in close. "You square with me? He's not gonna have to fight anyone?"

"If it goes to plan," Asti said. "Plan depends on your crack shot, though."

"Then I've got one more price," Helene said.

Asti ground his teeth. He had told her too much, let her know he needed her. "What's that?"

Helene grinned. "This crossbow you're going to get me, it's not just going to be any crossbow. Verci's going to make it."

That was surprising. And as far as Asti was concerned, an easy enough condition. "That's what you want?"

"You want me at my best, I need a Verci Rynax crossbow." Her voice purred when she said Verci's name. Asti always knew Helene had a soft spot for his brother, but he had no idea how much of one.

"I'll have to talk to him about it," Asti said. "But I think we can make that happen."

"All right then," she said. "We're in."

"Meet us in an hour. Stable of the North Seleth Inn. You know it?"

"Of course," she said.

"You have a flop for tonight?" he asked her.

"Good enough," she said. "Kimber has taken enough pity on us to let Julien sleep in the storeroom and give me a spot in her chambers."

"Nice of her."

"Nice, nothing," Helene said. "We've been doing her scullery and cleaning."

"We'll see if we can find you something better for tomorrow, all right?"

"I don't need you worrying about what bed I'm sleeping in, Rynax," Helene said. For the first time since the fire, her eyes lit up.

"It gives me something to think about at night."

"Well, keep it to thinking." She gave him a grim smile. "See you in an hour."

"See you then." He got up, glancing around the room. Greenfield sat alone in one dark corner, an untouched plate of stew in front of him. Asti walked over, tapped on the table to get Greenfield's attention. The man didn't look up.

"Win?"

No response. Greenfield stared blankly at the stew.

A soft hand—Kimber's, Asti knew instinctively— touched Asti's shoulder. "Everything all right?"

"Just seeing how Win is doing," Asti said, turning to her. "Heard you've been looking after the Kessers."

"Win, Helene, Jules . . . you."

"I don't need looking after," Asti said.

"So you don't need that room you've rented?"

"Didn't say that," Asti said. "I'll need that at least a few more days. And . . . I'll take Win's bill as well."

"You don't need to do that," Kimber said.

"I know but—"

"I ain't charging that man a tick," Kimber said. "Saints look poorly on someone who profits off of misery." She kissed the knuckles on her right hand and touched them to her chest.

"I get you," Asti said. "But if the time comes, I've got Win covered."

"Course you do." Kimber gave him a wan smile, patted his arm, and walked off.

Mila wasn't in the taproom. Asti wasn't sure where to find her now. He went back outside—no sign of her in the street. He wandered over toward Holver Alley. Maybe she had wandered back over there.

He was nearly at the alley when he sensed that someone was following him. The streets weren't too crowded, so it wasn't hard to notice the shadow keeping an even distance behind him.

A glance backward at an opportune moment confirmed what Asti had already suspected: Mila was tailing him. He wasn't sure why she was, but there was something amusing about her attempt. With a perverse glee, Asti turned down the alley and let her keep up with him.

Once he was halfway down the alley, he chose one of the more stable-looking wrecks and slipped inside. He quickly found a window that wasn't too singed to peer through.

Mila was walking down the alley, and doing a damn fine job of looking like she was going about her own business. Her glances at each home and storefront had the marked casualness of someone just paying attention to where she was going. Even in the dusky twilight, though, Asti could make out the hint of intensity in her eyes—she had lost her quarry, and she was intent on finding it, but she wasn't going to let anyone know a blazing thing about it.

She stopped in front of the building Asti was hiding in. She gave a quick glance about, and placed herself inside the empty doorframe, as if simply taking a moment to catch her breath. Her eyes went everywhere, but the rest of her face betrayed nothing.

Her hands went inside her ragged coat, played perfectly like she was doing it just for warmth.

Asti realized he was being far too cynical; she probably was doing it for warmth.

Still, the girl had raw skill, and it would be foolish not to cultivate it.

He snuck out of his hiding spot over to the doorframe. "Looking for me?"

If he had surprised her, she didn't let it show. "Could ask you the same, Mister Rynax."

"Yeah, but I decided to watch you work some more."

"Do I pass?"

"You'll do," Asti said. "So we need to change our plan. You want in?"

"In how?"

"In as in a part of the gig. Equal share."

"What's an equal share?"

Asti figured the numbers in his head. "One-fifty."

Now she looked surprised.

"Blazes, Mister Rynax. What . . . what are we doing?"

"Come on over to the stable, and we'll talk about it."

Verci had spent the better part of the afternoon up to his elbows in axle grease. Kennith seemed to appreciate the help, and appeared to be in a better mood when Asti returned with Mila. He quietly cleared off a worktable and brought it to the front room.

Shortly afterward Helene and Julien arrived. The two of them looked worse than ever. Their clothes were a wreck, torn and unraveling, clearly the same ones they had thrown on when the fire started. Julien didn't even have matching boots. Helene's face was covered with ash and scratches.

Verci whispered to Asti, "Are you sure about this crew for this job?"

"Positive," Asti said. "Shall we get started?"

"What is this gig, anyway, Asti?" Helene asked.

"And what do you need me for?" Mila added.

"I'll tell you." He went to the door and latched it. "Everybody, take a seat or something."

Verci sat on the workbench, letting Asti take the floor.

"What we're looking at," Asti said, glancing about at the people around him, "is a carriage job."

Helene groaned. "Those are the worst."

"Why are they the worst?" Mila asked.

"A lot of reasons," Verci said. "The big ones being you've got a small window of time to do the job, and the second being you're sure to create a quick rattle."

"Quick rattle?" Kennith asked.

Asti chuckled. "A rattle is the call put out when someone realizes he's been robbed. He cries out and the constabs come looking."

Verci added, "You do, say, a window job or a safe job in the middle of the night, the rattle may not come until morning. If you do it really well, it may be days before the mark knows he's been robbed."

"You hit a carriage, though, then they know right away," Helene said. "It almost always means a fight, Asti. You said there wouldn't be a fight."

"I said Julien won't have to fight," Asti said. "Big difference."

"I can fight," Julien said.

"I don't want Julien having to fight," Helene said.

"He won't have to," Asti said. "If the plan goes smooth, only Verci and I will be fighting."

"If it goes smooth," Helene said. "I don't like that if. What about me?"

"What you do isn't fighting," Asti said with a grin. "Fighting implies the other guy has a fair chance."

Verci laughed. "Then what you do isn't fighting, either, brother."

"Stop buttering us all and tell us the rutting plan, Rynax," Helene said.

"The plan is a statue, coming from the customhouse on Wheeler."

"Over in Keller Cove." Helene shook her head. "Sticks pay a lot closer mind to things over there. Especially by the customhouse."

Verci stifled a laugh. This was the big reason why a lot of crews stopped working with Helene, despite her being the best shot in westtown. She argued every point, tore apart every plan. There were other reasons, of course. She refused to work without Julien but refused to let him do anything that could get him hurt, which limited his use. He was one of the strongest guys Verci had ever known, but with his slow thinking he wasn't good for anything beyond heavy muscle.

Verci knew Asti didn't mind either thing. He liked the Kessers, especially liked having someone like Helene tear up his plan.

"That's a risk, of course," Asti said. "That's why we've got to hit hard and fast and bolt."

"Why not get it at the customhouse?" Helene asked. "Or at its destination?"

"You think I hadn't thought of that, Hel?" Asti asked.

"Statue is heavy," Kennith said.

"Not the sort of thing you can sneak out past security," Verci added. "Best shot is when it's in transit." Helene frowned at him. "Hey, I hate it, but it's the truth."

Asti nodded. "Shame, but there it is, and the money is too good to let it slip."

"Nine, six ways?" Helene asked. "Or is there some other cut?"

"That's the whole nut," Asti said, looking at Kennith. "Right?"

"Nine hundred is our share," Kennith said. "I don't know what the buyer is paying Josie."

"So how much each?" Julien asked.

Mila, who had been sitting quietly on the floor, responded. "One hundred fifty crowns." She glanced around at everyone. "I've never seen so much as ten crowns at once, and that was from you."

"That's gonna change soon," Asti said with a grin.

Helene scoffed. "So, carriage job. Hit the carriage, kill the guards, take the statue, and run like hell. That the gist of the plan?"

"In broad strokes," Asti said.

"Broad strokes," Helene muttered. She shook her head and went over to the wall.

"From what Kennith tells us, the carriage is heavily armored. We've only got a small window to take out the driver through."

Helene perked up, turning back to the group. "How small?"

Kennith held up his hands, making a rough box about a foot wide and three inches tall. Verci saw her eyes light up.

Helene nodded. "Someone will have to make that shot from far enough away that they aren't spotted."

"Tough shot to make," Asti said. "Hardly anyone could do it."

Helene laughed. "Don't need the butter, boys. Just the crowns."

"I thought she needed the butter," Asti said.

Verci looked her up and down. "You seemed like you were fishing for some butter."

"I want some butter, you'll know it," Helene said. "And your wife will worry."

"Helene!" Julien cried out, sounding scandalized.

"Blazes, girl," Asti muttered. "There's children in here, you know."

"Hey!" Mila snapped. She shot to her feet, jabbing two fingers into Asti's chest. "You call me a child, I walk." Asti bit his cheek, and Verci wasn't sure what his brother was holding back, laughter or the impulse to break the girl's fingers.

"I'm talking about my baby brother." Asti smirked and backed away from Mila.

"I've got very delicate ears," Verci added. Mila scowled back and forth at the two of them, then stalked over to another corner.

"Here's the big thing to worry about," Asti said. "We know roughly when this will happen, and we know what the thing will look like."

"We do?" Julien asked.

"I've got sketches," Kennith said.

"The big question on our plate is where," Asti said. He put a finger on the wall as if he expected something to be there, then gave the blank wall an annoyed glare.

"You need a map of the city, brother?" Verci asked.

"You have one?"

"Not on me," Verci said. "I'll add it to the shopping list."

"By tonight if you can."

"I can go grab one now if you like."

"It can wait," Asti said. Tapping his finger on the blank wall, he started mumbling.

"Can't hear you," Mila said.

"Question of where," Asti said louder, turning back out to the group. "We know they are going to go out east, but we don't know exactly how they're doing it. So that's the big challenge."

"Ferreting out the path?" Helene asked.

"Don't want to ferret it," Asti said, shaking his head.

"Takes coin and muscle," Verci said, nodding. "Getting someone to talk."

"More to the point, it makes noise. Word can get to the wrong people that someone wants to know the path, then the guard is up. No, we need to work out the possible paths and come up with a plan that can move."

"Plan that moves can't be too far from the customhouse," Verci said.

"Why not?" asked Kennith.

"Each block means a place things can change. Three blocks away, there're fewer than ten places the carriage could be. Five blocks, more than twenty."

"But too close to the customhouse, they yell for backup," Asti added.

"Have I mentioned how fun it is to be with you boys?" Helene said.

"This is it in the nut," Asti said. "Find the spot to hit, get the carriage to stop. That's Verci and Mila."

"Me?" Mila asked.

"Damn right, you," Asti said. "Take out the driver through his window. That's Helene."

"Hurrah," Helene said dully.

"Verci and I take out any other escort, signal the carriage. Julien and Kennith ride up once they get the signal."

"What's the signal?" Julien asked.

"I need to figure that out," Verci said. It needed to be something that could be seen from a couple of blocks away at night. Or heard. Verci scratched his chin and thought about it.

"I need to know what the signal is," Julien insisted.

"You'll know it, Jules," Helene said. "As soon as I know it."

Asti continued. "Julien and Kennith help Verci crack the carriage."

"Can't be cracked," Kennith said.

"What?" Helene asked. "What's the point—"

Verci held up his hand to Helene. "Ain't a thing made by human hands that can't be cracked. We'll get it."

Asti sighed in disgust. "Once it's cracked, Julien gets the statue out and loads it on our carriage, Kennith races it out. Meet back at the safehouse, make our seller drop, and split our shares."

"Easy as blackberry pie," Verci said. "What else do we need to do?"

"Go scout the paths," Asti said.

"I know where to start that," Helene said.

Asti had to admit, the view was impressive from the roof of the whitestone. It never seemed that tall from the street. Looking down, he realized it was at the top of the slope, giving him a clear sightline all the way to the river. This was two blocks into Keller Cove, and the customhouse, the gates around it, the streets leading away, everything was laid out in front of him. To the west, the crowded brick and wood houses of North Seleth, crammed up to the shore, and the ramshackle junkyard of Benson Court beyond it. Keller Cove stretched out to the east, the houses and towers brighter and cleaner, with bits of green vegetation peeking through. The larger buildings gave him easy landmarks— Tyne's Pleasure Emporium and the Hesker marketplace.

"How'd you find this place, Hel?"

"Shooter girl needs to know her nests. This is one of the best." She put her eye to a lensescope—she had made Verci give her one before she took Asti up here—and scanned along the streets. "I could hit as far as—Colman Street, if I had the Beast."

"The Beast?"

"Beauty of a crossbow, she was. Needed Julien to carry the blasted thing, but once I had it mounted, it was like calling down lightning from the sky."

"You don't still have it?"

"Nah," Helene said. "Not since Julien and I worked for Tresser. Remember Tresser?"

"What happened to him?"

"Don't know," Helene replied. "He vanished and I don't ask questions about it."

Asti nodded. That was all too common in this trade, same when he was in Intelligence. Of course, in those days friends vanished because something went wrong on a mission no one could talk about. In this business more often it involved getting thrown in the river over some petty mistake. Tresser was a good window-cracker and a half-decent planner, but he had a bad habit of bragging about jobs, usually loudly in public places. Asti wasn't surprised he vanished. Helene shrugged. "He had a ton of gear stored in his flop, and it all went away when he did."

"I lost a good pair of boots that way once."

"I'm gonna build a new Beast someday," she said wistfully.

"With what you're gonna get now, where could you hit from up here?"

"Pure distance, six blocks. Blazes, I could riddle the gates of the customhouse if I really wanted. But you want me to trim a flywing, and this ain't the nest to do that from."

"Where do you want to be?"

"That depends on where we hit, boss."

"Right," Asti said. Helene was mocking him. That was good, it meant she was feeling comfortable. He turned his attention to the streets below. "Kennith says the carriage is slow."

"Where'd you get that chomie, anyway?"

"Might wanna watch saying that in front of him," Asti said. "He came through the Old Lady."

"This is all tangled through that bun?" Asti heard a lot of anger in her voice, but when he looked back at her, her body was calm and relaxed.

"She's a useful one to tangle through," Asti said. "At least, as far as I'm in a position to go through anyone."

"She know you brought me and Julien on?"

"I didn't tell her," Asti said. "But knowing her, she's probably fully aware."

"That's not gonna do you any favors, Rynax."

"I'm not looking for favors," Asti said. "Just a clean job, good payout. I need it, and you and yours need it."

"True," Helene said. "Don't trust her, though."

"Never do," Asti said. "Hardly trust anyone."

"Me?" Helene asked.

"Not a chance," Asti said, smirking back at her. "I'm ready to throw you off the roof if you try anything."

"Good to know." Helene pointed down to the street. "Corner of Ginny and Hicks. Three blocks from the customhouse but out of line of sight, most direct path to head out east. Plus, there's some good alleys to hide in. I can get on the roof of that flophouse and knock the foam off your beer."

Asti took the scope from her and looked at where she was talking about. "I think you may have an eye for this sort of thing, Hel."

"Thanks, Rynax. Now get your hands off my scope."

"This is Verci's scope."

"It's mine now. Part of the deal."

Chapter 8

THE CHEMIST SHOP WAS still open, despite the rest of Holver Alley being deserted and empty. Verci figured Almer Cort didn't hurt too much for business, being on the corner of a proper street. When he went in, the place was still a wreck from the other night, shelves knocked over, broken glass on the ground. The little bell over the door rang as Verci entered, and Cort came right out.

"Rynax," he said with a nod. "What can I do for you?"

"Not sure," Verci said. "I know what I need, don't know if it can be done."

"What do you need?" Cort asked. He scratched at his graying beard. "You talking about doing something that strays from legal business?"

"Let's just talk hypothetically," Verci said. "As one scientific philosopher to another."

"Oh, science," Cort said. With a chuckle he hopped up on the counter. "I don't think I really see you with the Uni boys, discussing theories and lessons."

"I could have done quite well at University, given the chance," Verci said defiantly. True, he hadn't done much proper schooling, not since he was ten and his father dragged him out to "earn something and learn something" as he had said at the time, but his marks had always been strong.

"Done quite well cracking dormitory locks, perhaps."

"Almer, help me out here," Verci said.

"Fine, fine. What are your philosophical thoughts, Scholar Rynax?"

"This is a mistake," Verci said. Annoyed, he went back to the door.

"Verci, Verci, sorry," Almer said. "I'm just . . . it's been a rough few days."

"That it has," Verci said. "Asti said you found proof the fire was deliberate."

"Oh, it was, no doubt. Even showed it to a Brigade officer, who said he told some inspectors. All time and no crowns in that."

"No help?"

"Inspectors came. Bastards wouldn't even listen." Almer grunted. "Said I shouldn't be bothering decent folk. Knocking my hand, they were."

"Sorry 'bout that," Verci said. "Asti said the Fire Brigade chief had come into some money recently as well."

Cort grunted. "Yenner? Did he? That explains that."

"What?"

"Oh, after the inspectors, I went to the Brigadehouse to talk to that decent fellow again. He told me Yenner up and quit the day after the fire, bought a new house over in Keller Cove, and hasn't been seen since. They don't even know who's the chief right now."

"Bastard," Verci said.

"It's all a loss, anyway," Cort said. "There's a bunch of vultures, you know, buyers and reps from Whatever and Whoever, dropping coin on the empty lots."

"Yeah, I've heard," Verci said. "We'll probably sell ours."

"Money's good," Cort said. "I don't need to sell, but they're sniffing me anyway." He shook his head. "So what do you need?"

"Hypothetically."

"Hypothetically, what do you need?"

"Imagine it's night, and you're on one street corner. You have somebody waiting for you, a few blocks away, wanting to know real quick that you're there, and you're ready for them."

"A signal."

"Yeah," Verci said. "Something quick, though, so the guy waiting for it will see it, but it won't stick around for someone else to gawk at."

"I get you," Cort said. He hopped down off the counter and went in the back. A moment later he came back with a couple of clay jars and squares of cloth. He laid out the squares and began scooping small spoonfuls of powder onto the cloth. "These will do the trick, I think. Won't do nothing until they catch fire. Say, from a street lamp."

"And if one did throw it in the street lamp?"

"You're gonna get a green flame that will shoot up, a good hundred feet or so. Real fast and hot. Someone's looking, they'll see it flare. But it'll be quiet."

"No burst or pop?"

"Or boom," Cort said. "Most things like this would boom. That would get everyone's attention. No, unless you're looking for it, saw it out the corner of your eye, you might think there was some strange lightning or something."

"In theory that should work quite nice," Verci said. "How much?"

"Nothing today," Cort said. "Far as I'm concerned, I still owe you and your brother a debt." He tied off the cloth into small pouches. "That'll do?"

Verci thought about the plan. Cort probably had a dozen other things he could use, if he knew exactly what he needed. There was one big snare he kept coming up with — if he was going to have to see inside the armored carriage, he'd need light. "Don't suppose you have a way to make a tiny lamp?"

Cort grinned. "How tiny?"

Verci held his fingers a few inches apart.

Cort looked at the door, as if expecting someone else to be listening. "You didn't get this from me." He went into the back and came out with a vial of light purple liquid.

"Is that *effitte*?" Verci asked. He had no idea Cort dealt in that. That was something sure to bring the sticks on his head, or more likely the eastside bosses who owned that market.

"Not exactly," Cort said. "It's a key ingredient to this, though I seriously doubt many people know it can be used in this way."

"In what way?"

"It's reactive to heat and motion." He held it up gingerly, only using the tips of his thumb and forefinger. "You squeeze it, warm it with body heat, and shake it, and it becomes luminescent."

"You're joking." Verci saw no humor on Cort's face. "Almer, you could make thousands of crowns off this."

"I could, if the glow didn't die out after a few minutes. And if it didn't require smuggled substances to make."

"What do I owe you for this?"

"Also nothing. Except you and your brother keep your ears open, you know?"

"Always do," Verci said. "If you hear anything else about Yenner, or . . . anything else . . ."

"I'll let you or Asti know," Cort said. His face reddened, his jaw clenched. "No point in bothering with anyone else."

Mila imagined everyone was staring at her. She knew that wasn't true, but even with new clothes—old clothes from Miss Kimber, actually, but new and clean for Mila—she couldn't help but think she was a street rat girl pretending like she belonged sitting at the long tables outside the Wheeler Street Tavern. She even imagined they were watching her eat. She told Asti as much.

"It's pretty common to feel that," he said. "Every time I'm working a gig, I'm constantly noticing someone looking at me, and thinking, 'Did he just make me? Am I skunked?'" He pushed his half-eaten Heckie pie across the table. "You want that?"

"You're not hungry?"

He shook his head. "I only ordered it to blend in."

Mila was ravenous—she always was—and greedily took it. It was greasy and tough, but she didn't care.

"So what am I doing here?"

"We're checking out the routes the wagon will take."

"But why me?"

"Because I—here, humor me. Close your eyes."

"Why?"

"Just do it."

Mila sighed and closed her eyes. "Now?"

"Now, there are a few guys sitting at the farthest table. You saw them before, right?"

"Yeah," Mila said.

"Now, imagine those guys, and pick which one is the best one to rob."

Mila opened her eyes to glare at Asti. "Really? That's what you're asking?"

"Look at me," Asti said, meeting her with a hard gaze. "Which one?"

"The guy in the green cap," she said.

"Why?"

"Because he bought cider for the whole table, and his purse is still bulging. Plus he's had at least three himself. He also has stubby legs, so I could outrun him."

"Why not the old man? You could outrun him."

"Sure, with his missing leg," Mila said. "But he also has a hook for a hand, and you don't want him even getting a chance to swipe at you with that."

"And which one is the best mark to shake a hat at?"

"I don't know!"

"What do you think?"

Mila turned her head to get another glance at the table. Asti reached across the table and held her head in place. "Just look at me."

She slapped his hand away, but didn't turn back. "Gray coat."

"Why?"

"I don't know, he just . . . has the look, you know? Like he's got guilt he needs to purge."

Asti smiled. "And that's why you're here."

Mila didn't believe him. "You don't know me. You don't know what I can do."

Asti nodded. "You're right. Also, your pop was a good sort. He worked the grocer over on Ullen—"

"I know what he used to do," Mila said. She didn't want to talk about her father. Or any of her family.

"Fair enough." Asti seemed to take the hint. "So behind me is the customhouse gate. We figure the thing is going to head east from here, so what'll it take?"

"Probably this street here." She pointed off to the right.

"That's Dockside. You'd be right, except Tyne's Emporium is down that way. Even late at night, the street would be clogged in front of it. So then what might it take?"

Mila sighed and rolled her eyes. "The next one over there."

"That's Ginny. What else could it take?"

"I don't know."

"Well, that's what we need to figure out. Sun's about to set. Ginny is our best bet, so you'll take a nice walk up and down it. Be unobtrusive."

"Un what?"

"Unob—just try not to get noticed."

"Then say so."

"Pay attention to people on the street. Where it gets crowded at night. Where it doesn't. Find the best spot on Ginny to make the carriage stop. Get it?"

"I think. What'll you do?"

He got up from the table. "Check other routes. We'll meet up at the stable tomorrow morning, figure out our plan."

"Hey, wait!" She didn't realize he was already leaving.

"What?"

"Um . . . where am I sleeping tonight?"

"You mean you don't . . . blazes, you don't have anything."

She wondered why Asti could sometimes seem so smart, and yet miss such obvious things.

"All right," he said. "I'll make sure you have something at Kimber's. I'll take care of it."

"By 'take care' you mean . . ."

"It'll be paid for. You need to stay sharp, and that means sleep. So I've got it."

Mila let her eyes go wide, giving her best "thanks for the crown" look. "That's so sweet, Mister Rynax, buying me dinner and my room for the night."

He shook his head. "Oversold it."

"Just so we're clear, Mister Rynax, that room you're getting me better blazing well be a different room than the one you plan to sleep in."

"Saints, girl. Of course it is."

Mila couldn't help but be wary of those "of courses." Even so, she was starting to believe that Asti really wasn't trying to roll her. "So I'm off to scout it."

"See you in the morning." He left the table and went off down the street.

She would go scout the street in a minute. For the moment she had to deal with the serious business of finishing the Heckie pie. On top of that, the man in the green cap was looking like he was getting ready to leave in a minute. Asti was right about one thing: she did know how to spot whose pocket was the best to pick.

Verci had returned to Hal and Lian's house for dinner at eight bells—late, Lian had pointed out—with a satchel full of materials he had scraped together for Helene's crossbow. His plan had been to get a quick bite, have a few spare moments with his wife, and go back out to the North Seleth Inn.

Hal had quite neatly sabotaged that plan.

"Off again?" he asked when Verci picked up his satchel. "Where you going at this hour?"

"I—" Verci faltered. "No, I'm not going anywhere. It's just, I . . . got a commission to build something. And I have my tools and such in my satchel." As soon as he spoke, Verci knew it was a stupid thing to say. He should have just said, "Yes, I need to go meet Asti about something." Or even, "I just was getting something from my satchel." But now he was stuck.

Stupid Hal and his stupid questions.

Verci never had been good with thinking of things to say quickly. That's why he preferred just not getting caught anywhere. Hal caught him.

"So what do you need to build?"

Lying, at this point, was futile, at least, lying outrageously—if he was stuck building the crossbow here, it would reach a point in the process where what he was building would be undeniably obvious. Though he had learned his lesson of offering too much information to Hal.

"It's a crossbow. For someone from the neighborhood."

"Really?" Hal's eyes went wide. "You know how to make one?" The man appeared to be shivering with excitement.

"Yes," Verci said. "I've made a few of them before and—"

"Verci." Hal spoke with an intense, hushed voice. "I know I would never be able to help you, but I would really love to just watch while you worked."

"That's a great idea," Lian called from the kitchen. She walked over to the two of them, carrying the pot she had been scrubbing. "I, for one, would *love* to see you do some work, Verci."

Verci glanced over to Raych, nursing Corsi in the chair in the corner. She just gave him a wry smile, as if to say, "You're on your own here."

"All right," Verci said, putting the satchel on the floor. He sat down in front of it and started sorting through his supplies. There were a few things in the satchel he did not need Hal seeing.

Over the next three hours Verci only managed to do one hour's worth of work on the crossbow. Every time he picked up a tool, every time he attached a piece, every cut he made—each action earned a question from Hal. Sometimes two questions. Sometimes the same question asked multiple times. Verci answered each one with as much patience and reserve as he could manage.

At some point Lian came in from the kitchen and observed the pile of sawdust, wood scraps, and other detritus that had accumulated on the floor. "You are going to clean that up, yes?"

"Of course I am," Verci said. He looked to his wife, dozing in her chair with their sleeping babe in her arms. "Tell her, Raych."

"Of course he is," Raych said.

Lian leaned over to her sister. "I'm glad he's doing something . . . productive. But I'm not here to be his cook and maid, you hear?"

"Yes, Lian." Verci looked at her pointedly, the glare he'd

used to use to scare off street rats before they'd spoil a gig. "I will take care of it."

Lian stepped away, looking more than a little spooked. "Fine. Hal, you should come to bed. You have a job to go to in the morning, you know."

"Yes, of course, dear." Hal got to his feet and brushed the sawdust off himself. "Though I would love to—"

"Hal."

He glanced at Lian, then back to Verci. "You've still got some work to do here, yes?"

"A bit." Verci was more than eager to get Hal out of his hair, and in no way did he want to encourage him to stay just a few more minutes. "I'll get this cleaned up. Go on with your wife."

Hal nodded and went up the stairs with Lian. Raych pulled herself out of her chair, Corsi still held in one arm.

"You should go up with your wife soon, too, you know," she said with a warm whisper.

"Soon," he told her. He picked up the crossbow, checking the tension on the cords. "Half an hour or so. Including cleaning up."

"Such a good husband." She kissed him on the forehead. "Working so hard."

Spring tension on the trigger was off. "Yeah, well, Helene needs this in the morning, so she has time to get used to it."

"Oh, *Helene* does, does she?"

Verci heard the tone in his wife's voice. That tone couldn't be good. He looked up to see her eyebrow arched, her face cold.

"Yes, Helene. Asti brought her and Julien in on this. I told you."

"No, you didn't mention that," Raych said, her voice a blizzard.

Verci got to his feet. "Now, look, Helene is an excellent marksman."

"Woman."

"Excellent," Verci said, straining to keep his voice from rising. Last thing he needed was for Hal and Lian to hear this. "And we need her skill on this gig."

"Skill?"

"I mean with a crossbow, Raych."

Raych bit her lip, tears forming at her eyes. Then she started laughing. "Sorry, I couldn't keep it up any more. It's just so fun watching you squirm."

"Raych!"

She giggled some more. "'I mean with a crossbow.' You're so cute."

"You're horrible," Verci joked.

"And you love me," she said, kissing him. "I've seen how Helene Kesser looks at you, Verci. I know what she's thinking."

"Do you?"

She leaned in and whispered in his ear. "I'm usually thinking the same thing."

Verci's blood heated up. "This can wait until morning."

"Oh, no." Raych put her hand firmly against his chest. "You finish your work. And clean up." She went to the stairs. "Just don't take too long, all right?"

Verci didn't waste any more time getting the job done.

Helene preferred to hunt early in the morning, but that hadn't been an option. Verci hadn't shown up with the new crossbow until after nine bells, and then there was another hour wasted arguing with Asti about why she needed to take some time getting to know her new equipment and not spend it scouting travel routes for the blasted wagon. Then it was another hour to walk to the eastern edge of the city and slip into Carol Woods.

Strictly speaking, Carol Woods was private property, and Lord Carol would prosecute trespassers if they were caught. Helene knew from experience, though, that Lord Carol was never particularly vigorous about having the woods patrolled. The key to not getting caught was being smart about what to hunt. There was no way to sneak back into the city with a whole deer carcass, although Helene had heard plenty of stories of boar poachers.

That's why Helene always went for rabbits. They were Julien's favorite meat. Easy to sneak back into the city with a few rabbits, and one or two made a decent bribe if a stick or one of Carol's men caught her.

Plus they were blasted hard to hit with a crossbow, and Helene liked that. Good way to test her new toy.

It was past midday when Helene had finally found a clearing with what looked like a good-size warren, and hid herself in the brush. It would be a bit before any conies came out to feed.

Helene checked through the lensescope. Good sight. Verci did well choosing the lenses—she knew damn well he wasn't grinding them. She spotted a tree off in the distance, a big and knotty one. That would serve well. She found a nice round knot on the tree and took aim for dead center.

Right on target. So Verci had aligned the scope damn well. That's what she had expected. She wound the gear-crank to recock it. Verci had done a stellar job on that, too. She hardly needed to work to reload the crossbow, and could do it fast.

Good old Verci. There was a Rynax a girl could count on.

She checked out the tree again, and took another shot. Fast as she could, she wound, cocked, reloaded, aimed, and shot. Again: wind, cock, reload, aim, shoot. Again. She looked through the scope: five bolts in a tight pattern in the same knothole. That would do nicely.

She reloaded the crossbow and waited.

A buck came out of one of the holes. It took a few lazy lopes across the clearing, nibbling on the grass and clover. Helene got the critter in her scope. She let it take a few more hops. Let it relax, get engrossed with its feeding. She checked the distance between the rabbit and the hole. It would take him a few seconds to get back underground.

She lined up the shot, and started to pull back the trigger.

The snap of a branch cracking echoed through the clearing.

The buck's ears went up.

Helene turned her aim to the warren hole and fired.

The buck dashed back to the hole, reaching it just in time to take Helene's bolt square in its head.

Helene cranked and reloaded, trying to do it without looking, letting the action become a natural motion of her arms. She kept her eye on the clearing. The rabbit didn't move; it was a clean kill.

Something else was nearby, big enough to crack a branch like that.

Helene let out two sharp whistles.

Two more came from the other side of the clearing.

Helene raised up her crossbow and stepped out of the brush. Another woman came out on the other side. This woman looked like she belonged in the forest, even though she wore a coat and boots that were lined in fur, the kind a fashionable woman would kill for, and her black, lustrous hair fell gracefully past her shoulders as if she had just been primped by a score of dressers.

"Capital shot, dear," the woman said, her accent far more highbrow than Helene would have suspected. Helene wracked her memory: was there a Lady Carol? Was she the sort to tromp about in the forest?

"I thought so," Helene said. "You're going to let me take my rabbit?"

"By all means, dear. You killed the bunny, he's yours."

Despite her courtly manners, the woman moved like a predator. Helene noticed the knives strapped on her hips, and two more at her boots. Helene moved carefully as she approached the dead rabbit.

"You didn't snap that branch by accident, did you?"

"Never by accident." The woman looked over to the tree at which Helene had taken her practice shots. "But those shots were a bit closer to my blind than I liked. Petty, I know."

"I still tagged the buck," Helene said. She crouched down to pick it up, not taking her eyes off the woman.

"And well done at that," the woman said. "But you should probably take your bunny and get out of the forest."

"Why?" Helene asked. "Will Lord and Lady Carol have me arrested?"

"Possibly," the woman said. She reached into her coat and pulled out a rolled-up paper and passed it to Helene. "You seen him about?"

Helene unrolled it and checked the charcoal sketch. The guy pictured looked familiar. "Is that Cobie Pent?"

The woman nodded. "That is what it says. You know him?"

Helene ignored the writing. "Met him a couple times, few years back. Heard he was thrown in Quarrygate months ago."

"He was, but he got out. And the price on his head is very nice." The woman drew one of her knives.

Helene brought up the crossbow. "Hey, now. I'm just hunting. And I ain't seen him."

"I know," the woman said. "All the more reason to get gone before he finds you. I'd hate for him to use you as a hostage."

Helene decided that one rabbit was enough for today.

Chapter 9

ASTI FOUND THE SMELL of roasted rabbit distracting. The whole stable reeked of it when he came in. Helene and Julien were sitting on one bench, sharing the meat by themselves. Kennith was tending to the horses, looking more than a little annoyed at them.

"Blazes, Helene," he said. "And here I thought you were too busy to help us pick the routes today."

"Had to make sure the crossbow worked," she said, wiping the juices from her mouth as she spoke. "It does very nicely. I'll have to thank your brother."

"Hmm." Asti had some idea how Helene would thank Verci, had she half the chance. He went over to Kennith and the horses. "Kennith, how's the escape carriage?"

"Fine, fine," he said. He ground his teeth as he put a blanket over one horse. "I know we're planning a gig and all here, and I know we all are under the grace of the Old Lady in this place, but still—" He trailed off, focusing on vigorously rubbing the horse with the blanket.

"Still what?" Asti asked. Kennith was getting annoyed about something, and it was better to fix it now, before it blew up during the gig.

Kennith glanced over to the Kessers, and lowered his voice. "I live here, in the stable, you know? I know we're working together on this, but . . . this is my place. My cot, my bench. My stove."

Asti glanced back at Helene and Julien. "Got it." He lowered his voice to match Kennith's. "Those two, they . . . sometimes they don't always think about the rest of the world around them, you know?"

"I've noticed."

"And after tomorrow night, you're done with them."

"Fine," Kennith said. "I've got to get back to the horses."

Mila came in after a few minutes, followed shortly by Verci. Verci glanced at Helene and the rabbit. "Crossbow works well?"

"Perfect."

Asti stepped up to the center table. "Listen up. This is how the gig will go. Four steps. Stop the carriage. Take out the escort. Open the carriage. Get the goods."

"And run," Verci said. "That's step five."

"Always. So, stop the carriage. Verci and Mila."

"Me?" Mila asked. "How?"

Asti laughed to himself. "You two will do a Doxy Slap."

"A what?" Mila's voice went up an octave. "I told you—".

"Yes, you aren't a whore. But we'll dress you like one. Real simple. You and Verci are on our designated corner."

"Which is where?" Mila asked.

"I haven't decided yet." This was true, but the reason was that voice of distrust in the back of his head, that anyone else in the room might tell the sticks where they were planning on hitting the carriage. No one can betray you with information they don't have.

"And what do we do when I'm dressed like a whore?"

"You stage a fight, and then Verci slaps you so you go in the street. The carriage should stop to not run over you."

"Should?" Mila asked.

"Should, definitely," Verci said. Asti could tell he was biting his cheeks to keep from laughing.

"Should is cold comfort," Mila said.

"When it's stopped, Helene hits the driver through his little window. I'll take out the escort, Verci will help with that."

Julien raised up a hand. "You say 'take out.' You mean kill, yes?"

"If we have to," Verci said. "I'm not crazy about it, but these are paid guards. That's fair."

Asti nodded. That was one of Dad's rules: when you're doing a gig, if you have to kill a stick or a soldier or any muscle, it was fair game. They took the job. They knew the risks, they were armed and ready to defend themselves.

Julien pursed his lips. "I won't be there for that, right?"

"Right," Helene said sharply. "He won't."

"Right," Verci said. "Once the carriage is secured, I'll throw the signal in a street lamp. It'll be a green flare in the sky. Quick, no sound."

"Really, no sound?" Asti had never heard of anything that could do that.

"That's what Cort said."

Asti wasn't going to question that any further.

"So carriage stopped, escorts out, then Julien and Kennith come in on their carriage. We're ready with that, right, Ken?"

"I think so," Kennith said. "How you going to open the other carriage?"

Asti turned to his brother. "You got it figured?"

"Got it."

"All right," Asti said.

"But how is he . . ."

"Ken. Verci says he's got it. That's all I need to know."

"What does he got?"

Verci sighed. "I've got Julie and a crowbar, and a small window into the carriage."

"Provided the driver doesn't slam it down before Helene shoots him."

Asti shrugged. "Helene misses the shot, we're skunked. That's that."

"No pressure," Helene said.

Asti winked at her. "Once open, Julien loads it, we all bolt. Got it?"

"Got it," Verci said.

"All got," Helene said.

"So now what?"

"Now, everyone go home, or whatever you're calling home, and get some serious rest. Meet here at six bells at night. Be sharp then, because we'll be at it all night."

"All night." Verci moaned. "Oh, saints, I'm going to have to paint a story for Hal and Lian."

"Do what you have to do," Asti said. "See you all tomorrow."

Helene's fingers were twitching. Get some rest, Asti said. Like she could do that right now. She finally had a real gig, even if it was just a one-night deal. And a new bow. A Verci Rynax-made bow at that. The piece was a work of art. Needed to be, if she was going to make this shot that the gig hinged on. She wasn't worried. Anxious, though. Always was before a gig that hinged on her shot. Couldn't be helped.

They had all left the stable, save the chomie, who had kept shooting ugly looks at her and Julien the whole night. He could go roll himself, as far as Helene cared. She didn't need him or his stable, no matter what Asti thought of him. He was trouble. No one in the neighborhood knew him.

Asti and Verci had said their good-byes and split off, Verci heading home to his damn pretty wife. Lucky girl. She kept her pace with Asti, as Julien lagged behind. Asti didn't speak as they walked to Kimber's, and the look on his face told her he wasn't interested in chatting.

Neither was she.

"Rynax," she said. "Pass me a crown."

"Eh?" Asti looked confused. "What you need a crown for?"

"Do I need to explain money to you, Asti?"

"No. But why do you need one?"

"Never you mind. I'm good for it."

Asti dug into his pocket. "Fine." He rolled the coin over his fingers for a moment. "You're not going back to Kimber's?"

"Eventually," Helene said. "Julie, stay with Asti. I'll see you in the morning."

Julien didn't like it. "But where are you going?"

"I just need a few hours," Helene said. "I'll be fine." The last thing she needed was Julien going with her.

"Come on, Jules," Asti said, flipping the coin to her. "I'll buy you a cider, all right?"

Helene caught the coin and spun on her heel before Julien could object. She dashed off down to Elk Road.

She hadn't been to the Shack in months, but it looked the same as always: a run-down, dim tavern where every table leaned to one side. The bartender was new, though.

"What's the score, skirt?" he asked as she walked in.

"You tell me." She came over and leaned on the bar, which creaked with her weight.

"Wine or cider, since that's what we've got."

"Ain't drinking."

"That's all we got, skirt."

Helene leaned in closer. "Laramie whirl."

"I don't mix nothing like that, skirt."

This new bartender wasn't getting it. She lowered her voice. "Downstairs? Knuckle matches. That's the password."

"Don't know what you're talking about, skirt."

"It's all right, Gil." A rough hand clapped on Helene's shoulder. Nange Lesk came up close to her. Far closer than she ever wanted Nange Lesk to be. "Hel's on the nose, all right."

"You say so," the bartender said.

"Come on down," Nange said, his arm now working around her. "We don't mess with passwords anymore. It's all just the people we know."

"'We,' Nange?" Helene asked. "Since when do you run the Shack?"

"I wouldn't say 'run,' so much." He led her around the bar to the back stairs. Three boys, skinny street rats with scrapes and bruises all over their faces, lurked at the top of the stairs.

"Hey, chief, we got a—"

"Not now, boys," Nange said. "You go to Ren, I don't need to hear it." He took Helene down the stairs.

The basement was set up same as always. A few low-burning lamps hung on the ceiling over the chalk-circle ring. Two young girls—both of them could have been Mila's age, or younger—were knocking each other senseless. Benches surrounded the circle, with old men laughing and throwing down coins. Helene noticed at least two or three sticks in uniform as well. That was new.

"Friendly with the sticks, are ya?"

"The right ones." Nange flashed an ugly smile. "There are some good Red and Green who love a show, you know?"

The girls were really hammering at each other. Both their faces were bloody messes, but neither one yielded. That wasn't how the matches used to go.

"Harsh," Helene whispered.

Nange looked over at the girls. "Yeah, this is a special one. Winner gets to join the Scratch Cats up there."

"And the loser?"

"Honey Hut. How much she'll go for depends on the state of her face."

Helene shuddered. She'd fight like blazes to stay out of the Honey Hut as well. "Don't tell me you're running the Hut, Nange."

"Branching out, putting things together." He shrugged. "Things are shifting here on Elk. After the fire and such, we need to gather up, you know?"

"Know the feeling," Helene said. "So I came to get in on a match or two. But just the usual knuckle-dust, nothing like this."

"You wanna knuckle-dust, Hel?" He touched her face. Helene fought the instinct to wince and pull away. Definitely didn't want his hands on her, but she might as well play nice for the moment. "Wouldn't think you'd risk hurting your eye."

"Ain't that much of a risk."

"Your eye's worth a lot more than a few crowns."

Helene couldn't help smiling at that, even if it came from Nange.

"I'm not really doing it for the crowns," Helene said. "Just looking to blow some nerves, you know, before—"

"Before what?"

Blazes. She should have kept her trap shut. "Before I have to go and sleep on Kimber's floor again."

"Still no place, Hel? That ain't right."

"I'll have it sorted in a few days."

"We can get you sorted, you know."

One of the girls got the upper hand, putting her opponent to the floor. She pounced, slamming her knees onto the other girl's chest. Two more hard punches across the jaw, and the girl on the floor stopped moving.

"Julien and I will get ourselves set up soon."

"How is Julie doing? He keeping his head up?"

"Hey," the fighting girl shouted. "Am I a Cat now?" The crowd around her hooted and laughed.

"Nice work," Nange said, holding a finger up to Helene as he focused his attention on the girl. "You're a Cat. Go up to the boys, get your scratches."

The girl crossed over to the stairs, giving a sneer over to Helene. "I got my scratches." A few guys dragged the other girl off the floor, while the crowd jeered and whistled some more.

"Tough girl," Helene said.

"She'll need to be," Nange said. "I'm serious, though, Hel. I was thinking about you the other night."

The last thing Helene wanted to know was how Nange was thinking of her. "How so?"

"Well, like I said, me and my boys, we've got some interest in the Honey Hut."

"You finish that thought, and—"

He held up his hands. "No, nothing like that, Hel. Honest as a saint."

Which saint? Helene thought. "So what the blazes are you on about?"

"Well." He drew out the word, like he knew Helene might knock him down for what he was about to say. "The lady who used to manage the girls, she's not part of the new . . . arrangement."

Which probably meant she was facedown in the creek with a slit throat.

"You're kidding, right?"

"Look, a good joint . . . a profitable, clean joint like I know the Honey Hut can be . . . it needs two things."

"Girls and beds." Helene didn't need to hear anymore.

"Is the circle free for me to dust it?" She walked over to the chalk ring.

Nange grabbed her shoulder. "Any doxy pit can run on that. I mean to make it nice. Two things."

Helene suffered the idea of listening to him while she took off her coat and vest. "Two things, right."

"One is a lady—smart lady to keep the girls in line, keep the coins and numbers adding up. Stay on her toes while the rest are on their backs, you know?"

"You really thought me the type for that, Nange?"

"Not normally, no. But you're burned out, you know? Need to be flexible, you do. But there's the other thing we'd want at the Hut."

"What's that?"

"Someone who'll make the clokes think twice about trying anything funny with the girls. Big guy, make the place safe just by being seen, you know. But also a guy we can trust not to do anything funny himself, you know?"

Her and Julien. Of course. "It's not a bad package."

"Roof and bed and stove for the two of you, easy work."

"Hmm." Helene didn't like it a damn bit, but there was very little going on that she did like. Even this gig of Asti's would only get them back on their feet for a couple months. She'd rather get stable, even if it meant getting cozy with the likes of Nange.

"Just think about it, all right, Hel?"

"Give it all the thought it's due." She handed him her coat and vest. Flipping her coin into the chalk circle, she called out, "Who's ready to dust with me?"

Another coin dropped into the circle, and a woman in shirtsleeves, suspenders, and trousers stepped out. Helene recognized her from the neighborhood, but she didn't know her name. She was tall and blond—Waish or Bardinic heritage, likely—with arms like a blacksmith. She also wore a green fur-lined felt cap.

Helene planned to walk out of the Shack wearing that cap.

Chapter 10

ASTI SLEPT LIGHTLY, he always did, but for once his sleep wasn't uneasy. No dark dreams, no drenching sweats. It was well into midmorning when he finally rose, dressed, and wandered down to the kitchen of Kimber's.

Kimber was working hard at the stove, whistling and stirring. She barely glanced at his entrance. "I thought you were either sleeping all day, or had snuck out before dawn."

"It's usually one or the other with me," Asti said. "I don't suppose I could trouble you for some tea?"

"Only tea?" She flashed him a spark of a smile.

"I wouldn't hate breakfast."

She turned away from the stove to face him, wide smile on her round face. "I can manage oats with cream and honey."

Asti chuckled. "I think I would eat that without objection."

She moved in a bit closer, lowering her voice. "I might also have some peaches left in my preserves."

Asti's mouth watered despite himself. "If it doesn't put you out."

"Not at all. Get out there to the taproom. I'll bring it out in a click."

Asti went out to the taproom, which was mostly empty, save one table. Win Greenfield stared down at the table, scratching absently at the wood. Asti joined him.

"You sleep all right, Win?"

"I sleep," Win said flatly. "That's about it."

"Good, good. You ate already?"

Win shook his head. "Was hoping for some beet and carrot soup."

"That'd be a good lunch, Win," Asti said, unsure of what else he could say. Win kept scratching at the table, digging a small trench in the wood. "We could ask Kimber, don't you think? I bet she'd do that for you, Win, don't you?"

"Won't be the same," Win said. "You had my wife's soup that one time, didn't you, Rynax?"

"I did." Asti had no particular recollection, though Missus Greenfield had brought them dinner plenty of times. "Real good soup."

Win nodded slowly. "The best." His voice cracked.

Kimber came out to the table with Asti's breakfast.

"Kimber, Win was wondering if you could make a beet and carrot soup. You can do that, right?"

Kimber's eyes went wide and she turned to Win, who did not look up. "Of course I would. That sounds perfect." She gingerly reached out, almost touching him on the shoulder before he flinched away.

"Thank you, dear. I'll . . . I think I'll go up to my room." Win got up from the table and shuffled off to the stairs.

Asti watched him go. "I'm beginning to wonder if I didn't do him a favor."

"Don't you dare say that." Kimber took the seat opposite him. "You saved a life, that is . . . it's a sacred thing."

"Saved him, not his family." Asti dug into his breakfast. Excellent, as always.

"Could you have?" She looked at him pointedly. "Honestly, did you even have a chance?"

"No. I was going to try, but . . . Verci held me back. And he was right. By the time we were pulling Win out, there was no chance."

"Then you did what you could, and God didn't mean for you to do anything else."

Asti sipped his tea to cover his smirk. "I never liked trying to blame God or any saint for my failures."

"It's not about blame. Or failures. It's about accepting our limitations. And our blessings."

"I think we're pretty short of blessings here, Kimber."

She shrugged. "Blessings aren't always obvious."

Asti took another bite of his breakfast and deliberately steered the conversation away from religion. "Fewer people staying here now. Have most of them found somewhere else to go since the fire?"

"I hope so. A lot of them just left. Some bloke in a suit came around here—"

"From Colevar and Associates?"

"I think so. Who are they?"

"They're lawyers," Asti said. "Question is, who are they buying up Holver Alley lots for?"

"Don't know. Does it matter? People have a chance to move on with their lives."

"A fire is set—and it was set by someone, Kimber, I know this—and some mysterious person has lawyers buy land that's now freed up?" The look on Kimber's face was blank. Either she didn't get it, or she just plain didn't care. "That's suspicious. That isn't even pretending to not be suspicious."

"Maybe so, Asti," Kimber said, patting him on the shoulder as she stood. "But what're people like us going to do about it?"

"If it isn't us, then who's it gonna be?"

Tonight was the gig. Everything was set—primary plan, secondary plans, emergency backup plan, and a safe place to run to if things turned left. Despite that, Asti had an urge to do another walkaround by the customhouse, and check the routes one more time. He tamped it down. No need to do anything to spook the target at this point. Nothing good would come from it.

Stewing in Kimber's taproom until it was time to meet at the stable wouldn't do. He was too restless, he needed to keep himself busy or he'd lose it. He had to at least get out on the street.

Helene and Julien were sitting out on the stoop in front

of Kimber's, talking in low voices. Helene was wearing a ridiculous felt cap. They both hushed up when he came out.

Asti pointed to the cap. "You buy that with the crown I lent you?"

"Something like that," Helene said, giving him a sly grin. She pulled a crown out of her pocket and flipped it up to him. Scrapes and bruises on her hands. "Where you headed?"

"Clear my head, look around the neighborhood."

"Keep yourself out of trouble until tonight?"

"Something like that. You should do the same."

"Always do," Helene said. Her mood was definitely improved. Probably because she went to the Elk Road Shack and dusted her knuckles in the basement. If that kept her happy, and she could still make her shot, then Asti didn't care what she did. He knew not to say anything, though. All it would do was start a fight between her and Julien, and that was the last thing he needed tonight. He gave them a curt wave and walked off.

The newsboy shouted out from the corner. "Southwest Council meeting tomorrow!"

"What's the word, boy?" Asti asked. "Anything on Holver Alley?"

"Pay me the ticks and read it yourself," the boy said. "I'm wise to you."

"You've got a ways to go before you hit wise," Asti said, handing over the coins. The boy threw a newssheet at him and went back to his cry.

There was a story on the alley fire, finally, but it might as well have been nothing. "Fire damages several homes and shops along Holver Alley, leaving several dead and more displaced. Donations for help can be given at Saint Bridget's Church." Pointless. There was more space devoted to the series of tetchball matches. Today's game was Bricklayer's Guild against the South Kitchen Scullers.

That was as good a way as any to while away a few hours.

There was a decent crowd at the tetch pitch, though Asti recognized a lot of old Holver Alley residents hanging about. Some still dirty and singed. A couple with several kids sat on the outskirts, shaking their hats with half-hearted resignation. Kilmen? Kinsten? Asti couldn't remember. Dry goods store, two down from Greenfield. He threw the crown Helene gave him into their hat.

The match was in full swing, Scullers on the field. A burly Bricklayer was in place at the rail, tetchbat raised high. The arm tossed low, forcing the batter to flip under to knock the ball. He hit it weakly; it didn't even clear the jack line. Despite that, he ran out into the field, hoping to score at least one point. The bumpers were on him before he got five steps in. The bumpers piled onto him, but they only slowed him down, and he kept driving for the jack line. The arm rushed to the ball, and tossed it to the rail for the restore. The watcher didn't call the restore.

The Bricklayer kept charging forward, despite having two bumpers hanging on him. The jack warder tackled the Bricklayer's legs just before he reached the line. All four of them fell forward, the Bricklayer's hand stretching out over the jack line.

"Point, Bricklayer!" the watcher called out.

Half the crowd erupted in screams. The call was blatantly unfair; that could hardly be considered crossing the line, and the bowler had restored the rail long before.

Then Asti realized the watcher was Ren Poller. Nange's man.

And there was Nange, standing near the Bricklayers, tapping the side of his nose. He had a sizable crowd at his shoulders now, at least five.

Before Asti could move, Nange spotted him.

"Blazes," Asti muttered. Nange approached, three of his entourage with him. One was a tall blond woman, built like a draft horse. She had a pretty face, save the busted lip and black eye.

"Enjoying the match, pirie?"

"Trying to," Asti said. "You're tweaking tetchball games, now?"

"I don't know what you're talking about, Asti," Nange said. "Blazes of a point they scored there, wasn't it? Real screamer."

"Right," Asti said. Another glance at the crowd, where he saw a handful of young punks—including the ones from

Almer's shop the other night—slipping through the crowd, picking the pockets of people too focused on their own outrage to notice it. "You've got fingers in every pie, don't you, Nange?"

"You've got to eat the pie when it's warm. You know that, pirie."

"Some pies should be left on the sill."

Nange moved in closer, running a finger on the seam of Asti's vest. "Listen, pirie. I know you've got something in the oven right now. You and your brother, and likely the Kessers as well."

"I don't know what you're talking about." Asti cursed himself. They had been too sloppy, clearly, if Nange knew anything at all.

"Sure, sure," Nange said. "It's all just fine. That's just what we want to see."

"He's working with Kesser?" the blonde asked. Nange just gave a shrug. She sneered. "Tell that piece of skirt I want my hat back."

"Leave it," Nange said. "She's got a rage about the hat, you see. Hel won it fair."

"Why don't you go back to watching the match, Nange?" Asti said. "I don't think we need to say any more, do we?"

"No, we don't," Nange said. He ran a finger up Asti's vest, and then patted him on the cheek. "I can wait to see what you and yours put out on the sill." With that, he went back over to the rest of his goons.

"He can't seriously expect a piece of action on this, can he?" Verci asked. He wasn't sure whether to laugh or worry.

"Apparently he does," Asti said. Asti's brow was sweating. He actually looked nervous. Or sick. He waved over to Kimber to bring him another cider.

"We're not going to give him any, though."

"Blazes, no," Asti said. "At least, I have no intention to."

"Good."

"Here's the thing," Asti said. "Nange has all of a sudden gotten his hands on several people, working several angles. All right after the fire. He was ready for it."

"You think he had a hand in the fire," Verci said, though even as he spoke, he didn't really believe what he was saying.

"It's what it looks like to me."

"Let me be the sinner on your shoulder here," Verci said.

"That's a switch," Kimber said as she brought over two ciders. "I thought you were the sensible one."

"I am," Verci said. Kimber laughed and walked off. Asti took his cider and gulped it down with abandon. Verci leaned in closer and lowered his voice. "Let's just say that Nange was involved. He's got to be at the bottom of it. Someone paid off Yenner. Someone is using the lawyers. That's someone with money. That ain't Nange."

"You've got a point, but . . ."

"I'll also point out, we've not had our ear to the ground for some time. Nange could have been building his pots for a while and we never knew."

"Fair point," Asti said. "So there's the guy at the top, and that ain't Nange. But I bet you my left foot Nange is directly connected to whoever actually sparked the fires. He may have even lit them himself."

"Wouldn't be surprised on that. But we only have your gut on this."

"My gut is blazing good with these things."

"True," Verci said. "But I don't want to start a war with Nange over it, you hear? Not yet."

"And he's not getting a piece of anything. Not of our shares."

Verci nodded and sipped his cider. "And he knows Helene and Julien are in? We should warn them."

"Probably," Asti said. "Unless they tipped them off. Helene apparently lined up with him and his while she was knuckle-dusting last night."

"Blazes," Verci said. Helene shouldn't be knuckle-dusting, not when they were counting on her to make such a hard shot. Broken hand or swollen eye would ruin the whole gig. After a moment of stewing silence, he said, "We can't dwell on this. We've got to get to the stable. Gig is in a few hours."

"Right," Asti said. He put on a weak grin. "Saints know you need your gig night ritual."

Chapter 11

ASTI WAS NEVER MUCH of one for gig night rituals. Every gig he'd done, every crew he'd worked on, there was always someone who had their thing. Even in Druth Intelligence, doing a hot run of some sort, there would be other agents who wouldn't go out unless they kissed both rings or spun three times.

He glanced over to his brother, getting ready at the worktable. Verci was a man with a ritual, but Asti acknowledged it was one that made sense. His was all about packing equipment. He had already dressed for the action, save three items: his belt, his vest, and his bandolier. Those three items lay on the worktable, as well as two dozen different gadgets, devices, and God and the saints knew what else. Those he was moving around, looking at, moving around again, contemplating more, moving them around again.

"What are you doing with those?" Helene finally asked. She dropped her crossbow down on the other side of the workbench, grabbed a tool from Verci, and started making minute adjustments to her weapon.

"Just trying to decide what to bring," Verci said. He moved a gear-and-clamp device from one pile to the other.

"Bring what you need to do the job."

"Need is a tricky thing." Verci pointed to the pile on the

right. "Right there is what I know I need. The question is what else I might need."

Helene picked up a vise-like device. "Why might you need this?"

Verci snatched it from her, put it back in the pile in the center. "That's what I'm trying to figure out."

"Nothing else," Asti said. "Go light, go fast."

"Might need a drill," Verci said, moving the small drill over to the pile on the right.

"It's not a safe-crack," Asti said.

"Isn't it?" Verci asked. "When it comes down to it, that's what we got—a hit-and-grab safe-crack, with the safe on wheels."

"Safe on wheels," Kennith echoed. He laughed broadly. "Yeah, that's what it is."

"With guards," Helene said. "You need weapons."

"Darts on the bandolier," Verci said offhandedly. "Two knives, inside pocket of the vest. Another in the boot."

"Dad's first rule," Asti said with a smirk. "No matter what the job—"

"—Go armed," Verci finished.

"I hear that," Helene said. She finished tightening the trigger screws on her crossbow. The bells of the alarm wires jangled. Someone was approaching the stable. Helene immediately cocked the crossbow and loaded it. Verci pulled out three darts from the bandolier.

Asti stepped up to the door. Loud footfalls, crunching on the gravelly walk, approached at an even pace.

"Sticks?" Verci asked in a low whisper.

"Always possible, but they usually sneak or charge." Asti listened carefully. "One person, not trying to hide their approach."

"Someone actually coming to the inn's stable?" Verci shrugged. "It happens."

"Shush," Asti said. He gave a few quick hand signals to Verci, who drew two darts and got to one side of the door. Asti pulled a long knife out and took the other side. The footsteps came right up to the door. Then a few loud, sharp knocks.

"Sticks don't knock," Helene whispered.

"Kennith," Asti whispered. "Ask who it is."

"Why me?"

"Because you are supposed to be here." Asti was always amazed how some people missed the small but obvious details.

Kennith gingerly walked over to the door. "Who's there?"

A woman's voice returned. "It's Raychelle Rynax. Is . . . are my husband and his brother in there?"

"Your wife?" Asti whispered.

Verci shrugged and opened up the door, and with a swift movement grabbed his wife and pulled her in, slamming the door shut.

"Oh!" Raych squealed.

"Why is your wife here?" Asti snapped. "Why does she know where *here* is?"

"He told me," Raych said.

"You told your wife where the base was?"

"Why wouldn't he?" Raych demanded, getting up close to Asti.

"You never tell someone who isn't part of the gig where the base is, especially right before the gig goes hot!" Asti stormed away.

"How am I not part of this, Asti?" Raych asked. "You drag my husband into some shady business, I'm part of it, too."

"Feh," was all Asti could bother to say to her.

"Why are you here, love?" Verci asked.

"Well, you all are going to be working this 'gig,' and it'll be a long night." She smiled weakly and held up the wicker basket she was carrying, which Asti hadn't noticed until now. "Is anyone hungry?"

"Blazes, no," Asti said. "Never eat before a gig."

"Are you kidding?" Mila came out from the stalls, dressed for the gig. Raych's eyes went wide, as the girl was wearing a high skirt, cut stockings, and a half-laced blouse.

"Asti, what are you doing having this . . . child . . . dress like a common street whore!" Of course Raych would blame him.

"That's her disguise for the gig, Raych," Verci said calmly.

"And this poor girl is just skin and bones," she said. "Really, Verci, you should be more aware of such things." She put her basket on one of the tables and pulled out a loaf of bread, tore off a chunk, and handed it to Mila. "I have cheese and lamb in here as well, and plenty."

"Cheese?" Julien's whole face lit up. Asti sighed. There was no stopping this now.

"Three kinds, Julien," Raych said warmly. "I knew you were here." She started spreading cheese on the bread.

"Thank you, Missus Rynax," Julien replied, a childlike smile of contentment on his face.

"And you, Helene?" Raych asked, her eyebrow up. "Do you want anything I have?"

"If there's something I want, 'Chelle," Helene said, leaning over the table, "then I'll take it."

"Can we move forward, please?" Asti asked. "We need to get out there soon."

"By all means, Asti," Raych said. "You're not hungry, then?"

"That's not the . . . a bit of lamb, please, thank you . . . we do need to go over things one last time."

"Go ahead, Asti," Mila said, folding a hunk of lamb into her bread before cramming it into her mouth.

"Fine. Our primary spot to strike is Ginny and Hicks. If they aren't taking Ginny, then our secondary is Stokes and Hicks. Tertiary—"

"Tersha-what?" Julien asked.

"It means third," Helene whispered.

"Why didn't he say third?"

"*Third* is Keeley. If none of those are viable, we need to make this a chase. But that shouldn't be an issue. I'll start at the customhouse gate and track the carriage from a block away. Verci and Mila will be at the strike spot."

"You're with her," Raych said.

"That's the plan," Verci said.

"While she's dressed like that?"

"That's part of the plan. The whole idea is to distract the carriage driver and escorts with what they think is a scuttle between a doxy and a jake."

"And you're the jake?" Raych laughed.

"It was either me or Asti," Verci said.

Raych looked back at Mila, then raised an eyebrow at Asti. "Probably for the best, for her sake."

Asti let that go. Stay focused. "Helene took a room on the top floor of a doxy den half a block away. She'll have line of sight on me, the primary and secondary, as well as the customhouse. We change hit spots, she'll send a message by arrow."

"She's gonna shoot at us?" Mila asked.

"I won't hit you," Helene said. "Probably."

"Julien and Kennith are over at Yenks and Wheeler, waiting for the signal from Verci. When the carriage comes down, Verci and Mila do their bit to stop the carriage. Helene takes out the driver. Verci and I take out any other escorts. Verci fires the signal."

"Green flash in the sky, like lightning," Julien said. He had been repeating it all afternoon, like a prayer.

"Then I pound the escape carriage to the spot," Kennith said.

"Verci and Julien crack the carriage, Julien unloads the statue onto our carriage, Kennith bolts."

"And we all scatter to the winds," Verci said. "Meet here by one bell after midnight."

"When will you be home?" Raych asked.

"We'll have to do the drop and then split the cash. Probably four bells. Maybe five."

"All right," she said. "I'll have some tea on for you."

"Lovely," Asti snapped. "Is everyone done eating? We need to get to work."

The carriage emerged from the customhouse gate. Asti had to admit Kennith wasn't kidding about the thing. The carriage was a steel-skinned beast, trundling its way down Wheeler, pulled along by eight straining draft horses. The animals were probably the largest horses Asti had ever seen, but even they could barely manage to get the carriage up to more than a creep. They might as well have driven it with oxen.

Asti crept back in the alley. The speed of the carriage was perfect. If it didn't take the route they anticipated, they could easily move to a secondary position, stay ahead of it. At that pace, one could walk alongside the thing, just like the four armed men were doing.

Asti scowled. Four outside escorts. He hadn't anticipated that. He had hoped that they would have preferred discretion to security. He hated guessing wrong. At least they weren't in uniforms. Private mercenaries, in cheap vests and coats. Nobody that the sticks or marshals would get too ruffled over.

He stayed hidden in the shadow of the alley, waiting for the carriage to pass. At its pace, he was able to get a good look at the small window on the side as it went by. It was open, and there was definitely one man inside besides the driver.

Six men total to take out and take out quickly.

It could be done, but he hated having to change plans on the fly.

As soon as the carriage turned onto Ginny, Asti ran back down the alley to Stokes Street. The carriage was moving right on track, right to the position. Extra guards aside, it couldn't be going more perfectly. Asti tore his way around the corner. He would get into position, and as soon as the carriage came into sight, Verci and Mila would stage their fight, which should distract all the escorts, and Helene would take her shot. He and Verci could easily take out the four outside escorts with knives and darts. Everything would work.

He was so focused on seeing it play out in his head, he took little heed of his surroundings as he ran to the next alley. He whipped around the corner and barreled flat into a well-dressed gentleman. Both of them went down, falling over each other onto the cobblestones. Asti scrambled to regain his footing, about to mumble an empty apology, when two sets of large hands grabbed him and lifted him off the ground.

"How dare you?" the gentleman said from his position on the ground.

The two large men, clearly bodyguards with the gentleman, slammed Asti against the wall, pressing him on the cold brick.

"I'm very sorry," Asti said quickly. "It was a complete accident."

One of the bodyguards released Asti, going to help his master to his feet. The other bodyguard did not budge, holding Asti hard against the wall with just one meaty arm.

"Accident caused by trash such as you stampeding down the street," the gentleman said. His accent was as westtown as Asti's. Hardly matching his clothes. His back to Asti, he waved off his bodyguard's further assistance, dusting off his coat.

"Very true," Asti said, sounding as contrite as he could manage. "Now if you would be so kind as to let me—"

"Someone should teach you to respect your betters," the man said, turning around, and Asti finally saw his face. "Don't you have any idea who I am?"

Asti grinned, despite the sudden burning rage that ignited in his gut. "Oh, yes, sir. I know exactly who you are."

It was Fire Brigade Chief Holm Yenner.

"Then you should know well enough to—" was all Yenner managed to say before Asti's foot connected with his nose. Blood poured out of Yenner's face, but Asti didn't have any chance to enjoy the moment. The bodyguard, still holding him with one hand, punched him across the face. The man's fist was almost as big as Asti's face, and Asti had no leverage to roll with the punch. His ears rang.

Despite his blurred vision and fogged mind, Asti's hands went into his coat and came out with two knives. Before a second punch could come, he stabbed both blades deep into the arm holding him. The bodyguard screamed and dropped Asti.

Asti landed on his feet, still dazed from the blow. Instinctively he jumped forward and rolled away, anticipating the other bodyguard to come at him. It was a good plan, but one of the two men grabbed his foot and yanked him up by it.

"Stupid!" one of the bodyguards said. He dangled Asti by one ankle.

"True," Asti said. He drew out two more knives. Despite being upside down, he still could tell where his enemies were. He stabbed wildly at the man holding him. The knives found their mark, sinking into the man's belly. He let go, and Asti fell headfirst onto the street.

Then everything went red.

Chapter 12

"**D**O YOU SEE ASTI anywhere?" Verci whispered. The carriage approached, extra guards walking with it. The job was half-skunked already, then. No, it had to be fine. Asti would have given them a high sign if he thought they needed to pull out. Verci couldn't see his brother anywhere, though.

"No," Mila whispered. She glanced over her shoulder, just the barest turn of her head. Verci was impressed, she made it look like a demure act, a natural teasing ploy that a street doxy would do to rope in her client. Anyone seeing the two of them as they stood outside the pub would have presumed they were exactly what they were playing at. She looked back at him, running her hand up his arm. "He wouldn't just skip, right?"

"Never," Verci said. "Blazes, Asti drives forward even when he should skip. Always drive forward, he says. He's probably just staying out of sight until he strikes."

"So the four guards?"

"Asti and I can take them." He leaned in and whispered, making a show for anyone who might be watching. "But just in case, you can defend yourself, yes?"

"Look at the belt of my skirt," she whispered back. She

stepped away so he could admire her, playing her part just like a real doxy would.

"You hiding a knife in there or something?"

"No, it's a rope," she said, giving a fake playful giggle as she came closer. "I can have that off in a couple seconds."

"A rope?" he asked.

"I'm better with a rope than anything else," she said, running a finger down his chest.

"If you say so," he said. The carriage came closer to their spot on the corner. "They're just about in position. Ready?"

"Make it look good," she said.

"Just roll with it," he said. He pushed her away and swung his fist at her cheek. He only glanced her, he knew, but she threw herself to the ground like she had been clobbered. "That's what you get!" he shouted. Helene would hear that and take her shot. He hoped Asti was in position to strike.

"Oh, dear god and blessed saints," Mila cried. "He's going to kill me!" She scurried backward farther into the street, forcing the carriage to stop.

"Oy!" one of the walking escort shouted. "Get your whore out of the road!"

"Who are you calling a whore?" she cried at him.

"You're the whore, you stinking—" was all he got out before she jumped at him. Predictably, the other three guards starting laughing.

The small window to the back of the carriage was open. Verci dipped his hand into his vest and grabbed two darts. He threw just as he heard the sharp twang of Helene's crossbow. His darts hit true, taking out the man in the back. From what he could hear, Helene's shot was just as accurate.

"What the—?" one of the other guards said, looking around. Verci drew out two more darts. Mila had her rope belt off and wrapped it around the neck of her guard. Verci was impressed again. He threw his darts at the other guard on his side. The two on the other side, Asti would make short work of. Time was critical right now. Seeing Mila had her guard on his knees, clawing futilely at the rope choking

him, Verci took out the pouch Cort had sold him and tossed
it into one of the street lamps. It quickly caught fire and
burst, sending green sparks high in the air. Julien and Kennith would be racing up in a moment, and now it was just a
matter of getting the carriage open. The two little windows
were still open, so they must have successfully taken out
everyone inside. He walked over to the carriage, quite
pleased at how smoothly everything went.

He had only taken two steps when the other two guards
charged at him, rapiers drawn.

"Whoa!" Verci yelled, jumping and rolling out of the
way. He regained his footing a few paces away from the
men, coming up with a full spread of darts in both hands. He
threw fast, but both men were ready for him, ducking out of
the way. Surprise gone, Verci was losing any advantage he
had in the fight.

"You ain't pinching us, rat," one of the guards said. Both
of them were coming in at him with their swords, and Verci's only option was to keep dodging. Where the blazes was
Asti?

One sword came in close, Verci twisting his body so it
just missed skewering him. The guard thrust too hard,
clearly thinking he was getting a killing blow. He passed
Verci, showing his unprotected side. Verci grabbed the
sword arm with one hand and punched the guard in the
kidneys with the other. The other guard came in, and Verci
pushed the two into each other.

The escape carriage came around the corner. Verci
needed to end this, regardless of what had happened to
Asti. He drew a dagger and plunged it at the guard who still
had his back to him. The man twisted away, so he was only
stabbed in the shoulder. He screamed and pulled away, taking the knife with him.

Verci swore under his breath. He didn't need screams
just now. But he did need the knife.

Verci wasn't able to get away before the other guard was
on top of him. Verci fell back, desperately trying to keep
the sword from penetrating his body. He grabbed the
guard's wrist, attempting to force the blade away, but the
man was stronger than he was. Verci kept stepping back,

keeping the guard and the sword away, until his back was against the wall of the pub. He got his other hand on the guard's neck, but couldn't do anything more than hold the man back.

"Mila," he croaked out. He didn't dare glance over to see what Mila was doing. If she hadn't already saved him, she had good reason.

His arms started to give. The sword inched closer to his gut.

An arrow struck through the guard's throat. He dropped down in front of Verci. Verci took a deep breath. That was far closer than he had wanted.

Kennith and Julien were at the carriage, Kennith showing Julien exactly where the seam of the door was. Julien took his prybar and shoved it in as hard as he could. Mila had finished off the last guard.

Verci pushed the dead guard with his foot and joined the others. He looked over to Helene's sniping location and gave a small wave. "That could have gone better."

"Where is Asti?" Mila asked.

"That's a very good question," Verci asked. "You got it?"

"Not yet." Julien struggled, pulling with all his might as the veins in his massive arms bulged.

Verci grunted. He clambered up to the front of the carriage, peering into the darkened window. He couldn't see anything in the cabin. With one hand, he dug out the small vial Cort had sold to him. He gave it a squeeze and a shake and tossed it in the window. It started giving off a sickly glow.

"Clever, Cort," Verci muttered. He could see the latch now, holding despite Julien's efforts. Holding, but barely. Verci pulled out a short stick from another pouch. He gave one end a twist and pulled it out, telescoping it out to a five-foot-long pole. He slid the pole through the window hole, carefully aiming it toward the latch. He just needed to knock it a bit.

"You got it?" Julien asked. He grunted with the strain.

"Almost," Verci said. The pole almost touched the latch, though it was a challenge keeping it straight through such a tiny hole. Verci jabbed, and missed.

"Come on!" Mila said. "I thought I heard bells."

"Just what I need," Verci muttered. "Julien!"

"Not opening!"

Verci glanced over—Julien was really pulling. Behind him, Kennith had a strange smile on his face. The man was so blasted happy that they couldn't crack his carriage.

"Kennith!" Verci snapped.

Kennith seemed to realize what he was doing and sobered his expression. "Sorry."

"All right, Julien, give it a little more," he said. Julien strained. Verci lined up the pole again and gave a sharp jab. He tapped the latch. A sudden loud crack filled the air and the door popped open.

"Got it," Julien said with a sheepish grin.

"Get that statue and load it up." Verci pulled out his pole and collapsed it back down. Jumping off the carriage, he looked around the street nervously. Two blocks away he could see figures running toward them. "Hurry."

Julien grabbed the large green statue. It really was a bizarre thing, a life-size jade figure of a man with four arms and a screaming face.

"That's Acserian?" Mila asked.

"That's what they say," Verci said. Julien dropped it in Kennith's small carriage. Kennith jumped into his driver's seat.

"See you there," Kennith said. He cracked his reins and was off.

"Go," Verci told Julien. The big guy nodded and ran in a different direction.

"What happened to Asti?" Mila asked again.

"Go see if you can find out," Verci said. He picked up one of the swords from the dead men. Mila nodded and ran down one alley.

The two running men were coming closer. Dressed in suits like these guards, so not constabs or marshals. Good. Verci wasn't going to let either of them follow the rest. He looked back to Helene's nest, hoping she was still there. Hoping she had his back. He gave her a wave and held up two fingers, pointing to the approaching men. With everyone else out of sight, all he had to do was discourage them and get away.

Easy as blackberry pie.

Asti's head was split open, his brains pouring out of his skull. At least, that was how he felt. The pain was all he was aware of, unsure of anything else. He wasn't thinking about where he was, what he had been doing, what he should be doing, or how long he had been sitting tied up with a splitting headache.

He was tied up. That realization dawned on him slowly. He struggled to remember how that might have happened. He struggled with the ropes that bound him. Finally he opened his eyes.

Long dark hair and wide eyes greeted him. "Mister Rynax?"

"Mila?" He looked around. A dark alley. Three other figures lying on the ground. Blood.

"Are you . . ." Mila started hesitantly. "Are you . . . you?"

"The blazes you mean, Mila?" he asked. "My head is screaming."

She looked at him skeptically. "You were the one screaming a few minutes ago."

He blinked at her, trying to focus his blurred vision. "Screaming what?"

"Just screaming. Well, more like . . . barking. And then you came at me."

"I . . . I don't know anything about that."

"Well, I do." Mila held up her arm, which was bleeding from a deep gash.

Asti took a deep breath, closing his eyes. The pain was pounding at him, but he pushed it back, forced himself not to feel. "Start at the beginning. What happened?"

"You weren't in place for the job," she said.

"The job!" he gasped. "Is it skunked?"

"No," she said. "At least, I don't think so. Verci didn't have an easy time of it, but last I saw, he had gotten the carriage open and the statue out. He sent me to find you."

"And you found me, how?" Asti was terrified of the answer.

"Back here in this alley. You were cutting up one of those men. And you were ..." She trailed off, staring at the men lying on the ground.

"What?"

"Growling. Like a dog or something."

Asti closed his eyes, trying to hold back tears. It was happening again. It was getting worse.

"And then I came after you."

"I called to you, and you just ... launched at me, knives in both hands. I barely got out of the way. You were like an animal, so I roped you up."

Asti opened his eyes again, looking at her. He couldn't believe what she just said. "You ... you roped me up, when I was like that?"

"I wasn't going to let you kill me, Mister Rynax," she said, simple and matter-of-fact.

"That's ..." He was astounded. "That's amazing, Mila."

She stepped back, looking at him with harsh eyes. "Thanks."

"Now we have to get out of here. Untie me."

"How do I know you aren't going to try to kill me again?"

"Because I'm not ... not like I was before. Obviously."

"How were you before?" She leaned in close to him. Her eyes unsure. Untrusting. Smart on her part, but not very helpful right now.

"Like you said. Crazed. Animalistic."

She stepped back. "Why?"

"That doesn't matter," Asti said. He twisted his hands around, seeing what leverage he had. If she wasn't going to untie him, he'd have to get loose himself.

"Like blazes it doesn't matter," she said.

"It won't happen again, Mila. But we've got to get out of here before the constabs show up and find us with three dead bodies."

"Two," Mila said. "The swell there is just out cold."

"He's still alive?" Asti's heart leaped, racing with excitement. "Mila, I'm serious as the grave. Untie me, tie up him, and we have to take him and get out of here."

"Take the swell?" She went over and looked at Yenner. "We gonna hold him for ransom or something?"

"Information," Asti said.

"What?" Mila looked like she was about to laugh at him. "What does this tosser know?"

Asti could feel his head swimming again, anger boiling up. He beat it back down, refusing to let it take him over. Not again. "That man knows who had the alley burned."

Mila's face changed. "Had it burned? On purpose?"

"And they paid him off to let it happen."

Mila came back over to Asti, grabbing the rope and pulling him to his feet. "You knew? You kept it secret?" Her face was flush, tears in her eyes. "Why did you—"

"Because I didn't know enough yet. I knew that Yenner there knew something, but he was gone. And then . . . ."

"Then here he was," Mila said coldly. She undid the knots binding Asti. "Here's the deal. Whatever more you find out, I want to know. Whatever else you do, I'm in on it."

"Deal," Asti said.

"One more thing, Asti," she said. "You're going to tell me just what the blazes happened to you back there."

The ropes fell off Asti. His head was still swimming and pulsing with pain. "It's a long story."

"We've got time," she said. She picked up her rope and tied up Yenner's hands. "You've still got to figure out where to take this guy."

Asti grinned. "I know exactly the place."

Chapter 13

ASTI THANKED WHATEVER SAINTS were looking out for him that the streets were relatively deserted and that Mila was able to find an abandoned wheelcart and tarp to steal. No one was looking too hard at them. Asti figured no one wanted to think about what a bleeding man and a street doxy were doing in the middle of the night with a full wheelcart. Whatever it was, it was no good, and no one but a constab would want to stick their nose into it.

No constabs passed them as they made their way back into Seleth. Asti could hear some whistle calls in the distance—probably swarming around the wreck of the carriage job. But whatever fire that might bring down hadn't found its way to this part of the neighborhood.

"Talk," Mila said.

"Talk, right," Asti said. "You know I was in the service. Intelligence."

"A spy."

"A spy, exactly. How much you know about a spy's life, Mila?"

"Not much," she said.

"Not much. Who do you think we do most of our spying against?"

"Saints, I don't know." She shrugged. "Whoever we had that war with?"

"Exactly. The Poasians."

"So you would spy on the Poasiers, all right. What does that have to do—"

"Poasians."

"I don't care."

"You want me to tell you?" he snapped. He glanced down the street. Constab on horseback and a Yellowshield wagon were coming around the corner. Probably on their way to the carriage, but not in any big hurry. From what Mila said, Verci wouldn't have left any of the guard alive to serve as witnesses. Probably all the sticks were doing now was cleaning up the mess.

He turned the wheelcart down a shadowy alley that would keep him and Mila out of sight. "There's a lot of things in this world you've never had touch you, girl."

"I've seen a lot of damage, Mister Rynax." Proud and hard. He would have said the same thing when he was her age.

"I'm sure you have. That's only a sliver of what is out there. Magic, for one."

"Never met a real mage," she said. "Only teasing fakers like Hexie Matlin."

"Don't sell Old Hexie short. But magic's not the only thing out there. There's also psionics."

"Sigh-what?"

"Psionics, that's what the bosses at Intelligence called it. People who can do things with their minds." He tapped on his bleeding head. "Crazy stuff, I'll tell you. Some of them can pull the thoughts right out of your head."

"That's impossible." She started to crack a smile, but then it stopped, her face blanching. "Great saints. You're serious about this?"

"Completely."

"Whatever you're thinking?" Her eyes grew wide. "How do you fight that?"

"There's ways," Asti said. "Ways to shut off part of your mind, protect yourself, bury yourself. Go where they can't touch you."

"Can you teach me?" she blurted out.

Asti stopped walking and stared at her. "Teach you? To . . ."

"Keep them out of my head!" She stalked off to the end of the alley, checking the street.

"Clear?" Asti asked.

"Clear enough," she said as she returned. She still looked spooked. Asti couldn't blame her. The first time he . . . that wasn't something he'd ever forget. "Where are we going?"

"Back to Holver," Asti said. "We'll secure him, then you'll go get the rest of the crew."

"Leave you alone with him? No chance."

"You want to stay while I get them?"

"I—let's just get there."

Asti pushed the wheelcart over to her. No one walked about in sight. They trundled out onto Rabbit Road.

Mila waited half a block before speaking up. "So you trained how to block your thoughts from these psionits?"

"Psionics. Yes. Most ways are only good to keep them out of your head for a few minutes, which might be all you need. Others are needed for a prolonged invasion."

He pushed on silently for a bit.

"Is that what happened to you?"

"About a year ago. It was on Haptur, one of the Napolic Islands that the Poasians control. My partner and I were sent to investigate a Poasian compound."

"What for?"

"Suspicions about them working on a mystical or magical weapon of some sort. It doesn't matter."

"Why doesn't it?"

"Because . . . we didn't find anything."

"Doesn't mean there wasn't anything. Seems like it would matter," Mila said testily.

"Not to me. Not anymore." Mila glared at him while he ground his teeth, pushing the wheelcart toward Holver.

"Fine," Mila finally burst out. "It doesn't matter. None of it."

"I was captured," Asti said, the words almost impossible to push out his lips. "My partner, she . . ." Silence hung, he couldn't say the rest.

"She was killed?" Mila offered.

"Betrayed me."

"Oh." Mila shuffled along the road, her eyes to the ground. Her next word was meek, tentative. "Why?"

"Money. Free passage. Kicks. Don't know."

"Were you and she . . . did you . . ." she stammered, looking awkwardly at the ground.

"Were we lovers?" He had been telling her everything already. No need to hold back here. "Yeah. Terrible idea."

"Oh."

"You want some advice, Mila? Avoid entanglements like that on any job. It only causes trouble."

She looked at him funny. "So you . . . you really didn't bring me in on this because you . . ."

"Saints, girl. No." Hadn't he been plain about this already?

Her whole face changed. Relaxed and relieved. "You really thought I could do the job."

"Can we keep moving?" He pushed the cart down the road.

"So," Mila said, strangely bright now. "You were captured, she betrayed you. What happened?"

"I ended up in a place called Levtha Prison. Possibly the most horrid place you can imagine. Napolic heat combined with Poasian ingenuity in the arts of torture. I was beaten, baked, torn, and cut."

"Sounds horrible." Her brightness had melted off.

"That was nothing," Asti said.

Her face was worried, fearful. "Doesn't sound like nothing."

"You can learn to ignore what they do to your body. That wasn't what broke me."

"They broke you?"

"They broke me all right." Asti felt his breath quickening, his heart racing. He had never said any of this out loud before. Not to Druth Intelligence, not to Verci. "They had several telepaths battering at me. I don't even know how many. Pounding attack after attack on my defenses. They laid siege to my mind like my brain was Khol Taia."

"Khol what?"

"Do you know nothing about history?" Asti snapped.

"I can barely read, Mister Rynax."

"Hmm," he grunted. "We need to do something about that."

"What, put me in school?"

"Maybe," he said. "All right, most of the war was fought throughout the Napolic Islands. Our ships outclassed the Poasians, but once they took an island, they could dig in like a tick. But we had one big victory in Khol Taia, a coastal city on the Poasian mainland. In 1158 hundreds of Druth ships crossed the ocean in a massive, coordinated attack."

They reached the corner of Rabbit and Holver Alley. The charred skeleton of Rynax Gadgeterium still stood there, a near-useless husk of ash and wood. Asti went to the remains of the door. He tried the handle and snorted with laughter. It was locked.

She came up next to him. "You're avoiding telling me the rest," she said, her eyebrow raised. "About what happened to you, not some city."

No use putting it off. "For seventeen days they pounded on me, dug into me. They broke me." He felt hot tears pooling at the corners of his eyes. His voice choked as he continued. "I put up wall upon wall inside my mind, burying the rest of me, the real core of myself, so far down they could never get to it. So far down . . ."

"So far down you lost yourself?" she asked. Her own eyes found his, filled with sorrow and sympathy.

"Rational thought, memory, identity . . . I buried it under the most savage, primitive, angry part of my brain. Rage was the only weapon I had left. The telepaths hit into that wave of pure, thoughtless fury, and my whole world became red."

"So . . . how did you escape?"

"I have no idea."

"What?"

"I was in the cell, being torn up by the telepaths, and . . . red. The next thing I knew, I was on a small boat in the Napolic Sea, covered in blood. Too much blood to be mine. Slowly I regained my wits and navigated my way back to Druth territory. But I could still feel it."

"Feel what?"

Asti couldn't get the words out of his throat.

"Asti." Mila put a hand on his shoulder. "Feel what?"

"That red fury, that rage that I put up to protect myself. Do you understand what I'm telling you, Mila? Those bastards broke my mind, and I'm just holding it together. The rage, the beast they set free ... it's pushing inside me, all the time. Like a dog straining at a chain. I'm always holding on to that chain, keeping it from getting loose."

"Blessed saints," Mila said. "Is that ... that what happened back there? You let go of the chain?"

"Back there, it was more like they knocked it out of my hand," Asti said. He put on his best good-humored face. He was certain Mila wasn't buying it. Turning away from her, he reached through the broken window and opened the door from the inside. "Let's get him inside, and then you can tie him up real good."

"Mister Ry—Asti ... how can you ..." Mila stared at him, her face full of confusion.

"You know damned well how, girl," he told her. "You hold it together, you survive for those around you. Because you have to." He picked up the handles of the cart and pushed it inside.

Yenner was profoundly unconscious. Asti took a small comfort in that. He wanted to get Yenner bound and secure, and it was much easier if he didn't have to fight him anymore. Once he was in place, then Asti would wake him. He wanted to hear what the man had to say.

Mila really was a genius with a rope, tying a convoluted series of knots that Asti was certain Yenner could never escape from. Asti didn't think even he could escape from it without using a knife, and even then he wasn't sure if Yenner could maneuver his hands in a way to use them. Asti had never seen anyone so thoroughly tied up.

"There," Mila said, stepping back from her work. Yenner, astoundingly, was still out cold, despite hanging from his arms. "You sure you want me to go get the others?"

"They deserve to hear this as well," Asti said.

"Not sure if you should be alone with him."

"Then go to the chemist across the street, tell Cort to come join me."

"Really? Him?"

"Why not? Trust me, he wants to know what old Yenner here has to say."

"Always struck me as a bit narrow, you know?"

"He is." Asti nodded. "But he's our narrow, you know. Part of the alley."

"If you say so." She gave another look at Yenner. "Don't kill him yet."

"Wouldn't dream of it."

❋

"Where the blazes did he go?" Verci heard Helene shouting as he walked up the walkway to the inn's stable. Quiet and subtle, Helene was not. Verci remembered why no one else would work with her; she was incapable of bottling her temper. He chuckled to himself as he limped his way up to the door. He had heard of a few jobs that had almost gotten skunked because she had blown up over something.

"We all clear?" he asked as he walked in. Helene, Julien, Kennith, and the statue were the only ones present.

"Verci!" Helene said. "You made it!" The rage on her face melted away when she saw him.

"Thanks to your cover," he said.

"How bad is it?" Kennith asked, pointing to a wet red stain on Verci's tunic.

"Not sure yet," Verci said. He sat down on a crate and started peeling off clothes. "Not too bad, since I made it here."

Whatever calm his entrance had given Helene left her just as quickly. "And what happened to Asti? Where was he?"

"Don't know," Verci said, wincing as he pulled the shirt off over his head. "Didn't see him, haven't heard."

"He skunked us," she said.

"Job's done, sitting right there," Verci said. "It ain't skunked if you have the goods and are away and clear."

"Not clear until it's gone," Kennith said.

"Right," Verci said. He twisted to look at the wound on his right side. Only oozing blood at this point. It wasn't very deep, but it stretched from shoulder to hip. Verci muttered a few curses. If the cut had gone any deeper, his guts would have poured out onto the street.

"You all right?" Julien asked.

"I'll make it," Verci said.

"You look like you need the Yellowshields," Helene said.

"Not a chance," Verci said. "Yellowshields would only bring constab with them. We're far enough away there's no need to draw any attention this way."

"It's your back," Helene said.

Verci shook it off. "When do we hand over the goods?" Asti was the one who always remembered these details.

"Three bells after midnight," Kennith said.

"What about Mila?" Julien asked.

"She went looking for Asti," Verci said. "I was a bit busy covering our retreat." He pulled out a needle and thread from one of his pouches. "Who wants the honors? Helene?"

"I don't sew," she scoffed.

"Kennith?"

"Sure, mate," Kennith said. He took the needle and held it in the flame of one of the candles. "You want a swig of something first?"

"Nah," Verci said. "Better to stay sharp."

"Your choice." Kennith stood behind Verci and went to work stitching up the wound. Verci gritted his teeth. It hurt like blazes, but he wasn't going to let anything out.

"So now what?" Helene asked.

"We wait," Verci said. "Hope Asti and Mila show up. Hope the drop at three bells goes without a hitch. Hope we aren't stiffed. Hope we live to see the sunrise."

"Lotta hope," Julien said with a sad smile.

"Hope and prayer are our stock and trade," Verci said, quoting something his father had said many, many times. He winced as Kennith did another stitch. "This is why I hate the hit-and-grab runs. Give me a nice, quiet sneak job any day."

No one responded. Kennith continued sewing the wound. Helene paced back and forth, her jaw clenching tighter and tighter. Julien sat on the floor, his large hands folded in his lap. He was the one who eventually broke the silence.

"Hope Asti is all right. He's a good guy."

"He is, Julien," Verci said. "He'll be fine, I'm sure."

"He's at the Gadgeterium."

Verci's hand instinctively went to a knife before he saw it was Mila at the door.

"He's where?" Helene asked, her voice crackling with anger.

"He's at our shop," Verci said.

"The one that burned down?" Kennith asked.

"That's the one," Mila said. "He wants you all to come."

Helene snorted and walked away. "Why should we do what he wants, after he skiffed on us?"

"He didn't skiff, he ran into some trouble."

"What sort of trouble?" Verci asked.

"Swell with two guards gave him some business," Mila said. "Turns out, the swell is one Holm Yenner."

The surprise of that, combined with Kennith putting in another stitch, was more than Verci could contain. "What?" he shouted.

"Who the blazes is Yenner?" Helene asked.

"A man who recently came into some money," Verci said. "He was a Fire Brigade chief before that. The chief for the Brigade that didn't come to Holver Alley."

Helene stopped pacing.

"Did Asti kill him?"

"Not yet," Mila said. "We tied him up, took him to the Gadgeterium. Asti is there with him now."

"Alone?" Verci asked.

"Almer Cort joined him," Mila said, giving Verci a wicked grin.

"Oh, blessed saints," Verci muttered. He didn't think he even wanted to know the kind of damage Asti could do to someone with Cort's help. For all of Cort's mousy exterior, the man seemed to have a strangely vicious streak. "So he wants all of us, then."

"You crazy, Rynax?" Kennith asked. "We sweat and bleed for this ugly thing, and we're all going to go for a little stroll and leave it?"

"I'll point out only I bled, Ken," Verci said.

"That doesn't mean it's not stupid to leave it alone!"

Verci scratched at his chin. "Fair enough. Odds are against anything happening. But with this many crowns on the line, I don't like playing the odds. You good keeping watch, Julien?"

"The alarm bells set?" Julien asked. "Mila didn't ring them."

"I know where the cords are, Julien," Mila said, rolling her eyes slightly.

"I'll leave you a crossbow, all right, Jules?" Helene said. "I'll just be gone a little while."

"You really have to go, Helene?" Julien's big eyes went wide and soft.

"Yeah, Jules. I got to hear this, you know? For both of us." Helene cocked up a crossbow and put it on the ground next to Julien. She knelt in front of him, touching the side of his face. "You remember what I told you?"

"Center of the body, clean shot," he said.

"That's right." She smiled briefly, but her ice-hard face returned once she stood up and turned around. "What are we waiting for?"

"Kennith," Verci said.

"I'm not leaving this place or this thing alone, thank you," Kennith said.

"Jules is staying," Helene said.

"And so am I."

"Fine, fine," Verci said. "Two people keeping watch is smarter. You got a spare shirt you can lend me, Kennith?"

"Yeah." Kennith went in the back and came out a moment later with a shirt. Verci put it on and left with Helene and Mila.

The night was cool, and they walked at a brisk pace. Verci realized he had left his bandolier at the stable, and going unarmed made him feel exposed and naked. As they walked, his fingers absently found their way down to his belt, fingering the pouches. He touched each one, going over in his head what it contained, considering how it might help him should trouble occur. The telescoping stick would be all right to fight with, though he was never very good with a staff.

When they reached Holver Alley, Verci was struck by how eerie and quiet it was. Dark as well. Only a handful of lamps were burning on the side of the alley the fire hadn't touched. Verci even noticed a few doors boarded over, signs taken down. Cort's shop was one of the few that still held both sign and burning lamp.

The door of the Gadgeterium, or what was left of it, hung open, the dark husk of the shop inside beckoning them. Gingerly Verci led the other two inside. Mila walked right behind him, with a confidence he found a bit unbecoming in her. Helene took the rear, stalking like a wolf. A coil wound like she was would spring or break soon.

"Asti?" Verci called out.

"Back room," Asti's voice came back. The door, such as it was, was shut. Verci was actually amazed by how much of the building's structure was intact. Not usable, he thought in quick assessment, as the whole thing was surely unstable. If one wanted to build here, the whole thing would have to be razed and cleared away.

A soft light spilled out as Verci opened the door. At Asti's hissed urging, the three of them quickly passed in and shut the door behind them.

A few lamps were on the floor, and one hung up on a hook on the uneasy-looking ashen ceiling. Asti stood at the end of what would have been Verci's workbench, his attention focused on the unconscious man tied up on it. Asti was covered in blood, even his face, but he gave no sign that he noticed or cared. Almer Cort was crouched in the corner of the room, bottles clinking as he dug through a leather bag at his feet.

"He keeps passing out," Asti said. He looked at the three of them for the first time. "Where's Ken and Julien?"

"Stayed with the statue at the stable," Verci said.

"You got it safe, then?" Asti said, nodding.

"No thanks to you," Helene snapped.

"True, true," Asti said, holding an open hand to her. "Every right to be angry, Hel. Sloppy mistake on my part, but if it went well, all the better. We get him to spill some words, though, it should make up for it in spades." Asti's demeanor was energized, manic. He grinned widely at them, which unsettled Verci significantly. "Good show on you all, really."

"Thanks," Helene said. "What's with this bloke?"

Asti grinned and bent over the man, who Verci presumed was Yenner. "This man was paid very generously to let the alley here burn. I don't know about you, but I'm very curious to hear what he might have to say."

"As am I," Helene snarled.

Asti snickered as he pried his fingers into Yenner's mouth, another sign of strangely good humor that disturbed Verci. Asti leaned into Yenner's face, counting teeth in the man's mouth. Verci glanced around the floor and saw a few teeth scattered on the floor, and quite a lot of fresh blood. "Problem is Mister Yenner has no tolerance for pain. I try and get him to talk, and he goes out like a blown candle." He punctuated the last words with a succession of slaps across Yenner's face.

"This should do it," Cort said, coming over with a vial. He shook the vial and pulled out the cork, which he waved under Yenner's nose.

"Really?" Asti asked.

"Wait," Cort said. The chemist mouthed a count of three, two, one, and as he finished Yenner's eyes shot open, a scream erupting from his mouth. Yenner looked around desperately.

"Who's there?" he stammered out.

"Impressive, Cort," Asti said. He moved behind Yenner, crouching so he could whisper into the man's ear. "Some more friends, Yenner. Some more people you helped ruin."

"I didn't ruin anybody," Yenner sobbed.

"You ruined people. You let people die," Asti whispered. "You had a job, a duty to save them, but you passed that up for a well-lined purse."

Yenner's eyes searched over Verci and the rest. "Please, please . . ." he whimpered at them. "I have money, it's true . . . please . . . whatever you want, just save me . . ."

Asti clapped an open hand across Yenner's ear. "We don't want your blood-covered crowns. We want one thing, one little thing."

"No, there's no . . ." Yenner moaned.

"Wrong," Asti snapped at him. Like lightning, Asti reached into Yenner's mouth, bracing it open with one hand. He picked up a charred and rusty tool from the workbench and shoved it into Yenner's gaping maw.

"Asti, those are my pliers!" Verci said. Verci didn't like anyone touching his tools, even ones he had written off as lost.

"Waii!! Waiii!" Yenner yelled. Asti had his jaw pried open.

"Wait?" Asti said. "You want me to wait?"

"Ye, ye," Yenner pleaded. Asti let go of his mouth.

"Do you have something to say now?" Asti asked softly. His voice dripped with honey. "Because you have twenty-five teeth left, and every time you pass out, we can wake you up again. And after teeth, there are fingers. Toes. Eyes. All I need to keep working on your body are your ears and tongue."

"I . . . I was paid . . . to ignore the fire . . ." Yenner panted.

"Who paid you?" Helene roared this out as she leaped up on the table. Asti and Cort scrambled back from her as she savagely grabbed Yenner's head, her knee in his gut. "Tell us!"

"I . . . don't know . . ."

"Liar!" she screamed.

"Helene, really, there is an art to—" Asti protested.

"Shut it, Rynax! We lost our grandmother thanks to this slime! He's going to tell us who paid him!"

Verci was shocked. Neither Helene nor Julien had mentioned that, and he had thought that Old Missus Kesser had passed years ago. "Helene, what do you . . ."

"Her death is on your hands, Yenner! Who?"

"I didn't . . . I didn't know . . ." he stammered out weakly.

Helene broke completely, growling as she dove at his face. She clamped her teeth down on Yenner's prominent nose. Blood gushed forth as she came back up, spitting out the large chunk of flesh she had taken.

"Ah! Oh god!" Yenner cried out. "It was Tyne! Mendel Tyne!"

Helene crumpled as he said this, as if his confession had sapped everything out of her. She would have fallen off the table had Verci not rushed over to catch her.

"Really unprofessional, totally lacking in form," Asti muttered. Yenner kept yelling out Tyne's name.

"It worked," Cort said with a shrug.

"Yes, but it's the principle of . . . can you put him out again?"

Cort casually stepped over to the screaming man and poured the contents of another vial into his mouth. In a moment, Yenner was silent again.

"Tyne," Helene said. Her voice was muted, dead of any emotion. She still clutched onto Verci, her hands digging into his arms.

"Tyne, indeed," Asti said, shaking his head.

"Who is Mendel Tyne?" Mila asked.

Verci answered her. "Tyne's a rich man, in the Keller Cove neighborhood. Powerful, fingers in the black market and other illegal business. Smuggling, drugs, whores, and slaves. So they say."

"And gambling," Asti added. "He runs the other stuff out of his semi-legitimate gambling house. He's tangled in with big money and big names, as much as any man can be on the southwest of Maradaine."

"He's huge," Helene whispered. "He's untouchable. He's the most powerful man in five neighborhoods." She let go of Verci and walked to the corner of the room.

"Sweet saints," Mila said. She looked around the room. "What are we going to do?"

Verci looked over to Asti, and as soon as he saw his brother's eyes, he knew what the answer was.

"We're going to get him, of course," Asti said. "If you're in, that is."

Helene turned around, her eyes wet, blood still on her lips. She wiped her mouth, and with a muted nod said, "In. Julien and me."

"Good," Asti said.

"I'm in," Mila said quietly.

"You need me, I'm in," Cort said.

"Brother?" Asti asked.

Verci hesitated. Raych would hate this. It wasn't necessary. It was dangerous. It was foolish. Reckless. Everything about Asti she didn't like, everything she wanted him not to be. It was stupid, is what it was.

"It's impossible, you know," he told Asti.

"Probably true," Asti said. "You in?"

"In, damn it," Verci said. "Someone has to keep an eye on you."

Chapter 14

ASTI WAS FEELING CHEERFUL. An angry, vengeance-driven kind of cheerful, but still cheerful. The anger he had been carrying over the fire now had a target, a face, and removing the vague, directionless rage was like a weight off his shoulders.

"Raych is going to be very cross with me, you know," Verci said. It was nearly two bells after midnight as the four of them—Verci and Asti, Mila, and Helene—walked through the dark streets back to the North Seleth Inn. They still had to make the drop.

"The cash from this gig will sweeten her mood."

"Hope so," Verci said. His eyes narrowed on Asti. "You have a plan, and not one for getting Tyne."

His brother knew him too well.

"True," Asti said. "Well, it ties to Tyne."

"What is it?"

"Someone is buying up the lots in the alley," Asti started. He hadn't quite put things into words, the thoughts still coalescing in his mind.

"We've got an offer on ours," Helene said. "Not much, but with our share here, we can get someplace to flop for real."

Asti nodded. "Cort said he's got an offer. Lots of people

on the other side of the alley have them, and most are taking them and splitting."

"What, exactly, is Cort going to do with Yenner?" Verci asked. "He said he'd take care of him, but not kill him."

"I think you're happier not knowing," Asti said. He wished he didn't know what Cort planned. Cort had laid it out, a rather elaborate plan involving acids. Asti had seen plenty of horrible things, done some horrible things, but the cold, calculated way that Cort had spelled out his intentions gave him a shiver.

"Probably so," Verci said. "He'll meet us at the stable after?"

"Sure that's a good idea?" Helene asked. "We're gonna have a lot of cash there."

"I'm not worried about Cort in terms of the money," Asti said. "If he wanted that, he'd sell his lot. If it was just about money, we should all sell our lots."

"What do you think we should do?" Verci asked.

"We don't take any offer. We keep the plot, pay our debt according to the plan."

"Why?" Verci asked. "Raych will really hate that."

"Because it will be a stick in their gears," Asti said. "Tyne clearly wants the land, all of it, so we don't let him get it all. One plot is all it takes."

"So we should take our offer?" Helene asked.

"Unless you can afford not to," Asti said. "But it'd draw a lot of direct fire on you. Verci and I can take it."

"We can?" Verci asked. "Asti, I—"

"I'll keep it on me alone if you want, brother."

"Fire doesn't work that way, brother."

"I'll make it work that way," Asti said.

"Pff," Verci scoffed. "Josie couldn't keep fire off the alley."

"You're right." Asti laughed. Then he stopped walking and stared at Verci. He was right.

"Oh, blasted saints, Asti. You think—"

"What, what?" Helene asked.

"Blessed and blasted saints," Asti muttered. "Why didn't we see it?"

"See what?" Helene demanded. She and Mila stared at Asti and Verci.

"We even joke about it," Verci said flatly.

"What?" Mila asked.

"Like I told you, Mila," Asti said. "There's not a pot in North Seleth that the Old Lady doesn't have a finger in." It was obvious. The Old Lady had to have known about the fire, and Tyne.

"What do we do?" Verci asked.

"You two," Asti said, pointing at Mila and Helene, "go back to the stable and make the drop, like everything is normal."

"Is everything not normal?" Mila asked.

"Yes. It is fine," Asti said. "Come on, brother."

"Where are you two going?" Helene called as they ran down the road.

"To the sewers!"

"Blazes, this isn't right," Helene muttered. Mila trailed behind her like a lost dog. The night—the whole gig—was one of the most skunked she had ever seen, and she had seen some gigs that really had gone into the creek. The last thing she needed was to have to take care of a little girl as well as handle a nine-hundred-crown drop.

"I'm not a little girl, Helene."

Blazes, she had said that out loud. "You're underfoot."

"Was I underfoot when I helped stop the carriage? Or took out two of the guards?"

Helene spun to face Mila. "Keep your blasted voice down."

"What?"

Helene grabbed Mila by the collar and pulled her into the closest alley. Mila grappled at her hand until Helene slammed her back into the brick wall. Helene lowered her voice to a raspy hiss. "Would you mind not bragging about your role in a major crime in the middle of the street?"

"I—" Mila stammered and looked at the ground.

"That's what I mean by 'little girl.'" Helene let her go. "Come on. We need to not skunk up the drop." She left the alley and doubled her pace to the North Seleth Inn.

Mila caught up to her. "You do know where we have to do the drop, right?"

Helene didn't. "Blazes. Rutting well don't."

"Who does?"

"The chomie does, that's who."

They entered the inn's grounds and walked up to the stable, Helene not bothering to miss the tripwires. Julien and the chomie needed to know she was coming. Mila fell behind, avoiding the lines. Silly girl.

Helene gave the knock on the door, and in a moment Julien opened it.

"What's going on?" He still held the crossbow nervously.

"We've got to do the drop," she told him. She took the crossbow from him and went over to Kennith, sitting in the carriage with the statue. "Where is it?"

"What?"

"The drop," Helene said. "We've got to go do it."

"Where's Verci and Asti?"

"Not here," Helene said. "But it's nearly three bells, and we've got to get going. So where are we going?"

"We—wait. What happened to Asti and Verci?"

"It's a long story."

"They told us to do the drop," Mila said, closing the door behind her.

"Oh, they did?" The chomie didn't look happy.

"Yes, they did," Helene said.

"So first Asti doesn't show up at the gig. The little bird vanishes, then shows up and says, 'Oh, come see where Asti is.' You and she take Verci away and come back without him, and say, 'Oh, we need to do the drop!'"

"We need to do this, and, unless I'm wrong, we don't have much time."

"How do I know once the drop is made I won't end up in the creek like the Rynaxes?"

"They aren't in the creek you stupid cho—" Instinct made her arm twitch, raising the crossbow slightly.

Kennith jumped off the carriage and stepped to the side, grabbing her wrist and pulling out a small, curved blade. "Don't even think of pointing that at me!"

"Put the knife down!" Julien shouted.

"Where are Asti and Verci?" Kennith asked.

"We don't—"

"Knife DOWN!"

Julien smashed a fist against a support beam, cracking it. Kennith startled, dropping the knife and letting go of Helene's wrist.

Helene put the crossbow down. "Jules, honey, knife is down, all right? Crossbow is down. Everyone is calm."

"Yeah, calm," Kennith said, voice quavering.

"Listen, Ken," Mila said. "Asti missed the gig because he got grabbed, grabbed by the guy who let the alley burn down. He got the better of them, though. So he and I tied up that guy, and brought Helene and Verci over to hear him talk. He told us who had the alley burned down."

"So?"

"So they've got a plan to do something about it, and they had to check something out."

"Check what out?"

"I don't know, Ken. I really don't. They went to do that, told us—all four of us—make the drop. They did that because they know we can, all right? They trust us to get it done."

Kennith's shoulders relaxed. He nodded his head slowly. "Yeah, let's get it done. Julien, let's get the thing on the carriage."

Helene let out a deep breath. Mila did good, she had to admit. She bent down to pick up the crossbow. When she stood up, Kennith was right in her face.

"Let me tell you, lady," he whispered. "You call me what you almost called me there, your cousin won't get a chance to help you. Get it?"

"Got," Helene said. She held up the crossbow, careful not to even come close to pointing it at him. "We're going to need this, right?"

"Wouldn't hurt," Kennith said. "This is a big drop. Night can still get skunked."

"So," Verci said as they stood on the bank of the creek, looking over the sewer entrance, "what are we looking at?"

"You tell me," Asti said. "This is a hot run, no prep, with only a glance through the path."

"Target?"

"Getting into the inner sanctum of the most paranoid woman we know, without her knowing until we're right on top of her."

"And what, exactly, are we going to do when we are on top of her?" Verci asked.

"Confront her," Asti said. He was surprised it was even a question.

"Well, I had to ask," Verci said. "I didn't want to start asking questions while you're being stabby."

"No stabbing," Asti said. "Not at first."

"Good."

"All right, back to it," Asti said, rubbing his hands together. "This is a hot run, no prep, target always expecting something—"

"It's only hot if she's in there and awake."

"There's a nine-hundred-crown drop happening tonight," Asti said. "She's not sleeping until she knows it's done."

"Right," Verci said. "Easy as blackberry pie."

"What does that mean?" Asti hated when Verci said that, which he'd gotten in the habit of since he married Raych.

"Not that easy," Verci said, hopping down into the creek bed. "You've got to get the right balance of flour and lard in the crust, for one." He scanned over the stone masonry surrounding the sewer entrance, a hole in the bank only about five feet high. "Eggs, honey, and cream need to be just right. You have to control the heat of your oven precisely. Too cool, you end up with a soggy mess. Too hot, you scorch the whole thing before it sets." He pointed along the upper edge of the entrance. "Spider wire."

Asti crawled down. "You know too much about pie."

"Baker's daughter for a wife," Verci said. He leaned up close to the wire, a cord so thin Asti could barely see it stretched out across the top of the threshold. "If I were to guess, this just rings an early warning in her office."

"Right," Asti said. "City workers and such would have a legit reason to come in here, she can't do anything more."

"But she's probably got earhorns and peepholes rigged, so when the bells go, she can look and listen."

"So mouse quiet in there, eh?"

Verci nodded. "Mouse quiet." Gently he tapped the side walls of the entrance. "Spider wire will only be at the top. She wouldn't want any at ground level, or the water flow and rats would set it off constantly. That works in our favor."

"Anything at ground level? Spring plates?"

"Probably not in the sewer itself." Verci knelt down and put his hands in the waste-filled water, cringing slightly as he did so. He patted the stonework on the ground. "That would take more cash than she'd be willing to spend, too many people could notice it, and it would go off too often."

Asti nodded. The Old Lady was paranoid, but she was also thrifty. As many protective measures as she'd take, she wouldn't spend too much on them. "Her doorway is about a half mile in."

"We have to presume more spider wire across the ceiling the whole way there, so we have to crawl," Verci said, standing up again. "The passage between the two doors, though, is heavily alarmed. She knows we know about it. Probably several people know about it."

"What are your guesses about it?"

"For one, the whole floor is on gimbals. Slightly shifts with any weight on it."

"I didn't notice that."

"It's very subtle," Verci said. "You really would have to have a feel for it. I know it's not your thing."

"Thanks," Asti said. "What does it do? Defensive measures?"

"Don't think so," Verci said. "Last time through, I didn't spot anything."

"Were you looking?"

"Like blazes I was," Verci said. "I wasn't going to be caught like the stairs again. The passage is what she uses to let people leave, so she probably doesn't have it trapped. The floor rings alarm bells." Verci closed his eyes. "Yes, I remember now. A very light chime when we were walking out. And there are peephole lenses in the walls."

"So we can't step on the floor."

"I'm betting those doors aren't designed to be opened

from this side," Verci said. "And also to ring bells when they are opened."

"So we can't get in this way at all is what you're telling me."

"I didn't say that," Verci said. "It will just be very, very challenging."

"But what will she do if we set off an alarm?"

"My guess? Run. Hide in a safe room."

"How is that place not a safe room?" Asti asked.

"For Josie, the bunker under the bakery is almost a public storefront," Verci said. "If she wants to go completely under, she can. And then she'll send muscle for us."

"I know, I know," Asti said.

"If we get in there, and catch her, she might just send muscle on us anyway."

"I know," Asti said. "I was her muscle more than once."

"We're still going to do this?"

"Damn right we are," Asti said. "If I'm right, she rolled over as Tyne blazed our whole alley. She doesn't get to stay in her rabbithole after that."

"Let's do it, then," Verci said. "Mouse quiet, my lead. If I call skunk, we skitter."

"Your lead," Asti said.

Verci got back on his hands and knees and crawled into the darkness. Asti got behind him, matching pace. Both of them went slow and quiet, taking care not to even splash the fetid water.

✺

Helene kept finding her finger stroking the trigger of the crossbow. Driving back out the same night as a carriage smash with the merch was just stupid. Didn't matter that Kennith had redressed the escape carriage so it looked nothing like the one they had pulled the gig in. Fact was, they were still carrying a giant jade statue that every stick in the area would have their eye open for. Covering the thing in hay and canvas didn't help. Hay carriages don't ride through Keller Cove at three bells in the morning. Certainly not with four people riding on it.

The whole thing screamed stolen merch.

The ride had been quiet, though. They only passed a

handful of people, all on foot, all heads down. People who didn't want anyone noticing them, either. Not a stick the whole time. They were deep into Seleth, so the Keller Cove constabs might not even bother coming out this far, and the Seleth ones didn't care. Small blessing.

Kennith pulled up to a warehouse where the oil lamps out front were burning low. "That's it."

"All right," Helene said. "Here's the deal. I talk. You three keep your traps shut."

"Why you?"

"How many drops of stolen merch have you done, Kennith?"

He thought about this for a moment, and then nodded. "Fair enough."

"Good. Now take off your shirt."

"What?"

"Everyone knows Ch'omik warriors don't wear shirts."

"I ain't a Ch'omik warrior!"

She gave a nod over to the warehouse. "They don't know that."

Kennith glowered, but took off his shirt anyway.

"One more thing, Ken. Things turn left, we need to bolt. Do not get out of the driver's seat, get?"

"Got."

"Jules, grab the sledge, then go up and knock."

"What do I do?" Mila asked.

"Depends on how they play it. They might try and pinch us. Or not. We'll have to see."

Julien slung his giant hammer over his shoulder and knocked on the warehouse door. Last thing Helene wanted was a brawl, especially with Jules in the middle of it. But the sight of him holding that hammer might keep anyone from getting any ideas.

A moment later the door opened up, lamplight pouring out into the street.

"Get in here," a deep voice growled.

Kennith spurred the horses, and they went into the warehouse. Someone shut the door behind them. As Helene had predicted, there were a whole mess of blokes in here, most of them armed.

One man, the one in a swank suit with silver buttons, stepped forward. "Do you have it?"

Helene stepped down off the carriage, keeping the crossbow loose in one hand, hoping to give all these blokes the right idea: that she had it, she could use it, but she wasn't aiming it at anyone right now. "Wouldn't come here if we didn't."

"Let's see it."

"Money." Last thing she needed was to be stuck in a warehouse with a bunch of slugs with swords and only a giant statue and her crossbow as collateral.

"Show us you have it."

"Show us you have the money or my friend starts swinging his sledge." She cocked her head over to Jules.

The suit grinned. "We can take him down."

"Not before he smashes your precious statue."

The suit blinked.

After a moment he snapped his fingers to one of the other guys, who came up with a leather satchel. It was held open, full of notes of exchange.

"What—" Mila had opened her mouth.

"Good," Helene said.

"But that—"

Helene reached out and smacked Mila on the back of the head. "Walk over and get the satchel."

"Show us the statue," the suit said.

Helene looked over to Julien. "Show the man."

Julien brushed some hay aside and then lifted the canvas. The suit's eyes went wide and he took a few steps closer. "She's beautiful."

Helene thought the man had some strange ideas of beauty, but for nine hundred crowns he could think whatever he wanted.

"Girl, go get the satchel."

Mila sneered at Helene. She probably didn't like being called 'girl,' but that was better than using her name in front of these blokes.

"Unload it first," said the suit.

Helene tightened her grip on the crossbow. "Here's how it goes, bloke. First my girl takes the satchel. Then my driver turns the carriage around. Then you open the blazing doors. At that point, my bloke unloads. Get?"

The suit gave her a hard look, piercing eyes. "Turn the carriage. Then the doors. Satchel and statue at the same time."

"Done like a doxy," Helene said. She gave Kennith a whistle and a nod. With a quick cry to his horses, he turned the carriage around in a tight circle.

The cadre of armed blokes all stood real still.

"Door," Helene said.

The suit gave a nod to the two nearest to the door. They opened it up.

"Nice and easy now," the suit said.

"Absolutely," Helene said. She looked over to Julien. "Unload it."

Julien picked up the big, ugly thing, while Mila went over to the bloke with the satchel. He let her take it, no games.

"Bring it here, girl," Helene said. Mila gave her a look like she was about to strangle her, but she came over. "Open it." Mila opened the satchel up. It looked like good notes, looked like it could be nine hundred. Helene didn't trust the blokes, but she didn't want to spend one click longer in this warehouse than she had to. "Get on the carriage."

Mila jumped on, just as Julien finished putting the thing on the ground.

"You all have a good night," the suit said.

Kennith didn't waste time getting the carriage moving. Julien walked out behind him, and then Helene followed— walking backward so she could keep her eye on the whole room until she was out.

Soon as they were all in the street, the doors slammed shut.

"Did that go well?" Julien asked.

"If this counts to nine hundred, it went damn well," Helene said. "Hope whatever Asti and Verci are doing is going the same. Let's get back to the stable."

"Can I put my shirt back on now?" Kennith asked. "It's cold out here."

Chapter 15

ASTI BEAT DOWN HIS body's instincts, the urge to retch. It had been a half hour of crawling in near total darkness, the stench of the city's waste assaulting his nose, and he wasn't getting used to it. He could feel that dark rage clawing at the base of his skull. He wasn't going to let it take him. Not twice in one night. Not ever again.

Verci stopped, tapping Asti one time on the shoulder to let him know they had reached the spot. A moment later a pale sickly glow was coming from a vial in Verci's hands, providing only the slightest amount of light. Verci handed the vial to Asti and got into a crouched position.

Asti knew the doorway was right next to them, but he couldn't see it at all. If he hadn't come out this way before, he never would have suspected it was there. Verci ran his hands along the wall, cautious and gentle. His fingers lightly dusted the masonry, occasionally giving a nearly imperceptible tap on each stone. Asti always marveled at how deft and dexterous his brother was. After a few moments Verci found a point that satisfied him. He reached into the pouches at his belt and pulled out a couple of devices. Not taking his eyes off the stones, he assembled the tools blindly into a small drill. He put the drill against the grout and very slowly began to grind his way through it.

Asti counted time as Verci drilled. He knew he had to be patient, as Verci couldn't work too quickly, lest the drilling make a sound that the Old Lady could hear. Even as quiet as he was going, each turn of the drill made Asti's heart race, every noise from the drill and the sewer around them causing him a hint of panic. He pushed it all down into the back of his head, forcing himself to stay absolutely still, not letting the beating, pounding fear and rage find its way out. He was in control.

In the distance the church bells rang out three bells.

Asti had counted to 1,841 by the time Verci was able to carefully slide the brick he had been drilling at out of its spot in the masonry. Gently Verci reached into the small hole he had made.

Asti held his breath.

There was a very slight clicking sound. Sweat was beading on Verci's brow. He pulled out a small, thin tool with his left hand while his right hand stayed in the hole. He slid the tool in, passing it to his right hand, inching it in. Asti imagined Verci had his finger on a catch of some sort, holding it in place until he could get the tool into his other fingers.

Another faint click.

The door moved. It cracked open only a hint. Verci gave Asti a tap, and then pointed to two spots on the lip of the door. Asti understood, taking hold of the edge at the points his brother indicated. Verci held up his free hand, and silently mouthed, "Five."

He pulled in his pinky. "Four."

The two of them mouthed the rest together as Verci counted it on his fingers. "Three. Two. One."

Asti pulled the door open the rest of the way.

No other sounds.

Verci nodded, reaching into the doorway with his free hand. After a moment of fiddling, he pulled his right hand out of the hole.

Verci stretched his fingers out, breathing slowly. He flashed a grin to Asti, then stood at the threshold to the short passageway leading to the Old Lady's office. Asti watched his brother's face as Verci frowned and bit his lip.

After a moment he reached into one of the larger pouches on his belt.

He pulled out a complicated device, pulleys and clamps and rope. Asti was amazed the thing fit on Verci's belt. Verci adjusted it, then mounted it on the upper lip of the doorway, clamping it tightly in place. He clipped one end of the rope to his belt and handed the other end to Asti. He gave a sharp gesture, showing Asti to hold the rope strong and tight.

Asti pulled it taut, and Verci came up off the ground, suspended by the rope. He spun freely for a moment, and then caught himself on the walls of the passageway, braced with hands and feet. Slowly he crossed his way down the passage, holding himself up across the walls, Asti giving him only enough slack to move each step.

Thirty feet took ten minutes. Every scuff of hands or boots on stone, though nearly silent, made Asti wince. Twice the clamp slid, just by a hair, and Asti had to bite his lip to keep from crying out.

Verci had reached the other end of the passageway. Even in the pale light of Verci's vial, Asti could see that opening this door would be comparatively easy. This door had been designed to be hidden on the other side, so its mechanism was visible from this side. Verci, still bracing his body across the walls of the passage, pulled out two pins from the mechanism.

Verci turned back and gave a quick nod to his brother. The door was ready. This was the moment. As far as Asti knew, they had pulled off the run clean. In a matter of seconds they would be in the office, ready to surprise and confront Holt.

Verci held out his hand to count down from five. On three, he left it to Asti to finish the count while he put his free hand on a lever. On one, Asti dropped the rope and dashed forward across the thirty feet of hallway. The floor shook, bells jangled, and the door opened, even as Verci dropped to the ground. Asti dove through the open door, drawing out two knives, expecting to see the Old Lady dashing toward one of her secret escapes.

Josie Holt sat on a soft leather chair, her head

surrounded in a cloud of sweet smoke, a long pipe hanging from her mouth. She made no move at all as Asti landed in front of her, save to draw from the pipe and blow out more smoke.

"Took you long enough."

Asti's heart was racing, his palms sweating, the muscles in his arms tensed and ready to release. Everything he was feeling, everything he was prepared for, suddenly had nowhere to go. All that energy ended up channeled through his mouth, which gave voice to the only word he could think of to say in this situation.

"WHAT?"

"Sooner or later you boys would put a few pieces together," Holt said. "And when you did, you'd come in here, using whatever sneak-and-surprise method you could come up with."

Verci had stepped into the room, absently rubbing at his fingers. Asti was breathing hard, unsure of where to look or what to do. Finally, out of sheer frustration, he flung the knives into the ground, imbedding them in the wooden floor.

"Asti Rynax, there's no need for that," Holt snapped. "You're both upset, I understand that."

"You knew we were coming?" Verci asked.

"To be fair, I knew you had gotten hold of Yenner tonight. And that you weren't at the drop of the statue tonight. Which went fine, by the way."

"Good," Asti said. He didn't know what else to say.

"I figured you were on your way here, so I waited for you. I will give you boys this, that was excellent work. I didn't hear a thing until you made your charge. You've still got the touch."

"Thanks," Verci said, the slightest hint of a smile pulling at his lips.

"That doesn't—" Asti sputtered. He was thinking so many things, feeling so many different things he could barely get it all out. "You knew . . . the alley, Tyne . . . all of it."

"Not all of it," Holt said, taking another puff from her pipe. "Not beforehand." She slowly pulled herself up out of her chair, grabbing her cane as she rose. "I knew Tyne was spreading some crowns around the neighborhood, he was planning something. But not until the alley had burned did I realize what he was doing."

"So you didn't let the alley burn?" Asti asked.

"No," Holt snapped. She scowled at Asti, but then her expression melted. "I can see why you'd think that, though. And I don't blame you for wanting to cut my throat if I had." She hobbled over to the cupboard and poured out a few glasses of wine. "Have a drink. Or don't."

"So what is going on, Josie?" Verci asked.

She sipped at the wine as she slowly made her way back to the chair. "Tyne, he's been chipping away at my network, my system, my people for months. The fire, though, was the first blatant move he's made."

"What's he doing?" Asti asked.

"Making a move into North Seleth for some reason," she said. She took another sip of the wine, sinking deeply into her chair. "I figure he burned the alley just to show me he could."

"He can't," Asti said. "Not and get away with it."

"You gonna stop him, Asti?" She snorted with laughter before taking another sip of wine. "The two of you? Against Mendel Tyne?"

"The two of us," Verci said. "Plus our crew from this last job."

"Bit presumptive of you," she said.

"They're all in," Asti said.

"Oh, well then, that's different," she said. "The two Kessers, who are covered with the stink of failure, a Ch'omik driver, and a beggar girl. There's the team to take out one of the most powerful men on the south bank."

"Damn right they are," Asti said. They were his crew; he wasn't about to hear ill of them.

"You're serious," she said. She looked up at Asti, really looked him in the eye for the first time since he came in. She put down the drink and picked up her cane. "Sweet saints, you are serious."

"Have you ever known me not to be?"

"No," she said. She got up and crossed over to Asti,

limping along with her cane. With her free hand, she cupped his face tenderly. "I should have known it would be you two."

"What do you mean?" Verci asked.

"I had no shot at taking on Tyne," she said. "I had no one I could trust. No one he couldn't buy out from under me. And he did, Rynax. Oh, blessed and blasted saints, did he ever. So I threw out a few breadcrumbs—like having Mersh point you at your old Poasian friend—to see if anyone would take the bait and follow through. No one else bothered. Or they found out and switched over."

"Or started to carve out their own little empire?" Asti asked.

"Lesk," she mused. "He's at least honestly trying to make himself a boss. He's a rat, but I can respect that." She shook her head in disbelief, then gave them both a wide smile. "I should have known, though. You two."

"You don't trust anyone," Asti said. "Especially us."

"I don't trust you," she said. "But I trust that you want this. That you can't be bought. You've got a fire in you, Asti Rynax, and I know Tyne doesn't have enough crowns to put it out."

"So . . . what does this mean?" Verci asked.

"I mean your crew, your plan, whatever it is, to take on Tyne . . . I'm in." She straightened her back. "You need capital, equipment, whatever, I've got it. I'll deny it all if things come to a head, but . . . I can't have him taking anything else away from me. So you boys are my only chance."

"We're not doing a run for you, Old Lady," Asti said. He was chapped that she was trying to horn in on them like this, treat his revenge on Tyne as her own gig.

"We don't work for you," Verci said.

"Your crew, your run, your play," she said. "I'm just your bank."

"How much?" Asti asked.

"Within reason, boys. You do have a plan, yes?"

"Of course not," Asti said. "We only decided to do this an hour ago."

She snorted. "Fair enough. Whatever you do, though, I want a return on my investment. As in money in my pocket."

"You'll have taken down Tyne," Verci said. "Isn't that payment enough?"

"Notoriety is an empty belly, boys," she said.

"Fine, fine," Asti said. "We make arrangements through Mersh?"

"Forget that," she said. "The bakery is too hot, too known. I even have constabs sniffing around it. Time has come to cut away the fat. You won't find me here any longer."

"Where you moving?"

"Not telling," she said. "But we'll meet through the Birdie Basement. Over by the docks?"

"You have your finger in the Basement?" Asti asked.

"Everyone's had a finger in those birds." Verci chuckled.

The Old Lady smacked Verci across the back of his head. "Don't be disrespectful." She went over to her table and filled her pipe back up. "They've got quiet rooms. I'll let the madam know you aren't to be hassled."

"Or hustled," Asti said.

"Or muscled," Verci added.

"It'll be fine. Leave word there for me, and I'll get it." She lit the pipe and took a long draw of smoke. "Now get out of here. You both stink."

Mila had never seen so much money in her life. Before tonight she wouldn't have guessed that a satchel full of paper could even be money. Money was solid coins, copper and silver. Occasionally gold. Not paper.

Helene scolded her when she questioned accepting the paper. Actually, during the drop she just cuffed Mila across the head and told her to shut it. Once they got back to the stable, she said, "Do you have any idea how much silver nine hundred crowns is, girl? How much it weighs?"

"Not really," Mila said.

"More than you can carry away."

"How much would it weigh?" Julien asked.

"A pound of silver is ten crowns," Kennith said. "So, ninety."

"I could carry that."

"You couldn't run with it," Helene said.

Julien creased his brow in thought, then nodded.

"Each share—one hundred fifty crowns—that's fifteen pounds' worth of silver. Carry that through the streets of Seleth and you'll get your throat slit."

"So what is this?" Mila asked, taking out one of the sheets of paper. There was a lot of writing on it, an embossed seal, and the number 20. It didn't make any sense to her.

"Notes of exchange from a goldsmith." Helene snatched the paper from her and put it back in the bag. "Lester & Sons. Decent reputation."

"What does that mean?"

"It means if you take one of these to their exchange-house, they'll give you twenty crowns." Helene was talking to her like she was stupid. She didn't talk that way to Julien, and Julien—Julien wasn't stupid, but he wasn't that bright. Mila found it annoying. Helene held up the paper. "Note. Exchange. Crowns."

Kennith stepped over. He cleared his throat and spoke softly. "Means those notes are as good as crowns."

"Seems silly," Mila said. "You could easily make fakes. Blazes, you could just call yourself a goldsmith and write a bunch of those up."

"People try," Kennith said. "That's why the reputation of the house the notes are from matters."

"Most folks will honor Lester & Sons at near full value," Helene said.

Kennith shrugged. "Nineteen-five on the twenty."

"So we got cheated!" Mila said. She wasn't that good with numbers, but it sounded to her like they weren't getting all their money.

"It's all there," Helene said. "At least it should be."

"We're going to count it, right?" Julien asked.

"Course we count it," Helene said.

"The way Asti said we count it," Julien said. He glared hard at his cousin. "The fair way."

Helene sighed hard and nodded. "Teams of two. Mila and I count the money and split it into shares. Then you and Ken count the shares and put them in the sacks."

Mila nodded and sat down in front of the sheets of paper. "Each note is a twenty?"

"Each note ought to be a twenty," Kennith said. "And they all ought to be from the same house. You find something that don't look right, let us know."

Mila's hands shook, just a little. She didn't want Helene or anyone else to notice. She picked up a stack of the notes and started counting, best as she could. Slowly, carefully. She didn't dare make a mistake. Not in front of Helene. Not when Asti had trusted her enough to bring her into this.

The alarm bells jangled. In a snap Helene grabbed her crossbow and loaded it. Mila uncoiled her rope from her waist.

There was a knock on the door. "It's Almer Cort."

Kennith looked to Helene. "Who is it?"

Helene nodded over to Kennith to get the door. "He's from the alley. Asti wants him in on the next gig."

"What next gig?"

"The—" Helene bit her tongue. "Just get the door. Rynaxes will explain when they get here."

Kennith opened it slowly while she kept her aim trained on the door.

Cort stuck his spectacled face in the crack in the door. "Just me!"

Kennith opened the door a bit farther and let him in, latching it as soon as the mousy man was inside.

"You take care of Yenner?" Helene asked.

"Oh, yes." Cort giggled, almost like a girl. Mila found it unsettling. "He's not going to be any trouble."

"Dead?" Julien asked.

"He wishes." Cort giggled again. "Oh, Mister Yenner would be praying for death if he could."

"What did you do?" Mila asked.

"You, pretty little thing, do not want to know." He grinned widely at Mila. Helene's fist cracked across his jaw. "What the blazes was that?" He rubbed at his face, but stepped away from Helene.

"You don't talk to her like that," Helene said.

"Where's Asti? And Verci?"

"Not here yet," Helene said.

"Where'd they go?"

"Somewhere else," Mila said. "They get here when they get here."

"Fine," Cort said. He went over to the far corner of the stable, dragging a wooden chair with him, and slumped down in it with a dull thud.

"What's this about?" Kennith asked.

"Let's get back to counting," Helene said, returning to the table. "We should have it all sorted and done before the Rynax boys get back."

When Asti and Verci got back to the stable, the count was done. Mila had kept watch while everyone else was dozing, save Cort. He sat nervously, his eyes darting to every corner of the room, reacting to every creak and rustle. Mila refused to take her eyes off of him.

Asti made no attempt to keep quiet as he approached the worktable. He started throwing the planning models from the carriage job into a burlap sack. The rest of the crew roused, slowly approaching him and rubbing their eyes, then covering their noses once they got close.

"Blazes, Rynax," Helene said. "You weren't kidding about the sewer."

"Can't be afraid of a little stink to get the job done," Verci said.

"So," Asti said when everyone gave signs of being awake, "we did one job and got paid. All good?"

"All good," Mila said. She pointed over to the six bundles lined up by the door. "Everyone's share."

"So now we're on to a new job," Verci said.

"What's this new job?" Kennith asked. "Nobody is telling me anything."

"You didn't tell him?" Asti asked.

"Thought you'd want to," Mila said.

"This come from the Old Lady?" Kennith asked.

"After a fashion," Verci said.

Asti stepped over to Kennith. "This is the deal. Holver Alley was burned down on purpose. We know who did it, and we're going for him. But this is a big dog, a lot of barking. Long watch, long plan."

"What does that mean?" Kennith asked.

"It means that our target has a lot of money and a lot of security, so we don't rush it," Asti said. "Frankly, most people wouldn't touch this job. For us, it's personal. But I'd understand if you want to walk out."

"I ain't walking out," Kennith said. "I live here."

"No, right," Asti said. "I meant that—"

"I get what you meant," Kennith said. "And I mean it. I live here. May not have been my home that burned, but it's still my neighborhood. This last gig was personal to me, and you all jumped on. So I'm in."

Asti grinned. "Good. But you get this is pretty damn crazy. Near impossible."

"So was tonight's job." Kennith nodded with a big smile. "But I expect a fair cut. This will pay well, yeah?"

"We pull it off, big money. But we might not pull it off at all."

Helene nodded to the bundles. "Lucky we have this payday."

"We've got a bank for this gig now as well," Asti said.

"Missus Holt?" Julien asked. "She's helping us?"

"And that doesn't leave this room," Asti said. "I'm not going to mix any honey with this, folks. This is a risky gig, trying to filch off a man like Tyne. Risky gig, big money."

"This ain't about money, Asti," Helene said.

"No, it ain't," Asti said. "We all could walk right now with our bundles over there and live good clean lives from this day forward."

"I get a bundle?" Cort asked.

"No!" Helene snapped. "But you've already got a nice clean life all set."

"True," Cort said.

"Whatever we need to do, Asti," Mila said. She wanted Tyne to burn, burn like Jina had burned. Burn like Mister Greenfield's family. Like Asti's shop.

"All right," Asti said. "Verci and I are going to hold on to our shop space. Helene, you and Julien hold on or cash out, your choice. But find yourselves a flop somewhere in North Seleth. Public and respectable. Try and get work that's the same."

"Work?" Helene asked. "Like what?"

"They're hiring on the docks," Verci said. "It doesn't matter what. It's got to look like you're going clean."

"Or open a shop," Asti said.

"What kind of shop could we open?" Helene asked.

"A butcher shop," Julien said from the corner. His eyes were wide, and Mila had never seen such a smile on the big man's face. "We could do it, Helene. You could head out of the city and hunt deer and rabbits and bring them back to the shop and we'd sell the meat and the fur. Like we always used to talk about."

"Crazy dream, Julien," Helene said.

"You don't have to be a big success," Verci said. "Just look clean."

"Right, right," Helene said. "Look clean. Wear a pretty dress."

"Me?" Cort asked. "What do I do?"

"Talk to the people about selling your shop," Asti said. "But drag it out best you can. They're hot to buy, and you don't have a debt, so you can mess with them."

"That's it?" Cort looked disappointed.

"For now."

"What's my job?" Kennith asked.

"This stable is going to stay as our base, if that's fine by you, Ken."

"Fine," Kennith said. "That's all?"

"Start working on a carriage for us," Verci said. "We don't have a plan yet, but I can bet we'll need to get away quickly when we do the job."

"Fast carriage." Kennith nodded. "I can do that."

"What are you boys doing?" Helene asked.

"Scouting the job," Asti said. "When we know more of the plan, we'll tell you what you need."

"Wonderful," Helene said, rolling her eyes.

"I don't have a job," Mila said.

"Get a flop in Keller Cove," Asti said. "Low digs, spend as little as you can. Make sure no one notices you."

"No one ever notices me," Mila said. "And then what?"

"Then get yourself some street boys. From Seleth if you can."

"What for?"

"To run and deliver things and to ask no questions as long as they get some silver. You know some good ones?"

"Yeah," Mila scowled. "I know a few. Then what do I do?"

"I'll tell you when you're up."

Mila didn't like that answer. Asti was saying he didn't have a plan, but she had a sense he knew exactly what he planned for her next, he just wasn't telling her.

"Fine," she said. "Are we done tonight?"

"Money up and get out," Asti said. "Leave word where to find you here at the stable. Kennith is the center."

"I'm the center?"

"Until we tell you otherwise, all messages through Kennith. Now, good work, get out, get some sleep."

Mila grabbed a bundle and opened the door. It was already getting light outside.

"Long night," she said.

"Damn long one," Verci said as he took his bundle. "Raych isn't going to be pleased."

"You're bringing home a pile of money, brother," Asti said. "Women like that."

Chapter 16

VERCI DIDN'T MAKE IT back to Hal and Lian's house until well after sunrise. He found Rusch sitting on the steps of the front stoop, cradling Corsi in her arms.

"You're later than you said you'd be." A cup of tea sat on the stoop next to her. She slid it over to Verci as he sat down on the steps. She leaned over to kiss him, then pulled away. "And you smell terrible."

"The night went a little different than planned." The tea was cold, but he drank without complaint.

"Bad different?"

"In some ways," Verci said. "Mostly just different."

"Did you do the job?"

"Yes."

"Did you get paid?"

Verci held up the bundle of bills. "Yes."

"Are the Constabulary looking for you?"

"Don't think so."

"So it didn't go too bad."

Verci grinned and took another sip of tea. "True enough. Any one you get away from is a good one, as Dad used to say."

"The less yeast, the better," Rusch said.

"What?" Verci asked.

"That's what my dad used to say," she said.

Verci laughed and leaned over to the baby. "You listen to your mother, young man. Learn about bread instead of the trade."

"But bread is boring, Dad," Raych said in a baby voice.

"Bread is safe, son." He touched Corsi's cheek. This boy wasn't going to do anything like what he had to do last night. Not if he could help it. "Bread is clean."

Raych looked back up at Verci, her eyes wide and wet. "So is this it then? We're clean, we're set, we can get on with our lives?"

"Not exactly."

Raych's face fell. "Verci, I . . . I've been sitting out here on the stoop since five bells. Lian thought I was insane, Hal didn't know what I was doing, and I couldn't very well explain it to them. My heart raced with every single person I saw come around the corner. I've been a mess, Verci. I don't think I could take another night like tonight."

"I don't think I could, either," Verci muttered.

"But you're saying you aren't done?" Her voice cracked.

"Asti and I learned something tonight, Raych."

"About time for him to learn something."

Verci chuckled wryly. Sometimes he forgot how much his wife disliked his brother, how little respect she had for him. Raych often overlooked his own faults, the sins of his past, but she clearly placed the weight of those sins on Asti's shoulders. Raych conveniently ignored the fact that Asti had gone straight, sought some kind of redemption, long before Verci ever had. Asti was paying a higher price for the path he chose than Verci could ever imagine.

"We know who had the alley burned."

Raych swallowed hard. "What can you do about it?"

"We're going to get him, Raych."

Raych's voice went hard, her eyes narrowed. "Get him how, Verci?"

Verci shrugged. "Not sure. Break him. Rob him blind. Make him pay for what he did to us. To the whole alley. All our friends."

"Our friends, Verci?" Raych's voice went up an octave. "What about our family? You, me, and Corsi?"

"What about Win Greenfield's family? Who's going to get justice for them?"

Raych faltered. Clutching the baby tight to her body, she looked down at the ground. "So ... so go to the Constabulary."

"This man bought out the Fire Brigade, Raych. The law won't touch him. If they could get him, they would have done so a long time ago."

"He's that bad?"

"Yes."

"That powerful?"

"Yes."

Raych smacked him across the head. "Then what makes you think you and your stupid brother can do a blasted thing to him?"

"Who else can, Raych? Who else is going to? This man has to pay, and the only people who could possibly do it are people like—"

"Like you and Asti? Desperate and too clever for your own good?"

"Well—"

"Your brother has nothing to lose. Can you really say the same?"

Verci sighed. He'd known she would say something like that. "I can't abandon him. Not for something like this. There's ... there's too much at stake."

"Our lives are at stake, Verci. Our family, our life together." She was on her feet, pacing back and forth as her voice grew louder. "Just let him go, let it all go!"

"That's not fair, Raych. That's my brother."

"And I'm your wife!"

"And if I told you to throw Lian off a bridge for me, would you?"

Raych paused. She bit at her lip. "No, of course not."

"If your sister needed you, you'd want me to back you up, wouldn't you?"

Raych nodded silently.

"And I would, Raych." Verci got down on one knee in front of her. "I've got to do this. Not just for Asti, but for me. That man ... that man ruined my plans, my dreams. I want to get him. I want to make him pay. Don't you?"

"Of course."

"Good," Verci said. "That's settled then."

"Promise me, Verci," Raych said. "Promise me you won't do anything too stupid, you won't get yourself killed."

"Of course," Verci said. "I want justice, but I'm not stupid."

"Good," Raych said. She sighed and looked up at her sister's house. "Can we at least move out of here and get our own place again?"

"You're damn right we can," Verci said. "We do have a sack full of money, after all."

"Thank the saints for that. Now go find a bathhouse before you come inside. I don't think you want to explain to Hal and Lian why you smell so blasted awful."

Asti came down from the upper rooms of Kimber's Pub with all his belongings in the world slung over his shoulder. Kimber stood at the bottom of the stairs, her face sad.

"I was getting used to having you around here, Asti," she said.

"I'm not someone you want to get used to, Kim," Asti said, putting on his warmest smile. "You know that."

"Where are you heading to?"

"I've got a new flop, all mine, over in Keller Cove." A terrible flop, purely for the purpose of scouting this job, but it made for good appearances if anyone was paying too close attention to him.

"Keller Cove?" Kimber's eyebrow went up. "I didn't think you'd east up." Her voice cracked a little when she said that, hitting Asti in the heart. She thought he was abandoning the neighborhood.

"No, Kimber . . ." he faltered. "That ain't it at all."

"You left once already. I got that," she said.

"That was joining Intelligence."

"I know," Kimber said. She turned away and walked over to the bar. "That was service, not easting up. Plenty of North Seleth boys went Army or Navy. You pulled Intelligence. That ain't leaving us."

"I'm not leaving you."

"You're flopping in Keller Cove!" she snapped. Her eyes were red and welling up.

"No, it's . . ." Asti stopped himself. He liked Kimber plenty, but he couldn't tell her about the job, about Tyne, about any of that. "This neighborhood is always my home, Kimber. I ain't walking out on it."

Kimber scoffed as she picked up a cloth and wiped down the bar. "Just a single job, real quick, then you'll come back, right? I've heard it before."

"Kimber, did we get married at some point and I've just forgotten?" Asti said. "Why are you taking it so personal?"

She shook her head, not looking at Asti. "It's nothing, nothing. I'm being stupid."

"You're doing all right, right?" Asti asked. "I mean with money and everything?"

"Could be better," she said. She went behind the bar, her head staying down, never looking Asti in the eye. "Always the story in North Seleth, right? Always could be better."

"That's the truth," Asti said. He moved closer to her, reaching out but nervous to touch her, like she might explode if he did. "But you're not in trouble, right?"

"No," she said. She stood and faced him, wiping at her wet eyes. "Not in trouble, not yet. I don't have to take any offers. I don't want to."

"You've got offers?" Asti asked.

She nodded. "A couple. Nothing much. Nothing worth leaving home for."

"Don't take any," Asti said hotly.

"And why not?" she snapped. "If you're easting out, why do you care?"

"Because I'm not," Asti said. "I swear, Kimber. This neighborhood is my home. I'm coming back to it. I'm—" His voice faltered, dropping to a whisper. "I'm fighting for it."

Kimber's wet eyes went wide. "Fighting? How?"

"I can't talk about it." He glanced at the few people in the pub's sitting room. "Just trust me."

She looked at his eyes, quietly contemplating him for what felt interminably long. "The day after tomorrow, I'll go to service at Saint Bridget's. You'll be there."

"What?"

"You will be there, Asti Rynax. In decent clothes."

"Why?"

"Because you want my trust," she said. "That's how you'll get it."

Asti couldn't help but grin. Kimber played clever cards. "Fine. Day after tomorrow."

"Nine bells, no later."

"Yes, ma'am," Asti said. He wondered why he was letting Kimber get under his skin, letting her dictate terms to him. It wasn't like he fancied her or anything like that. She was a nice enough girl, sure, but never the type he would pursue. She was too much mother, despite being the same age as him.

She was the neighborhood, though. Hardworking, earn every crown, decent folk. She was what he and Verci were hoping to be before the fire. She was what they were going after Tyne for. She was what Win Greenfield couldn't be anymore.

"Is Win still here?" Asti asked.

"He is, up in his room."

"How's he doing?"

"He hardly speaks. But he comes down to eat every day, which is an improvement."

Asti nodded. "Keep him here as long as he needs it, all right? I'll pay for room and board."

"You don't need to—"

"He covered for Verci and me when we needed it. Blazes, when Raych gave birth, he paid for the doctor, knowing we needed every crown for the shop. I owe that man."

"You saved his life. Helene told me."

"All the more reason I owe him." Asti went back to the door and picked his pack up off the floor. "Day after tomorrow."

"You better be there." She was smiling again.

"Wouldn't miss it," he said, and walked out. Chuckling to himself as he walked down the street, he muttered, "Haven't been in church in fifteen years. What are you doing to me, woman?"

Verci woke disoriented, wondering where the blazes he was and why he was wet. It took him a few minutes to remember that Raych had forced him to clean up before coming into Lian's house and, after the eventful night, he must have fallen dead asleep in the baths at Larton's Bath and Shave.

No one else was in the baths, which was unusual. He wondered how long he must have slept. He couldn't possibly have slept so long that Larton had closed up. Larton would have woken him and kicked him out first.

Just the fact that he had slept undisturbed for as long as he had was strange. Nobody would have left a man sleeping in the pool for too long without at least jostling him.

His fingers were heavily wrinkled. It had to have been hours he was in there.

He hastily grabbed a piece of soap and scrubbed himself clean. After this long he had to attend to his purpose for coming.

Rinsed off, he exited the pool and grabbed a cloth to dry himself.

Just one cloth hanging by the steps. Also unusual.

There was a pile of fresh clothes on the bench by the door. Pressed and neatly folded. Not the ones Verci had come in with, but similar.

"Larton?" he called out. "Hello?"

No response.

He could either go out into the front room in only the drycloth or in strange clothes.

Drycloth it was.

The front room was surprisingly crowded, given the emptiness of the baths. Larton stood at his barber chair, hands trembling and sweat beading across his brow. The rest of the assembled persons were clearly there together: Nange Lesk, with Essin, Poller, Bell, and a muscled blond woman. All of them looked unhappy, save Lesk, who looked far too happy.

"There's the man," Lesk said, his rotten grin wide and ugly. "Did you rest well, pirie?"

"I suppose," Verci said, unsure of any other way to respond.

"Because you had a big night, didn't you?" Lesk approached, arms wide. "But look at you. Still wrapped in the drycloth. We brought you fresh clean clothes, didn't you see them? Essin, go get Verci's clothes."

"It's quite all right, I—"

"Nonsense," Lesk said, leading Verci over to the barber chair. "Have a seat."

"I don't need—"

"Have you looked at yourself, Verci? You're something of a fright of scruff. Isn't that right, Ia?"

"Fearful," the blonde woman said flatly.

"Your lovely wife," Lesk said, his voice dropping a register. "She just couldn't bear you coming home looking like that. Of course, that home is really her sister's. Lian, right? And Hal is her husband. Decent, hardworking folk, aren't they?" Lesk pushed Verci back into the chair.

"Larton, you don't need to . . ."

"Never fear, Mister Rynax," Larton said, his own voice cracking with terror. "I'm a steady hand at this." He proceeded to lather up Verci's face.

"Now I'm sure," Lesk said, "that Hal and Lian, being the decent, hardworking folk they are, are not the types to be involved in the sort of thing you and your brother got into last night, right? They wouldn't want the consequences coming to their doorstep."

"I'm not sure what you mean, Lesk."

The blade came onto Verci's cheek.

"Look," Lesk said. "I can be reasonable about things. Something ugly went down across the creek in Keller Cove. Ten dead bodies, Verci. Ten. That'll keep the sticks over there busy for a while."

That didn't sound right. Verci did a quick count in his head: driver, five guards, two more in the street after. How did it get to ten?

"Whoever did that sort of thing, well, someone like that will want some friends. Someone to keep the sticks from looking their way."

"I'm sure someone like that has already cleared town or such."

"Even still," Lesk said. "He'd want to keep his friends . . . happy with him."

"I'm sure," Verci said calmly, "that the people he considers his friends are quite happy with him. And that's all he would concern himself with."

Lesk frowned. "A smart man keeps a wide circle of friends, Verci."

"That's quite a gash you got there on your back," Poller added.

Verci fought the urge to twist his head around, and Larton was scraping the blade over his cheek. "Got hurt during the fire," Verci said.

"Of course," Lesk said. "The fire. That was some bad business all around, don't you think?"

Verci couldn't read Nange's face. He always had that smug look on it, and Verci couldn't tell if he was being smug about the fire or just in general.

"That's all it was to you?"

"It's bad for all Seleth, pirie, and I'll tell you why. Now we got people sleeping on the street, we got less business being done. That means Seleth is looking less like Keller Cove and more like Benson Court. People are gonna start to think the slums start at the creek. I don't want that, do you?"

The blade was far too close to Verci's mouth to dare respond.

"That sort of thing is bad for decent people living here. People like Hal and Lian. People like Larton here."

Lesk moved in closer. "You and your brother, you're doing what you have to do for you, and I get that. And you're doing what the Old Lady needs, and that's good, too. She's important here. It's, like, a legacy or something."

Verci didn't know what was more disturbing: the razor at his neck, or the earnest look on Lesk's face.

"So we've got to build something here, Verci. Our alley got burned down, and someone has to rebuild. Everyone has to do their part, do you understand?"

"I understand, Mister Lesk," Larton stammered out. He gave one more swipe. "Smooth as when he left his mother, like you asked."

Lesk clapped him on the shoulder. "That's awfully good of you, Larton. Isn't that good of him, boys?" The rest of Lesk's crew nodded. Lesk turned his focus back to Verci.

"You see, a man like Larton here knows to do his part." Lesk pulled Verci up out of the chair, leaving the drycloth on the seat.

Verci chuckled under his breath. If Lesk thought that was going to intimidate him at all, he'd be sorely mistaken.

"I'll do my part, Lesk," Verci said calmly. "I intend to have the Rynax Gadgeterium up and running as soon as possible."

Lesk and his crew all laughed at that. "Gadgeterium. Of course."

Essin stood by the back door, the pile of clothes in hand.

"Hand those over, Essin," Verci said, keeping his voice as calm and level as possible. "I would hate to catch a chill here." Essin blankly held out the clothes, which Verci grabbed.

"You and your brother," Lesk said coldly, "you'll need to respect what's going to happen in this neighborhood."

Verci dressed quickly. "Don't you worry, Lesk. The neighborhood has my respect." He leaned in and whispered in Lesk's ear. "And my brother and I will deal with anyone who hurts it. Anyone."

With a quick snap, Verci pushed Lesk away. The others all tensed up, hands to belts and pockets. If things suddenly went to blows and weapons, Verci would be in a bad spot. Best choice would be to dive for the front window. A few cuts from the glass would be preferable to Bell and Ia carving him up.

Fortunately Lesk held up his hands, easing back. The others relaxed.

"There's no need, pirie. We can all be friends." He gestured to the door. "Why don't you go see your pretty wife?"

Verci brushed through Lesk's crew and left, resisting the urge to grab their purses on the way out. He could have. It would have been far too easy. But it would have also changed Lesk's veiled threats into something Verci didn't need right now.

Right now, all he needed was to relax with his wife and son until Asti was ready for things to move forward with the Tyne gig.

Chapter 17

THE NEW FLOP WAS a mess of molding wood and crumbling plaster, a breeding nest for mice and bugs. It was four floors up, reachable only by a rotting stairway populated by whores and addicts. For the past four days a dead man had lain here, only discovered this morning. The sickening odor of decay was just slightly mitigated by the pungent splash of vinegar the landlady had thrown on the floor. It was vile, and, even at the pittance of a half-crown a week, it was overpriced. All that didn't matter to Asti because the place had a window with a clear view of Tyne's Pleasure Emporium.

The Emporium was a monstrosity, taking up an entire city block. The front door was twenty feet high, and there were two muscular goons who stood watch at it, not to guard it as much as open it for the people who were going in. Asti knew from reputation that the ground floor was a restaurant, one of the finest on the south side of Maradaine. People came from all over the city to dine there. The back half of the building was a huge stable where Tyne's valets parked the carriages of his clients.

Asti also knew, or at least understood from rumor, that there were other floors—above and below—where select clients could gamble, hire companionship, or engage in whatever sort of debauchery they had the money for. A lot of crowns went into the Emporium every day. Somewhere, probably in the lowest levels, there had to be a safe or a lockroom full of those crowns. Asti would keep his eye on the place until he figured out just where those crowns were, how to get them, and how to get away with them. He didn't know how long it would take, but he wasn't going anywhere.

There were no windows, at least not on the side Asti could see. If there were any, they would surely have steel grates covering them. There had to be a service entrance somewhere, but that was likely well guarded. The building was the tallest in the immediate area; so getting on the roof wasn't an option. Underground, be it from existing passages or sewers, might be the best path. Asti sighed. He hated underground entrances. He still felt disgusting from the crawl through the Old Lady's sewer the other day. If he kept up this lifestyle, he'd never get the stink off.

Keeping one eye on the Emporium, Asti reached over to his satchel on the floor, dragging it to him. He took out a clothbound journal and charcoal pencil, placing them on the sill in front of him. Next he took out Helene's scope. She'd be riled fierce that he pinched it, but it couldn't be helped. He needed the thing to see as much detail as he could from here.

Asti mused that he probably could have asked her. Riling her was more fun, though.

He kept close watch on the Emporium. Not much activity at this hour, far too early. Absently he took out a knife and sharpened the pencil.

A mule wagon came up to the door, its wares covered with a tarp. The guards waved to the drover friendly enough. Long-established pattern. One guard lifted the tarp in a cursory manner, giving no more than a glance before letting it drop. Familiarity bred a casual attitude, poor habits. Asti grinned. That was a good sign.

Scope to his eye, still watching the door, with his free hand he jotted in the book, *Joram 3, 4 bells. Drover up, waved around back. Blond hair with gray temples, middle years. Brown coat, no patches or badges. No guild. Guards know and trust to a degree.*

The wagon went around to an alley, to the back entrance. Asti couldn't see farther in. He needed to get some eyes closer to it.

He needed to put Mila on the street.

He didn't want to have to do that, not yet. She wasn't ready for this kind of work. Even he felt rusty, still occasionally glancing at the page as he wrote the minutiae of the guards' activities. A year ago he could write out the whole journal without once actually eyeing the page, just watching his target.

Not as sharp as I used to be, he thought. *Haven't really been sharp since Haptur, since Levtha. Not since that same hot stink of the recent dead had been his close companion, harsh voices, hammers on his skull, breaking, breaking. Hot sun high in the sky bearing down while screams surrounded him, knives in hand, blood to the elbows, everything red—*

Asti startled. His skin clammy, his pulse racing. Back in the flop. Slow breaths. He hadn't gone anywhere. Memory had swept him up for a moment—memory so strong it felt like he was there again. That hadn't happened before.

That was new.

Asti put the pencil and scope down and slumped to the floor.

Was this how badly broken his mind was? Not only could he not trust his temper, but he couldn't trust himself to stay present, to be in reality?

In the key moment of a gig, timed to the second, could he even trust himself to be aware enough to do what he had to do? He had already screwed up one gig, barely pulled from the fire by Verci.

He still couldn't catch his breath, shallow and fast. He wanted to run. He wanted to leap from the window. He wanted to cut the throat of the next person he saw.

You are Asti Rynax. He forced the thought across his brain, like jamming his foot on a door he refused to let open. *You are in control of yourself. No one else in here but you.*

Long, slow, deep breaths. Asti thought of nothing but filling his lungs. He didn't even care about the rancid, stringent air.

"You all right?"

His body went into action before thoughts could be formed. On his feet, knives drawn, lunging at the source of the voice.

Mila.

He pulled back mid-swing, slamming the blade into the doorframe.

Mila jumped back, her hand at the rope on her belt. But her eyes were calm, piercing.

"How did you get here?" he asked.

"Followed you from Kimber's."

He hadn't noticed. Sloppy on his part. Impressive on hers. "Nice. What do you want?"

"I want to know if you're all right. What you just—it wasn't a fight or anything."

"No. I don't . . . you weren't scared?"

"I knew you were in your right senses this time. For the most part."

"Not so sure about that." He sheathed the knife and went to sit on the bed. He glanced at it, and thought better, moving back over to the window. Mila came and looked out the window.

"Good view."

"We'll need better. You, shaking a hat on the corner there."

She nodded. "I can do that."

"How are you doing with gathering up some street boys?"

Her confident air fell. "I . . . haven't started yet."

"Why? You said you knew where to find some."

"Where, sure." Her eyes darted about the room, looking anywhere but at him. "But how am I going to get them to listen to me?"

This was a problem he could solve. "Do you know where they squat?"

She nodded.

"Then you walk right in. Change your look around a bit first. Tie back your hair, wear a different coat than usual, whatever. Create the person who you're going to be when you walk in." He took off his coat and gave it to her. It actually wouldn't be too big on her at all.

She put it on. "What good is this going to do?"

"That's just to give you the character. If any of them know you as Mila, you don't want them to recognize you. Do any know you well?"

"No."

"Good. Use that. Make a name for the character you're being. Be that person who is going to walk in and take over."

"This sounds like sewage, Mister Rynax."

"I'm serious. Then you figure out who the old boss is, and knock him down."

"Just start a fight with the leader?"

He tapped a finger on his temple. "No. I'm talking about outsmarting him. If you just go for the brawl, the rest might pile on."

"Insult him."

"Tear him down. You want all those street boys to want to follow you instead of him. You want them to think they're lucky that you're giving them the time of day."

"All right. I think I can do that." She went to leave.

"One more thing," Asti said. "Once you have them, don't give them an inch. Tight leash."

"Got it." She paused at the doorframe. "That isn't how you treated us."

"That's because I like you all."

She laughed, a low, hoarse chuckle. "You all right here, by yourself and everything?"

"I'll be fine."

"Listen, I—" She stepped back into the room. "I haven't told anyone else about what really happened to you the other night. As far as they know, you got jumped by Yenner's guys and that held you up."

"I appreciate that." The last thing he needed was the crew to think he couldn't handle this gig.

"Does Verci know?"

"Of course he does," Asti said. "I couldn't keep it from him. But everyone else, they . . ."

"They deserve to know what's going on with you. We all have to trust—"

"Shouldn't trust too much, Mila," he said. "Count on your crew to do their jobs. Trust is something else."

Her eyes hardened. "I'm trusting that you're going to keep your rolling head in one blasted piece. Let me know if you can't blazing well enough to do that." She stormed off.

Asti let out a breath he hardly realized he'd been holding in.

Mila was right. He was barely keeping his head together. He couldn't let something like this happen again, and he'd be damned if he'd let anything like it hurt the people around him, or stop him from doing what he had to do. He'd get this gig done, he'd do right by his crew. Once that was handled, he could slip quietly out of town and toss away whatever scraps of sanity he still clung to.

He turned to the windowsill, taking the scope and pencil in hand.

4 bells 10, he wrote. *One guard uses alleyway for water closet. Other guard pretends not to notice.*

Mila tracked a handful of street boys to a shabby wooden bridge crossing the creek past Scal Road. Tiny bridge, only wide enough for one person to walk across, rotted through in several spots. The bridge didn't lead anywhere. On the Seleth side there was only a lot with patches of grass clawing through the broken cobblestone, boxed in by buildings on all sides. A perfect place for a bunch of boys to stay out of sight and get into mischief.

A dozen boys at least. None of them older than twelve. Perfect.

Mila buttoned up Asti's jacket. She had on slacks and boots, and her hair was pulled back, so she almost looked like a boy. Almost. She'd never fool them, but they'd know she wasn't the kind of girl to mess with. Especially with a knife on one hip and a coiled rope on the other.

She crossed the bridge, strong, confident strides, even though the wood groaned with each step. The boys paid her no mind, focusing their attention on throwing rocks at an upper floor window—the only one intact.

How would Asti take control here?

She picked up a rock, and gave a sharp whistle. The boys all turned to her.

She hurled the rock. Strong arm, true aim. The window shattered. "Looks like you've got nothing more to break over here."

"What's that about, skirt?" one of them yelled. In the center. Tallest. Leader, in as much as these boys would have one. They weren't a gang, not yet, though every one of them would probably end up that way.

"This your idea, pip?" She walked up close, getting into his face. "Breaking windows in an empty lot?"

"What of it?" His breath was hot and rancid.

"Waste and sewage, that's what it is. Was this his idea?" she asked one of the littler ones.

"Yeah."

"Shut it," the older boy hissed.

"You'd think if you're gonna listen to him, he'd have better ideas," she said to the little ones.

"Who the blazes are you, skirt?"

She patted his cheek, just hard enough to insult. "Someone with ideas, pip."

"I got an idea." He gave her a wicked grin, and lashed out with a wild punch. She easily stepped out of the way, putting one hand on her rope. He turned back to her and charged. Sloppy and ugly. She dodged and tripped him up, sending him flying to the ground. Before he could get up, she knelt down on his back.

"Scrap and break, that's all you have?" She shook her head, looking up at the other boys. They all seemed to be waiting for one of the others to do something. "No wonder you just hide back here."

"We ain't hiding," one of the other boys said.

"You ain't doing anything. Because this one doesn't think of anything." She dug her knee between his shoulder blades for a moment, and he cried out. Then she got up again. "None of you think of anything."

"Stupid skirt," the eldest muttered.

"Never mind," she said, walking away. "Waste your time. There might be some boys over on Calder Way who want to make a few crowns."

"Oy!" one of them called. "You didn't say anything about money."

Hooked.

She turned back. "You want to make some money?"

They all nodded.

"Then you'll listen to what I tell you, hear? You listen, you say, 'Yes, Miss Bessie,' and then you do it. Hear?" Bess had been her mother's name. Them calling her that sounded good to her ear. It sounded like being in charge.

She looked at the eldest, still lying on the ground. "We hear."

"Hmm?" she asked, giving him a pointed look.

"Yes, Miss Bessie." He spat out the words, but he said them. She had them.

"All right. Who's fast?"

The little boy raised his hand up, proudly, eagerly.

"All right, pip," she said. *Call them all pip,* she thought. *Then I don't have to learn any damn names.* "You're gonna run up to a flop over in Keller Cove and deliver a message . . ."

Chapter 18

MILA HAD NO REAL CLUE what she needed to be doing now that she had her cadre of boys. Scouting, Asti had said. Move herself and her boys into the blocks around the Emporium and shake their hats. Keep watch and find out what they can. But the boys weren't supposed to know what they were looking at or why. Far as they knew, they were keeping an eye out for sticks and other trouble.

So she shook the hat for a day and a half, even though she couldn't care less about what she got. It was hard to fake that level of need when she had several dozen crowns in her dress. She knew she was eating today, she knew where she was sleeping. And she could give the boys a fair share out of her hatshake. That should keep their loyalties square. From what Asti said, that was what mattered most right now.

They were all a good bunch of pips, and they all thought she was grooming them for a proper gang. That's why they took the money and asked no questions when she sent them to run between her and Asti.

She glanced over to the Emporium, where a couple of well-groomed swells were going in for lunch. Another one came out, shook hands with them, talked to the valet. She could get well-groomed and have lunch if she really wanted.

Not here, though. She'd be damned if that blasted Tyne would get one tick of her dressful of crowns.

"Oy." Another valet came up to the swell. "Ecrain wants to talk to you."

The swell shuddered and rolled his eyes. "Just bring more food."

The valet shrugged. "Said you."

"Why?"

"Didn't ask." The valet looked a little spooked.

The swell shook his head. "Mages." He stomped back into the place.

That sounded like the sort of thing Asti needed to know.

"Mages," Verci muttered.

"What was that?" Hal asked from the sitting room. Verci knew Hal was already in a bit of a snit over a "street rat" delivering a note to his house. An inquisitive snit.

"Just a message from Asti," Verci said, holding up the note. Hal wouldn't be able to read it—no one other than Verci knew how to read Asti's scratch code—but if he could he would probably ask why Asti was writing. "Possible mage on staff."

"What's Asti doing?" Hal asked suspiciously.

"He was looking for a new flop, wasn't he?" Raych called from the kitchen. Bless her, thinking on her feet.

"Right," Verci said, shaking the note vigorously before putting it into his pocket. "He was just letting me know he's found one, out in Keller Cove."

"Easted, did he?" Hal pursed his lips. "That delivery you made across the river must have paid well."

"Well enough," Verci said.

"Speaking of," Raych said as she came out of the kitchen, brushing flour off her dress, "we should start looking. And I'd prefer to stay in the neighborhood if we can."

"Going to be tough," Hal said. "I heard up on the docks that a lot of landlords are hiking their rents."

"That's pretty low," Verci muttered.

"Must make hay when the sun shines," Hal said. There was another knock on the door. He grumbled incoherently as he got out of his seat and went back to the foyer.

"What's the news?" Raych whispered.

"Just some news Asti found about the gig. Nothing to worry about." It was a big wrinkle, actually, but an obvious one, now that he thought about it. Mages for hire cost quite a few crowns, but for someone like Tyne, it would be worth the expense. They had to assume the mage was part of the security, and that would be another problem to solve.

"Verci," Hal called from the foyer. "Someone else to see you."

"See me?" Verci asked.

"Mister Chell?" Raych asked.

Verci shrugged and went to the door, Raych right at his hip. To his surprise, the visitor was Mersh.

"Begging pardon, Mister and Missus Rynax," Mersh said, taking his white cap off and holding it to his chest. "I was wondering if I could have a few words." He glanced out at the street behind him. "Perhaps in private."

"Yes, of course," Verci said, holding his arm open to welcome the man in. "Hal, this is Mersh, the baker from Junk Avenue."

Hal's eyes brightened. Verci knew the way Hal thought—if he knew Mersh was a working merchant, he would be far more approving of the man entering his house. "Of course, yes. I'm sorry, Mister Mersh, I didn't know you." He laughed nervously as he patted his ample belly. "I'm afraid with my wife, I don't have much call to visit your bakery."

Mersh nodded with humble sympathy. Verci noticed how much the man was putting on a show, though he wasn't entirely sure whose benefit the show was for.

Hal led them all back to the sitting room, and with a slight prod from Raych, he went to the kitchen for tea.

"What can we do for you, Mersh?"

"I have a brother in Kyst, and I've just received word that he is very ill. He's a family man, many children. I've decided I need to go out and help them all, and I should leave right away."

This sounded a bit rehearsed. Verci was wondering what

he was—no, what Josie was playing at here. "So you'll be shutting down the bakery."

"If that's what has to happen," Mersh said. "I'd prefer not to have to. The bakery serves the neighborhood, you know, and in times like these, I'd hate—*no one* wants to see another shop shut down." He hit the words "no one" strongly, locking eyes with Verci, so Verci would know exactly who "no one" actually was.

"Of course," Verci said. Raych, sitting next to him, had taken his hand, and began to squeeze it tightly.

"I've heard rumor that your wife—and please scold me if I'm talking out of turn, Missus Rynax—is quite gifted in the baking arts."

"Why, thank you," Raych said.

"What we were—" Mersh stumbled, then bit his lip. "I mean, I was hoping that the two of you would be willing to take over the bakery during my indefinite leave. Of course, there are rooms upstairs for you to stay in, and plenty of extra space for you to work on your little projects, Mister Rynax."

Raych squeezed so hard she nearly broke his hand.

"I think that would be agreeable," Verci said. "Don't you think so, Raych?"

"Quite," Raych said, her face covered with a wide smile.

"Good," Mersh said, standing up. "I'll have my factor come to you with the details . . . let us say, rent purely as a percentage of profits?"

"More than fair," Verci said.

Mersh went for the door. "Then I'll be leaving early tomorrow morning. You can move in any point after that."

"One thing," Verci said, following him out. "Just that, um . . . a bakery could be a . . . *dangerous* place. You know, for a small child. I just worry that someone might grab or pull something. Get hurt. You understand."

"I understand," Mersh said, clapping Verci on the shoulder. "I'll make sure I leave everything dangerous locked up tight. It shouldn't be a problem."

"Good then," Verci said, opening the door. Mersh nodded in farewell, and went out to the street.

Raych was at Verci's side. "What just happened? Are we bakers now?"

"We are, I guess," Verci said. He grinned deviously at his wife. "After all, it's very important that the community sees we have a legitimate business, don't you think?"

Raych narrowed her eyes and whispered, "So they don't ask where our money comes from?"

"Something like that."

"To make sure there's no questions, it better be a damn good bakery." Her grin was impish, and her excitement infectious. She turned to the kitchen. "Lian! I'm going to need the book!"

Joram 5, 8 bells 50. Milk delivery. Milkman gives a bottle to the guard. Quick heated conversation between them. Suspect milkman tried to court a favor, failed. Asti put down the pencil and rubbed his eyes. He'd been at watch for almost two days now, and with only a few naps and scraps of dried beef to keep himself going. He felt terrible, but he was relishing how bad it felt, how real, how much he loved feeling like this from working.

Almost nine bells, he thought, *then the guards change. I'll note who's working and take another nap.* He was pleased with his plan when the words "nine bells" drifted across his brain again.

Kimber.

"Bloody rutting blazing saints!" he swore as he pulled himself on his feet. He had completely forgot. He tore into his knapsack, pulling out a clean shirt and vest. He quickly stripped out of the ripe one he was wearing, used it to polish his boots, and threw on the new one.

He bounded out of the flop, leaping down the stairs five at a time, smashing his way past two dozing doxies at the bottom stairs. He hit the street and broke into a dead run. The streets were full of people, most of whom were paying enough attention to see him sprinting like a madman down the street and get out of his way.

This is not the way to lay low, he thought as he crossed over Wheeler into North Seleth.

He crossed the creek bridge into Bridget Square just as the clock tower over the church started to peal out the time.

A few dozen people milled about the square, some of them looking like they'd been sitting there all night. If not longer.

Strolling across the square was Nange Lesk, with no fewer than six flunkies walking with him. Past Lesk and his men, Kimber stood at the bottom of the church steps, wearing a bright but sober dress. Her eyes lit up as she spotted Asti across the square.

Asti ran over, no way to do it without Nange seeing him.

"Rynax," Nange called out. "I need a word."

"Another time," Asti said as he passed, ducking out of the way of Nange's big-armed goon. "Have to get to church."

Without slowing down he closed the distance to the church steps, reaching it just as the ninth bell rang out.

"Well, well," she said with a warm smile. "I'm genuinely surprised."

"You didn't think I'd forget, did you?" Asti asked, breathing deeply through his nose.

"If you hadn't, you would have walked," she said, patting his cheek. "Come on, let's hear the sermon."

"The sermon," Asti repeated. "Right. You sure about that, Kimber?" He glanced back at Nange and his crew. They all looked fully riled up, ready to cause him trouble. Still, he'd rather ball his fists and dive into the lot of them instead of go up the steps.

"Completely," she said sternly. She looked him in the eyes, looking deeper and longer than he felt comfortable with. "I'm certain of only a few things, Asti, and most of them have to do with food or drink. But I know that you are a man in great need of spiritual guidance. So come on."

She walked him up to the church. Asti hesitated at the threshold. He didn't know what was stopping him. He knew, fully in his head, that walking in and listening to the sermon was little more than an hour of his time, a reasonable price for the good grace he had gotten from Kimber. Still, his heart pounded. Sweat started to bead on his brow.

Kimber's soft hand curled into his, and she pulled him inside. Asti felt an instinct to lash out at any hand pulling on his. He would never want to do anything like that to Kimber. Despite that, the urge raged strongly within him.

"Kimber, I—" he started.

"Shush," she whispered, pointing to the reverend, who was already well into his sermon.

"The community has suffered, my friends. Suffered a grievous blow, a wound deep into our collective side. Is this wound fatal? It feels like it."

Kimber led Asti to the pews and sat him down, then took a spot next to him.

"Oh, my friends, it feels like we would never recover from this injury. Each morning, every morning for the past week I have walked through Holver Alley and, my friends, I have wept. Wept at the devastating loss that has been suffered. The loss of life and of livelihood."

A wrenching sob burst forth next to Asti. He turned to find Win Greenfield sitting next to him, tears streaming down his face.

"But we must remember that there is always hope in any tragedy. Those who live should honor those who died, by doing everything they can to strive, to rebuild. To make the best out of what they can be. Else all this pain will have been to no end."

Another hand took hold of Asti's. Win grabbed it and held it tightly and looked at Asti, eyes pooling up.

"Asti, I—" he whispered.

"It's all right," Asti said. "Neither of us has to say a thing, right?"

Win nodded. Asti looked back to Kimber, who gave him a little smile and nod. Asti couldn't help but smile back.

The smell of Asti's flop almost killed Verci the moment he walked in. "You actually sleep in here?"

"I've slept in worse," Asti replied, staying at the window, not even glancing at his brother. "But I don't sleep much. I'm here to work."

"Right." Verci fought down the bile rising up his throat. "How's that going?"

"Eh," Asti said. "A few days of observation is nothing. The place is a fortress, I can tell you that. I don't think we could have picked a harder target in Maradaine."

"The King's Palace?"

"Please," Asti said, finally turning away from the window. "I could get in there while clapped in irons."

"Quarrygate Prison?"

"Getting in is simple." Asti winked. "Out . . . that would be a challenge."

"So what's the plan?" Verci asked.

"Still far from one," Asti said.

"Where's the crew at?"

"Mila has a flop above a barber's right by Evans, but she also has a crash in an abandoned mill with her Bessie's Boys."

"That what she's calling them?"

Asti shrugged. "It works. The Kessers rented one of the whitestones on Kenner. How about you and Raych?"

"We've . . . moved into an apartment on Junk Avenue. Above the bakery."

Asti raised an eyebrow. "Renting from the Old Lady?"

"Indirectly." Verci shrugged. He wasn't sure how Asti would take this. "Josie pretty much cleared out of there, locked down most of her rooms."

"She said she would."

"With her not there, Mersh left town . . . I think she sent him away. And he came to us . . ."

"Mersh came to you?"

"I think Josie had him come to us. But he offered it to us, and Raych thought . . ."

Asti snorted with laughter. "Raych wants to run the bakery? Did you tell her that it's, you know, not a real bakery . . ."

"It's a real bakery!" Verci snapped.

"Yes, Mersh actually bakes, and what he bakes is always very good. But he didn't have to actually, you know, run it. Like a real shop."

"He ran it pretty well."

"Yeah, but he didn't have to actually do real business, turn a profit."

"Well, neither do we!" Verci had his back up, and he knew it, but sometimes Asti really pulled his strings.

"True," Asti said. He bit at his lip for a moment. "No,

you're right, you're right. We probably should have some kind of front. Or at least you and Raych should. If we're going to be making debt payments on our lot, we don't want too many questions about where that money is coming from."

"I know that," Verci said. "Raych is actually quite excited."

"Good," Asti said. "That's real good for the two of you."

"So what's the next step?" Verci asked.

"Well, we've got to get some other looks at this place. Mila is on the street level, where she can see around the back."

"You think she's up for that?"

"Girl knows how to shake the hat," Asti said. "She does that on that corner, gets a good view, with her boys keeping watch for trouble for her."

Verci glanced out the window at the corner Asti indicated. "There weren't any serious hatshakers there already?"

"A few old saucers, who usually get chased away by the valets in the evenings." Asti glanced back. "They aren't making a stink about claim. At least, they haven't yet, and if they do, they're nothing Mila can't handle." Verci had to agree with that. They were old men, all bones and beard, long since broken with rotten cider.

"Point," Verci said.

"Besides, what kind of crazy hatshaker would claim the alley outside Tyne's place?"

"So let me get this straight," Verci said, struggling to put the ideas buzzing in his brain into words. "No one would set up serious shop rattling the hat out on Tyne's alley there because it would be dangerous and crazy and possibly get Tyne's attention?"

"Exactly." Asti looked like he didn't even know why he was in this conversation.

"And that's why it would be perfectly safe for Mila to set up shop there?"

Asti sputtered. "Yes, of course it is!" Verci sat down on the bed, ignoring the fact that it was disgusting, and spread his arms as if to invite Asti to explain his reasoning. Asti looked back out the window. "It'll be safe because she's not gonna muscle in or anything like that. She's just a scrappy girl trying a different corner. As long as she doesn't make too much noise, Tyne's thugs won't care."

"Fine," Verci said. "She's the one who figured out about the mage, isn't she?"

"She overheard something," Asti said. "I figured there was a good chance of it already. We'll have to figure out how to deal with that."

"All right." He didn't like Mila being the one most in harm's way. He didn't like anyone in harm's way.

"You've got something else to tell me, don't you?"

Verci was showing it on his face. "I had a bit of a thing with Lesk."

"Define 'a bit of a thing.' "

"He knows we did a job for the Old Lady."

"What he knows—or thinks he knows—doesn't matter."

"And he wants a slice."

"He doesn't get one."

Verci bit his lip. "He's got quite a few people with him. And he's made Larton's Bath and Shave one of his places."

"Is that where he twisted you? Larton's?"

Verci nodded. "He's implied he's got other places in his coat."

Asti scowled. "He's just a distraction. Focus on this job."

"All right. What else do we need to do?"

"We need to look inside, of course."

"How are we going to do that?"

"The way anybody else does," Asti said. "We're gonna get dressed up in our best and take our girls out for dinner."

Verci was surprised at that. "You've got a girl?"

Chapter 19

"**A**RE YOU COURTING ME now, Rynax?" Helene's dark eyebrows arched, her whole face betraying her amusement.

"Of course not," Asti said. Though he had to admit, now that Helene was bathed and dressed in new clothes—a tight purple blouse and vest with matching slacks—she looked more than good enough for a man to want to court her. The sitting room of the Kessers' new apartment was sparsely furnished, but it was clean and bright with sunlight, overlooking Fawcett Avenue just a few blocks away from Holver Alley. Helene looked oddly at ease, even relaxed, as she lounged back on the lone chair in the room.

"You're asking me to a fancy dinner," she said. "Sounds like courting."

"Sure does," Julien said from the kitchen. The big man was sitting on the floor, spreading soft cheese over a huge chunk of bread.

"Julien, what are you doing to me?" Asti asked. "This is about business."

"Courting business." Julien giggled.

"Eat your cheese," Asti grumbled.

"We live right over the cheese shop!" Julien said with wide-faced glee.

Helene gave Asti a bittersweet smile. "The little things that make us happy."

"I never knock good cheese," Asti said. "In all seriousness, this is about scouting the job."

"Never been much of one for scouting, except for finding the best nest for the job."

"I need your sharp eye, Hel," Asti said.

"Speaking of, you can give back the scope you pinched anytime."

"You'll get it back," Asti said.

Helene leaned forward. "So right now your plan is to walk right through the front door of the place we're hitting and pay for dinner for two?"

"Four," Asti corrected. "Verci and Raych will be there as well."

"Isn't that romantic?" Helene said, her smile turning impish. "And the baby?"

"The logistics of that aren't my problem."

"You're slipping, Rynax." Helene shook her head. "We're really hitting Tyne where it hurts by putting crowns in his pocket."

"We need to get a good look at the inside, Hel."

"Fine, fine," she said. "Tonight?"

"That's the idea."

"All right, then. I told you I'm in on this whole job."

Asti smiled. "Never doubted it."

Helene's face fell a little. She glanced over to Julien, and then beckoned Asti closer. "There's something you need to know."

"Nange Lesk is spreading his fingers? And he wants to try and pull you and Julien in?"

"You knew?" Helene's face, for once, looked worried.

"I suspected. He's been butter-or-bashing his way around the neighborhood. For me and Verci, it's been the bash."

"You figured he'd give us the butter?"

"What did he offer?"

Helene rolled her eyes. "Running the Honey Hut. The man's an idiot."

"I presume you politely avoided giving a direct answer?" Asti asked.

"That's the best strategy with him. I don't want to think about it. He makes my skin crawl. Let's just do what we have to for the job."

"Good, let's go," Asti said.

"Go already?" she asked. "It's hardly one bell in the afternoon."

"Right, which only gives me six hours to get you in a proper dress, not to mention suiting myself up."

"Dress?" Helene shrank in her chair. "I really have to, don't I?"

"Got to look the part."

"What do I do?" Julien asked, still gorging on the cheese and bread on the floor.

Asti came over to the kitchen and crouched down in front of Jules. "You know what I need you to do? Go over to Kimber's tonight and sit with Win Greenfield. Talk to him, make sure he's doing well."

"I can do that," Julien said.

"Good," Asti said. "Come on, Hel."

Helene grumbled as she got up off the chair. "Stupid dress."

✺

"What a dress!" Raych exclaimed. She took hold of the yellow and white elaborately embroidered satin dress with a plunging neckline, inlaid corset, and lace collar, all of which Verci had been assured was the very thing all women of substance were wearing this spring. "Verci, that . . . you didn't steal this, did you?"

"Of course not," Verci said. "Stealing a dress would just be pointless. You can hardly get the dressmaker to size it first before you steal it."

"How did you size it?" Raych asked.

"I was asked your measurements and I gave them."

"How do you know my measurements? I've never been measured for a dress like this."

"I know every inch of you, love," Verci said, moving closer to his wife. He gently placed one hand on the top of her head. "Height, five feet four inches." He ran his hand down her dusky hair to the nape of her neck. "Neck, twelve inches around. Shoulders, eighteen inches across." His hands moved around to her chest. "Bust—"

"Stop." She laughed. "All right, Verci, I'll go put this on, and we'll see how good you are."

"You're going to look beautiful, regardless," he said.

"Keep up with the butter and cream," she said. "Just because I'm letting you take me to a fancy dinner doesn't mean I approve of your latest criminal enterprise."

The carriage had been an issue. Asti knew full well they had to arrive as well-appointed as possible, give the full appearance of being people with money, if not birth and substance. Tyne's Emporium really only cared about money. That meant driving up in a carriage or cab. Asti had considered the cab, but that meant a cab number that someone could track down, if they were so inclined, and a driver with no loyalties who could be easily bought or beaten into saying where he had picked up his fare, what they had said, names dropped, and so forth. Not worth the risk. That meant getting a carriage from Kennith. He had quickly repainted the North Seleth carriage so it bore no identifying marks to lead back to the inn, so that hadn't been an issue. The issue was in the driver.

"You telling me I can't drive the carriage?" Kennith paced around the stable, shaking his head in frustration.

"Sorry, Kennith," Asti said. "It'll have to be Almer."

"Why does it have to be me?" Almer asked. He was sitting over at one of the workbenches, mixing up some foul-smelling concoction.

"Because you look wholly unremarkable," Asti said.

"While the Ch'omik would stand out," Kennith snapped.

"You would," Asti said. "Look, Ken, that's just something we're going to have to face here. This is a public scout. Something skunks, or at least pulls the line, there'll be questions. Questions like, 'Oy, didn't their carriage have the dark-skinned driver? I wonder how many Ch'omik carriage drivers there are in West Maradaine.'"

"Bound to be a few," Kennith muttered.

"I'll tell you how many, Ken," Asti said. "There're four,

and two of them work for Tyne, one is an old man with one arm who drives Hennimore Cab 432, and there's you."

"How do you know that?"

"Because I make a point to know these things!" Asti shouted.

Verci stepped forward, putting a hand on Asti's shoulder. "Point is, Ken, that one question brings a handful of thugs pounding on that door. Then we're skunked for certain."

"Fine. Almer drives," Kennith grumbled.

"I hate driving," Almer scowled. "Horses don't like me."

"You'll do fine," Asti said.

"Don't crash it," Kennith added.

Verci stepped forward again. "Ken, I've made some sketches I want you to take a look at."

"Sketches of what?"

"Of that spring drive we talked about."

"You're crazy. That'll never actually work." Kennith bit his lip for a second and then shrugged. "Let's have a look." He and Verci went over to the back table.

"Over here, Asti," Cort said. Asti headed to the mousy man.

"What are you working on?"

"You wanted to know about underground paths into the Emporium. This'll help us find one."

"Really? How?"

Cort held up the rancid-smelling liquid. "Drink it."

"You're kidding."

"Nope." He handed it to Asti. "It's pretty awful, so knock it back fast."

Asti brought it to his lips and his gag reflex kicked in. He bit back the bile in his throat and, holding his nose, threw the noxious concoction down his throat.

It took every bit of strength he had not to vomit.

"Gah," was all Asti managed to say once he could breathe again.

"Now make sure you use the water closet when you're in the Emporium," Cort said. "Much as you can. It won't be easy."

"Why won't it?"

"Because that stuff is going to make your piss like honey. Or maple syrup."

"What?" Asti shouted.

"Also it'll be blue."

"WHAT?"

"And glow in the dark."

Asti had no response to that.

"You should also know that you won't be able to stand to for a day or two," Cort said, waving a hand in the direction of Asti's crotch. "Hope you didn't have any plans along those lines."

"He doesn't now," Helene's voice came from the back stables.

"Shut it, Hel!" Asti yelled back. He wasn't sure who to strangle, her or Cort. "How the blazes will this help?"

"You're going to go into the Emporium and piss in their water closet, get it?"

"And it's going to be glowing, blue, and thick."

"Right," Cort said. "Making it easy to find and track in the sewers. Bright, shining goop leading back to the source."

"These are the things you think of, Cort?"

"I'm also trying to think of a way to deal with the mage problem you mentioned."

"You have anything on that?" Verci asked. "My best idea is avoid the mage and pray."

Asti chuckled. "That plan never works. Anything you got, Cort, I'd love to hear it."

Kennith spoke up. "Probably the best thing to do is find some way to take the mage out of the action before things get started."

"Right," Asti said, "but without anyone knowing we have. That's the key. We can't just drug him or get him drunk, you know?"

Cort's eyebrow went up. "Maybe we could."

"No, it's too obvious."

Cort raised a skinny finger, almost bringing it to Asti's lips, as if to shush him. "Not if the drug doesn't affect him in a way anyone notices. Get it?"

"Yeah, I get it," Asti said.

"Not tonight he won't!" Helene called out.

"Sweet saints, woman!"

"Real shame, too," Helene said as she came out from the

stables. "The one time he's got a girl who looks this good."
Asti stopped short when she came into view, and every
other man in the stable stood agape. Her purple dress hung
off her shoulders, exposing pale skin down to her ample
cleavage. The side of the dress and the petticoats were slit
up the side, showing off her bare leg with each step.

Asti had no idea Helene could look like that.

"Blazes," muttered Cort. "She is a woman."

"Damn right," she said. "Verci, lend me a few darts to
hide in my décolletage. I feel positively *naked* without any
weapons." She clearly shot that one word at Asti, and her
aim was as true as with a crossbow. Where was this coming
from? As long as Asti had known her, she had made hot eyes
at his brother, but suddenly she was giving him everything.
Of course, it was only because of his predicament with Cort's
potion. Once it wore off, she'd surely be back to normal.

"You're just cruel, Hel." Verci laughed as he gave her the
darts.

"You laugh now, Verci," Asti said. "You're the one who's
gonna trudge the sewers with Cort tracking my piss. You
want to go with them, too, Hel?"

"You won't make me, Asti," she said walking up to him.
Patting his cheek she added, "Since you've got such a *soft*
spot for me." Damn her. Still, it was good to see her acting
light and making jokes, even at his expense. If it made her
happy for this gig, he'd take every jibe she threw.

"Kennith, hitch up the blasted carriage. Almer, suit up.
And you're wearing the hat."

"The hat is awful," Almer said.

"If I'm pissing blue honey, you can wear the blazing
hat!" Asti shouted.

"Fine, I'll wear the hat."

Kennith put Verci's sketches on his workbench as he
went back to the stables. "That might be something that
could work," he said to Verci. "I'll see if I can hammer
something together from the design."

"Well," Helene whispered to Asti, "at least someone will
be hammering tonight."

This was going to be a long night.

Chapter 20

CORT'S CHEMICAL WAS CHURNING in Asti's gut as the carriage approached the Emporium. The feeling was not unlike having swallowed a frog. He obviously wasn't doing a good job masking it.

"You all right, Asti?" Raych asked. She looked splendid in the dress, Asti had to admit. Raych was a fine-looking woman, any man would think so, though he never could quite parse what it was Verci saw in her beyond that. Not that he had had the chance to ask his brother at the time. When he had first met Raych, Verci had already married her.

"Fine," he said.

"Just something he drank," Helene added.

Raych looked at the three of them, then looked like she'd decided not to ask anything else.

The carriage came to a stop, and moments later the door was opened by a large man. Asti recognized him as one of the regular front gate guards at the Emporium.

"Good evening, gentlemen, ladies," he said in a distinguished tone that didn't match the westtown accent. "Welcome to the Emporium." He extended a hand to Raych, who took it gracefully as he helped her step out of the carriage.

"Thank you," she said demurely. The valet offered the same assistance to Helene, and then stepped back to allow Verci and Asti to exit the carriage. Asti took a quick glance around. The massive doors were open just enough to allow single-file entrance. Down at the corner, in front of the back alleyway, he saw Mila sitting on the walkway, wrapped in a ratty blanket, blending in with the other hatshakers.

"Round back that way," the guard told Cort up in the driver's seat. "There's a carriage house, and the other drivers. Cards, stew, and cider 'til you're called."

"Wonderful," Cort said. He tipped the driver hat at Asti. "Until you call me, sir."

"Thank you, driver," Asti replied.

"If you will enter here to the coatroom." The guard indicated the open doorway. "Enjoy your visit to the Emporium."

"Thank you," Asti said, offering a coin to the guard.

"I must decline," the guard said. "But I thank you for the thought."

They passed into the coatroom, richly furnished with green velvet and dark oak chairs, and several mahogany wardrobes with gold trim and ivory fixtures. Verci let out a low whistle.

"What you figure?" he whispered to Asti. "Those are an easy hundred crowns each. Just in the front room."

"Valet doesn't even take a tip," Asti whispered back. "Well-bought loyalty here."

A man and a woman worked the coatroom, both dressed in simple elegance. Presentable, but nothing that would outshine the clients, Asti thought.

"Good evening," the man said. "Your pleasure tonight would be?"

"What are our choices?" Asti asked.

"Ah," the man said. "Your first time?"

"Yes," Asti said, "so what can we—"

The woman interrupted him, her voice as sweet as honey. "Then tonight your pleasure would be the dining room."

"Of course," Asti said. "But there are other—"

"Perhaps after you visit the dining room," the gentleman offered, "further membership options can be discussed."

"Wonderful," Asti said, putting on his best fake smile. "I'd be thrilled to discuss it. Then the dining room for the four of us, please."

"Certainly," the woman said. "Your coats and wraps, please, and we can proceed."

"Of course," Verci said, taking off his coat and handing it to the man. The man took it, and with a light and casual motion, he gave Verci's suit a light swipe, as if removing lint or dust. He did the same to Asti, and Asti understood—the man was checking for weapons, if ever so discreetly. He had found none, but only due to the cursory nature of his search. Asti had two knives in his boots, and he knew Helene had hidden a couple darts in her bodice. The woman found nothing on her search of Helene or Raych.

"Very good," said the man. "This way, please." He led them through a heavy velvet curtain into a large room filled with candlelit tables. Most of the tables had couples or groups, all finely dressed, most of whom barely looked up to acknowledge Asti and the rest passing through. Asti recognized several faces by reputation, including two Constabulary District Chiefs, a City Alderman, and a Member of Parliament. The last, he also noted, was definitely not with his wife.

"Is there a problem, sir?" the man asked Verci. Asti noted that his brother had stopped and tapped the floor with his foot.

"Sorry, no," Verci said. "My shoe was loose for a moment there. I think I've fixed it."

"Very good, sir." The man took them to a table in a back corner, where they were mostly out of sight of the rest of the patrons. Asti realized this was probably meant as a slight, but the seating suited him just fine. He could see the whole room, be ignored, and sit with his back to a wall. No one would sneak up on him. That was good.

"Your server will be with you in a moment," the man said. "Perhaps you would like to start with wine, or something else?" The man let the words hang there, like a challenge.

Asti was about to speak when Raych answered the server, her voice a solid punch of confidence and nerve.

"Bring us a bottle of Nitella Red, nothing younger than 1209."

"Yes, of course, miss. I will return shortly."

As soon as he was gone, Raych let out a heavy breath. "Verci, I really hope this plan pays off, because I just ordered a forty-crown bottle of wine, I think."

"Excellently done, Raych," Asti said. "It lets us play the role of contenders without being too ostentatious."

"How is a forty-crown bottle of wine not ostentatious?" Raych asked.

"For most of these people, that's a small token, the least one should pay for quality wine," Verci said.

"Our whole meal will likely cost on the order of two hundred crowns," Asti said.

"That's a lot of outlay for a scout job," Helene said.

"Can't be helped." Asti looked around. "A lot of coin does come through here."

"Good thing we have a backer on this," Verci said.

"What was that about memberships and other options?" Raych asked.

"There're many other choices of depravity here," Asti said. "Girls for hire, boys for hire, a wide gambling floor. Above us, I think."

"Above?" Verci said. "Oh, no, brother. The gambling floor is definitely below."

"You noticed something when you fixed your shoe?"

Verci nodded. "Large hollow space beneath us. Buzzing with activity."

"You'd think they'd muffle it somehow."

"I think there's a layer of cork in the floor," Verci said. "But there's a lot of people."

"Is this going to be shop talk all night?" Raych asked.

Helene grinned. "Probably so."

"Hush it, Helene," Asti said. "Keep your eyes open for people going downstairs."

"As you say, boss."

"You really call him boss?" Raych asked.

"Only because it annoys him."

"That's fine." Raych smiled. "Waiter approaching."

As Raych had noted, the waiter came over with a bottle

of wine. With a nod and polite greeting, he opened the bottle and poured out a sample for Asti. He waited patiently, expectantly, until Asti remembered the protocol and tasted the wine.

It was explosively excellent. He wasn't prepared for that.

"Quite good," he told the waiter.

The waiter nodded and filled the other glasses. "Very well, sir. If I may tell you about tonight's menu?"

"Please," Raych answered, her eyes glowing with anticipation.

"Our chef, as you may know, is one of the finest of the great archduchy of Linjar, brought up special from Yoleanne by Mister Tyne."

"Of course," Asti said. He had to fight down the angry growl that wanted to be released at the mention of Tyne's name.

"So the menu is representative of his specialties. We have a dedicated fleet of fishing ships bringing in fresh catches of sea bass, oysters, and shrimp daily. Any fish you eat tonight was swimming in the Avolic Ocean yesterday morning."

"Impressive," Raych said coolly. "You have shrimp?"

"Yes, madam. Sautéed in a traditional Linjari-style red pepper sauce, served over rice with simmered spinach and beet greens."

"Well, I don't need to hear anything else," Raych said.

"Excellent," said the waiter. "The sea bass is also fresh, grilled with vegetables and Linjari rice."

"You mentioned oysters," Asti said.

"Yes, sir, as a starter course, we have broiled oysters, served to the whole table."

"That sounds excellent," Helene said. "And the sea bass for me."

"What else is there?" Verci asked, "Perhaps in the area of fowl or game?"

"There is both pheasant and rabbit, succulently roasted—"

"Rabbit," Verci said quickly.

"Pheasant," Asti added.

"Very good, sirs," the waiter said. "We hope you enjoy

everything here at Tyne's Pleasure Emporium." He walked away.

"Well, this should be very interesting," Raych said.

"Our work does seem to have some perks, love," Verci said.

"One or two, it seems." Raych smiled and sipped at the wine.

"This is work, though," Asti said. "Eyes sharp, eh?"

"Eyes sharp," Verci returned. "How tall is the building?"

"I figured eight stories," Asti said. "I'm starting to think a lot of that space is employee barracks. Quarters for all the people working for Tyne."

Verci glanced about. "Possibly. What leads you to that?"

"I watched the place for a few days straight, and I've got Mila on the back alley. I didn't see a lot of the kind of movement in and out that you'd expect for a place with this much activity. I see two score servants and waiters just on the floor here. Then there's the kitchen, which would have to have as many. The gambling floor, as we've heard. Not to mention—"

"The whores," Helene said.

"Yes, exactly," Asti said. He turned to her. "In fact, you hear plenty about how Tyne has a wide variety of women."

"Foreign and exotic," Verci added. Raych glared at him, and he shrunk away. "It's what I hear."

"But where are they?" Asti asked, half to himself. They weren't evident in the dining room, nor had he seen any sign of them coming in and out. If they existed, they had to live at the Emporium all the time. Same with Tyne, whom he had yet to see.

Verci leaned forward. "We need to get a better look around. What are the goals?"

"Coin, frankly," Asti said, shaking off his earlier thoughts. "I couldn't care less about who lives here and does what. A lot of money comes in here and apparently stays here." If Tyne had sent large sums of cash out the door, Asti had seen no signs of that, either.

"Where do you think?"

"Best guess, if the gambling floor is below us, that's

where the big money is moving. It goes down there and stays down there."

"Safe?"

"Vault," Asti said.

"Fair enough," Verci said. "How do we size up the underground?"

"You and Cort are going to trace the sewers, for one," Asti said. "We need to figure out how to get to the gambling floor."

"Membership," Helene said. "How do we get one?"

"That I don't know," Asti said.

"Air flues," Verci said absently.

"Air what?" Asti asked.

"There're no windows on the outside, right? And a fair bit of space below ground, which we figure has plenty of people going in and out. Plenty of people need to breathe. They need to see, so that means oil lamps. Blazes, look." He pointed to the candles burning in chandeliers above them. "Fire needs to breathe, too."

"So fresh air has to get in there somehow." Asti nodded. "That a way in?"

"Probably not," Verci said. "You'd have to be pretty foolish to build flues big enough for a man to crawl through."

"So what good is it?"

"If they aren't big, then there has to be a lot of them," Verci said. He looked around the dining room and casually pointed at a part of the wall. "See, they cover it with a pretty silver grate, but there's one of them there."

"I don't get what he's talking about," Helene said.

"Flues and chimneys draw bad air out of the gambling floor," Raych said.

"Yes, I understand that, Raych," Helene said. "How does that help?"

"You obviously never lived in a tenement house or above a shop floor," Raych said.

"No, just the house that Tyne burned down," Helene snarled.

"Ladies," Asti snapped.

"It's pretty simple," Verci said. "There's sure to be plenty of ventilation flues that lead down to the gambling floor, if that is indeed what's below us. And where air flows, so does sound."

"Find a flue, press your ear to it," Asti said, nodding. "We can hear what's going on downstairs."

"Might be nothing," Verci said. "But it would at least confirm what's below us."

Asti stood up. "I guess now I'll do my part."

"Water closet?" Verci asked.

"Water closet," Asti said with a grimace. "I'm not looking forward to this."

Asti walked off across the dining room floor. His insides were churning, even burning, making it rather difficult to focus his attention on anything else. Searching for a water closet gave him a good excuse to innocently walk through wrong doors, stick his nose places he shouldn't. He wouldn't even have to lie, since he didn't know where the water closet was.

What he didn't want was for a server to ask him what he needed because then they would direct him to the water closet. So he went to a curtained corridor in the back of the dining room with a fast, confident stride. Anyone glancing at him would see a man who knew exactly where he was going and how to get there. If caught, he'd just have to play the part of a man certain that this was where the water closet was and too arrogant to ask anyone for confirmation.

The servants here probably had ten men like that a night.

No one stopped him on his path to the curtain, leading Asti to think that perhaps, indeed, this was just the way to the water closet. The corridor had several doors, all of them rather ordinary looking. He took this to mean that he was someplace he wasn't supposed to be, which was exactly where he wanted to be.

He tried one door. Locked. The next door was as well. He walked briskly down the hall, trying each door briefly without slowing down. Locked, locked, locked, unlocked. He opened that and peered inside. Shelves of clean linens, servant uniforms. No flues, grates, or pipes. He shut the door and moved on.

The next door was unlocked. This was a laundress press-room, with drying racks and stoves for heating the presses. The room was quiet and cool at the moment, but there were plenty of pipes lining the wall. He grabbed a candle off the wall and slipped inside.

With quick motions, he touched each of the pipes. Water was running through them, some hot. There were probably furnaces in the basement. Another pipe was larger and felt empty. He placed his ear to it.

"Twenty! Twenty on blue!" he heard. "That's the winning spin. I'm so sorry, sir. Thank you, thank you. Place bets again, double on color, double on color."

The sound echoed from below. That clinched it. The gambling floor was definitely on a basement floor.

"Three thousand on fifteen-red!" said another voice, an older man. Accent implying high privilege and from a northern archduchy. Possibly noble birth, at least educated.

"Fifteen hundred on twenty-blue!"

"Four thousand on five-no white!"

"All bets in, all bets in, spinning!" the dealer called. Asti could hear the spinner whirling, the rattling of something rolling. "Five! Five on white!" A jubilant cheer.

"Big winner!" the dealer called out. "I have a payout here!"

A sharp step approached, and a deep voice spoke. "What's the payout?"

"Four thousand on a match with double-color," the dealer said. "So that comes to . . ."

"Thirty-two thousand crowns," said the deep voice. "Congratulations, sir. If you will come with me, we will go see Mister Tyne."

Tyne was down there. The vault was down there. Asti was certain of that.

Asti checked more pipes until he found another empty one, and heard two voices.

"Blazes is that?"

"Two duck plates, one rabbit plate, and three orders of bread. For Ecrain."

"That's the second order."

"Where does it go, you know? Ecrain is so blazing skinny."

That clinched it—Ecrain was definitely the mage. Asti didn't know a lot about mages, but he did know, the more they ate, and the skinnier they were, the more powerful they were. A powerful mage meant Ecrain was definitely Circled, though if they were working here, it was one of the more morally flexible Circles. Asti didn't know which that would be, but it didn't matter. This Ecrain was going to be a big problem.

Someone was in the corridor. Footsteps stopped right outside the door. Asti crossed the room and got to the door just as whoever was out there started to open it. He took the handle and yanked it open as strongly as possible.

"Where the blazes is the water closet?" he asked in his most belligerent voice. The serving girl stumbled from the door being yanked away from her. She looked up at Asti in confusion.

"Sir, you . . . you shouldn't be—" she stammered out.

"I've been wandering up this hallway looking for the blasted water closet. You think you could put a sign or something. I don't have all night, you know!"

"Of course, sir, of course," she said, her head bowed. She was a young girl, no more than eleven or twelve. Her skin was lightly golden, her eyes narrow. It occurred to Asti she was of mixed birth, part Druth, part somewhere eastern. Imachan, Xonoca, even Tsoulja. "This way, if you please, sir." She cowered as she spoke, like she was expecting to be hit.

"Thank you," he said, suddenly feeling guilty for shouting at her. He wondered if she was the child of one of the "exotic foreign" women that Tyne specialized in.

She led him out of the corridor back to the curtain. She stood back once they reached it, clearly refusing to cross through it to the dining hall floor. "Out there, there's a green door near the entrance. That will bring you to it."

Asti gave her a coin and went back out to the dining floor. Once out there, two servers came over to him, with looks of troubled concern on their faces. He mouthed "water closet" and pointed to the green door. They both nodded, and one of them walked with him as he went over. Fortunately, they did not actually escort him into the water closet. The last thing he needed was someone watching him for this.

"How did it go?" Verci asked when Asti returned.

"That may have been one of the most uncomfortable experiences of my life," Asti said. "And I've been tortured by professionals." He took a piece of bread from the basket on the table.

"That bad?" Helene asked. For once she actually looked legitimately sympathetic.

"Yes," Asti said. "But like the man said, glowing blue and thick as honey."

"Lovely," Raych said.

Asti noticed the empty plates on the table. "Did you eat all the oysters?"

"They were delicious," Helene said.

"I hate you all."

"What did you learn?" Verci asked.

"Gambling floor, the mage, Tyne, and the vault are definitely below us," Asti said.

"We saw someone go down to the gambling floor," Verci said. "There appears to be a password."

"Did you hear it?"

"No," Verci scowled. "They whispered it closely."

"The chef is not from Linjar," Raych added. Everyone looked at her.

"How do you know that?" Asti asked.

She took a piece of bread from the basket. "This is a heavy bread, the dough enriched with cream and butter."

"It's delicious," Asti said.

"It is, but it's not Linjari. A Linjari bread is only flour, water, salt, and yeast. This bread is from a chef from an inland archduchy. Monim or Oblune."

"Are you sure?" Asti said.

"I know bread," she said.

"She really does," Verci added.

"So . . . why would they lie about the chef?"

"I don't know," Raych said. "I'll tell you more when I have the shrimp."

"Does that help you?" Helene asked.

"Every bit of information helps," Asti said.

"How about this, then," Helene said. "Why is that guy looking at you?"

Asti looked where she pointed. The guy in question was wearing a uniform of the Emporium. He was definitely looking at Asti. He was definitely walking closer. He was definitely . . .

"Blazes," Asti muttered.

"What?" Verci asked.

"Miles Kinter," Asti said. "Formerly Druth Intelligence."

"Are you saying?"

"Yes," Asti said through gritted teeth as he forced his face into a warm smile. "I just got made."

"Asti Rynax," Miles said as he walked up to the table, his hand outstretched. "What in all blazes are you doing here?"

Asti stood up and took Miles's hand. "Miles, I could ask the same."

"Had to go somewhere when I left the service," Miles said. "Assistant head of security for Mister Tyne."

"Very nice," Asti said.

"I'd suggest something for you—Tyne is always looking for good heads—but if you're sitting in here for dinner you must be doing all right."

"Pretty well," Asti said.

"I heard you were going into toys."

"Gadgets," Verci said with a reflexive defensiveness.

"Yes," Miles said. "Your brother, if I'm not mistaken. Verlin?"

"Verci."

"Of course," Miles said. He grinned warmly, but Asti knew Miles—or at least the kind of man Miles was—far too well. He was humoring them, getting a read, and not buying a word they were saying.

They were skunked.

✧

"Are we skunked?" Verci asked in the carriage ride back.

"I think we may be," Asti said.

"We bailing, then?" Helene asked.

"Like blazes we bail," Asti said hotly.

"But you said—" Raych started.

"I know what I said," Asti said. He was fuming. "Miles will figure that something is up, but there's no way he can know what. He'd probably figure we are scoping the place as a first step to muscle into the territory, find out what kind of racket we could squeeze into the neighborhood."

"So what do we do?" Verci asked.

"Play the part," Asti said. "Let's let them think we are some hot-blooded small-timers trying to make a mark in protection or street rattle or doxy trade or anything."

Verci nodded. "And the last thing they'll think is that we'd actually try to crack their vault."

"Because it's a crazy thing to do?" Raych asked.

"Pretty much," Verci said.

"Verci Rynax, what kind of insane, godforsaken, stupid thought goes through your blasted mind that makes you think that I'd ever get behind such a stupid plan?"

"Raych," Asti said, as calm as he could make his voice. It still came out as a bark, startling her into silence. "What do you want to do? Don't you want to stop Tyne? Make him pay for what he did? Keep him from doing it again to another part of our neighborhood? Kill more people we know? Kimber? Hexie? Your sister and Hal? There's not a person he wouldn't think twice about stepping on."

"And no one else crazy enough to go after him," Raych said, her voice losing volume and confidence.

"Except me," Asti said. "And you can say it, Raych, and say it to my face, because I know damn well you think it."

Raych stammered, her eyes filled with tears. "That's not what—"

"You think it because it's true. I am hair-ripping, bug-eating, elbow-deep-in-blood crazy. I know it, Raych. You'd probably be safer sharing a carriage with a hungry bear."

"Asti, you aren't—" Verci started.

"Yes, I bloody well am, brother," Asti snapped.

Helene spoke up, her cold eyes locked on Asti. "Are we talking that you're a bit wild and unpredictable, or more that we're going to have to lock you in a box before much longer?"

"The box," Asti said.

"No, Asti," Raych said, reaching across the seat to him, but holding back before she actually made contact. "I'm sure it's not as bad as that."

"I've got all my springs wound up and ready to pop, Raych. Best chance we've got—best hope I have at all—is to hold myself together long enough for you all to aim me where my madness might do a small bit of good."

There was no sound for several seconds, save Asti's own heavy breathing and the creaking of the carriage wheels.

Helene finally broke the silence. "We've got a gig to plan, then, don't we?"

Chapter 21

ASTI WAS BARELY ABLE to stand in the morning, the pain in his stomach was excruciating. Sleep had been in fits on the bench in the stable, with Helene regularly bringing him water and a vile-tasting brew Almer had left for him.

Helene had surprised him, spending the whole night in the stable, keeping an eye on him. Verci and Almer had left almost as soon as they had gotten back to the stable, off to plumb the depths of the sewer system beneath the Emporium. Asti had wondered how much sleep she managed to get herself, between his moaning and Kennith's tinkering in the back of the stable.

"How bad are you?" she asked when the gray light of dawn came through the window.

"I've been sicker," Asti said. "There was a mission I was on—"

"No," Helene said. She touched his forehead. "How bad are you? Should I be getting a box ready?"

"I can hold up," Asti said. "I can get this job done."

"And then the box?"

"And then the box," Asti said. "Though I'd rather . . . I'm gonna put something on you, Hel."

"I thought Cort's potion kept you from doing that," Helene said.

"That's not what—"

"I know," she said, her voice low and warm. "What do you need?"

"If it comes to that point, where I need to be locked up? If I'm just gone, and I'm not coming back . . ."

"You want an arrow in the head," she said flatly.

He nodded. Verci loved him too much, he could never do that. Helene, he knew, only liked him enough to do him that kindness.

"I'll do it, but I'd rather it didn't come to that," she said, sitting down on the stable floor, her back to him. "After all, if I kill you, Verci would never speak to me again."

Asti laughed, but laughing tore up his insides more. Helene gave him more of Cort's recovery brew, and he drifted into another doze.

Julien arrived shortly after sunrise, bearing a basket filled with cheese, bread, and cured lamb. Asti risked eating some of the bread. He recognized it as Raych's handiwork, light and crisp, and it made him feel far better than anything else he had tried.

"Did you see Win last night?"

Julien nodded. "Sat with him in Kimber's all night."

"How's he doing?" Asti asked.

"He didn't talk much," Julien said. "Neither did I."

"That's fine," Asti said.

"He eats slowly," Julien added. "But he kept eating all night long. Four bowls of stew!"

"His appetite is back," Asti mused. "Did he say anything? Ask you anything?"

"He asked me when he could go home. I didn't know what to tell him." Julien shook his massive head. "What's home going to be for him, Asti? He can't live at Kimber's for the rest of his life."

"I don't know yet." Asti sat up on the bench, his guts flaring when he moved. "Verci and Cort damn well better find something in the sewers."

"I'm not gonna drink anything Cort gives me ever," Julien said.

"Wise plan," Helene said. "Are we going to do something for Win, boss?"

"We're doing it, ain't we?" Kennith called from the back. He came out, his leather smock covered in grease and dirt. "Isn't this whole plan about doing right for everyone hurt in the fire?"

"Yeah, but—" Helene faltered. "Where do we stop? I figure, we pull this off, we'll have a fair pocket of scratch, sure, but where does that stop? We set Win up? What about everyone else?"

"Do we try and rebuild the alley?" Julien asked.

"Pff," Helene said. "Alley was a hole."

"It was our hole, though," Julien said.

"And our people in there," Asti added. "I don't know yet. There's . . ." He stopped. Pieces didn't all add up. Missing connections. Something he wasn't seeing.

"There's what?" Julien asked.

"Not sure," Asti said.

Someone pounded on the door, four short, two long, one short. Kennith went and opened it. Mila strode in, holding up a hat full of silver.

"I had a good night," she said. "That's a damn good perch, but I got a few ugly glares from the valets."

"They try and knock you?" Asti asked.

"Nah," Mila said. "But they made it clear not to get too close to the front doors. Or to wander down that alley. Could never get a good look in there. Verci and Almer are coming up the lane, by the way. I ran ahead because they stink."

"I'll get some hot water," Kennith said. As he went in back, the two of them came in. They were covered in filth and dirt, and the stench was awful. With his stomach the way it was, Asti almost threw up when the scent hit him.

"I hope to all the saints that was worth it, Cort," Asti said.

"Wasn't easy," Cort said.

"I've had enough of sewers for a long time," Verci said. He pulled off all his sewer-soaked clothes, showing no care about any modesty. Mila gasped and turned around. He threw the clothes into a pile. "We should just burn these."

"Right," Cort said. He tentatively followed Verci's lead in undressing, giving a nervous glance to Helene, who was only smirking with a raised eyebrow as she kept her gaze on Verci. After a moment of indecision he collected the clothes Verci dropped and retreated to the back of the stable. Kennith came back with a bucket, filled to the top with hints of steam curling off of it. Verci grabbed it and poured it over his head.

"So what did you learn, brother?"

"That Tyne is serious about his security," Verci said. He took the sponge Kennith had silently offered and vigorously scrubbed at his hands and arms. "We found the trail of piss you left for us, just like Cort planned, and we found where the water closets from the Emporium empty out. Was not pleasant. It's all lead piping, heavy brick masonry. Metal grating everywhere. Not a crumb of it is crumbling."

"No way in through there?"

"Not really," Verci said. "I do have some good news, though."

"We really could use some," Helene said.

"Is he dressed yet?" Mila asked, her back still to the rest of the room.

"Not at all," Helene said.

Asti ignored the women. "What's the news?"

"The water closet pipes carry sound pretty well, long as you don't mind putting your ear to them."

"Ugh," Mila said.

"Couldn't hear much," Verci said. "But I got enough to figure that the gambling floor is all along the western half of the building. The counting offices and the vault are somewhere in the southeast."

"That's something," Asti said, "but hardly good news."

"Ah, but I learned that underground, the eastern edge of the basement abuts another basement. A wine merchant from across the street."

"That is something," Asti said. He went over to the slate board and started sketching out a rough map of the Emporium and the area around it. "We can't do too much more scouting, you know."

"Not anymore," Verci said.

"Why not?" Mila asked, turning to the group and then quickly turning back when she saw Verci.

"Calm down, girl," Helene said.

"He's married!" Mila hissed at her.

"Lucky wife," Helene muttered.

"Helene," Asti said, giving her a signal to turn around.

She laughed a little and shook her head. "I've got no problem here."

Asti didn't need her games on top of everything else. "Seriously, brother, put something on, would you?" Asti said, throwing a pair of Kennith's trousers at Verci. "I doubt Raych would approve."

"You'd be surprised," Verci said, giving far too impish a grin for Asti's taste. Despite that, he pulled the trousers on.

Mila was still resolutely facing the wall. "Why can't we scout anymore?"

"I got made," Asti said. "Part of the security team was an old colleague from Druth Intelligence."

"A former spy works for Tyne?" Mila asked.

"It's common," Verci said. "Lot of his guards are probably ex-army."

Asti drew the wine merchant's shop on his map. "All right," he said. "We get into the wine merchant's shop and find the abutting wall. What then? Knock through it?"

"So it's a punch-in job," Helene said.

"Can't just punch in," Asti said. "He's got too many guards. We start hammering that wall, they'll not only line them up on the other side, they'll sent a squad into the wine shop. We'll be pinned."

"We don't hammer," Almer called from the back. He skittered out, a burlap sack wrapped around his naked waist. "I've got a different idea."

"How fast and quiet can it get through the wall?" Asti asked him.

"Very fast," Almer said. "But, ah . . . not quiet."

"How not quiet?"

"Deafeningly loud."

Asti sat back down on the bench.

"Won't work?" Verci asked. "Do we . . ."

"Just hush a second," Asti said. "Fast and loud, all right.

So then it really is a punch in." Ideas were slamming through his head, scenarios playing. He ran a plan in his head. That one failed. Tried a different one. Failed. He moved pieces around. Still failed. Another. Failed. Another. Failed.

"Here're the problems," Asti said. "We need to get some people inside quiet, onto the gambling floor. Other people will hammer through from the wine shop. We need to be able to hit in hard, at the same time keep the guards from getting to where we hammer in. Give ourselves two routes of escape. Clear the ways to bolt with the crowns. Get them to our carriage and make a fast escape that they can't follow."

"How do we get to the gambling floor quiet?" Verci asked. "We'll need a password and someone to go down there."

"The password is 'Queen Mara,'" Mila said.

"How did you know that?" Asti asked.

"One noble couple was discussing it before they went in," Mila said. "They probably didn't realize I could hear them. Or care."

"Chalk one up to rich and stupid," Helene joked. "We still need to get access to the wine shop."

"Right," Asti said. "The rest is pointless if we can't get in there."

"Any ideas?" Verci asked.

"There's the fast and easy way," Asti said. "Muscle in, crack some heads, take it over."

"No," Julien said.

"I was just—" Asti started.

Julien pounded a massive fist on the table, cracking it. "No! That's what they did when they burned us out. We'd be no better!"

Julien Kesser was rarely an angry man. His large, muscular body and brutish looks made him frightening in appearance, but his demeanor was usually so calm that Asti had never before felt threatened by him. In that moment, a jolt of fear shot its way up Asti's spine, hitting him deep in that chained beast in the back of his skull. He stumbled back away from Julien, grasping at the wall.

Verci must have spotted something was wrong with Asti. He quickly stepped in front of Julien, placing a hand on the big man's arm. "No, you're right, we can't do that. We wouldn't do that. It's not the code, right, brother?"

"Right, right," Asti stammered out, fighting off the urge to lash out, fighting his own racing heart.

"What code?" Kennith asked.

"Dad's rules," Verci said. "About who you can do something to. Like, he said it's all right to kill guards, because they know what they signed up for. It's fair. This wine merchant, he's just doing business. He doesn't deserve to get hurt because he's in our way."

Asti wasn't listening to his brother. The panicked rage was still pounding at his skull, barely contained. He forced himself to breathe slowly, to sit back down on the bench.

"You all right?" Kennith asked.

"Cort's drink still doing a number on you?" Verci asked.

Asti was grateful for the cover. "Yeah. I . . . I just need a few more hours, and I'll be pure silk."

"Good," Verci said. "So we need to get unfettered access to the basement of the wine merchant, right?"

"Right," Asti said.

"Plus we're going to need to get someone credible on the gambling floor. Who can be a big spender, right?"

"Right," Asti said, now grinning. He knew where Verci was going with this. "So we're going to the theater today?"

"Blazes," Helene said. "Pretty dresses, fancy dinners, and now the theater? This gig is loaded with culture."

Verci hadn't taken a bath yet when they got to the West Birch Stage, and he didn't stand out from the rest of the audience. The farther west one went in Maradaine, the more water closets became a rumor. People who lived on this block would claim they lived in Seleth, but people in Seleth would say this was Benson Court. The cobblestone road was riddled with cracks and holes, which were filled with proof of the lack of proper sanitation in this neighborhood.

"You sure he's here?" Verci asked.

"Sadly, yes," Asti said.

The West Birch Stage was a rickety, rotting mess of moldy wood and tattered curtains. Verci imagined that the whole thing would come crashing down if it got knocked too hard. A misspelled sign in the front advertised that the show playing was *The Marrage of the Jester*.

"I'm fairly certain that *Marriage of the Jester* is banned in the city," Asti said.

"Maybe that's why they are doing *Marrage* instead," Verci suggested. "Maybe that's a different show."

"Maybe." Asti snorted with laughter. "Instead of the whole cast rolling each other onstage, they disembowel the jester."

"The audience will love that," Verci said. They paid the bored-looking porter two ticks each and entered.

The scene on the stage confirmed that it was the banned performance, as most of the actors were in the process of ripping the dress off the bride. The actress playing the bride was in even worse shape than the theater, likely a *phatchamsdal*-dosed doxy well past her working prime.

Only one actor was not part of the scrum, an older man with a thin face and hair salted gray along the temples. Costumed as a priest, he was out on the front thrust, giving an impassioned speech on the sanctity of marriage, the importance it plays in society, and how two souls joined such were blessed beyond all others.

No one in the audience paid any attention to him. They were in a howling frenzy, fueled by the rest of the action onstage. One of them finally clambered up onto the stage to grope at an actress. Emboldened by the line being broken, the rest of the crowd charged up and leaped into the action. The older actor, clearly anticipating this, sprang to the side of the stage and grabbed a curtain. He dropped down to the ground, away from the screaming mob.

Despite being offstage and the audience being in a sex-crazed fit, he finished the speech.

Verci had to admit, it was a good speech.

Shaking his head, the man walked to the door of the theater.

"Isn't there some axiom about leaving them wanting more, Pilsen?" Asti asked.

The man looked up at the two of them, standing alone in the back of the theater, and his sad eyes brightened immediately. "Well, now! This is quite the surprise! How are you, boys?"

"Seen better days," Asti said.

"Haven't we all." Pilsen glanced back and forth at the two of them. "The answer is going to be no."

"We haven't asked you anything yet!" Verci said.

"I am aware of that." Pilsen gave a disgusted look at the debauchery up on the stage. "You know I once played Maradaine the First at the Kester?"

"I remember," Asti said. "Dad took us."

"Your father was a decent sort," Pilsen said.

"Why are the constabs not shutting this down?" Verci asked. Shows like this were banned for a reason, though they rarely played anywhere other than in the poorest parts of any city.

"A few coins—and preferred seating—to a few of them does the job for now." He sighed. "Sadly enough, that's all it takes." He gave another glance at the stage. "Fine, boys, let us leave this fetid pit of copulation and go someplace where you can tell me whatever stupid plan you have, so then I can tell you no properly."

"Why do you think the plan is stupid?" Asti asked. He looked more than a little offended.

"It would have to be," Pilsen said with a shrug. "It's brought you to me."

Pilsen gave a slight wave to the porter as they walked out into the street. "Ah, West Birch. Where everything good and decent in the human spirit goes to die."

"I'd ask you not to be so dramatic," Asti said.

"But then you remembered who you were talking to, hmm?" Pilsen said. "There's a place around the corner where the beer isn't completely rancid."

"Well, Pilsen, when you sell it like that, how can we possibly refuse?" Verci said.

"I'm nothing if not charming," Pilsen said. He leaned closer to Verci. "Have you been swimming in the sewers, boy?"

"Yes, I have."

"Whatever for, Verci?"

"He was tracking after my piss," Asti said.

Pilsen stopped in the middle of the square. "Are you both playing with me?"

"Not at all," Asti said.

Verci put on his best little-boy voice. "Swear to the saints, Mister Gin."

"I never bought that when you were a kid, Verci," Pilsen said with a laugh. He led them around the corner into an alleyway. "Oh, I should mention before we go in, address me as 'reverend.'"

"You're conning them for bad beer?" Asti asked.

"I use every resource I have at my disposal," Pilsen said, gesturing to his outfit. "Though, to be fair, they assumed I was a man of the cloth before I ever suggested it."

"Which you didn't discourage," Verci noted.

"Blazes, no."

They entered the dingy pub, a cramped space dug out of the foundation of a tenement, with a dirt floor and a mélange of tables and chairs, obviously built from scrap wood. The old man behind the bar shouted, "Door!" when they came in.

"Close it," Pilsen whispered. "He has a thing."

Verci shut the door behind him. The old man hobbled closer, one leg a wooden stump. His face was almost consumed by an enormous shaggy beard, but a scar running over one eye was visible under it all. "You ever serve?" he shouted at Verci.

"Serve?"

"In the war!" he roared.

"The war?" Verci asked, glancing over at his brother.

"Against the Poasians!"

"No, I . . . I was nine years old when the war ended."

"That's no excuse! I was on a ship where a boy of seven killed five of them! With his bare hands!"

"Now, Hentle," Pilsen said. "You know you shouldn't—"

"And you!" The old man's gnarled hand lashed out and grabbed Pilsen by the front of his priest outfit. "I was told what you are! An actor in that filth around the corner!"

"I give ministry to those poor souls—"

"You owe me thirty crowns!" he bellowed. "Pay me now or I'll crack your fool head open!"

"Thirty?" Pilsen asked. "I couldn't . . . perhaps, boys, you could . . ."

"Blazes, Pilsen." Verci started fishing into his pockets, but before he got any farther, Asti had leaped onto the old man. Verci reached out to stop Asti from killing him, not sure what he could do if his brother was in another fury.

A second later the old man was on the floor, and Asti had stepped away, his face completely calm. In his hands were the man's beard and wooden leg. Verci looked back to the man, who clearly wasn't as old as he had first thought, and had no scar, and possessed two perfectly good legs.

"Really, Pilsen." Asti shook his head disapprovingly. "You were trying to shake us for thirty crowns?"

"Same as I would anyone else." Pilsen shrugged and pulled himself to his feet. "Consider it a test to see if you were worth working with at all."

"Did we pass?" Verci asked.

"He saw through my disguise!" the barman said. "I thought it was very good!" He looked on the verge of tears.

"It was very good," Pilsen said, kissing the man on the forehead. "Asti, tell him it was very good."

"It really was," Asti said. "Future reference, old sailors never call it 'the war with the Poasians'. It's usually 'the Island war.'"

"And that's why I tell you, research, research, research," Pilsen said to the barman. Now that Verci got a good look at him, he really was quite young.

"All right," the young man said. "Beers all around?"

"Yes," Pilsen said. "So, boys, as you can see, I've got a comfortable little niche carved out here in the bowels of the city. So whatever crazy, stupid thing you are doing that you need my inestimable skills for, I am not interested, and nothing you will say will change that."

"We're robbing Mendel Tyne," Asti said.

Pilsen's eyes flashed with hate. "Then I'm in."

"I expected more argument," Verci said.

"Tyne and I go very far back," Pilsen said. "Before you boys were born. You're going after him, I want a piece of that."

Pilsen's young friend put a hand on his shoulder. "Is he the—"

"Yes," Pilsen said hotly. He turned back to Asti and Verci. "What's my part?"

"Two parts," Verci said. "First there's a wine shop where we need unfettered access to the basement."

"And we don't want to go the hard muscle route," Asti added.

"Why?"

"I think it's because of morals," Asti said.

"More of a code," Verci said.

"Morals? Code?" Pilsen raised his eyebrows at the two of them. "The two of you?"

"Consider it a matter of degrees," Verci said. "We've got reason for going after Tyne. But this wine merchant . . ."

"Doesn't deserve to get caught in the middle of it," Pilsen said. "So you need to get in his place without actually hurting him or his business." He nodded approvingly. "I can think of a few ways to do that. Have you scouted him at all?"

"Not yet," Asti said. "We should put Mila on that."

"Better eyes than you?"

"No, just . . . I have to limit my exposure in the neighborhood."

"Tyne's security made him."

"I don't remember you being sloppy, Asti."

"I wasn't sloppy!"

"He wasn't," Verci said. "One of Tyne's men worked with Asti before."

"Ah," Pilsen said. "Fair enough. Had more than one job soured by that. What's the second part?"

"We need someone to go into the gambling floor at Tyne's," Verci said.

"Play the big money." Pilsen's eyes sparkled. "A man of substance. Title. Position." He nodded eagerly and got to his feet, pulling off his priest coat with a flourish. "I will accept the role!"

"Do you need another . . ." the young man asked from behind the bar.

"No, puppy," Pilsen said, holding up a hand to his friend. "This is a job for the big dogs."

"I can—"

"I said no," Pilsen said sternly. "I couldn't stand it if you got hurt."

"All right," he said. He looked quite put out.

"Besides, I need you to keep the store open here," Pilsen said. "This will take a few days."

"What about the play?"

"Pff," Pilsen said. "I doubt they'd even notice I was gone. If you really want, you can go play the priest."

This seemed to please the young man.

"Good," Pilsen said. "So now what?"

"Meet us tomorrow morning in the Birdie Basement up in North Seleth."

"There?" Pilsen said. "That's a worse hole than this place."

"That's the place," Asti said with a shrug. "We didn't pick it."

"All right, go," Pilsen said. "See you there. I've a bruised ego to mend."

"This is coming together, right?" Verci asked as they walked back up Junk Avenue.

"It's coming," Asti said. His head was throbbing. The effects of Cort's potion had passed, at least the most noticeable ones. Now he just needed sleep. He had been going on pure willpower for days now, resting only in spare moments. If he was going to finalize a solid plan of what exactly they would do so that they had the best chance of success and survival, he needed a solid night of pure, untroubled sleep.

At least, as untroubled as he ever got nowadays.

Verci cleared his throat. "One thing I'm worried about—"

"Only one thing?"

"One thing that's standing out. Presuming we get to the vault, that's got to be a serious lockbox. We have no idea what he's got in there."

"Yeah," Asti said. "I'd been thinking about that. You don't think you could crack it?"

"Maybe if I knew what 'it' was, exactly, I could give you a meaningful answer."

"Right." Asti looked down the street. The bakery was just a block and a half away. Standing a further half block away from it were four men, all tall and imposing. One of them was Miles. None of them were specifically minding the bakery. Instead they were watching the crowd in general, moving methodically along the street.

"Verci," Asti hissed. "You found a back way into the bakery?"

"Well, sure," Verci said. "There's a ton of secrets in there, of course, I haven't gotten a chance to—"

"Use it. Get Raych and the baby down below."

"What is it?"

"Go!" Asti was off in a run, down a side alley. Once he was behind a wall, he glanced back to the street. Verci was gone. He would get in there and get his family secure. Asti relaxed a little. That was the most important thing.

He peered around the corner. Miles and his men were continuing to walk down the street, past the bakery. Were they scouting it or just checking the whole neighborhood? Asti considered the possibility that their presence had nothing to do with him. It was unlikely, but Asti couldn't discount it. If he just ran, just hid, he'd never know.

If they were looking for him, then he'd need to know why.

Blast.

He checked over his coat and vest. He was carrying only two knives. He made a mental note to not go anywhere without being heavily armed. He wasn't even wearing his father's belt.

"Stupid, stupid, stupid," he muttered to no one in particular. They were almost to the junction of Junk and Rabbit. Rabbit gave him a good, straight run away from Junk and the bakery. He palmed one of the knives and slid it up his sleeve. He walked back onto the street, taking a quick pace to reach the corner before they noticed him.

He stopped at an apple cart right on the corner. He put on the air of walking casually, stopping to muse over the apples while going about his day. The shop window behind the cart was dirty, but it still reflected well enough to see

Miles and his men. Sure enough, after a moment, they spotted him and approached.

They made a slow approach, walking with purpose but without drawing notice to themselves. Asti was impressed. It confirmed that their intentions were not in his best interest. Miles knew well enough not to sneak up on Asti unless he actually was trying to sneak up. If he really wanted a friendly chat, he would have called out to Asti by now.

Time to make a move.

Asti grabbed an apple and spun, throwing it as hard as he could at the biggest, tallest one of Miles's bruisers. It hit the man square in the forehead, and bounced back to knock Miles in the back of the head.

Asti hadn't planned that, but it was impressive. For a second he was so surprised he forgot to run.

Chapter 22

VERCI SLIPPED DOWN THE ALLEY to the backhouse, which looked like it had been nailed shut and
abandoned. He reached around the back to knock the catch
that opened the real door. In a moment he was inside and
latching the entry behind him. One thing he admired about
Josie's system—every secret entrance he found could be
completely barred off from the inside. This place could be a
fortress if he needed it to be.

He pounded up the narrow staircase that led to the
apartments. "Raych! Raych!" He called out before he even
emerged from the hidden entrance into the rooms.

"Saints, Verci, what is it?" She came into their sitting
room, clutching the baby to her chest.

Verci stopped, glancing her over. He had to actually see
that she was fine. "Just you and Corsi here? No one else?"

"No, of course not. What—"

"No time," he said. He brought her over to the hidden
stairwell. "I told you this place is full of secret places."

"I know, it's kind of—what are you doing?"

"Getting you where it's safe. Come on."

"Safe, what?"

He brought her to a room he figured was Josie's lock-
down room—hidden away by the ovens. It would be nearly

impossible to find even if someone took a hammer to the brickwork.

"Someone came looking for Asti, and me. And that means you and the baby."

"But Verci, I thought—"

"In here you'll be safe," Verci said. He pointed out the various features of the room. "There's a tap for the well, a water closet right there, you can stay in here for days if you need to."

"Days?"

He didn't respond to that. "Over here there's a cone and a lens. Put your eye to the lens, you can see out into the front room of the bakery."

"Really?" She took a look. "That's amazing. How ..."

"Ear to the cone, and you can hear what's out there. Now this is important." He went to the door. "No one will find you two in here. There isn't even a way to open this door from the outside once you pull this bar in. Which you'll do as soon as I leave."

"Leave?" She shook her head in disbelief. "Why would you leave?"

"Asti was going to draw those guys away from here. But he won't be able to handle them alone. He needs—"

"I need you, Verci! Don't leave me here ..."

"This is the safest place you can be. I need to know you're safe. And I need to know Asti is as well. You two and him are all I have."

Raych nodded. "Go."

"When I come back, if I don't ring the bell over the doorframe twice, do not come out. Do you understand?"

"Don't come out unless you ring the bell twice. Yes. What if you don't come back tonight?"

Verci thought about it for a moment. "If I'm not back by dawn tomorrow, then Asti and I are both dead. But I will be back."

"Go," she said. "Go while I still can let you."

He went out the door, back into the hidden staircase. In a moment he heard the click of Raych pulling the bar.

She and Corsi were safe. He went back out to the alley, and prayed to the saints it wasn't too late for Asti.

Asti didn't run, but only for a second. Then he turned down Rabbit and bolted as fast as he could. A shout from Miles and the scuffle of boots let him know the four of them were right behind him.

Rabbit was a crowded road, filled with pedalcarts and street sellers, wooden signs and cloth awnings, and score upon score of people. Hawkers, buyers, newsboys, dicers, hatshakers, doxies, and dozers. Several hundred things to trip him up when what he needed was some clear distance between himself and the bakery. It was a hell of a run to have to make, especially since he needed to make it look like he was trying to lose the bruisers, without actually losing them.

Lucky this was his neighborhood. Three blocks south, he'd have been totally skunked.

Five steps into his run, he ducked under the elbow of a woman carrying a basket of cabbages. Two more steps, he bounded up onto a mulecart, used it to ramp up his speed so he could leap onto the stone doorframe ledge of one of the whitestone tenements. The ledge was little more than a foot's width, but it was enough for him to take four more steps and jump down. He just landed on the iron banister with the ball of his foot and flipped down to the cobblestone street. Two more steps let him roll under a passing carriage and spring up on the other side, right in front of Jonet's Clay Bowl. He glanced back at his pursuers, still trying to barrel their way through the crowd, and dashed into the restaurant.

Hot paprika and roasted garlic—the pungent odors of Fuergan cooking—assaulted Asti's nose as he burst through the door, immediately arching backward to avoid colliding into a tray full of noodle bowls. He spun around and darted in the tight openings between the tables. Jonet ab Gessin yelled a few harsh, accented words at him as he pressed his way through to the back stairwell.

Seconds after he had left the floor, he heard the crash of bodies and the shatter of clayware hitting the floor. Asti bounded up the steps as more shouts in Fuergan were accompanied by the sound of several punches.

Asti chuckled. Jonet and his co-husbands wouldn't care whose men the bruisers were. Never knock over a Fuergan's food.

Asti sprinted down the corridor, pounding through the nearest bedchamber—which clearly surprised one of Jonet's wives—and leaped out the window. Fortunately the window of the next apartment was open—Asti hated to crash through glass. He rolled to his feet and went right back to running as he flew out of the confused family's apartment.

He ran down another corridor to the end of the white-stone, out another window, leaping onto the gutter drain of the next building. In the narrow alley he slid to the ground and rounded back out onto Rabbit.

He glanced back to see the four men still being ha-rangued by angry Fuergans and bolted off down toward Fawcett. Near the corner he glanced back again. They had spotted him and were back in pursuit. Good. If he had ac-tually lost them he'd have to do something really obvious to get their attention. That would have been unseemly.

Asti dashed back down Rabbit, ducking and weaving past the various human and inanimate obstacles that appeared in his path. He could tell by the clamor behind him that Miles and the others were coming like a cattle stampede.

He was only twenty yards away from Holver Alley, from the Gadgeterium. That was as good as any place to let him-self get caught. He could even make it look natural.

He leaped up to grab a protruding beam from the husk of the building, choosing one that looked like it wouldn't take any weight. It snapped as soon as he took hold of it, sending him back down to the ground hard. He was more than ready for it, rolling with the fall while keeping the bro-ken beam in his hand. As soon as he was on his feet one pair of hands grabbed hold of his shoulders.

Asti smashed the beam across the bruiser's head. The big man went down. Left with only a small piece of wood in his hand, he hurled it in the face of the next man racing at him. That one took it in the eye, and he dropped down, squealing in pain.

The third bruiser charged in with his fists first. Asti

dodged to one side, grabbing the man's wrist, then used the man's own charge to throw him through the wall of the Gadgeterium.

Then Miles was on him. The other three were grunts; he could spar with them all day without breaking a sweat. Miles was a different story. He delivered a rapid series of blows at Asti's head and body, which Asti barely repelled.

Asti struck back with a few powerful swings, which Miles efficiently blocked. Asti didn't have time to drag this out. It wouldn't be long before one of the bruisers was back in the game, and then he'd have more of a fight on his hands than he was ready for. He'd have to go for the kill, and there were already too many people watching, people who knew exactly who he was. The last thing he needed was for the constabs to get into his nose, and a few dead heavies would do exactly that. He had to take the whole business off the street.

Miles punched again, a little too strong, giving Asti the opening he needed to dodge to one side and grab his arm. He swung Miles's whole body around, but Miles didn't let him let go. They both went flying through another part of the wall of the Gadgeterium.

Clutching onto each other, the two of them went rolling along the cracked and ash-strewn floor. Asti used the confusion to draw the knife out from his sleeve and get it to Miles's neck. At the same moment Miles pressed a knife to Asti's neck.

"Good chase, Rynax," Miles said.

"Not my best work," Asti responded. Despite the lightness in both their voices, they kept their blades pressed firmly against each other's necks. Miles only needed a hint more force to break Asti's skin.

"So what are you doing, Rynax?"

"Me? I'm just buying apples when four guys try to press me."

"Don't even try," Miles said. "You lost your place here, and you know the scraps of westtown aren't worth spit. So like any pirie, you get greedy and think no one will notice you trying to carve a slice from a better pie."

"Keller Cove is a pretty big pie," he said.

"Not so much that we don't notice you getting a flop, bringing in a group of running boys to shake the hat."

"It's a good place to shake," Asti said.

"Shake west of the creek, where you and yours belong."

"I don't belong anywhere, Miles," Asti said, his voice growling more than he intended.

Miles glanced over at his men, who were now grouped over by the hole in the wall. With a wicked grin, he looked back at Asti. "Oh, that's not true, Rynax. You didn't sell when you could have, so this place is all yours." In a flash he swept out one leg while swiping with his blade. Asti fell to the ground, slicing Miles with his knife only superficially. He grabbed at his neck, blood seeping through his hands. The wound wasn't bad, Miles wasn't going for the kill. It was just enough to keep him down long enough for Miles to get to the exit.

"It's quite fitting, Rynax. It may be a burned-out hunk of nothing. But it's your nothing." He kicked at one of the few supporting beams still standing, half ash and charcoal. It cracked through. He and his men laughed and ran out.

Asti clambered to his feet. Blood oozed from his neck as he made his way over to the hole in the wall. The walls around him creaked and cracked. One step smashed through the floorboards, his foot caught. With a wrenching yank, he pulled it free. The cracking and tearing sounds around him grew louder, more urgent. The old girl had taken all that she could. Asti stumbled out into the sunlight as the building crashed down.

Holding the blood in as best he could, Asti looked back at the collapsed building. He didn't know when he had started crying; he just knew that he had been for some time. The beast in the back of his brain strained at its chains, screaming incoherently for blood, for pain, for all the blasted tossers to die. He clamped it down, held himself in check with every ounce of self-control that he had.

A hand touched him on the shoulder. He almost lashed out, his head snapping to look at whoever dared to come close to him, see who risked losing that hand.

It was Win Greenfield.

"Come on, Asti," Win said. "Let's get that looked at, all right?"

Asti nodded, letting Win lead him down the alley. He noticed his pants were torn, so he reached down and ripped off a strip and tied it around his wound.

"Can you speak?" Win asked.

"Think so," Asti rasped out. "It's not as bad as it looks."

"Looks awful."

"They didn't want to kill me," Asti said. "I think if they had, they would have."

Win glanced back at the mouth of the alley. "Were they—did those guys have something to do with the fire, Asti?"

"Them specifically?" Asti shook his head. "Don't know. But they work for the man who had it done."

"I didn't know," he said absently. They had reached the other end of the alley. Win looked at the pile of ash and debris that had been his home and shop. "I guess they didn't care who died that night."

"They wanted it all cleared out," Asti said. "I don't think anything else mattered."

"Like clearing out bugs." Win laughed emptily.

"Where are we going?" Asti asked him.

"Kimber's. Doc Gelson is only half drunk by now."

"Good enough."

Kimber shrieked when Win carried Asti into her pub, and she quickly ushered the two of them to Asti's old room. Asti caught a glimpse of himself in a mirror and could easily tell why. Not only was he covered in ash and blood, he was as pale as a Poasian. Win helped Asti onto the bed, and a moment later Kimber brought in Doc Gelson. Asti could smell a lot of cider on the old doc's breath, but he still managed to sew a steady stitch. Win stayed sitting quietly on the edge of the bed the whole time.

"That's it," Gelson said when he finished stitching. "Rest up. I'll have Kimber bring you something hearty to eat and drink. That's what you need."

"This is ugly business you're in," Win said once the doctor left. "What's it all for?"

"I think you know what it's for," Asti said. "The man who did this to all of us, who took away our homes, our lives . . . there's no justice he's going to face. Not proper justice."

"So it's got to be you?"

"It's got to be done, Win."

"And you've got nothing else to lose." Win nodded. "How can I help?"

"Win, that isn't ..." Asti started, but he was interrupted by the door opening again. It wasn't Kimber, though. Verci was there with a fish pie and a glass of wine.

"I see you've been busy," he said.

"Raych and the baby safe?"

"Of course," Verci said.

"How'd you find me here?"

"Followed the trail of destruction to the alley and then the trail of blood here."

Asti chuckled. "I wasn't exactly subtle today." He told Verci briefly what happened with Miles.

Verci flashed a nervous glance at Win. "So what will we do now?"

"For one," Asti said, "you said you didn't know if you could crack the vault quickly. So Win's going to be our box-man."

"Your what?" Win asked.

"You can crack locks and safes, yes?"

"Well, sure ..." Win said.

"Then you're our box-man."

"Are you sure, Asti?" Verci asked. "I mean, with what went down today, we're pretty well skunked."

"We're not skunked."

"Are we not clear here, brother, on what we mean by 'skunked'? How can we possibly pull off anything now?"

"Because it's a degree of scale, Verci," Asti said. "They think we're small fish, trying to nibble their crumbs. They would never guess we're hunting the big cat."

"That had too many euphemisms," Win said. "What are you talking about?"

"We're not doing what they are expecting from us," Asti said. "They're never going to expect us to do the huge job we're trying to pull."

"I'm not sure we can," Verci said.

Asti cut into his fish pie and took a bite. "Oh, I'm pretty sure now. All the pieces are in place."

"You're crazy, you know?" Verci said.

"I'm well aware of that." He sipped at the wine. "Now, gentlemen, I'm going to eat this, and then I'm going to try and sleep until morning. Please let Kimber know of my intentions. Tomorrow morning the three of us, and the rest of the crew, will meet with the Old Lady at the Birdie Basement. Spread the word, brother, to be there at ten bells. You both better get some rest as well, because tomorrow night might just be the biggest gig of our lives."

Spreading the word had been easy. Finding Mila was the only challenge. Verci had kept his head low the whole time. Miles and his bunch of goons probably had their eye out for him, and he wasn't going to let them have a chance to do to him what they did to Asti. But the crew knew about the meeting, and he could relax—at least try to, given the circumstances—until the morning.

The sun was nearly down when he got back to the Junk Avenue Bakery. He stopped outside for a moment, staring at the sign hanging over the door. It could be easily repainted to read "Rynax Bakery". Or even "Rynax Bakery and Gadgeterium". He liked that.

Not a good idea, though. Had to keep a low profile. Look legitimate, but don't draw too much attention. Another one of Dad's rules for getting by. Dad was big on trying to blend in. Though Verci had to admit, Dad had never been good at it.

He went inside, shutting and latching the door behind him. Then he reached up and rang the bell two more times. "It's safe."

He went up to the apartment, lit the lamps, put the teakettle to boil. He was starting to pull some cold lamb and cheese out of the icebox when Raych emerged from the safe room, Corsi swaddled in her arms.

"Is this going to happen a lot?"

Verci answered as honestly as he could. "I really hope it doesn't."

"Hope?"

"I don't know what else I can tell you, Raych." He laid out the lamb and cheese.

She sat down. "I just . . . I can't live my life with people coming after us."

Verci went to the cabinet, pulled out a bottle of wine that Mersh had left behind. "I don't think we really have a choice about that, love."

"If you and your brother stopped this crazy . . . oh, saints. Asti is all right, isn't he?"

"He got hurt, but he'll live." Verci opened the wine and brought it over to the table.

"So you see? We have to stop now before . . ."

"Before what, Raych? Before they burn our home down?"

Raych bit her lip, then went to place Corsi in his cradle.

"These people were already after us, you see? It may not have been personal, but they came after us just the same."

"It's not the same."

"No, it ain't. Now we're not some shopkeeps and renters they can muscle in on."

"Right," Raych said acidly. She came over to sit at the table. "Now you're the Rynax brothers."

"Now we're ready for the fact they're after us. Now we're handing back to them."

"But why do we have to be?"

"Because this is where we live, Raych. It's where I live, where you live. Where Hal and Lian live."

"Yes, I know, but . . ."

"Do you want to move out of here? Head west into Benson Court or something?"

"Of course not."

Verci poured out the wine. "East up? Dentonhill? Aventil? Corsi will have his choice of street gangs there."

"Blazes, no!"

"Leave Maradaine altogether?"

"No."

"So we have a choice, Raych. Let these tossers put us under their boot, or fight the bastards."

"When does it stop, Verci? When are we safe?"

"I don't know. I do know, if we do nothing, these tossers will run rampant over the neighborhood, and we never will be."

Raych sipped at her wine.

"How long?"

"We're doing this tomorrow."

"So you could be killed tomorrow."

Verci drank his wine. "I could. I could regardless whether we go forward tomorrow or not."

"True," Raych said. "But you're going to do your damnedest not to, you hear?"

"Damned right I am," Verci said. "I've got plenty of reasons to live."

"At least two," Raych said. She grinned wickedly, and gulped down the rest of her wine. "I better make sure one of them is firmly on your mind tomorrow."

Like a spring, she burst from her seat and grabbed Verci by the front of his shirt and kissed him. He stumbled backward, barely staying on his feet from her passionate onslaught. He returned the kiss, while her hands tore down his suspenders.

For just a moment Verci considered that he needed to put his life at risk more often.

Asti dozed lightly. Nightmares of Levtha came with deeper sleep—not just the torture, but the layers of mental defense, the explosion of violence, visions of his hands pulling out the entrails of Poasian archers as they shot at . . . images were lost.

Someone knocked, then opened the door. Kimber stood there in her nightdress, carrying a candle. "Asti?"

"I'm sleeping," he said.

"I heard shouting. I wanted to . . ."

Asti sat up. "I've been asleep. No shouting."

Kimber came in, shutting the door behind her. "I heard you shout, Asti."

"What did I shout?"

"Little things. 'Come with me.' 'Go!' Things like that." She sat down on the bed.

"I . . . I must have had a nightmare."

"You think?" She leaned in, gingerly touching the dressing on his neck. "I wonder why that happened."

"Kimber, what are you doing here?"

"Worrying about you, Asti Rynax." Her eyes were wide, slightly wet.

"Really? I'm . . . not sure I even know what that means." He thought she was about to kiss him. He wasn't quite sure how he felt about that. "Why do you worry about me?"

"I saw you, the day after the fire. You were angry, and bristling. But you also had your eye on everyone. Win, and Helene and Julien. And Hexie. I saw how much you cared about this neighborhood. But . . . I could see in your eyes how much you . . ." She closed her mouth and turned away.

"How much I what?"

"Hated yourself."

Asti didn't know what to say to that.

"I could see it in you, Asti. You're the kind of man who will throw himself in front of an arrow to save a neighbor. But I think that's partly because you want that arrow for yourself."

"I don't want to die, Kimber," Asti said. He touched the dressing at his neck. "Came too damn close today."

"Maybe that was a good thing," Kimber said. "Sometimes to find God, you have to get pretty close to him."

"I don't know about that."

"Maybe for someone like you, it's more like getting too close to the blazes of damnation to know how hot it is."

That was the problem. Tomorrow he would have to go into Tyne's blasted pit. Maybe that was the only way he could do it—get in as deep as he could stand to, look the bastard in the eye.

"What's going to happen to you tomorrow, Asti?" Kimber asked, touching his hand gently.

"I . . . Verci and I have a bit of a job to do. Cross town."

"And when that's done, are you coming back here?"

"To your place?"

"If you need to. Or make your own here. In the neighborhood."

"That'd be nice. If I can do that, Kimber, I'd like to."

She nodded. "There's hope for you yet. You should try and sleep." She didn't make any move to leave.

"What are you going to do?"

"Keep watch."

Asti took her hand and held it tightly for a moment, and then let it go. He lay back down and shut his eyes. For the first time in months, he fell asleep quickly.

Chapter 23

IN HER TWENTY-SIX YEARS Helene had never been in a place like the Birdie Basement, though she had heard plenty about it. She praised whatever saint had watched over her life that she had never had to resort to going there to make a living. She didn't even want to step inside now, just to meet with Missus Holt and the rest of the crew, but this was where Rynax said to meet.

"Don't we need to go in?" Julien asked as they stood outside the door. The entryway was recessed at the bottom of a stairwell, half hidden under the offices of an import agent. She had always assumed the agent was a front for smugglers.

"Asti said ten bells," she told her cousin. "I'm not stepping in a second sooner than I have to."

"They might be in there already," Julien suggested.

"Then they'll wait for us." Helene glared at Jules, who had a far too eager expression on his face for her taste. "When we're in there you keep your blasted eyes down, you hear me? I don't want your eyes—or your hands—going someplace they shouldn't. Hear?"

"You were staring at Verci yesterday."

"I was not staring, I was—that's completely different."

"I don't really think it is."

"And that's why I do the thinking, Julien."

Julien pouted, making him look very much like a little boy, save for the fact that he was nearly seven feet tall.

"I'm guessing you two are waiting for the same people I am." An older gentleman, thin and drawn, approached the two of them. He was dressed in a suit that looked like it had been the height of fashion ten years ago, but was now threadbare and faded. His quick eyes darted at the two of them, and he gave them a quick smile.

"What do you think that for, old man?" Helene snapped.

"Because you're looking at the door of that place like you'd rather eat your own hand than go inside." He gave Julien another look up and down. "Aren't you a tall one?"

"Yeah," Julien said.

"Why don't you step off?" Helene said.

"Because, like you, I'm waiting for those charming Rynax boys, who said we were to meet in this ill-reputed establishment, though why here I have no idea."

"Who are you?"

"Of course, how exceedingly rude of me." He took Helene's hand and kissed it as he bent down in an extravagant bow. "Pilsen Gin, master of stagecraft."

"Stagecraft?" Julien asked.

"He's an actor," Helene said.

"Absolutely, my dear," Gin said. "Though I'm sure it is the baser aspects of my talents that our dear Asti and Verci wish to exploit."

"What did he say?" Julien asked.

"That he's a con artist."

"Guilty," Gin said. "Though I would never say such in a court of law."

The door of the Birdie Basement opened and Asti was standing there, glaring at the three of them. "Would you three stop blabbering out in the street and get in here?" Asti's neck had a horrible gash, crudely stitched shut.

"What happened to you?"

"Nothing that won't heal. Come on."

Reluctantly Helene stepped into the place. The inside stank of mold, sweat, and rotten perfume. The stone floor stuck to her boots with each step, and Helene didn't even

want to think what it was sticking with. Her eyes adjusted
to the dim candlelight, and then she could clearly see the
girls.

Two were on the crude stage, wearing nothing but stockings and corsets. One of them she figured to be Mila's age;
the other was old enough to be her mother. Both of them
danced with blank expressions on their faces, specifically
fixing their gaze on a part of the room where there were no
men. As for the men patronizing the place, they littered the
floor around the stage haphazardly, all of them regarding
the two girls dancing with as much interest as they could
muster.

The idea passed through Helene's mind that neither the
girls nor their clients gave a damn if they lived another day.

"Ah, depravity," Gin said from behind her. "One never
lost money supporting it."

Another girl walked up to Helene, slightly more dressed
than the two on the stage. "Oy, aren't you a pretty raven?"
she said with a Waish accent thicker than the paint on her
face. She reached up to touch Helene's hair. Helene slapped
the woman's hand away.

"Don't touch me," Helene snarled. She glanced back at
Julien, who was blushing furiously. He looked over at her,
swallowed hard, and ducked his head.

"We're seeing the boss," Asti said, leading them to the
back of the room and through a shabby curtain. They passed
through a dark hallway with several doors on each side. The
sounds from behind each door turned her stomach. Helene
was no maiden; she appreciated a good roll when the opportunity suited her. This struck her as nothing like that; the
sounds she heard were desperate, soulless. Pathetic. Nothing she wanted any part of.

Asti knocked three times on one door. After a moment
Helene heard the loud snap of a latch being undone, and
the door opened. Verci stood there, with his far too pretty
smile and piercing eyes. He stepped back and let them enter. The rest of the group were already around a small table,
lamps and candles all around. Mousy Almer Cort sat
hunched over one corner, fiddling with a few bottles of
some concoction. Mila, with her dark hair and darker eyes,

stood up against the wall, her expression showing she was as disgusted by this place as Helene was. Kennith, his black Ch'omik face lost in thought, probably piecing together some mechanical puzzle. Most surprising was Win Greenfield, looking for all the world like a rabbit with a sky full of hawks.

Sitting in a chair at the head of the table was, Helene presumed, the woman herself, the grand dame of the Seleth underworld: Josefine Holt. Helene had heard plenty of stories about her. As with the carriage job, she had worked on gigs that were for her; one couldn't help it in this neighborhood. But this was the first time she had ever seen her. She was surprisingly small and stout, but even sitting in a dingy room in the back of a depraved hole that couldn't even be considered a proper brothel, the woman had presence.

Pilsen Gin made straight for her. "Josie Holt, you glorious creature, I should have known you'd be in the center of this madness."

Holt smiled at Gin like he was a dog begging for scraps. "Pilsen. Asti told me he had brought you in on this." Helene noticed that Missus Holt had grabbed her cane when Gin approached her, clearly preparing to crack him across the face if he got too close.

"It's been far too long, Josie. Last time I saw you, you probably could have shown all those girls out there how things are really done on that stage."

"What?" Verci said incredulously.

"You boys are far too young to have known it, but in her day, Miss Josie here could dance."

"I had no idea," Asti said.

"She'd even make my knees shake, boys," Pilsen said, taking a seat at the table. "And that, I can tell you, is an accomplishment."

"Enough, Pilsen," Missus Holt said, her tone giving the discussion all the finality needed. Pilsen seemed chastised, nodding quietly to her. "Well, Asti. You think the gig needs to go tonight?"

"Tonight?" Helene was surprised. This all was happening a lot faster than she had expected.

"It's a hot iron kind of gig," Asti said. "But we've got to

hit all the parts like the church clock, you hear? No sloppy mistakes this time."

"It was your sloppy mistake last time, Asti," Helene said.

"True enough." He drew a deep breath. "First off, we have to secure the wine shop. I want that in place today, and have it clear all throughout the night. Pilsen, that's on you."

"It most certainly is," Pilsen said. "I hope you don't mind, I took the liberty of moving on that right away."

"Not at all," Verci said. "What did you do?"

"Well," Pilsen said, leaning back in his chair, "my poor little puppy was very put out that I wasn't going to let him play, so I decided to let him help with this one. Anyway, we did a variant on an old gag, a bit I'm going to call 'Caskets of Nitella Red.' I'm presuming there is some overhead available on this whole operation, yes, Old Lady?"

"What do you need?"

"Three hundred crowns is all," Pilsen said. "The usual scam involves getting someone who fancies himself an expert on something, and paying him a small fee to come and verify the quality of a product, and then there's a bit that turns left and boring, boring, boring, and in the end you have his money and he has a whole lot of nothing. This is actually much easier to pull off since we don't need the bit that goes south or the fake goods. Just my sweet boy leading the merchant to a warehouse all the way up on the north side of the city, where there will be no goods at all, and there may be some shouting and possibly the Constabulary and I'm talking too long. Simply put, at three bells this afternoon, the merchant will lock up and leave, and he won't be back until the morning. I presume, Verci, you retain the skills to get inside without further help from me?"

Verci seemed very amused by Pilsen's whole speech, but through his chortling he managed to nod.

"Excellent," Asti said. "Once we're in there, if my memory of the block is correct, there is a loading dock for the wine shop around the back. Kennith, you'll be staging our escape carriage there."

"It should be ready," Kennith said. "I could use Julien's help for the rest of the day to set it up."

"All right," Asti said. "After the carriage is ready, you, Cort, Greenfield, and Verci will be in the wine shop."

"And the rest of us?" Helene asked.

"Mila, I'm putting you on lookout at your hatshaking spot. Most of our trouble will come from inside the Emporium, but if something turns left out front, we need to know."

Mila nodded. "Got it."

"Your cadre of street boys ready?" he asked her.

"They aren't much of a cadre."

"I need them to do one job," Asti said. "I need Corgen Street clear when we give the signal, which should be just before midnight. Can you get that done?"

Mila nodded. "I think I can wheedle that out of them."

"What about Julien and me?" Helene asked. Asti seemed to be avoiding that, which couldn't be a good sign.

"You aren't going to like it," he said.

"What are we doing?"

"Pilsen will be going to the gambling floor, in disguise. You and Julien will be going with him."

"Inside?" Helene really hated that plan. She liked to work from at least three hundred feet away from the gig and didn't want Julien anywhere he might have to fight anybody.

"That's how it's gotta be," Asti said.

"I'll be playing my part of an important man with a lot of money to waste." Pilsen gave Helene a leer. "A man like that wouldn't go out without something pretty on his arm — and I'm talking a ripe piece of woman flesh like yourself — "

"You're disgusting," Helene said.

"And a bodyguard. That's your big boy there."

"Asti!" Helene snapped. "There's got to be another way!"

"I have always wondered," Missus Holt said softly, "what it was, exactly, that made people tell me you two needed to be blacklisted. Most people complain about Julien, that he can only do simple tasks. But that's true of so many big guys like him. So I really think he wasn't the problem."

The room went quiet. Helene was too terrified to say anything in response to the woman.

"No, I think the problem was you, Helene. You don't know when to shut your blasted mouth and do the damn job."

She never raised her voice. Not a hint. Helene would have preferred if she shouted. Then she could shout back or storm out. The calm, controlled tone of Missus Holt shook Helene to the core. That, and the confirmation of what Helene had always suspected: she and Julien had been put on a blacklist, and that's why no one had hired them for any gigs in a while. No one except the crazy Rynax boys. Helene looked back at Asti, who despite every bit of flack and lip she gave him, still believed in her and Julien. She had no idea where he got that confidence in her.

"All right," Helene said. "But won't they recognize me from the other night?"

"Not when I'm done with you," Pilsen said. "No one in this room will recognize you."

"Plus I made this for you," Verci said, pulling a corset out of his satchel.

"Your wife know you made me underthings, Verci?"

"This isn't just any corset," Verci said. He turned it around and opened up a seam. "Several hidden pockets for tiny arrows."

"And a tiny crossbow?" she joked.

Verci opened another hidden pocket. "It's flattened out, but it can be assembled pretty easily."

"Hand it over," Helene said, grabbing the whole corset. She dug out the clever little device and started snapping the pieces in place.

"I can't swear to it being especially accurate," Verci said.

Helene held up the completed device to her eyeline. It could easily fit in her hand, but there was no way to calibrate it. There wasn't much to keep the shot true. Every time it was flattened and refolded, its inaccuracy would increase. "That's for sure. Give me a couple hours to get a feel for it. But I wouldn't be able to hit much more than twenty feet away."

Cort coughed, but didn't look up. "I treated the tips of the arrows as well, so be careful with them."

"Treated them with what?"

"A compound that should give just about anyone severe itching and swelling," Cort said. "And fast, too. But I can give you a salve to counter it, in case you scratch yourself."

"That's not your big jobs, you two," Asti said.

"What're the big jobs?" Julien asked.

"First this," Asti said, holding up a necklace.

Helene chuckled. "Underwear, now jewelry?"

"The stones are fake," Asti said, pointing to the seven hanging pearls along the necklace. "When Cort does whatever he does to the wall, it'll make a lot of noise. We need some full-blown chaos when that happens. Throw one stone into any fire. Lamp will do just fine."

"And then what?"

"There'll be a loud crack and a ton of smoke," Cort said. "Those seven should be more than enough to fill the whole floor."

"That's not that big of a job," Helene said. "What else?"

Asti looked down at the floor. "You know that we've got a good idea there's a mage working for Tyne, named Ecrain."

"Oh, no," Helene said. She wasn't going to deal with a mage.

"This goes on all three of you," Verci said. "We need you to do it."

Verci asked, and that made her guts jump. She hated what she said next.

"So what do we do?"

Cort held up a little vial filled with clear liquid. "Almost no taste, hardly any odor. Get it in Ecrain's food or drink."

"What'll it do?" Helene asked, taking the vial from Cort.

"Magic requires a certain focusing of thought, from what I understand," Cort said, looking to Asti for confirmation. "He has that in his system, he won't be able to stay focused on anything. But subtle. He won't act strange, just seem oddly distracted."

"How, exactly, do you expect us to do that? Like how to spot him?"

"Pilsen, you can make a mage, right?" Asti asked.

"Quite well," Pilsen said. "Once I've found him, I'm confident this lovely thing will be able to distract him enough to slip him this little surprise."

Helene was really starting to dislike the old man.

Verci coughed. "Beyond those things, I also have a hunch they've got some kind of system for keeping people on the gambling floor when something goes wrong. Crash down gates or something."

"You want me there to open the gates?" Julien said.

"You'll want to," Asti said. "Once things go crazy, the three of you get out. Fast as you blazing can."

"And what are you doing all this time?" Missus Holt asked him.

Asti's eyes darted around the room, assessing each member of the team. "I'll be going in with Verci," Asti said. "And with any luck, we'll cut a path right to the man himself."

"But the money first, right?" Missus Holt asked.

"Right," Asti said. "Verci and I get Greenfield to the vault, he cracks it, and we get as much cash out as we can carry."

"Cort and Kennith as well," Missus Holt said. "I want us to clear out that vault if we can."

Asti scowled. "Cort, yes."

"Yes?" Cort chirped.

Asti nodded. "You can do it. Kennith I want ready to drive that carriage out. When we've got the money out and loaded, give Mila the signal, and she'll clear the path."

"What's my signal?" Mila asked.

Verci reached into his satchel and pulled out a big brass bell. "Ring it three times, Ken."

Helene couldn't help but laugh. "Simple enough."

"Sometimes simple is best," Verci said. "At this point we'll have bashed down a brick wall and smoked out a room, so we don't have to be subtle."

"It's got to be hard and clean, Asti," Missus Holt said. "We don't just give Tyne a bloody nose, understand?"

"I understand," Asti said.

Missus Holt shook her head at him for a moment. Helene got the impression she didn't have full faith in Asti or the plan.

"At the signal, everyone get out of the area, get yourself across the creek back into Seleth. We regroup at the stable."

"Not there," Missus Holt said. "Paper trail back to me is too direct."

"Then where?"

"There's a dock warehouse at the end of Junk Avenue," Missus Holt said. "Green walls, white awning, number seven. That's the spot."

"You're the boss," Asti said.

"What next?" Verci said. "Helene's got to get dressed and practice with her new toys."

"Do that at the stable," Asti said. "Pilsen will get her disguised. Kennith and Julien will work on the carriage. Cort, get all the supplies you need there. Mila, get yourself ready and then go keep an eye on the wine merchant, make sure that place is cleared out when it needs to be. When's sunset today?"

"Around seven bells," Verci said.

"Then we'll get into place around eight bells."

"Good," Missus Holt said. "Now all of you get out and do your jobs." She got to her feet and slowly limped to an alcove in the back of the room.

"Warehouse on Junk?" Verci asked when she left.

"She has her fingers everywhere," Asti said. "Everyone should walk over there and give the place a glance. Separately."

Helene flattened out the crossbow and slipped it back into the corset. "All right, let's go." The idea of running her part of the gig inside the place, having to deal with a mage, scared her more than she wanted to admit, but she wasn't about to let anyone else know that. She grabbed her cousin by the sleeve and pulled him along. Fast as she could walk she went down the dark corridor, out through the stage floor, brushing past the dancing girls, and kicked open the door. She had never been so happy to see the sunlight.

Asti didn't talk much with Win as they went back to Kimber's. Win didn't engage in idle chat, not anymore. All they needed to do was stop in, pick up Win's few belongings, and bring them over to the stable. Simple job, and then they'd be off the street until it was time for the gig.

Asti's mind wasn't much on chatting. Or anything but the gig. The brunt of the risk was on his shoulders for this gig. That was right, that's how it should be. If nothing else, if the night ended with him dead but Verci and everyone else getting away safely, he could accept that. He wasn't worried about what Tyne's men might do to him.

Kimber's taproom was crowded, surprising for the early hour. Asti started to go upstairs before he noticed out of the corner of his eye that it wasn't crowded with customers. Nine people, all on their feet, some armed. Kimber backed up against the bar. Only one person sitting down.

Enanger Lesk.

Asti went straight in. "Blazes is this?"

"This?" Nange asked, sipping on a Fuergan whiskey that must have come from Kimber's private stock. "This is just an understanding between local business people. Nothing to worry your pirie head about, Rynax."

"You all right, Kimber?" Asti asked.

"I'm not hurt," she said. Her face was full of fear.

"You want these folks out of here?"

"Please."

"You heard the lady, Lesk." Asti moved over to the table Nange sat at. "You and yours should get out."

"I have to say, Rynax, you've got stones in you." Two of his boys came in close to Asti, knives in hand.

"I know this bloke," one of the boys said. "He's the one what killed Poul and Tummer."

Asti sneered at the boy. "So you were one of the punks trashing Cort's shop. Lovely."

"Rynax," Nange said. "You're a smart man, and you understand that steps need to be taken. This neighborhood isn't safe anymore."

"Because of the likes of you."

"Me?" Nange got to his feet, picking up his whiskey glass. "Four blocks from here a carriage was smashed open and eight people killed. I had nothing to do with that, did I?"

"Asti?" Kimber asked.

"Just go in back, Kim," Asti said. He glanced at the doorway. Win was still standing there, dumbstruck. "Win, take Kimber in the back."

"Nobody is going in the back," roared one of Nange's goons. The tall bruiser. He was unarmed. Five young kids with knives, all with matching scratch marks on their necks. Scratch Cats. The blonde woman with massive arms. Two other thugs by the door.

"Easy, Sender," Nange said. "No need to shout." He sipped the whiskey. "Rynax just needs to accept how things are going to be from now on in Seleth."

"You're fooling yourself if you think you're going to be a boss in this neighborhood."

Nange whistled, and two fists flew at Asti. Asti ducked them both, grabbing one of his attackers by the wrist and throwing him at the other. The two punks fell in a heap.

"I don't go down that easy, Nange."

"No, you don't." Nange peered at Asti's throat. "Quite the nasty scar there. That from the little fracas you caused over on Rabbit?"

"You've been paying attention."

"I've been saying you'd be an asset. You and your brother. Sender here thinks I'm wasting my time. But I think you have value."

"Sender's right."

"I think it's a matter of motivation," Nange said. A flick of his head, and the blonde woman grabbed Kimber by the front of her dress and slammed her against the bar.

"Stop it!" Asti shouted. Win had stepped into the room, but the two other goons grabbed his arms.

"Just keep doing what you're doing, Rynax," Nange said, brushing imaginary dust off of Asti's coat. "And we take a piece. Just like Kimber here will give us a piece. For security. Seleth isn't going to be a mess any longer."

The beast was howling in Asti's head. It wanted out. It wanted to claw out Nange's eyes and eat them. Red was filling up the sides of Asti's vision.

"That isn't going to happen," Asti said.

"No?" Another gesture, and all five of the Scratch Cats jumped on Asti, grabbing his arms. Asti was too focused on holding the chain, keeping the beast held back; he couldn't throw them off. Nange laughed. "I really like your spirit, Rynax. That makes breaking you so much fun."

Asti laughed. A deep belly laugh he couldn't restrain. Two Scratch Cats let go of him in shock.

"What's so funny?" one of them asked.

"You think you're going to break me, Nange?" Asti manage to say once he could draw in enough breath. "You stupid man."

"You think we can't break you, Rynax?"

"It's not that," Asti said. The laughter stopped, sudden and cold. The beast was now slamming at his skull, straining at the chain. "It's that you have no idea how broken I already am."

"I think I'll have to see for myself," Nange said. The three Cats tightened their grip, and Nange wound up his arm, punching Asti with all his strength across his jaw.

"Asti!" Kimber cried.

Hot blood filled Asti's mouth. He wasn't going to be able to hold the beast back much longer.

And he didn't care either. Not with Nange's ugly face right in front of him.

"Nange," Asti whispered. It took so much just to hold on to the chain now, he could barely speak.

"What is it?" Nange asked, moving in closer. Smug look on his ugly face. "You have some smart comment?"

"Let him go already," Kimber said. "I'll pay it. He'll pay it."

"I want to hear it from him," Nange said. He lifted up Asti's chin. "What do you have to say to me?"

Asti could only get out one word.

"Run."

He dropped the chain.

Everything went red.

Chapter 24

ASTI BECAME VAGUELY AWARE that his hands
were wet. Wet and being brushed. Wiped with a cloth.
Slowly he opened his eyes.

Dim room. Lit by a few candles, no adornments. Just a
sleeping pallet and a blanket. And someone was washing
his hands.

His hands were covered in blood. So were his clothes.

"Who?" he croaked out.

"It's all right," said a familiar voice. The person washing
his hands looked up. Win Greenfield. "You're not hurt. Not
much, anyway."

"Kimber?"

"She's just fine. A bit shaken, but fine."

"And . . . you?"

"As well as I can be."

"Lesk? And his people?"

"You don't remember?"

Asti pulled himself up to a sitting position. "No, it's . . .
all a blur after I told Lesk to run."

"I think they're all still alive. Though I imagine none of
them will take that for granted for a few weeks." He chuckled drily. "I've never seen anything like that."

"Like what, exactly?" The last few spells had been

brutal, bloody affairs. Scared the blazes out of Verci and Mila. Win seemed almost amused by it.

"You thrashed those thugs like an artist. It was . . ." His face took on a bright, shining countenance. Asti had almost forgotten that Win could smile. "It was fluid, a dance of rage and blood. The way you moved, the way you acted—"

"Like an animal?"

"Like a saint. Pure of purpose." He stared up at the ceiling, as if searching for the words he wanted up there. "I'll tell you what is was like. A really brilliant lock, the best kind of lock, has several parts that need to move in concert. You try to pick it, and the tumblers move together the wrong way. Stays locked. But with the right key, everything spins together, lines up perfect, and slides open. That was you, Asti. It was like, the right key just turned in you."

The wrong key, Asti thought. *A very wrong key.* Asti looked about, desperate to change the subject. "Is this a jail cell or something?"

"No," Win mused. "This is Saint Bridget's. One of the sleeping cells for the order."

"How—how the blazes did we get here?" Asti lowered his voice, as if the priests might be listening. Or the saints themselves.

"Once you started thrashing, and Lesk realized which way the water was flowing, he—you have to remember the look on his face, Asti."

"Afraid I don't."

"It really was, the way it fell, I just . . ." He laughed, full and rich. "Saints, that was something to see, his whole air just collapsed like a bad cake."

"How did we get in the church?"

"Sorry, I'm getting to it. Anyway, Lesk ran, ran like blazes out Kimber's back door. You went after him, leaving the rest of his thugs bleeding and moaning on the floor. You chased him down the alley, out through the square, and up the steps of Saint Bridget's."

"Middle of the street, me covered in blood, him running?" Asti asked. "How am I not in shackles at the Constabulary?"

"Would you let me tell you?" Win shook his head. On

some level, Asti was thrilled. This was the most life he had seen out of Win since the fire. "Anyway, you were right on him, and I did my best to keep up with you. Right when he reached the top of the steps, you grabbed him by the neck and just picked him up off the ground like a doll."

Asti could scarcely believe that. "Seriously, Win, that's not—"

"I'm in a house of God and saints, Asti, and that is what I saw."

"All right, so then what?"

"You pulled him close, his ear right to your mouth—"

"I bit it off?" Asti's hand went to his mouth on instinct.

"No!" Win sounded shocked that Asti even suggested it. "You whispered something to him."

"What?" Of everything Win had told him, this shocked him the most. "What did I whisper?"

"If you don't know, then only Lesk and the saints do. I was at the bottom of the steps, still catching my breath. After you said it, you tossed him down the steps. He landed, broken and bruised, at my feet. And you just . . . crumpled."

"This is where the sticks should have grabbed me."

"They were there, but so were the priests. They were right at the door, and they pulled you inside."

"Why would they do that?"

"I'm not entirely clear, but the Constabulary did come running up to the church doors for you. The priests told them that you were under their sanctuary and that they would not bind you."

Asti was unable to comprehend why they would do that. Typically one would have to directly ask for sanctuary, and most priests would be loath to grant it to someone who had just thrashed another man on the church steps.

"About then is when I got involved, and Kimber arrived. She lodged a direct complaint against Nange and his friends, that they came into her establishment and drew weapons. She told them they were asked to leave, and then her employee used force to remove them."

"Her employee would be me?"

"I added myself as witness," Win said. "The long and

short is, the sticks had little choice but to leave you be and bind Lesk."

"Nange got bound?" Asti couldn't help but laugh a little at that. "That does put a nice cap on things."

"I thought it would cheer you," Win said.

"So . . . can I leave the church? Once I get cleaned up, of course."

"As far as I know. I have some fresh clothes for you here. Kimber brought them over."

"Kimber, she's . . . she's not here, is she?"

"No." Win picked up the bundle of clothes from the floor. "She put on a good show for the Constabulary, but you . . . this whole business really shook her. She didn't want to see you. She told . . . she told the priest she was afraid for your soul."

"She's not the only one," Asti muttered. He took the washbasin from Win. "I'll take care of myself here. You . . . you can go on, get ready for tonight. I'll see you at the stable."

Win hesitated. "Are you certain?"

"This . . . this isn't the first time the key has turned, Win."

Win got to his feet. "I'll see you there, then." With a quiet nod he left.

Slowly Asti washed the blood off his hands and face. Then he stripped off his clothes and dressed in the fresh ones. He made each moment, each act, deliberate. He demanded complete control over his hands and body. The beast would not get it again, even though he could feel it growling softly in the dark corner of his brain.

This time, this last time, he had gotten lucky. By all rights he should have woken up on his way to Quarrygate. He could have woken up to the dead bodies of Kimber and Win, massacred by his own hand.

Never again. He'd hold down that beast, even if it killed him.

Asti left the cell. Two priests, one much older than the other, stood waiting outside the door.

"You are well?" the younger priest asked.

"Well enough," Asti said. "I—I don't understand why you did what you did for me, but I'm grateful."

The older priest stepped forward and touched Asti's head. "Sometimes the why is all the reason we have." He patted Asti on the hair and walked off.

The younger priest looked embarrassed. "Please excuse Reverend Halster. He is quite advanced in years."

"It's all right," Asti said. "I really do need to go, though. If that's all right."

"Of course."

Asti stepped away, looking for the fastest way out of there, but something held him back.

"Listen, Reverend. You all are accepting charities for the victims of the Holver Alley fire, right?"

"We are," the priest said. "Were you a victim of the fire?"

"Yes," Asti started. "I mean, I'm not . . . I was just wondering. You are still accepting. And it is still getting to the people who need it."

"Always," the priest said.

"Thanks," Asti said, walking away again.

"Walk with the saints," the priest called after him.

Asti found his way to a set of stairs leading him down into the main chapel and face to face with the statue of Saint Bridget.

Saint Bridget was the water carrier, shown as a humble woman with two buckets hanging from a pole resting on her hunched shoulders. Asti never could remember her story, something about helping the helpless and climbing up a mountain. Coins and prayer tokens were scattered about the feet of the statue.

Absently Asti took a coin from his pocket and placed it at the feet, and knelt before it.

"I've never been much of one for prayers. Certainly not to you, but we're in your house, and your people here did me kindness. Dad was Kieran, so he never took to the church here, and Mother told Verci and me that if we were to pray, it should be to Saint Senea. Guardian of righteous outlaws, I think?"

Righteous outlaws, indeed.

"So I've got no right to ask, but between Saint Senea and you—you look over the destitute and oppressed—this is a job for the two of you. I don't want a blasted—" He bit his tongue. No need to blaspheme in prayer. "I don't want anything for myself, here. But I've got a crew of righteous outlaws, destitute and oppressed. Saint Senea, if you can hear this while I'm at Saint Bridget's feet, this is for you as well. I need all my people to come out all right. I need my brother to live through it, see his boy grow up. Have that boy grow up with a chance to be more than Verci and I ever had a chance of being."

Tears came to his eyes. He let them fall on the coins at Saint Bridget's feet.

"The rest of them, they all need any help you can give them. Get them through this night. I don't care what it takes from me, do you hear?" He took all the rest of the coins he had out of his pocket and dropped them at the statue's feet. "I'll take all the fire. Anything that's supposed to land on them, you give it to me."

"Blackberry pie." Verci leaned into the plate Raych had just placed in front of him. The scent was sinful. "You're too good to me."

"Damn right I am," she said, sitting down with him. "Still, I thought you needed a little reminder of what you had back home."

"I know exactly what I have here," Verci said. "The two most precious jewels in Maradaine."

"Glad you know." Raych looked around the apartment, wistful. "I don't suppose I should stay out here tonight, should I?"

Verci sighed. She was moving to more practical matters. He had hoped to avoid that.

"Honestly? I don't think you'll need to hide."

"Why not?"

"Because if things go badly, Asti and I will get squashed, and that will be that. I don't think they'd waste much time on further retribution."

"But yesterday you—"

"I may have overreacted." That was the best answer he

could give. He didn't want her afraid, not for herself tonight. "Something was happening and I thought it might be coming for you. But it was just about Asti, really."

"Hmm." She stood up. "Even still, it doesn't hurt to be prepared, right?"

"What do you mean?"

"Well, last time you rushed us in there. Nothing to eat or drink. It wasn't the best way to spend a few hours."

"Fair enough. So you want to prepare the safe room. Make it cozy?"

She smiled, if only faintly. "Something like that."

"It probably wouldn't be a bad idea to have the room ready so you can hide in there at a moment's notice."

"But you don't think something would happen to us here?"

"I doubt it," Verci said. He held his tongue on the ideas swirling in his head.

"But yet—" She could see he was holding back.

"One, there's the chance people might come here trying to get Josie. They wouldn't care that we live here now."

"And what would she do? If that happened?"

"Go in the safe room, use the drop chute to get into her lair in the basement, and then one of her exit hatches, leading to a different house completely."

"Drop chute?" Raych's eyes went wide. "Lair? Exit hatches?"

"I didn't mention all those?"

"No," Raych said. "Clearly you forgot all that."

"This is partially supposition on my part, mind you. Drop chute is real, lair is real. I'm only presuming she has exit hatches."

"You haven't found them?"

"Haven't found them *yet*. There's a lot to figure out here, and I haven't had the chance."

"I would hope, after tonight, you'll be spending many more nights at home."

"I'd like that," Verci said. He still hadn't gotten to eat the pie. It was just sitting there, slowly cooling on the table. That wasn't right. He took one bite.

Perfection.

"After tonight, if all goes well, we'll be secure and clean, here in the bakery. Just us three."

"Asti won't live here?"

Verci didn't want to say, even if all went well, Asti still might not make it. All going well was going to take a lot of blessing and luck. "I don't think he'll want to. You don't want him here, do you?"

She looked like she was about to pull her teeth out. "Of course he's welcome if he needs it."

"I appreciate that, Raych." He took another bite. "Almost as much as I appreciate this pie."

"You better really appreciate that pie."

"You have no idea how much."

"All right," she said, getting to her feet. "I need final instructions before you go."

"Final instructions, fine." He took a last bite of pie and got up. "If trouble occurs, go to the safe room. If you can't wait it out in the safe room, use the drop chute—"

"Define 'can't wait it out.'"

"If, for example, said trouble involves the building burning down."

Her face went pale and clammy.

"Just a worst-possible example, love," Verci said, moving closer to her.

"Which we've lived through once already."

He caressed her face. "I know. From the lair, there's at least one exit to the sewers. It's not ideal, but it'll get you out." He told her how to open that door.

"All right, when will I hear from you?"

"Ideally, before dawn."

"So at dawn, start to worry?"

"You're going to worry the minute I walk out the door."

"Yes," she said, brushing some crumbs off his vest. "But I want to know when it's no longer unreasonable."

Verci kissed her. "I really love you, you know that?"

"And I'm clearly crazy about you," Raych said. "Crazy to agree to let you do this."

Verci tensed, expecting an argument. "We've been over this . . ."

"And I agree. Crazy as it is, I'm behind you."

Verci kissed her again. "I should get going."

She grabbed his arm, "But let me make something clear. I understand you're going to walk through fire and blood for Asti. But if you have to choose between saving someone else and getting out of there, you *get out of there*. The rest of the crew can hang as far as I care."

Verci grinned. "Even Helene?"

"Especially Helene." She kissed him on the cheek. "Go on. Before I lock you in the safe room."

Chapter 25

ASTI WAS FEELING STRANGELY nostalgic about the stable of the North Seleth Inn. It hadn't been much of a planning base, but it had served their needs.

"You're thinking we need to drop this place?" Verci asked.

Asti grinned at his brother. "Yeah, a shame."

Kennith stuck his head up from out of the carriage he was working on. "What do you mean drop it? I live here!" His East Druthal accent flared up in anger.

Verci stepped in front of Asti, and Asti was more than happy to let his brother do the talking. "Look, Ken, this is a big job we're trying to pull. Thousands of crowns each, if we're lucky."

"So, what, I'll move out of here?"

"To be honest, this is the kind of job people would leave town after. Fires will be put to feet after this."

"Leave town?" Julien asked from inside the carriage. "Are you gonna?"

"No chance," Asti said. "Good or ill, this is where we live. This is our city, our neighborhood."

"Not gonna rabbit?" Verci asked.

"Did you think we were?"

"No." Verci stopped and stared at the ground for a moment. "I thought you were, though."

Asti was taken aback, but he couldn't lie to Verci. He stepped over to the corner, Verci right behind him. "We . . . it's likely we won't even survive tonight, let alone make off with the prize. But if we do . . . we'll be flush."

"Yeah," Verci said. "Flush with a hairy eye at us."

"Right," Asti said. He didn't want to say this, but Verci brought it up. It was harder than he thought it would be. "So it might be smart for us to go separate ways."

"Are you dosed?" Verci asked. "What the blazes are you talking about?"

"Verci, you know what I'm saying." He looked at his brother, Verci's eyes imploring and questioning. Asti tapped on his own forehead. "Whatever is going on in here, brother, it's getting worse."

"No, you had one slip during the fire, brother—"

"And another the night of the carriage gig. Came close a few more times. Sometimes over nothing."

"The past few days—"

"And today."

Verci stopped cold. "You came close again today?"

"No. I lost it today."

"Blazes," Verci whispered. He glanced about at the group, who were all too involved in one another to pay them much mind. "Where? How?"

"Nange and his people, they were putting the squeeze on Kimber. The whole neighborhood. And for a moment, I couldn't hold it back anymore." That wasn't true, and he had to let Verci know. "I didn't want to hold it back anymore. I wanted to let it loose, let it tear Nange's face off."

"Nange is dead?"

"No," Asti said, chuckling despite himself. "Some saint had his eye on me, because it ends with the sticks carting Nange away while I kept walking free."

"See?" Verci said, putting on his best face. "It's going to work out. You didn't kill him. You're getting better."

"Getting worse, brother. Every day it's like . . . a swarm of ants creeping up the back of my skull."

"The gig is over, things will calm down."

"Verci!" Asti snapped, trying to keep his voice from going too loud, keep Kennith or the rest from noticing their argument. The last thing he needed was to spook the crew right before a gig. "I could snap anytime. Any. You know that. You don't want me in your home, Verci. You don't want me around Raych or Corsi."

"Raych can—"

"Raych can what, brother? Handle me? Do you think you could put me down if I'm in a frenzy, trying to claw her eyes out? Bashing your son's skull open?"

Verci's eyes flared wide; anger flashed across his face. "That . . . don't say things like that!"

"It's the truth, brother. The ugly truth."

Verci shook his head. "No. No, brother. That's not going to happen. Raych understands that . . ."

"Raych has probably been far more understanding than I deserve, Verci," Asti said. "But I'm a danger to her, you, and your boy. And if anything happened . . ." Asti felt tears coming to his eyes. He didn't want to do this with Verci. Not now. Not today. "If I hurt any of you, I couldn't live with that. I . . ."

Verci grabbed Asti in a close embrace. "All right, brother, all right." He pulled back, touching Asti's face. "We'll just deal with tonight for now, all right? The rest we'll figure out when it comes."

"Sounds good," Asti said.

"Will you two stop sucking each other's faces?" Helene said as she came around the corner from the back. Asti glanced over to her, and his hand instinctively went for a knife; she didn't look a thing like herself. Her hair was blonde, pulled short to one side. Her olive skin was now alabaster fair. Even her nose looked thinner and smaller. Only her voice and her familiar dark eyes told him that Helene was standing in front of him. Pilsen had worked his craft like he had never seen.

"That's amazing," Verci said.

"You like?" Helene asked.

"Perfect," Asti said. "If anyone marked you the other night, they wouldn't recognize you now."

Pilsen came out from the back, Mila in tow. "I am amazing, I know."

"That should do it," Verci said.

284 Marshall Ryan Maresca

"I need to do the big guy as well," Pilsen said. "As well as myself."

"Are you going that severe?" Asti asked, nodding to Helene.

"Blazes, yes," Pilsen said. "I haven't seen Mendel Tyne for ten years, but he damn well would recognize me, I can tell you. So I've got to bury this beautiful face."

"What else do we need to do?" Verci asked.

"Mila needs to go get in her perch," Asti said. "We're burning daylight."

Helene shook her head. "Not before she helps me into that blasted corset."

"Anyone can help you with that," Asti said.

"No," Helene said. "That's going to be Mila. Then she can go to her perch."

"Fine." Asti looked around. "Anything else people need before Mila goes to her perch?"

"Yeah," Kennith said. "I . . . there's something I want to do. Since we're all here. One click." He went into the back of the stable, and came out a moment later carrying a clay pot. Win and Cort came out with him, each with a stack of bowls. Neither of them looked like they knew what was happening.

"What's this, Ken?" Asti asked.

Kennith put the pot on the workbench, turned to the whole group. "This is . . . *chr'dach*." The foreign word sounded like it scraped against his throat.

Verci grinned. "And here you insisted you were Druth, not Ch'omik."

"I am!" Kennith said. "But my pop did try and teach me a few old things. Not much stuck, except this."

Mila piped up. "What is krah-duck?"

"*Chr'dach*," Asti said, fairly certain he didn't mangle the word. "It's a Ch'omik dish, a sort of good luck before a fight tradition."

Kennith nodded with a half-hearted agreement. "There was more ceremony to it than that, a joining together of brothers-in-arms as they went out to face death. Mostly I remember the recipe." He spooned out the dishes and started passing them around.

Mila looked at her bowl. "But what *is* it?"

Asti poked at the creamy, spicy-smelling mess in his bowl with a spoon. He wasn't sure.

"They're a sort of meatball, cooked in cream and cheese," Kennith said. "There are some peppers in there."

"Do we just eat it?" Win asked.

"No, I . . . I never learned the words in Ch'omik, so I'll . . ."

"Just do the blasted thing, Ken!" Helene snapped.

"Right." Kennith held up the bowl. "Tonight we go forth. Tonight we are victorious, or we are dead. We accept both with full hearts. In the names of our fathers we do this." He brought the bowl back down to his face. "In the name of Nohtho Rill." He looked over to Verci expectantly.

Verci held up his bowl and brought it down. "Kelsi Rynax."

"Kelsi Rynax," Asti repeated.

Mila held up hers, choking her words out quietly. "Jono Kendish."

"Orton Kesser," Helene said.

Julien followed after her. "Holsten Kesser."

"Layton Gin," Pilsen said, holding up his bowl with one hand. "Miserable bastard."

"Quentin Cort."

Win started sobbing. "My girls, they . . . they won't ever . . ."

Mila came over to him, putting her arms around his shoulders. "They will, Mister Greenfield. Saints'll see to that."

Win sniffed and nodded. "Billthym Greenfield."

Kennith nodded solemnly and took a bite of the *chr'dach*. He closed his eyes, a smile across his lips.

The rest all took a bite.

Asti's mouth was on fire.

"Blazes, Ken!" Verci said. "*Some* peppers?"

The room was filled with coughing and swearing, which slowly evolved into laughter.

"Well," Pilsen said, putting his bowl down, "I suppose nothing worse can happen to us tonight."

"Maybe that's the point," Asti said. "Are we done?"

Kennith nodded. "Thank you. That . . . that actually meant a lot to me."

Pilsen clapped Kennith across the shoulders. "Then, my friend, it was worth it." He laughed as he pointed at Julien. "Come around the back, you."

"You need anything more, Kennith?" Julien asked.

"Not right now," Kennith said. "Before we head out, I'll need you to crank that up."

"All right," Julien said. He glanced at his cousin. "It doesn't hurt, does it?"

"No, Julien," she said with a laugh. "How does it look?"

"Like someone else," he said. He turned away quickly and went to the back of the stable.

"We should get ready," Verci said.

"All right," Asti said. "Let's get geared up. I want us to be in the wine shop before sunset."

Mila felt rushed. Asti had thrown a lot at her to arrange in a short order of time. Why the blazes were they moving so fast? Tonight! She had run over to the warehouse where they were supposed to go at the end of the gig, just so she would know where it was. It looked like a warehouse. She didn't know what else she should have expected, but for some reason it was just a boring building. She supposed it was better that she found it in daylight, instead of hunting around for it at night. What were the moons supposed to be tonight? She couldn't remember. That was the sort of thing she ought to be thinking about.

It was the sort of thing Asti would remember. Asti was always paying attention to those little things.

She worked her way through side alleys back toward the Emporium. Everyone else was getting dressed, getting ready. Helene would get a real pretty dress. Again. Helene would get surrounded by fancy people and good food and warm candles. Mila still was wearing rags, despite having a hundred crowns in paper notes inside her skivs. Those weren't going to be anywhere other than on her own person.

At least the spring nights had been warm so far.

Asti had been vague about the take for this whole gig.

He had said they should be bringing in thousands of crowns, if not tens of thousands. It was more than she could wrap her head around. How many of them were on the crew now? Nine people? Did Missus Holt count? Did she get a larger share? She had a whole slew of questions she had been afraid to ask Asti.

Her hands absently went to the rope tied around her waist, looking like a poor girl's makeshift belt. It worked fine, a fashion she had seen plenty of times in Seleth and the western neighborhoods. As she walked she untied the rope, pulled it taut, and tied it again with one hand. She wanted to make sure she could do it, anytime, as quickly as possible.

"What's the word, Miss Bessie?" A boy had walked pace with her, one of the ones she had recruited to be in her cadre.

"I'm gonna need that street flat we talked about, pip," she told him.

"What's the time?"

"Time is when I tell you, pip," she snarled.

"We gonna just stand around and wait?"

"No," she said, giving him an angry eye. She did her best to sound like Asti when she talked to these kids. "You do that the sticks and the other shakers will get the stink, you hear?"

"Yeah," the kid said, though he looked like he wasn't sure what she was saying.

"You be ready, pip, but look like you're all just standing around. The call comes, you'll know it, and you flat that street but quick."

"That's gonna be tough," the kid said.

"You can do it," she said, looking him up and down. "You do it good, there's ten crowns in it. You do it bad, you get my foot on your neck. You hear? Now scamper."

"Yes, Miss Bessie," he said. He ran off down the street.

She loved it when they called her "Miss Bessie."

The sun was hanging low. High time for her to get to her perch.

❖

Asti felt cramped in the back of the carriage. It was not a big space inside, with seven people, Cort's barrels, and

Kennith and Verci's contraption all pressed in there. Asti didn't like it, but he knew they had to stay out of sight while together in this neighborhood, and a single carriage with drawn curtains going down into the loading alley wouldn't look too suspicious. Seven people walking individually might draw someone's eye, and if that someone knew the wine merchant had gone up to the north side of the city, they might call in a constab to sniff around.

Kennith drove the carriage through the narrow dirt alley, the horses moving at a slow pace as he brought it up to the back dock of the wine shop. Verci popped out of the carriage and went right to the door.

"Locked?" Asti asked.

"Yes," Verci returned. He already had a tool out, fiddling with it. "But not anymore."

"That was easy," Win said.

"Figured it would be," Verci said. "We are sure he's gone?"

"Quite," Gin said. "My sweet boy did his job well enough."

"All right." Verci popped open the loading door. "Let's get in fast."

Asti glanced at the dirty windows that looked onto the loading dock. Flops and tenements all, probably no one in there to worry about. He grabbed one of Cort's barrels. "Let's get these in there."

Cort followed Asti's eyes up to the windows. "Think someone is watching us?"

"Maybe," Asti said. "But they'll see us bringing barrels inside. The main thing people look out for are robbers, right?"

"And robbers rarely load stuff into the place they're robbing," Verci said, taking another barrel.

"We should get moving," Gin said, indicating the Kessers. "I've made arrangements for a cab to pick us up at the Hotel Saint Gelmin."

"Did you get a room there as well?" Helene asked.

"Two hundred crowns a night, are you kidding?" Gin said. "We don't need to put up that much show. On the off chance, after the dust settles, someone traces us to our cab, the cabman will only know that's where we came from."

"And the trail runs cold there," Asti said.

"Very smart boy," Gin said, patting Asti on the cheek. "Let's move, though, so we don't have to run. Then we'll sweat, and that would ruin the effect completely."

"This is it?" Julien asked.

"Afraid so," Helene said. "You ready?"

"I think so," Julien said.

"You crank that thing as far as you could, Jules?" Kennith asked.

"Wouldn't move another inch," Julien said.

"Do we say good luck?" Helene asked. "Or does that jinx it?"

"I don't believe in jinxing," Asti said. "It either goes or it doesn't."

"And we have to go," Gin said, hopping off the loading dock to the dusty ground. "Come along now."

"Luck," Helene said.

"Same to you," Asti returned. The three of them slipped out the other side of the alley.

"Let's get inside," Verci said. Asti picked up a barrel and followed his brother.

Cort, Win, and Kennith were lighting lamps in the basement, which was filled with racks of wine. It was a dank, dusty place, smelling of mold. "Do we know exactly which wall we need to use?" Cort asked.

"Give me a minute and I'll figure it out," Verci said. Asti watched his brother's face screw up with concentration. His fingers moved as he pointed into the air, his lips mumbling inarticulately. "That way."

The five of them walked through the cellar until they came to a large wall covered with casks of wine. Verci sighed. "It's this one."

"Blast," Asti said. "We'll have to move all of these, won't we?"

"Yeah," Cort said, pushing up his spectacles. "Good thing we gave ourselves plenty of time, right?"

"Right," Asti said. "A few things. Ken, get the carriage set so you don't have to do anything else to bolt."

"I should be the first one up there once we move," Kennith said. "The horses won't just stay at the ready forever."

"Do what you can. Cort, Win, get moving the casks here."

"Heavy lifting," Win said. "Shame we sent Julien away."

"You can handle it," Asti said. "Verci, come with me to get the last barrel out of the carriage." He went back upstairs, leaving Win and Cort grumbling as they started to move the casks.

Verci was right behind him when he was back outside. "Why did you need me to come?"

"Because you're going to carry the barrel back down," Asti said. He pulled it out of the carriage and put it in Verci's hands.

"It's already time to go up to the watch flop?"

"No use putting it off, you know," Asti said.

"I suppose," Verci said. Asti could tell Verci was skeptical.

"We didn't say this before the carriage gig, brother," Asti started. "And we probably should have . . ."

"No matter what, drive forward?" Verci said. "Is that what you want to say?"

"Yeah."

"You did notice that I drove forward on the carriage gig, even when you nearly skunked it?"

"I noticed," Asti said. He laughed despite himself. "We've got a lot riding here, you know? So no matter what . . ."

"We're committed, brother," Verci said.

"One more thing, Verci," Asti said. "I want you to promise me, if you have to choose between getting yourself clear, and coming for me . . ."

"I'm coming for you."

"No, Verci. Get yourself clear. Get so blazing clear and back to Raych and Corsi and don't even think about me."

Verci scowled. "It won't come to that."

"Promise me!"

"Fine," Verci said. "If you're going to go, go."

"I'm going."

Verci heaved the barrel over his shoulder and went back into the wine shop.

Asti had no nostalgic feelings about the fifth-floor flop. If a place had deserved to get burned to the ground, it would have been that building. Looking around the room, he figured that it wouldn't take much to turn the whole place into a cinder. Even still, no matter how much of a blighted hole the entire building was, no matter what messes the squatters there were, they didn't deserve anything like that.

The view of the Emporium was still clean. It was all he needed. Then he could walk away from this dump.

Lens to the eye. The cab was coming up to the door. The valet came up, helped Helene step down. Smile and nod. Gin and Julien got out of the cab. All good.

The front door opened, the three of them walked right in.

Five minutes, they'd either be in, or sent out.

Unless it went really wrong in there.

Asti shook that thought off. There was no reason for things to go that wrong, not for them. Worst case, they'd be kicked out.

Asti counted off three minutes. He panned his scope over to the mouth of the alley. Mila was there, looking more like a dosed wastrel than a hatshaker. All the better. No one would look at her twice.

Five minutes. No action at the door. The three of them were in clean.

Asti slipped the scope back into his coat pocket. He did one last check of the room. Nothing left he'd need. He grabbed his pack and threw it over his shoulder. Five steps, he'd be out the door and never have to think about this room again.

Which was when the door was kicked in. Miles and six other goons stood in the hallway.

"Beautiful night, Rynax, don't you think?"

Chapter 26

$\mathcal{H}$ELENE FELT THE COLD, clammy sweat of fear all over her body. The valets were the same two people as had been in the foyer the other night. Neither one of them showed any sign of recognizing her, but she worried that they might be well trained at maintaining such a façade.

The old man showed no fear at all. He was fully in character, playing to the hilt the role of a visiting businessman from out east.

"Queen Mara," he told the valet with complete confidence.

"Excellent, sir," the valet said. "If you will step over here?" He brought them over to the side and gave Gin and Julien a more thorough pat down than any of them had received the night before. The female valet did the same to Helene.

Helene felt her arms tense involuntarily as the woman's hands went to her midsection.

"I love your dress," the woman told her.

"Thank you," Helene said. Gin had told her not to bother with an accent or airs of any kind. She should play that she was a West Maradaine girl who had ended up with a moneyed man. That was easy enough for her. "The secret is the corset." Helene couldn't believe that had just come out of her mouth. What was she thinking? Why did she say that?

"Very flattering," the woman said, finishing her frisk.

"Now follow me," the male valet said, opening a door that blended into the woodwork of the wall. A wide staircase, inlaid with marble tiles, led underneath the dining room. The three of them followed the valet down to the gambling floor. "I should remind you that tonight all tables have a hundred-crown minimum."

"Excellent," Gin said. The man nodded and went back upstairs.

The gambling floor was a sprawling room, with chandeliers hanging from the high ceiling and oil lamps along every wall. A great round fireplace drew Helene's eye, the centerpiece of the room. Gaming tables littered the place: dice games, wheel games, card games, every kind of game. Along the far wall there were further corridors, girded by red velvet curtains.

"Back offices, count rooms," Gin said under his breath, nodding to the curtains ever so slightly.

"You spot the mage yet?" Helene whispered.

"Not yet."

"What shall we be playing?" Helene asked in a louder voice.

"Over there," Gin said, pointing out a table on the far side of the room. The table was right under several oil lamps, close to the fireplace, but still somewhat secluded from the rest of the room. Most important to Helene, there were stools and a cloth skirting around the table. That gave her a good place to hide her hands.

✵

Moving the casks had taken a couple of hours. Verci had been glad, though. It was better to have something physical to do, something to burn the hours they had to pass before it was time to run the gig. Waiting was always the part he hated the most. It made his nerves build, made his hands twitchy. Cort had been complaining the whole time. Greenfield worked quietly, nodding occasionally with Cort's complaints. Kennith would move a few casks, then go back up to the carriage, do something up there, and come back down.

"The horses are nervous," he said the last time he came down.

"They ready to run, though?" Verci asked.

"I guess," Kennith said. He grinned. "We never really did test that thing, you know."

"I checked over everything you built," Verci said. "I couldn't see anything wrong. You did a fantastic job with it."

"Thanks," Kennith said. "Still there's something to be said about testing things out."

"Field tests are fine," Verci said. "I've had to do that many times."

"Makes me nervous."

"You two done yapping?" Cort asked. He put his ear to the stone and tapped it with a hammer. He moved over a few feet and repeated it. He gave a small nod. "We need to crack the barrels and drill some holes in the wall."

Verci opened up his satchel and pulled out two hand drills. One thing he liked about gigs like this, he could bring plenty of gear. "Where are we drilling?"

"Where is Asti?" Greenfield asked. "Shouldn't he be back by now?"

"Should be," Verci said.

"What do we do if he's not?"

"If he's not back when it's time to roll, we roll," Verci said.

"But without him?"

"We roll," Verci snapped. "We're burning time. Cort, where do we drill?"

Mila kept her head down sitting on the corner. She held out her cap to each passerby, but didn't shake very hard. Just enough to keep up the show. Eyes up, head down, like Asti had told her. She saw Helene, Julien, and the old man go in. They didn't come back out, so it must have gone clean. She saw her various pips strolling about the street, trying to look inconspicuous. Some of them had taken up a street game of tetch, which was a good strategy, Mila thought, had it not been well into moonrise. Kids playing tetch in the street would keep a clear path, letting them flat it fast when the signal came. But it was going to be around midnight when that happened; kids playing tetch then would look strange.

Nothing to be done about that. The porters at the door to the Emporium didn't pay the pips any mind, and that was what mattered.

She glanced back at the porters. No real change there.

A constable strolled through the street. He paid no mind to anything, save a friendly wave to the porters.

This night was going to drive her crazy with waiting.

She heard a grunt and a scuffle in the back alley leading to the Emporium's loading dock. No carriage had gone in. She risked scooting closer to the mouth of the alley to get a glance down it. The porters took no note of her. She craned her head around the corner.

There were a group of goons dragging someone to the back door, a guy with his arms and legs shackled, a hood over his head.

A short, muscled guy wearing Asti's coat.

"Blazes," she muttered.

She spun back around before the porters snapped at her.

If she just saw what she thought she saw, the job was skunked. Wasn't it? It would have to be.

Blazes.

She took the coins out of her hat, shoved them into her pocket and put the hat on her head. Only one way to be sure.

Head down, eyes forward, she shuffled off until she was out of the line of sight for the door porters. Then she ran for the wine shop as fast as she could.

"Double-tap!"

Helene was impressed with this old man. He had won several hands of cards in a row, and had a pile of several hundred crowns of winnings. He kept betting high. Already one disgruntled minor noble had stalked off, having been cleaned out by the stakes Gin was setting.

"That's how the bull hits you," Gin said, pointing two

forked fingers at the dealer. He gave a twangy, nasal laugh. "Ain't that the way, darling?"

"Sure is," Helene said.

Gin turned to the player on his right. "Now my cousin, he kept trying to speculate in silver up in the hills, and I kept telling him, I told him, the only thing you're digging up there is your own grave. Am I right? Am I right?" The other player nodded but seemed afraid to interrupt. "Sure, the silver can pay off big if you find it, but 'if' is too dangerous a game for this ranchman."

"You seem to like taking chances," the dealer told him.

"Cards ain't chances!" Gin laughed again. "Man has skills he uses to win here."

Julien kept eyeing the room nervously. He hadn't spoken since they entered the Emporium. Gin had told him he should keep his speaking to a minimum, but Helene knew how uncomfortable he must be. He hated new situations. She felt so out of place, but she clenched her teeth and kept her fake smile up.

The player next to Gin threw down his cards. "Blast! Too much for me."

"Oh, come on now, buddy," Gin said. "Can't give up yet. Night is still young. Barely ten bells, am I right?"

"It's halfway to eleven bells, sir," the dealer said.

"Eleven bells?" Gin asked, his eyebrows raised. He gave a pointed look to Helene. "Did you hear that, darling?"

"Still early. You haven't even spotted your old friend yet," Helene said.

"I know," Gin said, looking around the room. His eye stopped on a far corner. "No, it couldn't be."

"What?" Helene asked.

Gin leaned in to the dealer. "You'll forgive me, boy, but I think I spot an old family friend over in the corner there. That is, um, Miss Ecrain sitting there with the roast pheasant, am I correct?"

Helene turned. There she was, rail thin with stringy hair falling in her face. She sat at a table in the corner, gnawing on a piece of meat while staring out into the room with dead eyes.

Ecrain was a woman. Blast.

"Family friend?" the dealer asked. "I can't imagine her having many friends."

"Her mother was a lovely woman," Gin said. He turned to Helene. "Don't you think you should go say hello?"

"Really, dear," Helene said. "She was more your friend. I think you should do it."

"But you are the one who has her gift," Gin said.

"But I think she would take it so much better from you," Helene said. "I don't think she'd be as charmed by me as you are."

"You can't be sure about that," Gin said. "You should try."

Julien's large hand suddenly thrust into the pocket where the vial was. "I have it." Before Helene could say anything to object, he was already striding across the room.

"There," Gin said. "Now that that's taken care of, the rest of the evening can proceed. Don't you think?"

Helene laughed her best faking, trilling laugh and wrapped one arm around Gin. The other hand she dug into her dress. She was desperate to run over to Julien and drag him away. What was he thinking? How did he plan to give her Cort's concoction? She couldn't let herself watch, or even think about it, or sheer panic would overtake her.

With deliberate movements, the ones she had practiced all afternoon, she began removing the pieces of the small crossbow. She was going to have to assemble and load it with one hand. In the stable she could do it in five minutes.

In the stable her hands weren't shaking.

"Nicked pair, sir," the dealer said, flipping over his own cards. "Sorry, sir. Perhaps your luck is changing."

"Oh, I don't know about that," Gin said. "This night still has some luck, I think."

Mila ran to the back door of the wine shop, bursting through with more energy and noise than she had intended. She called out, "Asti? Asti?"

There was a crash and a few swearing voices below her. A moment later she heard pounding feet coming up the stairs. Verci came up from the basement, his face red with anger. Mila had the passing thought that, for the first time, he really looked like Asti's brother.

"The blazes is wrong with you?" he snarled at her. "You've got a post to watch!"

"I was watching it!" she said. "Where's Asti?"

Verci's eye twitched. It was a small thing, but she spotted it. "He's not here."

"I think they grabbed him."

Verci took a moment and then nodded. "All right. Get back to your spot."

"But—"

"Get back to your spot, Mila!"

"If they grabbed him, doesn't that mean we're skunked?"

"The last thing he told me was, no matter what, drive the gig forward," Verci said. "So get back out there and let me do my part!" He stalked back downstairs.

Mila stumbled out of the wine shop. They were going to move forward without Asti? And Asti was grabbed by those goons? And she was just supposed to keep watch on the door?

No chance she was going to do that.

She was going to have to get into the Emporium.

Chapter 27

HENRIETTA NOTARA OF ERINGASH really felt she should get to be called Lady Henrietta. She had money. She had land. She had both from her birth, and they had been in her family for three generations. She had more land than some baronesses she knew. She certainly had education and manners. She just lacked a hereditary title, as her family had only come into land and money in the past sixty years.

Her cousin Niya was now Lady Niya, thanks to marriage, a point Niya never failed to drum home at any opportunity. Henrietta would be damned if she was going to let Niya beat her out on a title. That was why she had set her sights on young Kesmin Jounce, to be Earl of Upper Kisan once his dismal father had done the world the favor of ceasing to breathe. Kesmin, despite his title, was lacking in both land and money, due to his father's unhealthy fixation with gambling. Unfortunately Kesmin had inherited this trait from his father. He was obsessed with coming into this dismal part of Maradaine for the privilege of giving away the little money he had.

Henrietta had the intention of humoring his vice only for as long as it took to get a bracelet on her wrist. As it stood, it had taken quite a bit of convincing to get him to leave that place while the night was still relatively young. She worried that she would have to make good on at least a few of her hinted promises. Enough to keep him interested, not enough to make him think unkindly of her virtue.

Not until she had that bracelet.

Kesmin wasn't wasting time as the carriage trundled away from the Emporium toward his apartments. The ride would take nearly a half hour. Fending him off for that long would be a challenge.

Especially with the carriage suddenly stopping in the street.

"What's going on?" she asked, pushing Kesmin's hand off her chest for the second time.

"What do you mean?" he asked, clearly with little interest in hearing an answer.

"Why did we stop?"

"I don't—" He was cut off by a strangled cry from the driver.

"What was that?"

"Well, it . . ." he stammered. All the blood had left his face, and his lip was quivering. Was he really afraid? That wouldn't do. A husband who frightened so easily was unacceptable.

A muffled thud. A sound she was sure was the driver's body landing on the cobblestones. Her heart jumped up to her throat.

"Go see what's happening," she whispered.

"I—yes," Kesmin said. It was clear how little he wanted to open that door, but he was doing it anyway. That was a good sign. His hand only trembled a little as he pulled the latch. The moment it came free, the door flew open. A second later Kesmin was clutching at his neck as he was yanked forward, out into the dark street.

Henrietta never even saw what had pulled him. Just, suddenly, he was gone.

She couldn't scream. She couldn't move. She couldn't even breathe. She was helpless with fear when someone jumped into the carriage, shutting the door behind her.

Her.

Henrietta had been expecting a large brute of a man, but

it was just a girl. A dirty waif of a girl at that. Even more, Henrietta was certain she had dropped a few coins in this girl's hat earlier that evening. There was peasant gratitude for you.

"Take off your dress," the girl said.

"What?" Henrietta hadn't been expecting that.

"Dress," the girl growled out.

"This is Turjin silk!"

The girl pulled out a knife from inside her bodice. "Get it off!"

The blade looked dirty and sharp. Henrietta was certain she saw blood caked on the edge. The girl's grip on it was hard and desperate.

"Don't—please ... I have money, I—"

"I don't want your money," the girl said. "Give me the dress!"

Henrietta started unlacing the front. As she undressed, the girl carefully took off her own rags, all the while keeping her sharp eye and sharper knife close on Henrietta.

"You don't expect me to wear your ... rags, do you?"

"I couldn't care," the girl said. "Sit in your skivs in here."

Henrietta pulled the dress down, crumpling the silk before giving it to the girl.

"And the shoes," the girl said as she snatched the dress away.

"I don't think they'll fit you!"

"I don't care what you think, give me the blazing shoes!"

Street girls and their filthy mouths. Henrietta kicked the shoes off. The girl pulled the dress on. Sloppy.

"Tie the laces properly," Henrietta said.

"Don't tell me how to dress," the girl snapped back.

"Clearly it's a subject you know nothing about," Henrietta said.

With one hand—since the other hand never dropped her guard with the knife—the girl deftly tightened the laces and tied them into place. Henrietta had to admit that was impressive. The girl had skills that would make her a good lady's maid, were she not a filthy street-rat of a thief.

"Better," Henrietta said. The girl jammed her feet into the shoes. Her feet were clearly too big, but she got them on. With a last sneer, the girl popped the latch open and stepped backward out of the carriage.

"The driver isn't dead," the girl said. "He should wake up and take you home shortly."

"Thank you for that small kindness," Henrietta said. She wasn't sure what she meant by it. The girl bowed with mock extravagance.

"Glad to be of service, my lady," she said and slammed the carriage door shut.

Henrietta couldn't help but smile. At least the girl had the decency to call her "my lady."

✺

Asti didn't need to see to know where the carriage Miles and his boys had thrown him in had gone. Even with the hood on, even with the trick turns and the roundabout route, Asti wasn't so spun around he couldn't tell where he ended up. He knew they had reached the loading alley of the Emporium.

Besides, where else would Tyne have him brought?

They pulled him out of the carriage and brought him inside. He gave them a decent struggle, as good as could be done wearing a hood and shackles, but he really couldn't do much to stop them pulling him inside. A few moments later they dragged him down some steps. He heard Miles's hoarse whisper in his ear.

"Normally, out of respect for the old days, I'd give you the dignity of dying here and now." Miles leaned in close, so Asti could smell his hot breath. "Unfortunately for you, Mister Tyne wants to talk to you first."

So he was in the Emporium, on the lower levels.

It wasn't exactly the preferred way to get there, but he was where he wanted to be.

He kept struggling as they dragged him down a corridor—he could hear he was in a narrow space—but just enough to make them think he was putting up a fight. He didn't want them to think he was interested in them taking him wherever they were taking him. Then they might do something else.

He counted steps, measured each turn. He wanted to be able to trace his way back out.

Asti used each pushed step to gauge his ankle shackles. The chain between them was long enough to walk, but not to run. Only about a foot to work with. The metalwork was solid enough, though the joint between his left shackle and the chain had a bit of play. A strong enough yank might make it give.

His arms were shackled behind his back, and his wrists were less than two inches apart. Very little to work with. He didn't dare feel about with his fingers, not here, not with Miles probably keeping a tight eye on everything he was doing.

Every other thug in this group dragging him along was probably a former soldier, or just street tough done good. He wasn't too worried about taking on any one of them, even with his arms behind his back. Miles was a different story. The past two days had reminded Asti that he was a gifted fighter. Asti couldn't afford to underestimate him.

A door was opened, and Asti was pushed inside. Wide chamber with a low ceiling. Wooden floor under his feet. Flickering light from warm oil lamps placed all around the room. Scents of roasted lamb and quality wine. Heavy breathing from three people in the room, two men and a woman. Asti was thrown into a hard wooden chair.

The hood was pulled off his head and Asti was looking into the beady eyes of a bald man with a pointed beard. He was in an office, seated in front of a large wooden desk, neat stacks of papers on one corner.

"So this is the dirty pirie who thinks he can match me," the man said.

"Pleasure to meet you as well, Mendel," Asti said.

Mendel Tyne chuckled drily, and then smashed the back of a closed fist into Asti's jaw. Asti spat out blood and a couple tooth chips. Tyne grabbed him by the chin and pulled his face back over to him. "Do not presume, pirie, that you can use my given name. That you and I are somehow equals."

"We're not equals, Mendel," Asti said.

"No, we are not, pirie," Mendel said. "You do know what that means."

"It's a shortening of 'imperial,' as a slur on my Kieran heritage."

Asti was hit in the face again. He was ready to be hit that time, rolling with it best he could shackled in the chair. He also yanked both legs as hard as he could in the moment. The bolt on his left shackle gave a little. "Not the word, Mister Rynax." Tyne was cool and calm now. "I mean that I am a man of substance, power, and connections, and you are a rat—a skilled rat, but just a rat—living in a dismal hole with the dead and dying."

"I was moving out," Asti said.

"You aren't doing anything, Mister Rynax. I do commend your ambition, though. Most people don't ever lift their heads from whatever rock they're born under. You tried to reach out, grab a piece of something more." Tyne leaned in and whispered to Asti. "I can respect that, believe it or not."

"I believe it," Asti said.

"Good. But it's important that you know your place, Mister Rynax."

"My place was on Holver Alley."

"Indeed it was," Tyne said. "You should have stayed there. Don't you agree, Josefine?"

The distinctive step and clomp of Josefine Holt's cane came from behind Asti. "You couldn't leave well enough alone, could you?"

"Missus Holt?"

Miles leaned in, hissing in Asti's ear. "You just keep getting betrayed, don't you? First Liora, now this."

Asti thrashed at Miles, giving his leg shackles another hard pull as he did so. The loose bolt nearly gave.

"Learn your place, and learn loyalty," Tyne said. "Josefine knows her place, don't you?"

"Yes, I do, Mister Tyne," Josie said, coming into view. She shook her head at Asti. "You know I had to give you up."

"I didn't think you'd have to," Asti said.

"Shows how little you know," she said. "There is an order to things in these neighborhoods."

"And North Seleth is nothing," Tyne said. "But Josie here was smart, she knew it's better to be the Queen of Nothing, instead of no one at all. I'm a generous man to people who are loyal to me."

"And I'm left under your boot," Asti said.

"That was the choice you made, Mister Rynax."

Asti turned his gaze at Josie. "You disgust me. You betrayed your people, your neighborhood, everything you were supposed to stand for!"

Josie's cane came swinging at his body, knocking him off the chair. He lay on the floor as she hit him again and again with it, against his sides, back, arms, and wrists.

"Josie, Josie," Tyne said calmly. "Don't hurt yourself."

Josie pulled back. Winded, she sat down on the desk, using the cane to support herself. "Sorry, Mister Tyne. He just—"

"Yes, he's an infuriating little rat," Tyne said. "I'm amazed you hadn't done that sooner."

"I tolerated him for his father's sake," Josie said.

"Loyalty is beyond people like this pirie," Tyne said. He brushed off his suit and offered a hand to Josie. "Come on now, Josefine. You can point out these spies on my gambling floor. Gentlemen, kill the pirie. Try and make it bloodless, though. I don't want to have to get the floor cleaned."

"As you say, Mister Tyne," Miles said from behind Asti. Asti had managed to roll over onto his back so he could see how many people were in the room. Eight, including Tyne and Josie.

"As I say, indeed," Tyne said.

Asti gave a hard eye to Josie. "We're not done here, you know."

"We all do what we have to, Asti," she said. "You should know that." She took Tyne's hand, and the two of them left the room. Miles and his men slowly circled around Asti, who still lay on his back, arms underneath.

With his arms under him, Miles couldn't see his hands. He couldn't see Asti work the lock pick in his right hand — the lock pick he had pulled off Josie's cane — to spring open the shackle on his left hand.

"So you're supposed to keep this bloodless," Asti said.

"That's what the man said," Miles said, leaning directly over him.

"That's going to be tough with that bloody nose, Miles."

"What —" was all Miles said before Asti rolled back and kicked straight up, pulling the chain on his leg shackles as hard as he could. The weak bolt snapped, shooting Asti's right foot into Miles's face. Blood gushed out his old colleague's nose.

The other five men were shocked still, just for a moment. A moment was all Asti needed to snap down and pop up onto his feet. His feet planted, he barreled his shoulder into Miles, who was still reeling from the earlier blow. Miles tried to grab on to Asti, to hold his footing, but the force of Asti's blow knocked him back. With a hard press, Asti pinned Miles to the wall.

With that spare second, Asti got his left hand out of the open shackle. He had hoped to have gotten it off completely before starting this fight, but these things never go the way one hopes.

Miles coughed out an inarticulate order while punching Asti in the kidneys. Asti swung out with his right hand, hitting Miles in the face with both the lock pick and the loose shackle. Miles dropped to the ground, gasping for breath.

Two of the goons made a grab for Asti. They were cocky, since they had taken him easily in the apartment. They had no idea he had let them win.

He spun and punched one of them, quick and hard, and grabbed the guy by the vest. He gave the guy a hard shove into the other one, and slipped past on the other side. Three more thugs between him and the door.

Not that he had any intention of taking the door with these guys still on their feet.

Three short swords came out from their belts. No more messing around. Blood was already on the floor.

For a moment Asti wanted to let go completely. Just unlock the cage in his mind and damn anything else. Let the furious beast tear these tossers to shreds.

No, he thought. *Better to die a sane man.*

One jabbed in with his blade, which Asti adroitly avoided, grabbing the thug by the wrist. He forced the follow-through of the thrust to skewer one of the first two who came at him. Hard elbow to the face, sword released. Asti helped himself to it. Yanked it out of the dying thug, hitting the exposed neck of its former owner on the backswing.

Two men still standing clean, two dying, one hurt, and one off-balance.

Asti still had a shackle attached to his right arm, and both ankles. Threw him off balance. That backswing went too far, left him open on the right side. One of the blokes with swords took advantage of that. He came in low and quick. Asti scrambled over to the left, while pushing the skewered man onto his friend. Let dead weight do the work for him.

Asti blocked an attack from the last man, and was about to stab him when another one yanked on the shackle. His arm jarred, the sword flew from his hand and skittered across the floor.

He gave a sharp pull with the shackled arm, yanking that man close to his friend's blade. The thug let go of the shackle too late to avoid getting cut, and the shackle shot out and knocked his friend in the face.

Asti grabbed that man's head and slammed it against the desk, scattering the pile of papers. The man struggled, grabbing frantically at the papers and trying to shove them at Asti. Asti ignored the letter that flew at his face, smashing the man's head against the desk again.

The one thug who hadn't been injured had managed to push his associate's dead body off, but hadn't gotten to his feet. Asti relieved the man he had just concussed of his sword and finished the two of them off with quick strokes.

The last man standing, holding his wounded side with one hand and a sword with the other, said something in a vain attempt to be threatening, but Asti didn't even listen. He batted the sword away and stabbed the man in the chest.

A flash of a memory of the scattered papers crossed Asti's brain. He didn't have time to reflect, as Miles had just gotten back to his feet. With a sickening wet sound, he pulled the lock pick out of his cheek and threw it at Asti's throat. Catching it was easy.

Doing anything else before Miles was on him wasn't an option.

Chapter 28

"QUEEN MARA."

The valet just raised an eyebrow at Mila, the rest of his face stone.

"I told you—"

"I heard what you said, little girl," the valet said. "I'm just not sure what you think it means."

"It means you let me down below," Mila said.

"I will admit," the valet said, "that when some people use that phrase, they gain admittance. However, that does not mean we would allow a child—one who clearly slipped away wearing her mother's dress, I might add—down to the gambling floor."

Mila clenched her teeth but took some small comfort in the fact that while the valet recognized the dress was not hers, he in no way suspected its real origins.

"Look," she said, making her eyes as wide and wet as she could manage, "I came here because ... because ... my mother just ran off with the cook. She was livid because my father is here with his mistress and I need to tell him and I needed to put on something and this was the only thing she left behind and—"

She had worked herself up into tearful hysterics, which weren't entirely feigned, and the valet was uncomfortably glancing around and urging her with his eyes and hands to be quieter.

"Your father . . . he's here? Downstairs?"

"That's where he said he would be," Mila told the valet. "If I could just go down and find him, that's all I need to do."

"I know I shouldn't," the valet said, half to himself. "What's your father's name?"

Blazes. What was the name that old man was going to use? She knew she had heard him say it earlier. Thressen? Tensen? "Thomas Tharen."

"Tharen?" The valet screwed his face in thought. "Don't recall that name off hand, but let's go have a look." He waved to the other valet to watch the door while he led Mila down a back stairwell.

The stairs opened up to a wide, sprawling palace of polished floors, warm candles, and table after table of finely dressed people playing at cards, dice, and wheels.

"You see him?"

Mila scanned the crowd, instinctively looking for Julien. He'd stand out in any crowd. Sure enough, there he stood by one wall, but he was talking to some crazy-looking woman. Where was that old man? She bit her lip, not sure how long she could stall. Finally she found Mister Gin and Helene, Gin playing cards and grinning like a cat. "There he is."

"Follow me," the valet said, bringing her over to the table. He tapped Gin on the shoulder. Mila noticed the old man tensing, ever so slightly.

"Mister Tharen, is it?"

"Yes?" He barely even glanced at the valet.

"This . . . girl says she's your daughter."

"She does?" He turned around and really looked at them both. "Well, dear, what are you doing in here?"

"There's a problem with . . . with Mother."

"Mother?" He shook his head sadly. "I suppose I should have expected it." He took one bill from his pocket and offered it to the valet. "Thank you so much."

The valet nodded, refusing the bill, and walked off. Helene gave Mila a small nod, but didn't do more than that. She had her hands occupied under the table.

"Dear girl," Mister Gin said, moving in close to embrace her. He then whispered. "Is 'mother' Asti or Missus Holt?"

"Asti," she whispered back. "They grabbed him."

"Blast," he said. "Not much to be done, I suppose."

"What are we going to do?" Mila asked.

"The cards have already been dealt, dear," he said. "I'm afraid we either play what we have, or we fold."

"What's Julien doing?"

"Taking care of our mage problem, I think."

"He is? How?"

"I think he's just doing a Front Door Knock."

"A what?"

Gin gave her a sly wink. "Sometimes the easiest way to trick someone into doing something is to make it no trick at all. Yeah, look."

Mila saw Julien take two wineglasses and then making a show of hiding—hiding from the room, not the woman—he poured from Cort's vial into both glasses. He then offered one to the woman and took the other. He drank his wine, and the woman drank her own.

"He drank it himself!" Mila said.

"What?" Helene asked, still at the table, keeping her voice low.

"Nothing, dearest," Gin said. "I'm sure it's fine. Cort said it was essentially harmless, right?" Mila could only shrug. Gin snapped his fingers and called Julien over, stepping away from the table with Mila.

Mila saw Julien say some polite words to the woman and then cross back over to them. Gin glanced at the woman, and then gave a hard glare at Julien. "You shouldn't wander away. That's not what I pay you for."

"Yes, sir," Julien said. The three of them went back to the table.

"What the blazes just happened?" Helene whispered. "Why is she here?"

"Just some trouble at home, nothing much," Gin said for the dealer's benefit. "Our boy got the job done, though."

"How?" Helene's eyes went wide.

"I figured she was bored," Julien said. "So I talked about being bored with being a bodyguard. She liked that. Then I said I had some stuff to help ease the boredom, but my boss wouldn't like me to take it. So I drank some and gave some to her. Easy."

"You drank it?" Helene looked like she was fighting the urge to shout.

"It's fine. I don't do magic."

"All right," Gin whispered. "We should go back to the game. Won't be long before the last hand of the night gets dealt."

Tyne was walking with a deliberate, slow pace, obviously his attempt to give Josefine the dignity of keeping up with him. She played up her need for the cane a little more than necessary, which served its function.

"You do have to admire the audacity of it all, of course," Tyne said as he walked down the hallway. "In my youth, well, I may have done something similar. I did do a few similar things, come to think about it, which made me the man I am today."

"I bet you pulled some good gigs," Josefine said, with her best good-humored sincerity.

"I've heard some stories of your youth, Josie," he said. "A few are the stuff of legend, you know."

"I was a blazes of a box-girl in the day."

"Artistry," Tyne said with a nod. Josie couldn't figure out if he was putting on a show of civility, or if he really meant it. She then decided she didn't give a damn. "Those gigs of old had craft. Dignity. This Rynax's plan was just a mess. Sneak a few people on the gambling floor, smash a carriage through the front door, and just make a mad grab for the cash? It's brutish. I respect you turning them in, Josie, because the whole thing is beneath you."

"I suppose it was."

"When we get out on the floor, just be discreet about who the spies are. We'll take them off quietly."

"Good," Josie said. "I'd hate to make a big fuss."

"What's the hour?" Verci asked.

"Three minutes since the last time you asked," Win

responded. He was tapping his fingers absently against his leg. Fingers anxious to be used. Verci was happy to see that.

"Are we ready to do this?"

Cort stepped away from the wall, wiping off his hands. "Yeah, I think so."

"So what do we do?"

"Is it time?"

"Ken!" Verci shouted up the stairs. "Is it eleven bells yet?"

Ken came halfway down the steps. "Saint Milster's hasn't rung it . . . but I think I heard Saint Bridget's."

"Close enough," Verci muttered. He couldn't take waiting much longer. "All right, it's time! Cort, what do we do?"

Cort took a piece of string dipped in lamp oil and held it up to the flickering flame of the lamp. Then he shoved it into one of the holes drilled into the wall, which he had stuffed with powder and grease. "It's set."

"What happens now, Cort?" Verci asked.

"Oh," Cort said absently, "we should probably get behind those shelves pretty quickly. And cover your ears if you want to hear anything for the next day or two."

Win's eyes went wide, and he scrambled over behind the shelves. Cort walked over calmly, wiping off his hands on his leather smock. Verci gave a quick look to Kennith, who bolted back up the stairs. Verci dove behind the shelves, hands over his ears.

He waited.

Nothing happened.

He glanced around the corner.

Nothing.

"Cort," he hissed, hands still over his ears.

"Wick's taking a bit longer than I thought," Cort mused. "It shouldn't be—"

The whole room shuddered with a crashing boom that was far louder than anything Verci had ever before experienced. Casks of wine fell down all around the room.

"There it is," Cort said.

"Sweet Saint Maria!" Verci swore. "You said it would be loud, but—"

Cort giggled in a high pitch. "Yeah, that was a good one."

"Blazes, would you look at that," Kennith said, coming back down the stairs.

Verci saw: a great big hole in the wall with a wide corridor beyond it. He grabbed his satchel.

"Come on, boys," he said. "We don't exactly have time to gape at this marvel of science. Let's run." He took off down the corridor and hoped they were right behind him.

Chapter 29

TYNE STUMBLED as the walls shook around him. "What the blazes was that?"

Josie chuckled. "About that brutish plan with the carriage, Mendel?" He turned back to her in time to see her cane swinging into his head. He dropped down to the ground like a sack of potatoes. She bent over his collapsed form. "I lied."

She limped back toward the office as fast as her bad leg could take her.

The whole gambling floor shuddered. Everyone in the place screamed.

Helene's right hand went for her necklace, unhooking the latch and putting it on the table. Her left hand kept the tiny crossbow at the ready.

"Keep calm!" someone called out from one of the doors. "If everyone could just—"

Helene freed one of the stones from the chain. A simple toss sent it into the nearest lamp. The reaction was immediate. Smoke poured out of the lamp, thick and dark.

People pressed for the exit. Others grabbed bills off the tables. Dealers and valets were urging people to be calm.

Helene threw four more stones. One missed the target, but the other three were true. The whole room started to fill with smoke.

Helene's eye went over to Ecrain. She stood up, hands raised, but her face showed mild confusion. Amid the chaos she looked like she was calmly trying to remember an old friend's name and failing.

"Lock it down!" a guard screamed.

"Now would be a good time to move," Gin said.

"But Asti!" Mila shouted.

"We can't do anything about that!"

Helene saw the panic in Mila's eyes. "We've got to get out."

A guard was blocking the exit stairs. Another ran over to a lever on the wall. Helene grabbed the remainder of the necklace and threw it into a fireplace. No time to waste.

The result was an enormous burst of smoke and flame.

The guard by the lever was distracted. Helene aimed her crossbow at him and took the shot. He went down, but not before he grabbed hold of the lever. He dropped and pulled it with him. A heavy metal gate came crashing down in front of the stairway.

The panicked screams rose to a fevered pitch.

"Julien!" she called to her cousin. He looked a bit distracted, but not as much as the mage. After a moment he focused on Helene, and pounded his way to the gates.

Two guards came at him, identifying him as a problem. Helene loaded another dart and shot down the first. The second reached Julien, but only got so far as to put a hand on his shoulder.

Julien's massive fist swung back, cracking the man in the skull.

The carpets and tables closest to the fireplace were aflame.

Julien pushed his way through the press of bodies, reaching the gate. He grabbed it with both hands and pulled it upward.

At first it didn't budge. Then there was a grinding sound, so loud it overpowered the panicked crowd, and a great metallic crack. The gate flew up.

"Come on!" Gin called, grabbing Mila's wrist.

"What about Asti?"

The crowd slammed through the open staircase. Even Julien's massive body could not hold them back, and he was shoved to the side. Helene ran to him, Gin right behind her.

Mila had yanked herself free from Gin's grasp and ran to the other side of the room.

"Mila!" Helene shouted. She reached Julien, who had fallen to the floor. "You all right?" she asked her cousin.

"Fine," he said.

"We need to go!" Gin said.

"What about Mila?" Julien asked.

"We can't do anything for her if she's going to be stupid!" Helene snapped at him.

Julien's eyes went wide. "You'd kill anyone who said that about me."

Helene felt all the blood drain from her face. Ashamed, she nodded. "You two stay here. I'll go get her."

Miles's attacks were furious. Blow after blow came to Asti's face and body, each one he could barely block. He stabbed Miles in the arm with the lock pick, but it broke from the abuse.

A punch came in too fast to counter, striking Asti directly in his right eye. A savage growl burst forth from his mind, voiced in his throat before he realized it. He lashed out, knocking Miles in the sternum.

Miles grabbed the chair Asti had been sitting in. Asti punched at him again, nearly incoherent with anger. Miles blocked the punch with the chair, getting Asti's arm caught in its wooden latticework. He spun it to one side, savagely twisting Asti's wrist.

The pain was too sudden, too intense. Red thoughts filled Asti's mind. Everything was about to go. The chain was about to break.

"No," Asti whispered.

"Oh, yes!" Miles shouted. He swung the chair back, knocking Asti in the head with it. Asti's wrist snapped from all the twisting of the chair, but his arm was free. The force of the blow sent him reeling toward the door.

"No!" Asti called out, beating back the raging beast wanting to blot out his mind.

Miles tackled him into the hallway, knocking Asti to the floor. He punched hard and fast in Asti's back.

"You think you can come after us, come after my place, Rynax?" Miles was on his feet, standing over Asti.

"No," Asti said, but it was entirely to his own mind. The creeping madness was beating through his skull, but he held it back. Despite the pain, he kicked out at Miles's knee. Miles jumped back, giving Asti the chance to stand up.

If he had to die right now, at least he'd die in his right mind, and on his feet.

Verci had known there was one deep, deep flaw to their whole plan: they had no specific idea where in the whole underground complex the money room actually was. It was a piece of information they had no way of learning until they actually did the gig. Asti's plan for finding the room was, on its face, filled with insanity, but it had a kind of logic to it, playing into the fact that Tyne would be expecting something.

"It's real simple," Asti had explained once they were alone with Josie in the Birdie Basement. "Josie goes to Tyne and turns us in. At least, that's what he'll think. She tells him that Miles and his boys can grab me from the watch flop at nine bells."

"What good will that do?" Verci had asked.

"They grab me, take me to Tyne's office. His office is surely right by his money room. He won't want to be far from it. So once I'm there, and we blow the wall, there's going to be a lot of chaos."

"So then what?"

"Then I'll find you, lead you to the money room."

"After you've been caught by Tyne's men."

"I'll get away."

"'I'll get away' is your plan?"

Verci really hated this plan.

Verci took the lead down the hallway, pair of darts in each hand. Cort, Win, and Kennith were all right behind him, but he knew none of them were really up for a fight. Ken might be able to scare away someone with a Ch'omik glower, but Verci had no idea if he actually had any skills in a fight. Win certainly didn't. Cort held a glass vial in one hand, looking ready to hurl it at anything that moved.

There was plenty of chaos going on, shouts and screams in the distance. He was more than a little surprised that, so far, no guards were running toward the loud noise that shook the whole building. Maybe none of them could tell the difference between it and the confusion Gin and the others were creating on the gambling floor.

The corridor ended in a tee. Most of the madness was to the left, but he could hear sounds of fighting to the right. The cries and grunts from that fight were distinctly familiar. He broke into a run, and the other three scrambled after him.

The hallway rounded another corner, where two figures were beating each other into bloody messes. One of them, though, was more than recognizable by his height, build, and jacket. Verci wasted no time throwing two darts into the back of the other one and following it with two more. The man turned around, more surprise on his face than anything else. When the man turned, Asti punched him in the head, again and again. The man dropped to the ground.

Asti dropped to his knees. "I had him," he mumbled.

Verci quickly appraised his brother's face. He was bruised and gashed, and his left eye swollen. Verci figured Asti could barely see out of it. "Sure you did. How bad?"

"Wrist is broken, I think," Asti said, holding up his left arm. His right one had a shackle attached to it, as did both ankles, though the chain was broken. "I was supposed to find you."

"You were supposed to get away," Verci said. Asti was a mess of blood and bruises. "Can you walk?"

"Sure," Asti said, looking a little dazed. He pointed absently to one of the doors. "That's the office, and I bet that's the money room."

Verci nodded. "Win, check it." Win went over to the door and started fiddling with the lock. Verci pulled out a small tool and opened up the shackle on his brother's wrist. "You did good, brother."

"Damned blazes I did," Asti said in a slur. He grinned and grabbed Verci by the head as soon as his good hand was free. "I held it together. I did. It tried to take me, and I didn't let it."

Cort crouched down next to them both, taking out a small vial. He opened it up and offered it to Asti.

"Blazes is that?" Asti asked.

"Numb the pain, clear your head, for a bit," Cort said.

Asti shrugged, took the vial, and drank it down. "Tastes of horse piss."

"Key ingredient," Cort said, rubbing Asti on the shoulder.

"This is quite the lock," Win said. "If this isn't the money vault, I don't know what it could be."

"My thoughts when I saw the door," Asti said. Verci glanced back over to his brother. His eyes were more focused, and he was looking at them as if really seeing them all for the first time. "How are we doing?"

"We're all here and alive," Verci said.

"Capital," Asti said, getting to his feet. "Someone should be coming soon to stop us from doing this."

"I think our confusion plan is doing its job."

"Good," Asti said. "How's that door, Win?"

"There're four different locks involved," Win said. "And when I got three open, one sprung back shut."

"What?" The last thing they needed was to stand around this hallway.

"It's very good craft. This may take a bit."

"One more minute," Verci mumbled. He dropped his satchel and opened it up, pulling out a few empty sacks.

Asti undid the shackles from his ankles and picked up a discarded sword from the ground. He started off down the hallway.

"Where are you going?" Verci asked.

"Going for Josie," he said. "Got to make sure she can get to the hole in the wall fast enough. Where is it, by the way?"

"Round the bend, thirty feet, left down to the end. Can't miss it."

"I'm off, then. Good luck." He sprinted off down the hall.

"Good luck, brother," Verci responded, but Asti was already out of hearing.

An ugly metallic crack ripped through the air. "Got it," Win said. He opened up the door. Verci grabbed a sack and looked inside. It was glorious. Piles upon piles of neatly stacked goldsmith notes, all from reputable houses.

"Get those bags stuffed, gents," he said, wasting no time dumping a pile into the one he was carrying.

Chapter 30

ASTI POUNDED DOWN THE hallway, pain fading thanks to Cort's elixir, but he was far too aware of his blind side from his swelling eye. He felt a howling scream, deep inside his skull. The beast wanted to come out, but he no longer had to keep it on a chain. His mind was a cage again, that great red animal was not going to be allowed to come out. Not tonight. Not ever again, had he a say in it.

"Get your hands off of me!" Josie's voice, just ahead. No time to waste. He pursued her voice, turning the corner to find three of Tyne's men grabbing her.

Asti stabbed one hard, savagely yanking the blade free. The other two men released Josie and turned to him. One leaped right at him, forcing Asti on the defense. The other stood frozen.

"Come on!" the first guard yelled at his friend. "Help me get him!"

"You!" the frozen guard said, staring hard at Asti. Asti was struggling, holding off the one man's attack. The frozen guard dropped his blade and backed away. "I can't fight you." He tore off down the corridor. The first guard seemed more surprised than anyone, dropping his defense. Asti took the opportunity to deliver a solid blow.

"You need me to carry you, Josie?" Asti asked as the man dropped.

"I'd ask you that," she returned.

"I'm fine," he said. "Nothing that can't heal. Let's get you out of here."

He took her arm over his shoulder and led her back toward their escape hole. Verci and the others were coming down the hallway, all carrying full sacks.

"How much?" Josie asked.

"More than I could count," Verci said. "And that's just what we could carry."

"Blazes," Asti said.

"And the rest?" Josie said. "You left it?"

"What else could we do?"

"We should burn the whole place down," Asti said.

"How do we do that?" Verci asked.

Cort put down his sacks and pulled a bag of powder out of his belt. "This should do it."

Asti snatched the bag from Cort. "All right. What do I—"

"Don't touch the powder with your bare skin. Pour it out and then drop a taper or flame on it. Then get out." Asti nodded in understanding. He gave the others a quick wave to head down to the exit, and Josie went with them.

Verci touched his shoulder. "Brother, we need to—"

A scream of rage came from down the hallway.

Miles.

"He's still alive?" Verci sounded more annoyed than anything else.

Asti pocketed the powder and drew his sword. "Go. I'll hold him off."

"You're crazy!"

"Established fact," Asti said. "Get gone."

"You mean . . ." Verci let it hang.

"Full escape. Meet you in the warehouse." Verci didn't move. Blazes. Asti pushed him away. "Go already!"

"Rynax!" echoed through the halls. Miles was coming.

Verci sighed and nodded solemnly, then ran off down the hallway. Asti watched until he was sure he was gone.

"Raise him clean, Verci," he whispered, then stalked back toward the office.

✷

Mila pushed her way through the screaming crowd, forcing her way to one of the roped velvet curtains that separated the back offices from the gambling floor. She had no idea if things were going well or badly, but her gut told her Asti was back there, and he needed help. She'd come here to help him, and she wasn't going to let him down.

She reached the curtain and was about to slip into the hallway when a rough hand grabbed her arm. She looked to the owner of the hand, an old, bald man with piercing eyes and an exquisite suit. "The blazes are you doing, girl?"

"I . . . I was trying to find . . . a way out to . . ."

The man's eyes scanned the people pressing to the doors, the smoke filling the room, the knocked-over tables, the flickering flames. "Amateurs, making a mess of my place."

"Your—"

He looked back at her, a hard, angry glare. "That isn't your dress."

She didn't have a chance to say anything. His other hand snapped like a snake onto her neck, tightening with a rage-fueled strength.

"You think you rats can come in here and crack *my* house? Do you know who I am?"

Mila's hand groped at the curtain behind her, grabbing the rope that held it open. With a flip of her wrist, she pulled it free. In one fell motion, she swung the rope around so it wrapped around Tyne's neck, at the same time driving her knee hard into his crotch. He let go of her throat reflexively, and she pulled the rope tighter.

"I know who you are." She had both ends of the rope now, twisting them with every ounce of strength in her arms. He was on his knees, clawing uselessly at the rope, his face turning a beet purple. She leaned in and hissed in his ear. "You're the man who killed my sister."

He stopped moving, and she kept her grip tight.

He was flat on the ground, and despite the screams and the smoke and all the chaos, Mila's world was silent, until a hand was on her shoulder.

"Come on," Helene said. "You got him."

"What about Asti?"

"He can take care of himself," Helene said. "But we still have a job to do."

"How are we getting out?" Mila said as Helene pulled her to her feet.

"With four magic words," Helene said with a wicked grin. She looked across the room. "Julien! Make a hole!"

Julien was caught behind one of the gambling tables, keeping the press of people off of Gin. He nodded back to Helene with understanding. Suddenly his expression changed, every muscle in his body tensed. He picked up the table, and holding it in front of him, pushed his way through the crowd, mowing a path through the swells and nobles until he reached the stairwell. Helene and Mila ran up behind him, joining Gin in the safety of Julien's shadow.

"Did I see you just kill Mendel Tyne?" Gin asked Mila. "You lucky girl!"

"Go, go, run!" Verci shouted to the others as they pounded up the stairs. He dropped his sacks on the ground and drew out four darts, spinning to watch the hole in the wall. No one came.

"Verci!" Win called.

Verci turned his head slightly toward Win, standing on the stairway, but never taking his eye off the hole. "What?"

"What are we doing?"

"Getting ready to pound out of here," Verci said. "Load my sacks."

"What are *you* doing?"

"Waiting for Asti, covering our retreat."

"For how long?"

"Until I say we pound out of here!" Verci snapped. "We're giving Asti as much time as we can."

Win came down and grabbed the sacks.

"Is Josie safe, Win?"

Win stood for a moment at the bottom of the stairs. "We have her in the carriage, ready to go."

"That'll do," Verci said. "Get up there and be ready for us."

Win carried the sacks up the stairs. Verci turned his attention back to the hole in the wall. No one but his brother would get through. He just needed to get here soon.

Chapter 31

HELENE COULDN'T BELIEVE THEY made it out to the street. On some level, she never believed this was going to work. But the place was burning down, Tyne was dead, and she and Julien were out in the open night air. Smoke-filled, panic-stricken open night air, but they were out. Mila led the four of them over to the alley, away from most of the crowd.

"Too many people out here," Mila muttered. "And Brigade'll be here soon. Don't know if my cadre can flatten this."

"Think of some way to do it," Helene said. "Our carriage is going to need to get through this in a click."

"I'd love to know how to disperse a crazed mob, Hel."

"You!" A shrieking voice pierced through the air. The crowd scrambled away from the source: Ecrain the mage, her hair smoking, her eyes red. A bony finger was pointed at Julien. "What did you do to me?"

Julien froze with fear. "Hel . . ."

Sparks sputtered out of Ecrain's hands, like a dying bonfire. "I don't know what you did. But you will suffer for it." A bolt, like lightning, jumped from one hand to the ground. She approached them with a shambling limp, as if the entire left side of her body was numb. "All the Firewings will make you pay!"

"Helene!" Julien shouted.

"I think she's getting her focus back," Gin said.

Helene drew up her small crossbow, bracing it with her other hand to stop it from shaking. Taking only a moment to aim, she shot a dart into the woman's neck.

Ecrain screamed, then tore the dart out. "Fine. I'll kill the trollop first."

Helene reloaded the crossbow as fast as she could, while the sparks around Ecrain's hand danced faster and harder.

"Hel!"

"Run!" Helene barked at the three of them. The shot was loaded.

The sparks grew into a sickly green ball.

Helene drew up her arm and snapped the shot. The dart struck true, buried in the woman's eye. Ecrain screamed and dropped to the ground.

Helene turned back to the other three, who still stood dumbstruck.

"I said something about running, didn't I?"

They didn't wait a second longer.

Miles looked as bad as Asti felt. His shirt was soaked in blood, red footprints behind him. He didn't hesitate when he saw Asti, charging full tilt, sword out. Asti was surprised he could move that fast. Asti barely blocked the thrust, Miles scoring a glancing slice along Asti's arm.

Miles kept up his furious attack, no banter this time. Pure rage, channeled into an onslaught of thrusts and kicks. Asti had no opportunity to counter; it took everything he had just to hold Miles off.

The hallway was getting hazy with smoke, screams and cries in the distance.

Asti ducked under a sword swing and darted down the hallway, closer to the office. He needed some distance to regain his bearings. Miles came at him, but he was ready. Sword up, he parried Miles wide and knocked the blade out of his hand. Miles grabbed Asti's wrist—the one that had been broken—and wrenched it. An intense bolt of pain replaced the dull ache, and Asti screamed. He dropped his sword. Miles hit him in the stomach, and then in the chest.

Asti punched back, only one arm strong enough to do any good. Miles didn't falter.

Miles struck again. Asti stumbled back, slipped in blood on the floor, and lost his footing.

Miles picked up the closest sword. Asti tried to get to his feet, but Miles stepped on his broken wrist. Asti beat back the pain, beat back it all. Held down the torrent.

Miles didn't speak. He simply raised up the sword, ready to slam it down into Asti's chest. Asti rolled to the left, the sword only piercing his coat, cutting open the soft lump of Cort's pouch.

Asti punched desperately at Miles's knee, knocking the man back. His broken arm free, Asti pulled himself up and took out Cort's pouch. Before Miles could stab him again, he threw the pouch at Miles's chest.

The pouch burst, gray powder covering Miles's body. Miles coughed and swatted at the dust around him.

Asti ripped one of the oil lamps off the wall and threw it.

Miles lit up with a flash of blue flame, which sparked and shot over the hallway. Asti dove away, through the doorway into Tyne's office.

The place was still a mess, with five dead bodies sprawled over the floor. Memory washed across Asti's mind. Something he saw on a paper, just for a moment. Something important.

Asti stumbled over to the desk. The papers had been knocked all over the desk and floor. Quickly Asti looked through them, as well as he could with only one eye working properly. All business things, inventory, accounting, the usual things expected.

Then he found the letter that had been in his face during the fight.

He gave it a quick scan, noting the key words that had gotten his attention. "Thank you for the services rendered." "Fire largely effective in acquiring property." "Our mutual friends will proceed." "Colevar and Associates."

He folded the letter and put it inside his jacket, and left the office.

The blaze had spread. Smoke filled the hallway.

Asti couldn't see, couldn't breathe. There was nothing but black and death.

Asti dropped to the ground, where the smoke was only marginally thinner. He crawled along, the pain in his arm piercing at him every time he put his weight on it. He held the injured arm close to his body and crawled using only the other one.

How far had he gone down the hallway? Thirty feet? He couldn't tell. Had he gone around the curve? Was he even going the right way?

He didn't know where the hole was. It didn't matter. Any exit would do. Any sign of fresh air.

The smoke was smothering, choking. There was nothing to breathe anymore.

Verci had made it out. He had sacks full of money.

He would be all right. So would Raych and little Corsi. They would do just fine.

A few more feet. Not that he was going anywhere anymore. He dropped down flat, unable to move.

Verci and his family would be good and safe. The neighborhood was avenged. Tyne's Emporium was savaged.

It would do.

Despite the suffocating horror, for just a moment, he felt calm. His mind was at peace.

Everything went black.

Chapter 32

SMOKE POURED THROUGH THE hole in the wall.
No guards were coming. Neither was Asti.

How much longer?

Verci was about to go back in for his brother when there
was a smash of wood and glass upstairs. Someone had
bashed through the front door.

Instinct put his feet in motion, bounding up the stairs. He
reached the top to see a handful of Tyne's men storming
through the front of the wine shop, all armed, all angry.

Verci threw a wild spread of his darts. Nothing would
likely hit them, but it would give them a moment of pause.
He raced out the door and grabbed the back end of the
carriage.

"Now, Kennith!"

Kennith didn't hesitate, snapping the reins. The horses
started off, far too slow for Verci's taste at this moment.

The first of the guards came out the door, grabbing at
Verci's leg. Verci snapped a kick at the man's face.

The carriage was moving faster now, heading out to the
main road. Tyne's men were keeping up, gaining ground.
Verci scrambled up on top of the carriage.

"We need to move!" he told Kennith.

Kennith urged the horses, and they gained speed. "We have to wait until we've got a clear path!"

"Let's hope Mila did her job!" Verci shouted.

"Get in place!" Ken said. They were now out in the main thoroughfare, passing in front of the Emporium. Smoke poured out of the whole building, and people were standing around dazed. Verci was reminded of the other night, when the alley burned down.

He stepped out onto the carriage yoke, keeping his balance despite the jostle and kick of the carriage. "Ready!"

Kennith grabbed the bell sitting at his seat and rang it, three sharp, penetrating peals. Some of the people stepped out of the streets. Up ahead a group of street boys perked up at the bell. One of them shouted, "Oy! Clear it!" In a moment the boys scrambled and pushed people away, and an open path of nothing lay ahead of them on the road.

"Now!" shouted Verci, praying to every saint and a few forgotten Kieran gods, just for good measure.

Ken pulled one lever, and the yoke dropped off the carriage. Verci jumped forward onto one of the horses at the same moment. He kicked it hard, and relieved of their weighty burden, the two horses were off like a shot. He turned back to see what happened next.

As the carriage slowed Ken pulled the second lever, and there was a terrible snapping sound. Then the carriage surged forward, gaining speed like Verci had never seen. It quickly caught back up to him and the horses, forcing him to spur them on faster to stay ahead.

The carriage kept going, nearly flying down Dockside.

Kennith laughed, even though his knuckles were white from gripping the stick that controlled the wheels.

"Spring power!" Verci shouted to him.

"Spring power!" Kennith returned.

Far in the distance behind him, the pursuing guards all lost the chase, heaving for breath, falling out of sight.

A minute later, eight blocks away, the carriage slowed down. The spring engine that Verci conceived and Kennith built had run out of torsion. Verci stopped the horses and hopped to the ground. Kennith jumped down as well, moving quickly to reconnect the horses to the carriage.

The door opened as Verci looked back.

"Did we lose them?" Josie asked.

"Think so," Verci said.

"Where are we?" Win asked from inside.

"Deep in North Seleth," Verci said. "Only a couple blocks from the safehouse." He stepped away from the carriage, back toward Keller Cove.

"Get in, Verci," Josie said.

"I have to find—"

"Get in the carriage, Verci!" Josie snapped her cane on the floor of the carriage. "We don't have time. Won't be long before constabs look for whatever tore through the street."

"Don't you tell me what do to," Verci said.

Josie gave a small sigh. "Either Asti made it, and we'll see him, or he didn't. Nothing you can do will change that."

Verci hated to admit that she was right. Asti didn't want him running back for him. He wanted Verci to get out clean. Swearing under his breath, he stepped into the carriage. Ken was already back up on the driver's seat. The horses were urged forward, going at a steady trot to the safehouse.

The warehouse was simple and unadorned, nothing to distinguish it from the scores of others along the street. Wooden frame, white walls, large set of barn doors for loading. Josie handed three keys to Verci, letting him go and open the place up. "There's a catch switch, knee high on the right side of the door. Make sure you toggle it before you open the door."

A minute later the carriage was in the warehouse, the doors shut behind them. The place really was quite nice on the inside. Stone floors, ample space, high ceilings. Workbenches along one wall, storage cabinets along another. A few wide tables on one end of the room. A metal stove in the corner. There was a wooden staircase leading to an oversight office. Verci looked around in surprise.

"You wanted to set us up here, didn't you?" he asked Josie.

"If you pulled this off, you'd be a crew to back," Josie said. "I'd be a fool not to get you out of that stable."

Win and Cort took the sacks of money out of the back of the carriage and loaded them onto the table. Verci went for the rest and found a full cask sitting in one of the seats.

"Who stole a cask of wine from the merchant, boys?"

"I didn't steal it," Kennith said. "I left a hundred crowns for it."

"Put it over in the kitchen," Verci said.

"The kitchen?" Kennith asked.

"Over by the stove."

Kennith carried the cask over. Verci took the last sacks of money over to the table.

"Let's start counting," he told the rest.

Counting took a lot of time. As they counted, Pilsen, Mila, and Julien and Helene eventually arrived sometime around one bell in the morning.

"Nice dress," Verci told Mila when they came in. "You steal it?"

"Yup," Mila said, sitting down at one of the tables. She pried off her shoes and rubbed her feet. "That lady had some small shoes."

"You've got big feet," Helene said, sitting next to her. "What's the take?"

"We're double-checking," Verci said, "But it's over one hundred thousand crowns."

Helene and Mila both let out low whistles.

"That's quite a pleasant evening, then," Gin said. "You should all know that the pig of a man is dead."

"Who?" Verci asked. "Tyne?"

"Tyne, indeed," Pilsen said, grinning like a schoolboy with candy. "This delightful girl here choked every ounce of life out of him."

"Mila?" Verci asked. He looked at her. She gave every appearance of being more concerned about her feet than anything else. "You all right?"

"Tired," she said. "Where's Asti?"

"We . . ." Verci faltered. "He hasn't gotten back yet."

"Oh," Mila said.

The whole room was silent for a moment.

Josie broke it. "Julien, why don't you roll that cask of wine over here. And there are some cups in that cabinet."

Quietly Julien brought the wine over. Helene and Pilsen got the cups. Verci cracked open the cask and served out some for everyone, including one for Asti.

"What are we drinking to?" Win asked.

"Nothing yet," Verci said. "We finish the count, and then we'll know what we're drinking to."

Verci had a sickening feeling that when they did drink, there would still be one cup untouched.

Chapter 33

ASTI'S WHOLE BODY WAS shooting with pain. He was aware of that before he was properly awake. His arm was in agony, his face a swollen mess, his breathing heavy and labored.

He was alive. That was the only way he'd be in this much pain.

He opened his eye. Only one responded at all. He was lying on a damp floor in a dark room. The scent of smoke was still in his nose, more of a memory than a living odor.

He tried to stand up. His whole body argued with the idea.

"Hey, hey, slowly," said a voice at his side. Older man. Two hands took hold of his shoulders, calmly and gently. Someone helped him sit up. "Didn't know if you'd make it."

"I don't remember . . . getting out," Asti slurred.

"You didn't," the man said. "I dragged you out."

Asti's eye focused on the man. At first he didn't place the face. There was something familiar. "Do you work for Tyne?"

"I guess I don't anymore," the man said. "I don't think there'll be any more work."

"The place burned down?"

"The parts that mattered," the man said. He was

definitely one of Tyne's guards, an old veteran by the looks of him. "Mister Tyne is dead, so that's the end of that."

"You saw him dead?" Asti asked. The man nodded somberly. "So why am I alive now? Last bit of revenge?"

"You don't recognize me, do you?" the man asked.

"Yes," Asti said, now placing him. "You were the guard who ran off earlier. Didn't want to fight me."

"No, not from tonight," the man said. He leaned in closer. "You might not. Last time I saw you, I was little more than a hairy sack of bones. But your face. Your face is burned in my heart."

Asti felt disturbed, threatened by the man's intensity. The man didn't seem hostile, though. He could have easily killed Asti if that's what he wanted. Unless he wanted to savor the moment, really drive home to Asti who killed him and why. The saints knew there were plenty of men out there who wanted him dead and for good reason. Perhaps it was his due.

"I'm afraid I don't," Asti said. "Whatever wrong I did you . . ."

"Wrong?" The man laughed. "No, no wrong at all, mister."

"Then . . ." Asti let his words hang.

"You saved me," the man said. His eyes were wet with tears. "I had been held in Levtha Prison for over a year."

"Levtha?" The word hit Asti like a hammer. "I . . . what did I do?"

The man sat back. "I had given up hope. I had been captured when my ship crashed on Haptur after a storm. Twenty-nine men, and by the end there were only four of us still alive. I was nothing but a wreck of a man. Hopeless, until suddenly there you were."

"There I was how?" Asti asked cautiously.

"You don't know?" the man asked.

Asti faltered. "I—I honestly don't remember anything about escaping Levtha."

The guard nodded, like he understood exactly what Asti meant. "I remember it like yesterday. You kicked open the door of our cell and you . . . you looked like something out of scripture. Like Saint Jontlen, 'red-eyed and anointed in blood.' And you told us to follow you."

"I did?" Asti had never thought he was anything other than mindless rage when he lost it.

"You fought our way to the docks. You fought . . . I've never seen anything like it. You got the four of us onto a small sailing skiff, and a group of Poasian archers came down. You went after them to cover our escape. We . . . we didn't see what happened to you."

Asti sat back, shocked at this narrative. Were his rages more controlled than he had thought? Was he capable of recognizing friends when he was in that mode? Could he make choices like sacrificing himself, saving others?

He hadn't hurt Kimber or Win. Or Mila. She had been able to subdue him. At the time he had only thought of it as a testament to her skill and determination.

The man continued his story, breaking Asti's reverie. "After a while me and the rest of the boys, we started to wonder if you had been real. My mother, she was a Waish woman, she had told me stories of *adshylla*, spirits of the dead who come to help people when they are in desperate need. And I prayed to God, sir, and you came."

"I'm no spirit of the dead, friend," Asti said.

"But you were a gift from God."

Asti let that sink in. He slowly pulled himself to his feet. "Thank you, sir, for all that you've done for me tonight."

"I have a debt to you," the man said.

"Not anymore," Asti said. He reached inside his coat and pulled out a few twenty-crown notes. "In fact, I think you should take this."

"I couldn't," the man said.

"I'll point out that you are out of employment now, and that is my fault."

The man shrugged in ascent. "You have a fair point." He took the bills. "You able to walk?"

"I'll make do," Asti said. "I did get off Haptur, after all."

Chapter 34

THREE BELLS BECAME FOUR BELLS. The money had been counted and counted again. Bills piled in neat stacks, each share set to the side in satchels. The cups were still untouched. Julien went out for a bit and returned with fresh clothes. Everyone in costume had cleaned up and changed. Some people had dozed off. Cort and Win were talking quietly by the stove. Kennith was working inside the carriage.

After hearing the distant peal of four bells from whatever church was closest, Verci decided they had waited long enough. He went back to the big table and picked up one of the cups of wine.

"All right," he said in a loud voice, holding up the cup. "Let's do this."

The rest of the crew all got to their feet and came around the table, a slow, weary stagger. Verci held his pose, and the others joined him one by one, until the last cup sat alone on the table.

"We had a good run tonight," Verci said. "All told, probably the best one I've had. But it was not without its costs."

A few heads hung down. Win bit his lip, looking like he was holding back a sob. Julien's wide eyes held back nothing; tears poured down his face.

"So before we go, let's raise our glasses to our success, and to the man who made it possible."

"To Asti," Helene said.

"To Asti," the rest echoed.

"That's very sweet." Asti's voice came from the door. Verci dropped his cup and ran over. Asti was even more of a mess, his face covered in bruises, angry red welts, and burns. One arm was an unnatural purple and swollen.

He was on his feet, though.

Verci grabbed him in a hard embrace, lifting his brother off the ground.

"Ow, Verci, let go!" Asti shouted. Verci put him back down. "I'm battered all over."

"You look like God himself beat you," Josie said.

"Hardly," Asti said. He limped over to the table and picked up his cup of wine. "In fact, I am a gift from God."

"You really got hit in the head, didn't you?" Helene asked.

"Quite a lot," Asti said, drinking his wine. The rest all did the same. "What was our take?"

"One hundred twenty-seven thousand, four hundred crowns," Verci said.

Asti let out a low whistle. "That's some serious money. We could give Josie her cut, set aside a good chunk for the neighborhood, still split the rest nine ways, and each of us can slip off and live pretty comfortable for the rest of our lives. No real worries, hmm?"

He sat at the table, put his cup down, and leaned back. Verci could see from the look in his brother's eye—the one that was still open—that Asti was up to something.

"Pretty clean and plush, we'd all be," Asti said. "We could move on, forget about Holver Alley. Forget about what was done."

"I'll never forget," Win said.

"Tyne's dead," Mila said.

"You're sure?" Asti asked her.

"By her own hand," Helene said.

Asti raised his glass to Mila. She returned the gesture and sipped hers.

"So Tyne is dead. And if this began and ended with Tyne, then we'd be done."

"If?" Verci asked.

Asti took out a piece of paper from the inner pocket of his jacket and tossed it on the table. "A letter from our friends at Colevar and Associates, thanking Mister Tyne for his help in securing some of the desired land in North Seleth for their clients."

"Their clients?" Verci asked. "Who?"

"That remains a mystery," Asti said. He sipped more of his wine.

"Tyne was a middleman for someone else?" Helene asked.

Josie asked, "Someone making a move in my neighborhood?"

"Apparently so."

"And 'some of the land' it says?" Josie snatched the paper away from Asti.

"So whoever hired Tyne, they're not done." Asti took another sip of his wine.

"What are you going to do?" Helene asked him.

"I am going to drink this excellent wine," Asti said. He looked over to Verci. "Spoils from the entry point?"

"Ken grabbed it."

"Well done, Kennith," Asti said. "After that I will have someone set this broken wrist, which hurts like blazes, let me tell you. If someone can get some ice for this eye, I would be very grateful."

Kennith looked up. "Missus Holt, is there ice?"

"There's an icebox back there, had it stocked up this afternoon," Josie said absently, attention still on the letter.

"You think of everything, don't you?" Asti said to her. He looked around the whole warehouse. "You thought we might need someplace after tonight?"

"The thought that this didn't end with Tyne crossed my mind," Josie said.

"And now we know," Mila said quietly.

"Now we know," Verci said. His brain was buzzing. He wanted nothing more than to go to his wife, his bed, and to sleep for ten days.

"So after I rest and heal up," Asti said, "I'm going to see this through until I find the absolute bottom of it."

Josie raised her cup. "If you're running a long game, Rynax, you've got this place to run it out of."

"And you behind it?" Asti asked.

"Don't ask stupid questions, Asti."

"You've got me to the end," Mila added.

"Thank you," Asti said. "Anyone else?"

"Are we in?" Julien asked his cousin.

"As long as it takes," Helene told him.

"You people are crazy," Gin announced. "But you do good work."

"You in?" Asti asked.

"Absolutely. I've missed this sort of thing."

"Win?"

The locksmith drummed his fingers on the table. "This wasn't about the money for me. This was about doing something, keeping occupied. Long as you have something for me do to, I'll do it."

"Kennith?"

The Ch'omik man furrowed his brow. "These clients of Colevar and Associates . . . they want more of North Seleth. We've seen what they are willing to do." He set his jaw; anger flashed in his eyes. "My grandparents fled Ch'omik-Taa because men of power ousted them from their land. Men who did what they wanted since no one would stop them."

"That's not the case here," Cort said.

"Not with us," Kennith said. "Not with me. I'm not going to be someone who doesn't do something when he can."

"Makes sense," Cort said. "These folks still want the land, and that includes my shop. So I'm with you."

"Verci?" Asti asked. "Are you with us?"

There was a huge temptation to take his sack and walk out. Asti would understand. Asti, of all people, knew that sometimes you had to walk away. Especially with a wife and child. With money, he had security.

Verci looked over at Josie. She had plenty of money, but only the security of fear. Even her money, her paranoia, hadn't protected her neighborhood. His neighborhood.

"Blazes," Verci said. "There's no safety here, for any of us or ours, until we dig this out all the way. Is there?"

"Probably not," Asti said. "But I'll look out for our family, if that's what you need."

"We'll look out for our family," Verci told him.

"Good then," Asti said. "Everybody get some rest. We've got work to do."